Praise for Lindsay Lovise

Never Gamble Your Heart

"Sensual love scenes and simmering suspense combine to make this a true page-turner."

—*Publishers Weekly*, starred review

"An enjoyable Victorian romance threaded with mystery."

—*Kirkus Reviews*

Never Blow a Kiss

"Lovise writes with a sprightly pen, her story bursting with cheek and humor while also remaining unrelenting in its twists and turns. An extremely promising debut, one that blends the best hallmarks of each of its genres…we can't wait to see what's next."

—*Entertainment Weekly*

"Edgy and enticing…Lovise is sure to win fans with this."

—*Publishers Weekly*, starred review

"Gripping and fresh…Will have you hooked until the last page!"
—Amalie Howard, *USA Today* bestselling author

"Deftly combines equal parts romance and mystery. A strong historical romance debut, for fans of Sarah MacLean and Erica Ridley."
—*Kirkus Reviews*

"The kind of fast-paced, sexy historical romance I love to lose myself in."
—Manda Collins, bestselling author of *A Governess's Guide to Passion and Peril*

NEVER SPAR WITH A VISCOUNT

Also by Lindsay Lovise

Never Gamble Your Heart

Never Blow a Kiss

NEVER SPAR WITH A VISCOUNT

THE SECRET SOCIETY OF GOVERNESS SPIES

LINDSAY LOVISE

FOREVER

New York Boston

This book is a work of fiction. Names, characters, places, and incidents are the product of the author's imagination or are used fictitiously. Any resemblance to actual events, locales, or persons, living or dead, is coincidental.

Copyright © 2026 by Lindsay Lovise
Cover design by Daniela Medina. Cover photo illustration by Sophia Sidoti.
Cover copyright © 2026 by Hachette Book Group, Inc.

Hachette Book Group supports the right to free expression and the value of copyright. The purpose of copyright is to encourage writers and artists to produce the creative works that enrich our culture.

The scanning, uploading, and distribution of this book without permission is a theft of the author's intellectual property. If you would like permission to use material from the book (other than for review purposes), please contact permissions@hbgusa.com. Thank you for your support of the author's rights.

Forever
Hachette Book Group
1290 Avenue of the Americas, New York, NY 10104
read-forever.com
@readforeverpub

First Edition: March 2026

Forever is an imprint of Grand Central Publishing. The Forever name and logo are registered trademarks of Hachette Book Group, Inc.

The publisher is not responsible for websites (or their content) that are not owned by the publisher.

The Hachette Speakers Bureau provides a wide range of authors for speaking events. To find out more, go to hachettespeakersbureau.com or email HachetteSpeakers@hbgusa.com.

Forever books may be purchased in bulk for business, educational, or promotional use. For information, please contact your local bookseller or the Hachette Book Group Special Markets Department at special.markets@hbgusa.com.

Print book interior design by Jeff Stiefel

Library of Congress Cataloging-in-Publication Data

Names: Lovise, Lindsay author
Title: Never spar with a viscount / Lindsay Lovise.
Description: First edition. | New York : Forever, 2026. | Series: The Secret Society of Governess Spies ; 3 | Identifiers: LCCN 2025038860 | ISBN 9781538740583 (trade paperback) | ISBN 9781538740606 (ebook)
Subjects: LCGFT: Romance fiction | Novels | Fiction
Classification: LCC PS3612.O8746 N486 2026
LC record available at https://lccn.loc.gov/2025038860

ISBNs: 9781538740583 (trade paperback), 9781538740606 (ebook)

Printed in the United States of America

LSC-C

Printing 1, 2025

To Heather. I couldn't ask for a better sister.

Content Warning

Ivy Bennett is a governess who teaches secret self-defense classes to women in the early Victorian era. As part of the story, there are off-page references to past domestic and familial abuse. If you are sensitive to this topic, please take care reading.

In the Secret Society of Governess Spies, there are rules one must follow, along with things one must never do.

    1. Never blow a kiss.
    2. Never gamble your heart.
    3. Never spar with a viscount.

Chapter 1

October 1838
Richmond, England

Ivy Bennett grabbed two fistfuls of skirt and hurried up the creaky, narrow stairs. She was late to the gathering, thanks to her employer, Viscount Brackley. She had known the newly minted viscount was horse-mad, but she had not expected him to practically move into the stables upon his arrival a week prior. The low baritone of his voice and the tread of his boots had sounded at every corner since, and his presence had made it impossible for her to sneak out at her usual time.

Fearing she would be trapped behind a barrel of oats for eternity, Ivy had finally made a dash for Tansy the Temperamental, the ornery mare she had adopted as her own. Then she had recklessly cantered into town sans saddle, praying no one would catch her riding bareback and astride at nine in the evening. Ivy could not afford for her father to catch even a whiff of scandal, *especially* considering where she was going.

Ivy burst through the second-floor door, and six faces turned toward her—including one she did not recognize.

"I apologize for my tardiness, ladies," Ivy said, ripping her hat off and tossing it atop a small table that already hosted a number of other reticules and hats. "Lord Brackley seems to have taken up residence in the stables."

There were murmurs of interest at mention of the new viscount. The elder Lord Brackley had died two months prior, leaving behind a second wife and eight young daughters. If it were not for his much older son produced by a first marriage, the estate would have been lost to a distant cousin.

Ivy rather suspected the new viscount wished it had been. If most noble properties were racehorses, the Brackley country estate was the companion donkey. To say it was dilapidated would be generous. The new Lord Brackley, who had made his fortune breeding horses abroad, would have to sink a pretty penny into it if he wanted to restore it to even a shadow of its former glory.

Perhaps it was the new lord's grunts, or the narrowing of his green eyes, or his surly manner overall, but Ivy was almost certain he would rather the old place burn than have to deal with it.

Ivy unbuttoned her gown and let it fall to her feet before kicking it into the corner. She continued stripping down to her chemise, which was tucked into a pair of molded buckskin breeches.

She glanced around the room, basking in the feel of standing in *her* studio. Ivy had rented the single-room flat over the modiste shop a year ago, before she had taken on the governess placement at Brackley Manor. Although she had cleared out the furniture, she had kept the thick navy carpeting—the better to muffle sound. The walls were papered with gold scrolls, and candles flickered in candelabras scattered around the room. Other than the addition of the women's various perfumes mingling with the slight scent of dust, the entire suite was bare.

Six women stood before her, their stocking feet sinking into the carpet.

"How is the governess placement working out, Ivy?" Mable asked. She was a slender redhead who had had two unsuccessful Seasons and was hoping for one more to pass so she could settle into proper spinsterhood.

Molly, a robust woman of sixty, snorted. "I would not want to be responsible for eight little girls, much less the Brackley horde. I hear their mama has let them run wild."

Ivy winced. It was true. The dowager viscountess had long ago succumbed to the allure of laudanum and rarely emerged from her bedchamber, leaving the girls almost entirely to their own whims.

"They are spirited," Ivy admitted. The three governesses before her had not lasted longer than a week, but here she was going on a month. Not that it had been easy—she would forever have the urge to check underneath her bedcovers, thanks to several instances of slyly placed wildlife during the first few weeks. "What do we say? Shall we begin?"

She scanned the remaining women. Besides Mable and Molly, there was Tabitha, a beautiful widow of thirty; Tulle, a shy newlywed; and Bertha, Molly's cousin. All five women were regulars, Tulle having been the last to join several months ago. But tonight there was a new face among them. The stranger was dressed in breeches like the others, but the quality of her clothing told Ivy she came from money.

A prickle of awareness chased up Ivy's spine. Her class was secret and by referral only, so she trusted that whoever had brought the woman here had done so with good intentions, and yet her instincts warned her that this woman was dangerous.

It did not help that the woman had not removed her half-mourning veil. The black veil was attached to a jaunty little cap pinned in place atop honey-colored locks. From what Ivy could see of the woman's face—which was very little—her eyes appeared to be silvery green and slightly tilted, like that of a cat's.

Ivy took a step closer and offered a dimpled smile. "I am Miss Ivy Bennett, instructor of the Ladies' Self-Defense Club."

"The Dove," the woman murmured. "It is a pleasure to meet you, Miss Bennett."

"Oh, do call me Ivy. The Dove is a...different name."

"That is what she goes by," Tabitha said with a hint of Irish brogue. "She is a friend of my cousin's. I did not think you would mind, Ivy."

"The more the merrier," Ivy replied cheerfully. "The stronger women are, the better the world will be."

"I fully agree," the Dove said, her voice husky and melodious.

"You may want to remove your mourning veil." Ivy took her place in front of the unlit fireplace, out of view of the windows. Although they were sealed with drapes, it would not do for anyone to see silhouettes moving above the shuttered modiste shop at this time of night. "This is an active class, and we will not hold you to mourning customs in this room."

The Dove nodded, but she did not remove her veil.

"All right, ladies, are we ready?"

There came a quiet cheer from the women in the room, and they spread out and faced Ivy.

"Today you are going to learn how to defend yourself from someone who is trying to strangle you. You will learn how to remove hands that are choking you from behind, from the front, and also what to do if an object such as a rope is used around the neck."

Ivy held out her palm to ask Tabitha if she would help demonstrate, and noticed the stricken expression on Tulle's face. The young newlywed was painfully thin, with bland hair and bland features. She kept mostly to herself, and her smiles were always self-conscious, as if she were embarrassed by them.

"Are you all right, Tulle?" Ivy asked gently.

Tulle pressed her palm to her chest, her cheeks paler than usual.

"Would you care to sit? Not every class is right for every person."

The other women exchanged curious looks, and a pit opened in Ivy's stomach. She suspected Tulle had experienced trauma, and anger swept from the tips of her fingers to the joints of her toes. *This* was why she risked everything to be here. Her own mother—Ivy cut the thought off. She would not go there.

Fighting was not always the correct choice or the safest choice, but Ivy wanted to make sure it was an option for every woman who walked through her studio door.

Tulle wavered for a moment, her eyes darting around the room, landing on everything but the other women. At last her attention was drawn by the Dove, and there it lingered. It was as if a transfer of confidence and power flowed from the Dove to Tulle, because Ivy watched as Tulle's spine drew upward and determination settled into the premature lines of her face.

"No, I want to learn."

"Then let us begin."

For the next hour, Ivy taught the women simple and effective techniques that might one day save their lives. Years ago, a killer named the Silk Stalker had targeted women of the *ton* and strangled them with a yellow silk cravat. And only a few months ago, the Evangelist had begun murdering streetwalkers. If their victims had had the skills to fight back, it was possible some of them might have survived.

Sweat was sliding down Ivy's back and sticking her chemise to her skin by the time they finished. Her students were enthusiastic, if unskilled. None excelled the way the Dove did. It was as if she had already known and perfected every move Ivy taught. Ivy was deeply intrigued by the time the clock struck half past ten.

When the women broke for the evening, the Dove made her way over to Ivy. "Lovely class, Ivy. I wonder, where did you learn your techniques?"

Ivy set her water glass on the floor by the wall and inelegantly wiped the back of her hand over her mouth. "I have six older brothers. I learned most of my skills by spying on them when they had fencing and boxing lessons. As the youngest, it was easy to instigate fights with the brothers closest to me in age, and that is how I practiced."

"I wonder if I might entice you into a private match? I am very much interested in your particular skill set."

Ivy cocked her head and assessed the woman. Ivy very rarely sparred with anyone for the simple fact that it was difficult—nay, *impossible*—to find female sparring partners on her level. She thought the Dove just might be the person to give her a challenge.

"Yes, I would like that."

Ivy said her goodbyes to the other women, who were chatting excitedly as they entered the stairwell. Once everyone had cleared out, Ivy and the Dove walked to the center of the room. "Rules?" Ivy asked.

"I do not need any, but if you would like parameters, I am happy to abide by them."

That was interesting. Ivy thought about it and said, "I suppose I do not have any."

Before the words were fully out of Ivy's mouth, the Dove had grabbed her arm, thrust her hip into Ivy's belly, and tossed her to the floor.

Air escaped Ivy's lungs as she stared up at the ceiling pattern. Heavens, she had not expected *that*.

Ivy rolled to her feet and narrowed her eyes. The Dove was not even breathing hard. She seemed as put out as if she had just swatted at a fly. "Again," Ivy said.

This time she was ready for the snakelike attack, blocking a blow to her belly and another to her throat, but leaving her feet vulnerable to the low swipe that knocked her onto her back again.

"You are far more skilled than I am," Ivy said, climbing to her feet. "Why did you attend my class?"

"You are holding back." The Dove's tone was mild as she ignored her inquiry. "You are afraid to hurt me. That is a mistake. This time, I want you to try and strike me."

"I do not think I could—"

Ivy's breath was cut off by the Dove lightly uppercutting her rib cage. Ivy groaned.

"Hit me."

Ivy inhaled deeply through her nostrils and then she let loose, just as she had when she was smaller and fighting her larger brothers.

She fared much better, eventually slipping a punch past the Dove's defenses and connecting with her face. As soon as Ivy's knuckles made contact with the other woman's veil-covered nose—not hard enough to break it but certainly hard enough to make it smart—Ivy shrieked and clasped her hands to her mouth. "Oh my heavens, I am so terribly sorry. I did not mean to do that."

When the Dove dropped her hands, she was smiling widely. "Miss Bennett, I would like to offer you employment."

Ivy bent to collect her water glass from the floor and drank greedily. "I am sorry, madam, but I already have a job."

"Yes, as a governess for Viscount Brackley's younger sisters. That is exactly why I require your services."

Ivy lowered the glass. The Dove continued speaking as she stepped into a skirt that concealed her breeches, and tucked her shirtsleeve tails into the waist. Ivy could smell the expensive peony scent that clung to the woman's skin despite the exercise.

"Perhaps you have heard of Perdita's?" the Dove asked.

It sounded familiar to Ivy.

"Perdita's is the most exclusive governess school in all of England. We supply more than ninety percent of the *ton* and upper classes with governesses."

That was why it had rung a bell. When Ivy had told her mother she was going to decline her father's latest suitor and become a governess instead, her mother had paled and begun to tremble. She had been terrified of what Ivy's father and society would think about the granddaughter of a marquess taking *employment*. She had tried to talk Ivy out of her decision by claiming it would be impossible to find a position without a letter from Perdita's, but Ivy's mind had been too set to ask questions.

"I own Perdita's," the Dove continued, sitting on the floor to pull on her boots. "My governesses do more than educate the young minds of the *ton*. They also listen and collect names and bits of gossip, and then pass the information to me."

Frowning, Ivy wrapped her corset around her ribs. "For what purpose? Blackmail?"

"No, Miss Bennett, but I am pleased you had the nerve to ask. I collect the information to help deliver justice. Who is holding the lords and ladies of the *ton* accountable? Who can stop a lord with a title, fortune, and connections, if he has done wrong? Very few have that power, and that is why I help even the score. When pertinent, I forward information to the Metropolitan Police. But when there is an issue where the courts are incapable of exacting justice, I take matters into my own hands."

Ivy gaped at her. "Are you telling me you have an entire network of spies in the homes of the *ton*?"

"I am." The Dove straightened, and when she patted down her veil, Ivy realized with some awe that the woman looked as put together as if she had just stepped fresh from her dressing room.

"What sort of issues require you to take matters into your own hands?"

"The law is very clear about what constitutes a crime, but it rarely takes into consideration what constitutes a crime against womanhood. Recently, there were a number of progressive and outspoken women who were compromised into marriages in order to secure their dowries and silence. It was not illegal, so no law could hold those men accountable."

"The Dowry Thieves!" Ivy exclaimed. She had closely followed the scandalous exposure in the newspapers over the summer, repulsed by the behavior of the "gentlemen" involved. "Were you responsible for exposing them and ruining their reputations?"

"Yes, along with Mrs. Francis Jones. She was one of my governesses, and she uncovered the entire operation."

Ivy nearly let out one of the whistles her brothers were allowed but women were not. "That is impressive indeed, but what could you possibly need *my* help with? I have only been a governess for a month. I do not—" Ivy's heart stilled. "Lord Brackley. You suspect him of wrongdoing."

The Dove hesitated. "It is more that I have developed an interest in him."

Ivy pulled her dress over her head. "He has only just arrived from Prussia. How could he have landed himself into trouble already?"

"Just because he has not previously been back to Brackley Estate does not mean he has stayed out of the country. In fact, over the years he has occasionally visited England in order to complete business." The Dove paused, tapping her fingers against her skirt as if considering how much to share. "Do you keep abreast of the news?"

"Oh, yes," Ivy said, lacing her riding boots with one knee propped beneath her chin. "I keep up with all the news *and* all the latest gossip."

"Then you will have heard of the curious cases of madness that have begun to plague London. The *madness* presents itself as mental confusion, memory loss, and lethargy, and it has affected women almost exclusively."

Ivy nodded sadly. "The headlines today called it hysteria. A number of women have been committed to institutions, and there appear to be more displaying symptoms each day." She did not want to imagine the conditions the committed women would face.

The Dove's lips pursed. "I do not believe in female hysteria. The idea that women's minds are delicate and easily manipulated would be laughable if there were not very real and devastating consequences for those beliefs. I plan to expose the truth behind the 'hysteria.' I have been going through the information provided by my governesses, and some interesting patterns have emerged. In particular, many of the affected women's households were visited by a certain man within the year leading up to their 'madness.'"

"Do you mean to say Viscount Brackley called upon those women's homes, and then they later became hysterical?"

"More than seventy percent of the 'hysterical' women received a visit from his lordship."

"That is…how could…" Ivy's mind floundered. What could Lord Brackley have *done* at those visits? Why had he been in London so often? "That seems to be more than a coincidence."

The Dove tugged on her black gloves. "Indeed. That is why I need you."

"How can I help?"

"I want you to listen to the servants and the household gossip."

Now, *that* Ivy could do. Gossip was as essential as air to her.

"But more than that, I want you to spend time with Lord Brackley. I want you to assess his character, witness who he deems worthy of his time, and write down his rendezvous."

Ivy's nose wrinkled. That sounded far less appealing. So far, Lord Brackley had been as charming as a flea.

"Lastly, any correspondence, notes, or other written materials that you happen to lay eyes on could make all the difference in solving this puzzle."

Ivy noted the time on the mantel clock and began walking toward the door, deep in thought. This woman, whom she barely knew, wanted her to spy on her new employer. If Brackley were in some way responsible for what was happening in London, then it was the right thing to do. And if he were innocent, then Ivy would be *helping* him clear his name. Either way, she could not turn her back on the Dove's request.

"You will be fairly compensated for your time," the Dove

continued, pausing at the top of the stairs. "And I wish to make a second request. I would like to hire you to teach a self-defense class at Perdita's."

Ivy jumped up and down with excitement. "Oh, I would love that! But I would not be able to travel into London weekly. 'Tis too far."

The Dove waved her hand. "The class would coincide with the Season, when I presume the Brackley family will be in the city. Think it over. In the meantime, will you join us and take on the mission with Lord Brackley?"

Would Ivy join the Dove's secret society of governess spies? How could she not? The women plagued by "madness" needed her, and Ivy had never been able to walk away from a woman in need.

She stuck her hand out, and the Dove shook it firmly.

Chapter 2

Owen scrubbed his palm down his face, feeling the scrape of two days' worth of beard. He had been dodging his new, overzealous valet for days, which meant he had not had a proper shave. He could not stand to be fussed over, and yet he did not have the heart to relieve the man of his duties and livelihood, so instead he had been avoiding him. He would eventually have to speak with him, but valet problems were so low on Owen's long list of disasters that had to be dealt with, he simply hadn't found the time yet.

Owen rocked with the gait of his horse and cursed his wretched father for dying and forcing him to return to England. If there was one place Owen did not belong, it was among people who gave a damn about the bloodline that ran in their veins, and documenting lineage was practically the national pastime here.

Now, the blood that ran through a horse was a different matter entirely.

Worse than having to return to Richmond, a town that held far too many unpleasant memories, was having to deal with the source of his childhood darkness itself: Brackley Estate. The last time Owen had seen the estate, he had been turning his back on a well-kept manor. When he had returned a week ago, it had been to find crumbling walls, peeling paint, and an absent stepmother. Hell, even the mice were mangy. If the estate were not responsible for the livelihoods of dozens of servants and eight little girls, he would raze the entire thing and be done with it. There was nothing there for him but a bad taste in his mouth.

Owen nudged his horse into the street with the ease of a man who had spent more time on horseback than on his own two feet. The visit into Richmond proper to see Lord Terthon had been necessary, as the peer had been an old and good friend of his father's, but the requested nightcap had worn him out. Owen required a heavy amount of alone time, which was one of the reasons he found solace in horses. *They* did not require frivolous rituals. All of the formal bowing and proper words, the things not said but implied, and the notorious cuts with sugar drove Owen half-mad. He was not designed for London society. He was too blunt. Too uninterested in playing nice. He had known it from a young age, and so had his father.

That was why they had put into place The Plan. The viscount had allowed Owen to leave the country with the understanding that should the old man sire another son, Owen would surrender the viscountcy through whatever means necessary. Owen had happily agreed.

Then his father had proceeded to have eight girls.

Saxony nickered, and Owen stroked a calloused hand down the horse's neck. An October breeze lifted strands of the stallion's mane and brought with it the scent of wood smoke, making Owen grateful for the wool overcoat he had chosen last minute. Winter was fast approaching, and the manor was drafty and ill-suited for such a long stretch of cold, as were the stables. He briefly closed his eyes as he thought of the enormous sum it would take to restore the buildings. He was a wealthy man and could afford the repairs, but that did not mean he *wanted* to. He balked at the idea of investing in the thing his father had loved so much, and that he hated with equal passion.

Owen's thoughts drifted from the redesign he was considering for the stables to his half-sisters. Until he had arrived a week prior, he had never met them, and when they had been assembled into a line in the formal parlor to receive him, he had been so exhausted he had barely seen them beyond noting that, although they had the same caramel-colored hair as he, they took after their mother with their mischievous hazel eyes, for which he was grateful. He was not sure he could have borne eight miniatures of his father.

He had been told the girls ranged from the ages of three to ten, and by all accounts they were wild and unmanageable. According to the whispers he had overheard, because God forbid anyone say anything outright, the only person the children seemed inclined to mind was the new governess: Miss Ivy Bennett.

Owen scowled as he remembered his one and only run-in with Miss Bennett. He had briefly met the governess before she had known who he was. She had been charmingly disheveled, with light brown hair, a sprinkle of freckles on her pert nose, and eyes the color of clover honey. With a conspiratorial smile, she had proceeded to warn him about the "grumpy" new viscount who was due to arrive. When he had enlightened her to the fact that *he* was the grumpy new viscount, rather than looking chagrined, she had smartly saluted him. Was her impertinence why his young sisters adored her so? Or was it because she was a Bennett?

Owen's jaw clenched at the possibility that Miss Ivy Bennett was related to *Barnes* Bennett. Might in fact be the man's cherished baby sister. His former school friend had many talents, one of which was witty impertinence. Based on Owen's brief encounter with Miss Bennett, he thought the likelihood of their relation high.

Despite how his friendship with Barnes had ended, Owen still occasionally thought of the man. A decade ago, he and Barnes had been inseparable friends at Harrow, until the day Barnes had bloodied his nose and told him he never wanted to set eyes on him again. Before Owen had recovered from the assault, Barnes had packed his belongings and fled the school without another word. Owen had ridden to Barnes's house to *demand* an explanation, but his closest friend had refused to speak to him, and Owen had been too proud to keep begging. With no further reason to stay at Harrow, Owen had packed his own bags ten days before graduation and left the country, his traitorous friend, and his miserable life behind.

Owen was mulling over the bitter memory, when he spotted a shadowy figure on the road ahead. The streetlamps flickered in the wind, casting dancing shadows across the packed dirt and the silhouette of a woman trying hopelessly to squash a hat atop her head as her horse ambled forward. What was a lady doing riding unescorted on a country road so late at night? Any manner of ill fortune could befall her.

Owen urged his horse into a trot. The woman must have heard him coming up behind her, because she paused and turned beneath a streetlamp, her plush lips falling open and her honey eyes widening with surprise when she realized who he was.

"Miss Bennett," Owen said sternly, "what are you doing in town at this time of night?" His gaze fell to where a good four inches of her stockings were visible beneath her cape. She was riding astride, which in his expert opinion was the only sensible way to ride a horse, *and* bareback. He knew for a fact his stable possessed a number of good saddles.

"Lord Brackley." She smiled widely at him, and a crescent dimple appeared in her right cheek, which was rosy from the October chill. Tawny curls tumbled down her back, and her hat was askew on the crown of her head. She appeared entirely disheveled and breathless, as if she had just come from healthy exercise.

At the thought, Owen's hands seized on the reins. There was only one explanation for her presence on the street at this time of night, and in this state of dishabille. "I repeat, what are you doing in town?"

"Visiting a friend."

His jaw clenched. It was not his place to care whose bed his governess saw fit to visit, but he had to consider his sisters' reputations and the fact that every nosy person in this damned country *did* seem to care about what others did.

Then there was the small, niggling voice in the back of his mind that told him if Barnes knew, he would murder the man who dared tarnish his sister's reputation. Owen did not owe Barnes his allegiance, but he was Ivy Bennett's employer, and that made him responsible for her safety at the very least.

"You appear mussed, Miss Bennett."

"Oh." Ivy glanced down at her misbuttoned gown and laughed. "My friend is the modiste, and she and I were trying on gowns. What is the point in owning a modiste's shop if one cannot sample the wares when the business day is done?"

Owen's shoulders eased with that bit of information. "Is it not late to be calling upon an acquaintance?"

Ivy's lips twitched. "Pray, what are *you* doing in town, my lord?"

Owen's scowl deepened, even as he grudgingly thought, *Touché*. "I did not know governesses were taught to question the master of the house."

"Oh, I suspect they are not."

Flippant, just like her brother. "Although the country is generally safe, there have been recent reports of marauders traversing rural areas. It is unsafe to visit your friend after dark. Alone." His eyes involuntarily fell to the curve of her calf. "Without a saddle."

She squirmed atop her horse at that, but did not respond.

"I will escort you home. Watch for holes and loose stones that could hobble your horse."

"The moon is full." She tilted her head, letting her face bathe in the silvery glow. Her little navy hat slid farther down her hair, and he was irrationally relieved that it was not one of those brightly colored monstrosities that were all the rage in London at the moment, with the garnishing and ribbons so green they hurt the eye. "I believe it is bright enough that my horse will be fine."

She swayed atop her gray mare. The air was crisp, but she did not appear to be cold beneath her cape. Rather, she seemed enthralled by the night. She smiled and lifted her arms at her sides as if she were flying.

God, he despised chipper people. What the bloody hell was there to be so happy about all the time?

"How are you finding Brackley Estate, my lord? I imagine it must be very strange returning home after all these years."

"It is fine," he said curtly. "I have been intending to visit the girls again, but it has been a chaotic week. How are they doing in their studies?"

"Splendidly."

Owen grunted. "What are your qualifications, Miss Bennett? I am sure the dowager viscountess already questioned you, but I too would like to know the woman responsible for shaping the minds of my young sisters."

She studied him for a moment, her gaze running over his shadowed jaw. "I excel at needlework, French, watercolor, the harp, and calligraphy."

"What of hostessing and dancing?"

"Those as well."

"Your father is the second son of the Marquess of Rothford?" He silently begged her to deny it, to claim that she was a Bennett entirely unrelated to his former friend.

A dark cloud briefly passed over her face before she smiled with extra teeth. "Yes."

Owen stifled a groan. "You have a brother."

"Six, actually. Do you know one of them?"

"Barnes. We attended Harrow together."

She nodded, as if she had expected that. "When one has six brothers, one cannot throw a stone without striking a person who is acquainted with one of them."

They rode in silence for a few moments while Owen's tongue worked around the taste in his mouth. "How is he? Barnes? We did not keep in touch."

"Barnes is Barnes," she replied, which told him nothing except that he was still alive.

"Does he know you are employed here?"

Ivy's honey eyes fastened to his and held. "Barnes is out of the country at present."

Again, it was a non-answer, but Owen had discussed the topic for as long as he could stomach. Besides, he strongly suspected the answer to his question was *no*. Considering his final altercation with Barnes, he was certain his former friend would burn down heaven and earth before he let his baby sister live in the same manor as Owen.

Struggling to find small talk to fill the silence—God, he hated this—Owen said, "What drew you to the occupation of governess?"

Ivy caught her bottom lip between her teeth before releasing it, and in the moonlight her plush lip glistened. Owen's groin tightened, and he instantly looked away, horrified by the unwelcome dart of attraction. He quickly began cataloguing horse breeds in his mind to quell the involuntary response.

Shetland, Highland, Clydesdale.

Owen had left a woman behind in Prussia, one who had not wished to make their arrangement more permanent. On the trip to England, he had decided there would be no more women for him, at least for a while. He had not loved Heidi, but the way she had laughed when he had offered her his name still stung.

"We have had a good time, Owen, but this was never going to be more. My father already has a suitor waiting. I have been meaning to tell you but...I was enjoying myself too much."

Owen shook Heidi's voice from his memory and gritted his teeth. No, he was done with women. And even if he were not, he should be ashamed of that single, brief flare of arousal. *Was* ashamed. Ivy Bennett was his employee *and* Barnes's sister, no matter what had happened at Harrow.

Cleveland Gray, English Thoroughbred, Suffolk Punch.

"It was better than the alternative," Ivy muttered, returning his attention to their conversation. Then, seeming to realize that was not the best answer, she straightened and added, "And I have always loved teaching."

Owen stroked his hand along Saxony's shoulder, finding comfort in the slightly oily smoothness of his coat. He had removed his gloves during his visit and had forgotten to reapply them. Fortunately, it was dark, and should they pass anyone on the road he doubted his faux pas would be noticed. "What was the alternative?"

She wrinkled her freckled nose. "Marriage."

"You do not wish to marry?"

"Not the man my father chose."

She hunched her shoulders, as if preparing to hear a lecture about how it was her duty to marry whomever her father thought suitable. Owen gave zero damns about what English society thought was proper, and yet he was now responsible for eight little girls who would have to navigate those very infuriating and restrictive rules, so he supposed he should start caring.

"What was wrong with him?" he asked, curious despite himself.

She slid him a cautious look. "He simply did not suit me."

"Your tastes in a husband shall not impact my opinion of you as a governess, Miss Bennett."

Ivy flashed him a smile, and he noticed in the bright wash of moonlight that one of her eyeteeth was slightly, and adorably, crooked. "Do you know Mr. Marthin?"

He shook his head no.

"He is thrice my age and has little tolerance for women with, and I quote, 'big mouths and spirit.' He likes them, and again I quote, 'broken.' My father thought he was perfect for me."

Owen's knuckles whitened on the reins. Her statement packed a subtle punch and revealed more than she probably realized. At the very least, Ivy's relationship with her father was strained, if not troubled. A memory of Barnes's cheeks flushing with hatred as he talked about his father leaped to the forefront of Owen's mind. If anyone could relate to despising their father, it was Owen, and he *had* related at the time. Unfortunately, it seemed Ivy's experience with her father was no better than her brother's. "So you became a governess to my sisters to avoid marriage?"

"Yes, and I have not been happier. The girls might be a bit wild, as I am sure you have heard, but they have kind hearts. If you will allow yourself to know them, I am certain you will adore them as much as I do. Would you like to visit the schoolroom tomorrow? They would be delighted to see you."

With his father's death, Owen had gone from a carefree bachelor to a man responsible for the livelihoods of dozens along with the well-being of eight girls who might one day be married off to men three times their age who wanted them *broken*.

Over his dead body, he thought with cold resolve. He did not even know those little girls, but they were *his* to protect now.

This situation, the viscountcy, the house, his stepmother—it was everything he had spent a lifetime avoiding, but he was here now. This was his future, whether he liked it or not. So he would visit the girls and get a handle on the situation, and the strange hum of anticipation that slid through his veins had absolutely nothing to do with the fact that he would be seeing the annoyingly cheerful woman riding bareback beside him again tomorrow.

"I will be there."

Chapter 3

"Shall we show Lord Brackley how we sword-fight?" Opal asked. She lifted her wooden sword and jabbed it forward, keeping her left hand on her hip and her spine straight. The six-year-old's hair had tumbled from its pins and swung wildly around her shoulders. She had the same toast-colored locks as all of her siblings—including the viscount—but where his eyes were jade-green, the girls shared the wide-set hazel eyes of their mother.

"Oi! No, put that away, Opal," Ivy cried, racing around the schoolroom and straightening supplies. "Olivia and Odette!" The eight-year-old twins bounced over, ribbons trailing from their pinafores. "Will you please neaten the younger girls? Ophelia, be a dear and hide the swords."

The eldest at ten, Ophelia snatched up an armful of wooden swords and carried them to a cabinet in the corner.

When Ivy had first arrived at Brackley Estate, she had assessed the eight disheveled girls, whose skills ranged from rusty curtseying to banging away on the piano, and she had just *known* she was meant to be there. Everything she had told Lord Brackley was true: She would teach them hostessing and French, watercolors and reading, but more important—at least to her—she would teach them how to defend themselves and stay safe in a world that valued them less than their male counterparts. For every delicate tea party, there was a sword fight. For each stitched rose, there was a lesson on grappling. With every dance tutorial, there came an opportunity to practice balancing, ducking, and dodging.

The girls had taken to her lessons without an ounce of hesitation, as eager and excited to take part in "boy" activities as they were to finally have someone pay attention to them. They were sharp and sassy, and Ivy was unsurprised that their mother had been unable to keep a governess. These were not average children. They had been left to run wild, and as a result had cultivated a resourcefulness most noble-blooded children lacked. They needed more mental and physical stimulation than sedately reciting poetry could give them.

She knew this about them, because she had *been* them as a child.

A small hand wrapped in Ivy's skirts and tugged. "What if our brother does not like us?" Oriana's tiny oval face looked up at hers, her eyes wide with worry. "Mother says that if he does not care for us, he shall turn us out and we will live on the street."

Ivy paused in surprise, a smudged chalkboard in hand. "You spoke with your mother?"

"She came into the nursery this morning," Ophelia explained, slamming the cabinet doors shut before the swords could tumble back out.

"She came to see you this *morning*?" Since Ivy's appointment, she had only glimpsed the dowager once, and it had been late in the evening. To the best of her knowledge—and the healthy gossip of the servants—the lady kept to her rooms, sleeping off her drug-induced haze until the afternoon and then eating before beginning all over again. What could have possessed her not only to awaken early, but also to visit her children? Could it be that she was realizing how absent she had been? Granted, many nobles handed their spawn off to wet nurses, nannies, and governesses, but the dowager had been more inattentive than most.

Ivy's gaze fell on the youngest girl. Octavia was only three years old and was unusually attached to her nanny. Ivy wondered if she had even recognized her mother that morning.

"Did she say anything else?" Ivy wondered.

The twins shrugged and glanced toward Ophelia. Being the eldest, Ophelia was their unofficial spokeswoman.

Ophelia wrinkled her nose, as if she smelled something foul rather than the sweet-smelling harvest of hay blowing in from the open window. "She told the maid we are expecting an *important* visitor, and then warned us that we had better be on our best behavior if we want to stay here."

What visitor? Ivy had not heard any gossip from the servants about expecting a guest. Regardless, she thought it unkind that the dowager had reappeared in her daughters' lives only to make them feel unstable.

"Well," Ivy said carefully, trying her best to remember her place, "if you ask me, I do not think you need to worry about if your brother likes you or not. Why would the viscount want to visit the schoolroom if he were not interested in you?"

"He is not interested in *us*," Ophelia said darkly. "He is interested only in how good we can be."

Ivy opened her mouth to protest, but closed it again. Was that not the truth? Women and girls were only noticed for two things: how good they were, or how bad they were. If it were the latter, it would ruin the young lady's reputation, along with that of her family. It left only the choice of being *good*.

Ivy glanced at the clock on the mantel and gave a little shriek. "He will be here any moment. Girls, please do your best to remember your lessons and manners, and I implore you, I *beg* of you, to forget our secret lessons. Do you understand?" She looked specifically at the younger girls, who had not yet learned to temper their honesty. But the little ones nodded their heads, and when there was a knock at the door the girls scrambled into age order and folded their hands in front of them.

Ivy nodded once in approval and flung the door open. Filling the doorway, one hand pressed to the frame and the other on his hip, was Lord Brackley. His hair was mussed, but his cravat was crisp and perfectly knotted, and his navy-blue morning coat brushed.

She opened her mouth to greet him, but the words died on her lips. His jade eyes were angry, his unshaven jaw taut with tension. That was when she noticed the dowager viscountess at his side. Ivy's eyebrows climbed up her forehead. The dowager stood as if a board had been shoved down the back of her corset. Her black mourning gown bared enough of her bosom to draw the eye, and her dark hair was neatly braided and pinned atop her head. The dowager's hazel eyes landed on Ivy and narrowed. That was when Ivy realized that not only was she staring, but she was also blocking the doorway.

With a hurried step back, Ivy half-curtseyed to both the viscount and the dowager. "Lord Brackley, Lady Brackley."

The dowager swept into the room like a queen while Owen entered slowly, his gaze riveted on the eight fidgeting girls. A bead of perspiration slid down Ivy's spine.

"Mother!" Olena cried in excitement. She was four and had not yet learned that she was expected to hold her tongue unless spoken to. "What are you doing here?"

"Why would I not be here?" her mother asked coolly, raking the girl over with sharp eyes. "I am your mother."

Because you are never here, Ivy thought.

Olena's hopeful face fell at her mother's harsh dismissal, and Ivy's stomach clenched.

The dowager frowned at the display of admittedly poor-looking stitched-rose pillows on the settee. "Young ladies, the viscount has arrived to assess how well you have been absorbing your lessons. I suggest you do not disappoint him. If you are to make yourselves useful with an advantageous marriage match, your training must begin now."

Ivy could not help darting a look at Owen. A flush spread across her cheeks when she caught his green, half-amused eyes studying her as if she were fidgeting as much as the girls.

"Parles-tu français?" the dowager snapped at Ophelia.

Ophelia glanced quickly at Ivy, and she nodded to the girl. That irritated the dowager, because she snapped her fingers in front of the eldest girl's face.

"You will answer to *me*. Unless you are so stupid that you do not know a single phrase in French?"

Ivy's cheeks heated further, and not because she was embarrassed. She was suddenly grateful the dowager was usually in her chamber. The girls' lives were difficult enough without enduring this type of abuse from their own mother.

Ophelia's hazel eyes flashed. "Je ne suis pas stupide, sorcière."

A quiet groan escaped Ivy's lips. *I am not stupid, you witch.*

The dowager's eyes widened, and Owen coughed into his fist. "I do not understand French," he said, his deep voice a soothing contrast to the sharp and bitter tone of their mother, "but it sounds to me as if the girl does indeed speak it."

Ivy thought it unlikely he did not understand French based on the amused laugh he had tried to disguise with a cough, but she appreciated his attempt to save Ophelia from the wrath of her mother.

The dowager stared daggers at her eldest daughter before turning her attention to the twins. "Are you able to add? Subtract? Divide?"

The twins nodded silently, and the witch moved to the next child and demanded she recite a poem for her.

When the inspection was over, with the dowager completely ignoring her youngest two, she turned to Lord Brackley and smiled. When she spoke to him, her tone melted into something false and warm. "What intelligent young sisters you have, my lord."

Lord Brackley had leaned against the cabinet with his arms crossed over his chest to watch the dowager scare her children into shadows, and Ivy was terrified that when he moved, the doors would pop open and spill wooden swords everywhere.

"It appears the governess has done well. Excellent choice, Lady Brackley."

The dowager preened.

"Yet," Lord Brackley continued, "I have not heard from the girls how the governess makes them *feel*."

A line pinched between the dowager's brows. The girls exchanged confused looks but did not move from their perfect line.

"Their feelings do not matter." The dowager rubbed a ruby at her throat with trembling fingers. "Their accomplishments and agreeable dispositions are what is important."

"I disagree." He stepped away from the cabinet, and Ivy braced herself, but the doors remained shut. He approached Ophelia and bent so that he was face-level with the ten-year-old. "I am your brother, Owen. What is your name?"

"Miss Ophelia, my lord."

"Please call me Owen," he said. "Ophelia, if you could use one word to describe how Miss Bennett makes you feel, what would it be?"

Ophelia thought for a moment. "Happy."

Owen nodded and patted her on the shoulder with his calloused hand before moving to Olivia and Odette. "How about you two?"

"Special," Olivia said.

"Bright," Odette added.

Ivy's heart thundered in her chest. She did not know the purpose of this exercise, but her blood warmed with each word the girls spoke. She had not known the regard they had for her. She wished she could scoop all eight into her arms and squeeze them tight.

"Silly," Opal said with a laugh when Owen gently tugged on one of her curls and gave her a smile.

Ollie braced her fists on her hips. "Strong!"

"Happy," Oriana said, repeating her eldest sister's word.

"Fun!" Olena cried.

"Yes, the Bennetts do tend to have that quality," he said.

Ivy frowned. Certainly he wasn't talking about *Barnes*, who was perhaps the only other person she knew as cranky and brooding as Owen.

When Lord Brackley reached the youngest, Ivy watched in astonishment as he knelt on the schoolroom floor before the child. The dowager's fingers fluttered at her throat, appalled to witness the viscount kneeling before the three-year-old she had so cruelly ignored earlier. "Hello, darling," Lord Brackley said, his voice so deep and kind that Ivy's stomach made a strange, slow turn. "You must be the new pony I heard about."

Octavia giggled. "No! I am a girl."

"Are you certain?" Lord Brackley cocked his head. "I was told one of you was a pony. Spin around and let me see if you have a tail."

Octavia whirled around and waggled her bottom at him. "No tail."

"No tail indeed," he agreed solemnly. "I must have been misinformed. Well, Octavia, how do you feel about Miss Bennett?"

Octavia scuffed her little shoe on the floor, and from the corner of her eye Ivy saw the dowager barely restrain herself from admonishing the girl. Octavia said something so low that Lord Brackley had to lean all the way forward.

"What was that?"

She repeated it, again so quietly that he practically had to press his ear to her mouth.

"Yes, I can see that," he said with a nod, and rose swiftly to his feet. "Thank you, young ladies. This has been a lovely demonstration of your knowledge. I expect you all to join me for supper tonight."

Their mother gasped. "The children eat in the nursery!"

"I would like them to join me one night a week," Lord Brackley repeated, winking at Olena. "I want to hear about their lives."

The girls wiggled with extreme delight. This was the most exciting, most mature thing they had ever been invited to, and Ivy knew she would have her work cut out to retain their attention the rest of the day.

"My lord, I have invited our neighbors, Lord Pithins and Lady

Pithins, to supper tonight to welcome you back to England. The children cannot be at the table. It is simply not done."

Lord Brackley's gaze met the dowager's, and although it was blank, Ivy sensed the steel beneath it. "Do not fret, Lady Brackley. I am sure the Pithinses will delight in the children. Thank you for accompanying me this morning." The dismissal was obvious, and the dowager swept from the room without sparing a single glance for her children.

"Miss Bennett," Lord Brackley said, his green gaze meeting hers, "I should like to speak with you privately about your employment here."

Chapter 4

While Ivy situated the older girls with watercolors and the younger ones with wooden dolls, Owen wandered the schoolroom with his hands behind his back, pretending to study the sloppy needlework pillows and smudged charcoal flowers while he thought over what he had witnessed.

That morning, his father's wife had made an appearance for the first time in the week Owen had been back. She had joined him in the breakfast room, gaunt in her black mourning gown and as pale as a sheet. He had noticed her hands trembling even though she had taken care to try to hide it, and it had been painfully obvious to Owen that Millie was withdrawing from the laudanum. He assumed that was why she had not greeted him upon his first arrival.

Millie had taken the thinnest slice of toast, and Owen had been struck by how young she was. His father had wanted a younger wife the second time around, one who could bear him a legion of sons. Despite her illness, her dark hair had been perfectly coiffed, her hazel eyes bitter and fearful. Was she afraid of him? Or afraid that he would turn her and her daughters out?

Aiming to ease her worry, the first thing he had told her was that she and the girls would always have a home at Brackley Estate. A line had appeared between Millie's brows, so he had added that his solicitor was already in the process of drawing up generous dowries for his sisters.

"What of when you take a wife?" she had asked slyly, glancing at him from underneath her lashes. "Will she take kindly to such charity?"

"This is my sisters' home," he had repeated firmly.

"And what if your future wife takes issue with you living with a beautiful woman?"

It had taken him ten seconds to realize she was not speaking about Ivy, but herself. He had not been able to think of a delicate way to respond, so instead he had sipped his strong coffee, which he had learned to enjoy on a visit to Turkey, and said nothing.

When he had excused himself to visit the schoolroom, Millie had exasperated him by insisting on coming with him. And yet when the door had swung open to the sunny schoolroom and his eyes had landed on Ivy, he had forgotten all about the annoyance of having Millie tag along. Ivy's cheeks had been flushed as if she had been hurrying to ready the children, her hair in disarray. She was wearing a soft mint gown that had chalk smudges along the forearm. Her mischievous honey eyes had met his, and it had felt like a hit to the stomach. His visceral reaction to this woman was unexpected and entirely unwelcome. He did not like people with sunny dispositions, instead preferring jaded souls who wielded wit and irony like weapons. So why did he find Ivy's cheer so damned enchanting?

Then she had stepped aside, revealing eight little girls standing in a line, and this time he was not exhausted from travel and *really* saw them. And he had fallen flat in love.

During their mother's interrogation, he had quickly learned that although he might have loved the girls on sight, their mother did not. His sisters were wary of their mother, and the eldest downright hated her. When she had called her a witch, he almost failed to conceal his bark of laughter. It became equally apparent that they adored their governess. Their little hazel eyes kept darting to her for approval and reassurance, which they *always* received in the form of a smile, or a slight nod, and once even a discreet wink. He had not needed the girls to tell him what they thought of Ivy—it had been more than obvious—but the flush of pleasure that had stolen across Ivy's cheeks when they had spoken had made him grateful he had.

When he had reached the littlest, her words for Ivy had cemented a decision he had made the moment he had seen the girls with their governess.

At last, the girls were occupied and Ivy was able to slip into the corridor with him. Owen shut the door and guided her away so they would not be overheard.

"Have I passed your test, my lord?" She brushed a loose strand of hair from her face, and before she could drop her arm, Owen caught it. Her pulse beat in the hollow of her throat when he slowly rubbed his thumb over her sleeve, wiping away a smudge of chalk.

"What test?"

"You were assessing me as much as you were your sisters."

There was no point in denying it. He released her arm and stepped back. "The girls appear happy."

"They have two wonderful nannies who have been with them from the beginning, and they are very attached to them, especially the youngest. The staff here love them, from the butler to the head housekeeper. Although the girls can get into quite a bit of trouble, no one really minds."

"I notice you did not mention their mother on the list of people who love them."

Ivy hesitated and hedged with, "I have only been here a month."

"And I have been here a week, and the answer to that question is already quite clear. It is equally clear that the girls adore you."

"You wish for me to stay then, my lord?"

Owen rubbed his hand over his stubbled jaw. He had awoken that morning resolved to send Barnes's little sister on her way. Owen's new role was complicated enough without the baby of the Bennett family heaping more worries onto his plate, but after what he had witnessed in the schoolroom, he knew it would be not only stupid to let her go, but cruel.

He dropped his hand and sighed. "I not only wish you to stay, but I beg you to. You are everything my sisters need."

A small sigh of relief escaped Ivy's lips. "What did Octavia say to you?" she asked curiously.

"That is a secret between Octavia and me."

"You cannot leave me in suspense."

"If you insist. She called you an ogre."

"She did not!" Ivy planted her hands on her hips, and in her schoolmarm voice said, "Tell me what she said right now, my lord."

Commanding little thing, but Owen had spent a decade handling the wildest beasts with nothing but a firm touch and a deep voice. "I can see you are used to giving orders," he said in a low tone, stepping closer. The scent of lilac and mint filled his nostrils—*her* scent. "But are you adept at taking orders?"

Ivy blushed.

Bloody *hell*. He hoped to God she thought he had said that in the capacity of an employer, which he was. He was her employer and she was the sister of his former friend, and what on *earth* had he been thinking saying something like that to her in such a tone? Owen almost always kept that part of himself tightly under wrap. So why had it felt so natural to speak to sweet, innocent Ivy in such a way?

Because he was a rotter. There was no other explanation. If Ivy Bennett was to remain in his employ, and for his sisters' sake she must, then he would have to stay far away from her.

"I apologize," he said neutrally, inserting space between them. "You are doing a splendid job with the girls. Carry on as you have been."

Before she could speak, he turned on his heel and strode away.

Ivy was exhausted by the end of the day. The girls had been flushed with excitement ever since the viscount's visit and could not stop talking about how lovely they had thought their brother.

"I wish he were our father," Opal had whispered to her twin, Ollie. There were two sets of twins among the eight children, and all of them had names that began with the letter O. Ivy supposed the lady of the manor had thought it a cunning tradition, but in truth almost no one could tell the horde of girls apart, and even if they could, they could not remember which name belonged to whom.

"I do not remember Father. Do you?" Ollie asked.

Ivy was wiping the chalkboard with a rag, and slowed her motions to listen to the girls. The twin six-year-olds were cuddled together in a patch of sunlight, looking over a nursery rhyme picture book while they whispered.

"Only that he was scary," Opal answered. "Scarier than Mother."

"I heard Mother say he almost killed Octavia when she was born because she was not a boy."

Opal traced her fingertip over the colored drawing of a rabbit. "Boys are better."

Ivy opened her mouth to speak, but before she could, Ollie said, "Miss Bennett does not think so. She says we are lucky to be born girls because we are stronger than anyone knows."

"Maybe our brother will like us as girls, too," Opal said hopefully.

Ivy's heart was cracking in two when the nannies and maids swept into the room to gather the girls and ready them for supper.

As the girls usually supped in the nursery, and the dowager viscountess took her meals in her quarters, Ivy had made a habit of eating in the kitchen, mostly because it was a hot center of gossip and Ivy dearly loved to listen in. She was not a servant, so her choice had been unusual at first, but the maids and footmen had grown used to her presence and no longer curbed their tongues around her. Ivy had proven to be a vault with their secrets, and in doing so had earned their respect.

The kitchens would be the perfect place to start spying for the Dove. If anyone knew about Brackley's personal business and the goings-on of the manor, it was the servants.

Ivy was settling down at a rickety corner table with a plate of chicken and stewed vegetables, when one of the maids, Eliza, stormed into the kitchen, her eyes bright and angry. "That—that—that *wench*!"

Several of the cook's helpers were arranging heaping platters of food, but paused in excitement to see what had stirred Eliza into such a froth.

"What happened?" one of them asked, a sprig of dried rosemary forgotten in her hand.

"The dowager," Eliza spat. "She is in a horrid temper. Worse than usual."

A footman was leaning against the sideboard in full livery, his arms crossed over his chest. He was young and handsome, and Ivy knew that at least two of the maids were having affairs with him, unbeknownst to each other. "That is saying something. Two weeks ago she slapped Earnest right across the face, she did."

Eliza turned to him and paused, smoothing her apron and pasting a soft smile on her face. "I did not see you there, Thomas."

"What did the dowager do?" another maid prompted.

Eliza's misty expression dissolved. "She has been snapping orders at me and the other maids all day. I do not think she has taken a single breath in between demands. 'Twas almost better when she was in a fog. She is plotting something, the lady is. I know it by the look in her eye."

Interesting, Ivy thought, but she kept her head down and pushed a slice of chicken across her plate with a fork, discreetly breathing in the mouthwatering scents of the roasted lamb and mint that were warming for the guests. Perspiration gathered on her spine, and she did not know how the cook and her helpers were able to tolerate such heat all day, especially in the summer.

"Do you think she is scheming to marry the viscount?" the footman asked.

"She had best not be." Eliza was about to say more when the head housekeeper swept in. At once the servants snapped straight and scurried off, including the footman.

Mrs. Akers's sharp eyes scanned the kitchen and landed on Ivy. "Miss Bennett, I thought I might find you here."

Ivy gulped and straightened in her chair. Even though she did not answer to Mrs. Akers, she found the woman intimidating, with her tightly knotted hair and no-nonsense mouth.

"Lord Brackley has requested that you join the family for supper tonight."

Ivy's lips parted. "Are you... are you certain? I do not think the dowager would want—"

"It is the lord's house and his decision," Mrs. Akers interrupted. "I suggest you hurry. The first course begins in half an hour."

Half an hour was not nearly enough time! Ivy yelped and raced to her chamber, sorting through her gowns in her mind. She typically wore serviceable dresses for teaching, since she so often ended the day covered in chalk and any other matter of art material, but she had brought with her an entire trunk of much nicer gowns—mostly as a ploy to smuggle in her piles of breeches and fighting clothes. Now she was grateful she had, even if most of them were last season's designs. She doubted anyone would notice, except perhaps for the viscountess.

It was a miracle Ivy was able to find a gown that did not need steaming. She dressed herself and did her hair in record time, cursing the viscount's last-minute invitation as she pulled a rope of braided silver over her neck and tucked the enameled pendant into her gown.

She took a moment to study herself in the looking glass atop her chiffonier. Not for the first time, she lamented her body type. She was not tall and willowy, and she did not possess the delicate wrists and idle fingers of a high-born lady. Her cheeks had seen too much sun, and she was healthy from regular exercise. Her body shape was as unfashionable as the sunny yellow gown she was wearing, with the tiny red butterflies sewn onto the tulle overlay of the skirt.

She lifted her chin. Unfashionable, yes, but her body was capable of amazing things, and she must not forget that.

The gong rang, and Ivy made her way down the stairs, marveling at the number of repairs that were already being made to the house. The banister had been stabilized and shined with a new coat of lacquer. The peeling and stained wallpaper in the main rooms was slowly being stripped and replaced with fresh paint. The chipped brick façades were being mended by masons, and the floors were being buffed and the rotted boards replaced. For a man who had done nothing but growl about the role he had been handed, Lord Brackley was jumping into the task of restoring Brackley Estate with a commitment that surprised her.

Ivy slipped into the parlor, where the guests were already enjoying drinks. Although slightly shabby in the daylight, in the evening the formal parlor held an air of old glamour. Flames flickered in sconces and in candelabras, while a fire roared in a limestone fireplace. The soft lighting gilded oil paintings and danced across the tiny rosebud pattern on the wall.

Lady Pithins was seated on a scalloped-back settee, a cup of tea in hand and her lips pursed so tightly she looked as if she wished to whistle. She was a dignified woman with graying hair and a sour countenance that was only rivaled by her husband's. The Baron and Lady Pithins lived on a small estate across town, and were notoriously conservative. Ivy had met them twice in passing and had disliked them immensely. Lord Pithins was a snob, and his wife was nearly puritanical. They would *not* take pleasure in dining with children, of that Ivy was certain.

The dowager countess sat across from Lady and Lord Pithins, a drink in her finely trembling hand. She flinched as one of the girls shrieked and shoved her sister, all while Ophelia played the piano, her off-key notes adding to the chaos. The girls were dressed and curled and buffed to within an inch of their lives, but they had not been taught how to behave in formal company, something Ivy realized she would have to remedy immediately if the viscount intended to keep his word about having them for weekly suppers.

"You came."

Ivy startled at the sound of Lord Brackley's voice behind her shoulder. She had not heard him arrive, which meant he was either light of foot, or she was losing her touch. After a childhood suffering under the pranks of six older brothers, Ivy had long ago learned to keep an unconscious ear out for sounds behind her.

Ivy spun to face him, and not for the first time was reminded of the nearly foot of height difference between them. His curly brown hair was tousled as if he had just come in from a ride, his green eyes piercing beneath thick brows. His nose was unbroken—a marvel considering his line of work—and his mouth was surprisingly soft and sensuous. It appeared he had finally allowed his valet to shave him, revealing a strong jaw and a wide throat that was not fully concealed by his cravat. He smelled of the shaving cream, something spicy and warm.

Ivy continued her discreet perusal, taking in the expensive coat that stretched over his broad shoulders, the intaglio pin he had slipped through a buttonhole, and the trousers that hugged muscled thighs. Her gaze snagged on his lax hand, the blunt and calloused fingers slightly curled into his palm.

Could this man, with his work-roughened hands and love of his sisters, truly have something to do with the hysterics in London? Why had he been visiting the women who had gone mad? Had they been his lovers? Or had he been there for business dealings with their fathers?

Ivy did not know how she was to discover the answers to those questions, but the Dove had asked her to spend as much time with the viscount as possible and to collect as much information as she could, so she said, "You summoned. I came."

He inhaled slightly, but sharply enough that she noticed.

"Is that your family crest?" she asked, nodding to his pin.

Owen tore his widened pupils from her face and flattened his hand against the pin. "No. Well, in a manner of speaking. It was my mother's."

Before she could think of further prying questions, he said in a low voice that pulled shivers from her skin, "I am hoping you will be able to ameliorate some of the dowager's sharpness with my sisters over supper." He glanced at the gaggle of girls and the drawn face of Lady Pithins. "And perhaps do some shepherding."

Ivy had assumed that was why she had been summoned, and she nodded without speaking. Owen's deep voice had cast her back to the scene in the corridor earlier that day. The way he had asked her if she knew how to take orders had made her feel shivery and strange in a way she could not quite understand. Ivy was adept at *thwarting* orders—with six interfering brothers, a meek mother, and a father who wanted to marry her off to the nastiest man he could find, Ivy had perfected the art of getting what she wanted under all manner of circumstances. And yet when he had asked her if she knew how to take orders, she had felt the strangest, most incomprehensible desire to do just that—for him.

"I shall do my best," she said. "See, I can take orders."

Some emotion she could not name flickered in his gaze. "I suspect, Miss Bennett, you only take orders that please you."

She grinned, because he was absolutely right.

A sharp voice cut into their quiet and intimate conversation. "What is *she* doing here?"

Chapter 5

"Lady Brackley." Owen inclined his head to the dowager. Millie was dressed at the height of fashion, but her coloring was off, and her entire body trembled. He made a mental note to ask the family physician to stop by the next day. Owen had known men who could not live without liquor, who had *died* when it was taken from them. He worried that Millie might suffer a similar fate if she went about removing laudanum from her life in the wrong way. "I asked Miss Bennett to join us."

The piano stopped, and that was when Owen realized they had an audience. His sisters were squirming as if they had ants in their drawers, and the Pithinses were watching him with undisguised censure. Remembering his manners, he strode to Lord and Lady Pithins and welcomed them to his home. After pleasantries had been exchanged, Lady Pithins said sharply, "In my day, children ate in the nursery. They were taught to be seen and not heard."

It was a popular sentiment, but not one Owen felt the need to adhere to. His boyhood had been nothing but silence after his mother's death, and he did not wish the same suffering on his sisters.

Besides, now that Miss Bennett had arrived, she was calmly putting the girls in order so that they were seated and quiet, her gentle, almost inaudible corrections immediately met with their desire to please.

Before Owen could figure out a polite way to reply to the lady, the butler appeared at the door to the dining room. "Supper is ready to be served, my lord."

Lord Pithins escorted Millie, while Owen took Lady Pithins's arm and guided her into the dining room. Millie muttered bitterly about upended seating plans and children, and then, to his surprise, insisted that she and the Pithinses sit near him. The girls primly marched into the room and trembled with childish glee when a league of footmen pulled out their chairs for them. Miss Bennett entered last and, with some confusion at the seating arrangement, sat at the opposite end of the table where typically the lady of the house ate.

During the first course, Millie and Lord and Lady Pithins kept up a steady stream of conversation that required his constant participation, while Ivy laughed and chatted with the girls at the other end of the table. By the second course, Owen was beginning to feel frustrated. He had invited his sisters so that he might get to know them better, and yet here he was making small talk with Millie and the confounded neighbors she had seen fit to invite, and growing grouchier by the minute.

"Lord and Lady Pithins, where is your lovely daughter tonight?" Millie asked slyly. Before the proud parents could reply, she turned to Owen and said, "Miss Pithins is a dear friend of mine. There is not a lovelier woman in Richmond."

Lady Pithins flushed with pleasure, while Owen considered the source of the praise. With parents like the Pithinses and friends like Millie, he suspected he knew exactly the type of woman Miss Pithins was.

"She has a prior engagement. Her company is in *extremely* high demand. When she came out last Season, she turned down *four* proposals. She is waiting for the perfect suitor." Lady Pithins dabbed at her mouth with a napkin even though she had barely touched her food.

"She is a fine horsewoman, is she not?" Millie nudged.

"Indeed!" Lord Pithins puffed up his chest and adjusted the monocle in his eye. "Just like her father, I shall add."

Owen had a sudden, sinking feeling he knew where this was going. Millie had to know he would never marry *her*—the very thought of touching a woman his father once had nearly made him lose his first course—but it appeared she was determined to have a hand in arranging a marriage for him that would be advantageous to her.

When the third course was served, he had heard enough about the perfect Miss Pithins, who was not only an expert horsewoman, but had also made a jam the queen had complimented as "extraordinary," and was as beautiful as the "sunrise on the ocean." He deliberately ignored Millie, who had not stopped asking about Miss Pithins the entire time, and said loudly, "Which one of you is Olivia?"

A girl who could not have been more than eight shifted nervously and said, "I am, your lordship."

"Owen," he corrected.

"Owen," she repeated, the ghost of a smile touching her lips.

"Did you know, Olivia, that I once had a horse with your name? Olivia Peppersnort the Third."

The girls smiled, and Millie made a derisive noise.

"We always give our horses *proper* names," Lady Pithins sniffed.

Owen ignored her. "Olivia Peppersnort the Third was a very

special horse. She had undocumented lineage that many found inferior, but I knew there was something unique about her, and I was proven right the day she saved my life."

The table was silent now, all eyes glued to him with rapt attention. Even Millie, who was pushing food around on her plate, was paying attention.

Owen settled back, his goblet in hand, and met Ivy's eyes. She was smiling at him, as if anticipating a good story. For a moment he had a flashback to Barnes, who had always been able to spin a tale that could keep a man teetering on the edge of his seat. He wondered if Ivy had a similar talent.

Feeling much more in his element now that he was talking about horses, Owen refocused on Olivia, whose cheeks were pink with the excitement of being singled out.

"What happened?" one of the children cried. Perhaps Oriana, or maybe Olena. Owen could not keep them straight for the life of him, although he vowed that by the end of the month he would. If Ivy could keep track of them, so could he.

"I was riding Olivia Peppersnort the Third through the woods hoping to get a sense of her abilities and temperament when it began to cloud in. We turned to head back, but before I knew it, we were caught in a flash storm. When the thunder growled overhead, I thought a hellhound had been let loose by the gods."

One of the girls squealed in excitement.

"Thunder and lightning scare many a horse, but did it bother Olivia Peppersnort the Third?"

"No!" the littlest one cried.

Owen nodded at her in approval. "No, it did not. Olivia powered on through, not once faltering or shying. I knew she was a keeper then, but that was not what made her a hero. We were traversing a heavily wooded area when suddenly there was a crack, and a tree limb knocked me right off Olivia's back. I struck my head, and when I came to, I was pinned beneath the limb with a broken arm, Olivia nowhere in sight."

The table went silent.

"She abandoned you?" Oliva whispered, crestfallen by the actions of this horse that shared her name.

"I thought so at first," Owen admitted. "I thought I was going to die out there, with the sky weeping over my body. Night was beginning to fall, and I knew that would leave me vulnerable to attacks by wild animals. But then do you know what happened?"

Olivia's fingers were gripping her fork so tightly the tips were white. Owen met her eyes and said, "I heard a whinny, and a man shouting my name. I mustered the energy to call back, and then appearing through the curtain of rain was Olivia Peppersnort the Third, followed by my friend on his horse. She had galloped back to the barn, and when he saw she was without rider, my friend followed her back to me. He told me he had never seen anything like it, and neither had I."

"Olivia is a hero!" Octavia, the three-year-old, cried out.

Olivia blushed with delight.

Owen nodded. "Olivia Peppersnort the Third went on to be the best horse I ever owned. In fact, she is so special to me that I am having her brought here from Prussia."

The girls could not contain their cries of delight, eliciting a smile from Owen. When he met Ivy's warm honey eyes again, they were filled with approval, and for some reason, that meant more to him than it should have.

Chapter 6

Ivy did not see Owen much over the next week. Despite her best attempts to end up in his path, he was almost always accompanied by the dowager. Ivy had even slipped into the stables early one morning, certain she would catch him alone, but when she had approached the open tack room door, she had heard him grumbling to the stable master.

"She is everywhere," he had growled. "It is as if there are triplicates of her. I do not understand how she manages it."

Ivy pressed her ear to the wall. Who could he mean?

"'Tis not my place to comment," the old stable groom had replied, "but it does appear that Lady Brackley has multiplied."

Owen, or perhaps the horse, had snorted, and then there had been no more talk. When she heard footsteps coming her way, she had slipped from the barn and returned to the house. She was certain the Dove would contact her soon—perhaps even come to her class again that night—and so far she had been entirely useless in unearthing any information about the viscount, other than the fact that his intaglio pin was of his mother's family crest, suggesting a particular fondness for her.

As for listening in on the servants, the gossip had run from admiring—"Did you see the front parlor? Brand-new carpet!" "Our wages were paid on time this week, and Mrs. Akers said there might be an increase in the future!"—to scornful—"How does he not see what the dowager is plotting?" "Master best watch himself if he dun't want to end up wed to that viper Miss Pithins."

None of the chatter had been useful, other than the confirmation that the dowager was indeed attempting to arrange a union with Miss Pithins. Ivy needed more information, and since she was apparently not going to get it from the man himself, she would have to pivot her strategy.

She got her chance later that day. The children were eating their noon meal in the nursery with the nannies when Ivy looked out the window and spotted the viscount frowning as he held the bridle of a horse. The dowager and Miss Pithins were standing with him beneath the drifting maple leaves and gesturing toward the stables.

Ivy took a moment to study Miss Pithins. By now, she had heard the woman's praises sung so continuously that she half-expected her to be an angel. And although she did appear lovely from afar, with fair hair, smooth skin, and a fashionable riding habit, Ivy did not think there was anything particularly extraordinary about her. She wondered if the viscount agreed or if he had been swayed by the dowager's opinion.

Everyone was occupied, and Ivy realized she might never have a better opportunity to snoop for information.

She hurried to the second-floor east wing where she knew Brackley kept his quarters. She tried to appear natural in case any of the servants spotted her, but her heart was pounding in her chest and her palms were sweating. Give her an opponent with a fencing foil over this clandestine nonsense any day!

Her feet were soundless on the worn, once red and now pink carpet. When she reached his chamber, she paused outside the heavy door, looked left and right, and twisted the knob. She half expected it to be locked, but to her surprise it turned easily, and the door swung inward with a whisper across the carpet.

Ivy quickly closed the door behind her, her heart so loud in her ears that she could barely think. The drapes had been opened, allowing afternoon sunlight into the room. His quarters lacked all personality, and aside from the trunk pushed against the wall, could have passed as any other guest room in the house. Lord Brackley had flat-out refused to take his father's quarters or his boyhood chamber, instead claiming one of the dozen guest rooms even though it was far less grand. The servants were still scandalized that the master suite sat empty.

The tall, four-poster bed took up most of the space in the room, and opposite was an empty fireplace, wood stacked beside it and ready to burn for when the viscount returned that evening. If Owen were in the viscount suite, he would have a number of other rooms connected to his own, but this was a guest chamber, so it suitably narrowed down the places she had to search.

Ivy went to the desk first, her fingers trembling as she pulled open a drawer. She found the typical objects: a letter opener, a well of ink, pens, wax, and matches. In the second drawer there was a stack of blank paper printed with the Brackley crest.

Atop the desk, a half-written letter lay open. She bent close so she could read it without shifting the paper, afraid that if she did, he might notice that the angle of the unfinished letter was no longer perfectly suited to his hand. It was a missive to his property manager in Prussia, requesting that some of his horse tack be sent to the estate.

Ivy made sure all the drawers were closed and turned her attention to the trunk. Distaste at riffling through someone else's possessions coated her tongue, and yet she lifted the lid anyway. Immediately Owen's scent filled her nostrils. Although most of his clothing hung in the wardrobe, there were still a number of starched and folded cravats in the trunk, along with a bottle that she was sure was the source of the scent: something clean and light and woodsy.

Ivy gingerly searched through his belongings, until at the bottom of the trunk she found a neat bundle of letters tied together by a string. She pulled it loose and sat down, hugging the bundle to her chest. Did she have time to look them over, or should she take them to her chamber and return them later?

The thought of trying to sneak back into his bedchamber was too unwelcome, and it was possible he would notice the letters missing in the meantime. Her mind made up, Ivy untied the bundle and quickly began to sort through them. Most of the letters were correspondence between Owen and his various solicitors and property managers, and the rest were about equine sales he had made, all of the buyers seeming pleased with their transactions. There was no evidence that he was cheating his customers or being unscrupulous in his business practice.

Ivy was about to return the bundle when she spotted a letter stuck to the back of a request for a mare by its wax seal. She peeled the letter away, and her heart blipped when she read the salutation:

My Dearest Lover,

The bell chimed the time, and Ivy started with alarm. She was expected back in the schoolroom *now*. She stuffed the private letter down the bosom of her gown, quickly retied the bundle, and returned it to the chest. She bit her tongue when she cracked the door and peeked into the corridor. To her enormous relief it was clear, and she raced down the carpet to the schoolroom, the letter burning against her skin.

Chapter 7

Ivy itched to read the letter so badly she could barely get through the day. At last, the maids came to prepare the girls for supper, and Ivy dashed upstairs to her chamber. She threw open the window, allowing a burst of cool air to ruffle the shawl she kept on her wingback chair, and plunked onto the foot of her bed. With trembling fingers, she unfolded the letter and tilted it toward the lamplight, her stomach in knots.

> *My Dearest Lover,*
>
> *I do not wish for us to part on bad terms. We have found comfort in one another these past two years, and we have had many exhilarating evenings doing what you do best.*

Ivy read the line twice and her mouth popped open. *Oh!* She had overheard many conversations between her brothers over the years, ranging from crass to subtle innuendo, and her cheeks would have flushed at reading something so personal that was not meant for her eyes if she were not also intensely curious to know what made the viscount so *good* at such a thing. Ivy had been kissed before, but she would not describe it as exhilarating. She could not fathom how it could be done differently, and she found she very much wanted to know.

For the briefest moment she pictured how Lord Brackley might kiss. He would angle his head, and those intense, green eyes would never leave her face. He would press one wide, calloused hand to the small of her back and draw her closer, until she could feel the heat of his body and smell the saddle polish and leather on his clothes. His stubborn mouth would soften as he slowly brushed his lips across hers. Perhaps he would not have shaved, and she would feel the rough bristles against her skin.

Ivy rested her fist on her chest, alarmed by the intensity of her heartbeat from simply imagining a kiss. She quickly shoved the feeling down and returned to reading the letter.

> *I know you wished for me to accompany you to England, but my world is here. My betrothed is here. Although I am a noblewoman, I was not made for life under your new queen.*
>
> *Do not be vexed with my decision. I should feel horribly if the way we parted was your last memory of me. You have been good to me—faithful, persistent, and focused. As I endure my new marriage bed, I shall remember you fondly.*
>
> *~Heidi~*

What a witch! Ivy thought, creasing the letter with force. The viscount had asked his lover to come with him to Brackley Estate, and she had not only turned him down flat, but had also boiled their two-year love affair down to something tawdry she could use as fodder while lying with her new, and by all implications boring, husband. Clearly Brackley had felt affection for this woman, but she had not returned it, appreciating him only for what he could give her.

The last line had been unnecessarily cruel, and Ivy wondered why he had kept the letter instead of burning it. It deserved to be ash. Or, perhaps, since she had found it stuck to the back of another letter, he had not meant to keep it at all.

After a few more moments of sitting with her indignation, something occurred to Ivy. She reopened the letter and scanned it for the word that had stuck in her mind: *Faithful*. The woman had said Viscount Brackley had been faithful.

The Dove had asked Ivy to collect information to help her assess Brackley's character. Ivy supposed he could have taken other lovers while with Heidi, but Heidi did not seem to think so, and from what little Ivy had observed of the viscount, she had to agree. He did not seem the sort to spread himself thin with shallow dalliances. He was a man who would pledge his time and energy to one woman, and his devotion would be relentless. Or, as Heidi had phrased it, *focused*.

Ivy tucked the letter back into her dress. She would bring it to the Dove tonight and see if the woman found it helpful.

The next morning Ivy and the girls hiked to the northern field to collect autumn foliage. While the girls sought the crispest, most vibrant leaves, Ivy gazed into the distance and thought about her class the night before. The Dove had been in attendance, and her eyes beneath the mourning net had sharpened with interest when Ivy had handed her the letter.

After she had scanned it, the Dove had asked if she could keep it before tucking it into her cloak.

"Two more women were committed to the sanitorium yesterday," the Dove had said in her low, smoky voice. No one would know by looking at her that she had spent an hour practicing what Ivy now realized were very elementary self-defense moves to her.

"I am sorry I do not have more for you. Aside from the Pithins family, he has not had any visitors. He spends all of his time in the stables."

The Dove nodded thoughtfully, as if Ivy had said something that snagged against a bit of knowledge in her brain. "I will attend your class next week if possible. If I do not, please write to me with any further findings."

A breeze ruffled Ivy's gown now, and a maple leaf drifted from above and landed on her shoulder. She did not feel as if she were helping the Dove or the women being incarcerated. The newspaper headlines that morning had suggested fathers and husbands consider whether the females in their lives should stay in the house, lest the hysteria be "catching," and it had made her feel like a failure.

A hand appeared and plucked the leaf from her shoulder. Ivy yelped and spun around, pressing her palm to her wild heart. "You frightened me, my lord."

Brackley stared quizzically down at her, the sun pulling golden highlights from his short, curly locks. His eyes were greener in the harsh, natural light, the cut of his jaw more angular, the fine lines at the corners of his eyes more visible.

"Saxony and I were as loud as a thundering army. You were lost in thought."

Saxony was indeed nearby, happily grazing on the short, yellow grass.

One of the girls squealed in delight, and three others raced over to see what she had found.

"A lesson?" Owen asked, lifting a heavy brow.

"We are going to identify the leaf species and make prints." Ivy waited for him to admonish her for taking the girls outside.

"It is good for them to breathe fresh air."

On second thought, she should have expected he would approve. In the past week she had rarely seen the viscount indoors, and when he was, he appeared to be more of a restless prisoner than a lord at ease in his domain.

Ivy's thoughts involuntarily returned to the contents of the letter from his mistress, Heidi, and her cheeks reddened.

His eyes traveled over her cheekbones. "You are wind-chapped, Miss Bennett."

"It is chilly."

His gaze roamed her face for a moment longer, then returned to the girls. He slapped his gloves against his powerful thigh. "They seem happy. Stronger, somehow, than even a week ago." He did not speak for several minutes as the wind ruffled his hair. His brows were drawn, his mouth hard as his gloves continued to slap against his thigh.

Slap, slap, slap.

"I fear I have some uncomfortable inquiries to make of you, Miss Bennett."

Ivy gave him a gentle smile. "I grew up with six older brothers, my lord. You would have to work quite diligently to fluster me."

For some reason, the reference to her brothers made him frown harder. "It is ironic that you should mention them, as that is what my first inquiry is about. Do your brothers know you are employed here?"

Ivy pulled her cloak tighter. "Most of my brothers are gallivanting around the world and pursuing lives of leisure. They are not here to monitor my daily life."

Her brothers were experiencing all life had to offer, while *she'd* had to become a governess to avoid marriage. Early on in life, her father had made it clear her only value to her family lay in her ability to make an advantageous marriage. When she had first entered society, her father had strongly suggested a number of suitors, each more unpalatable than the last. When her third Season had ended and she had remained unbetrothed, her father had written her a scathing letter in which he had informed her that he was tired of funding her "frivolous lifestyle," and therefore she *would* marry the next suitor he chose.

Then he had selected a monster.

Powerless, Ivy had not known where to turn. All she had known was that she could not, *would* not marry Mr. Marthin.

Days later, she had glimpsed the advertisement for the governess position at Brackley Manor, and felt as if her prayers had been answered. If she were a governess and her father no longer had to support her existence, then perhaps she would not have to marry. Perhaps he would leave her alone. Perhaps she could be *free*.

She had written to her father, declining the marriage to Marthin and explaining that she would no longer be a financial burden, as she had taken a position as a governess. Her mother had cried for days afterward and taken to trembling every time the front door opened. Ivy had known her father would not visit, but she had accepted the mail with a sour stomach for weeks afterward. So far, her father had not contacted her. Although Ivy was tentatively hopeful, she knew her father and feared there was still misery on the horizon.

When she realized her shoulders were hunched at the thought, she forced them down. She was safe and happy for now, and she would *never* cower before her father again, whether in person or in thought.

And she would not ever marry his monsters.

In fact, there was only one person Ivy would accept a proposal from, but during her three Seasons she had not once caught the man's eye: *Lord Hartford.*

The youngest marquess in the *ton*, Lord Hartford was in his third decade of life and had eyes the color of molten chocolate. She had only been near enough to hear him speak once, at a country ball three years ago. Ivy had witnessed an old servant woman spill a glass of port on the marquess's coat sleeve, and Ivy had frozen to the spot, terrified of what would come next: his face would redden and his eyes would glitter with malice. He would strike as swiftly as a snake and leave the servant's cheek bruised.

But that had not happened. Ivy had watched with astonishment as Lord Hartford had kindly begged the woman not to fret, and then had asked the host to borrow a coat.

Hartford had treated the servant with more kindness than Ivy's father had treated his own wife. In that moment, Ivy had known that if she were forced to marry, she wanted her husband to be Lord Hartford. Not because of his title or visage—although he was beautiful in the way of a painting or a sunset, he had not once made her heart flutter—but because he was kind. Unfortunately, Hartford was a marquess while she was not even a lady. Her dowry was painfully modest, and there was the not-so-insignificant complication that he did not even know she existed.

One of the girls squawked with surprise as a gust of wind ripped through the clearing, pulling leaves from the trees and cycloning them over their heads. They raced around, trying to snatch them from midair.

Brackley cleared his throat and rubbed the back of his neck, pulling her from her memories. "I do not think your brother—Barnes—would be pleased to know you are here."

"Why?"

His jaw clenched. "Our friendship did not end on the best of terms."

She dearly wanted to ask more even though it was not her place as a governess to pry into the viscount's personal relationships. Then again, the Dove had asked her to discover as much as she could about his character.

"Barnes can be difficult," she said cautiously, waiting to see if he would take the subtle invitation to expand on his rift with her brother, but he remained silent. Realizing he was not going to elaborate, she added, "Fortunately, he does not know about my position here, nor does he need to."

Brackley's lips twitched at her defiance. "Very well. There is one other matter I wish to discuss. Have you... have you noticed anything out of the ordinary when it comes to the dowager?"

"Out of the ordinary? I did see her use a spoon to eat a piece of lamb. 'Twas quite awkward."

Brackley gave her a frustrated look. "No. I am asking if perhaps she seems focused on a particular goal to you."

Ivy knew exactly what he was hinting at, but she could not help teasing him a bit more. He was so grumpy and gruff all the time that she found perverse pleasure in needling him. She nodded solemnly. "Yes, indeed. We are all aware of Lady Brackley's plans."

He inhaled sharply.

She lowered her voice to a whisper and canted her head. "The lady *despises* the drapes in the breakfast room, and I do believe she is plotting to have them ruined."

Brackley's green eyes met her dancing gaze. "Are you playing with me, Miss Bennett?"

"I am simply answering your uncomfortable inquiry, my lord."

He made a rumbling noise, never removing his eyes from her face. His presence was imposing, his height blocking out the thin autumn sun at his back, and yet Ivy did not feel a single flicker of fear. A man who treated his eight sisters with care and compassion was not the sort of man a woman had to fear.

"I must warn you that it is *I* who prefer to do the playing."

Ivy's breath hitched at the dark undertone of his voice. He had not said anything untoward exactly, but the way he had imbued his words with a hint of something mysterious and forbidden made her mouth go dry and her heart skip a beat.

"What...what do you like to play, my lord?"

Olivia raced up to them and held out a fat red maple leaf to the viscount. "Brother, this is for you!"

Brackley tore his eyes from Ivy and accepted the leaf. Ivy staggered backward as if she had been released from a spell. There was something intoxicating about Owen Brackley's intensity, something that made a woman feel as if an earthquake could not shake his attention from her. Perhaps that was what his Prussian mistress had found so compelling.

Once Olivia had given Brackley a leaf, all the girls decided they must as well. It could have turned into a lesson on different tree types and other useful information, but when Octavia threw a handful of leaves at her older sister, a gleam entered the viscount's eyes. Before Ivy could protest, and she had to be honest, it would have been a token protest at best, he was engaged in a leaf fight with all eight girls. They screamed and giggled as he roared and swung them around, leaves showering them in a fall of gold, red, and russet.

Ivy watched from the side, a smile hovering on her lips. She could not believe this man, who chased a three-year-old through the leaves and tickled her until she collapsed with laughter, had anything to do with the hysteria in London. His prior visits to the affected women in London *had* to be a terrible coincidence, and she needed to prove it.

Chapter 8

The girls had a thousand questions about Saxony, stroking and touching the ever-patient horse, until at last their well of questions ran dry. When it was time to return to the manor, they ran ahead while Owen walked beside Miss Bennett, the stallion at his shoulder puffing clouds of steam into the cool autumn air.

Owen broke the uncomfortable silence first, seeing as he was the reason for it. For a second time he had lost all sense of gentlemanly decency and had made a comment to his governess that was entirely inappropriate.

Bloody hell, the woman was becoming a problem. He could not stop thinking about the sprinkle of freckles on her nose, or the maddening half-moon dimple in her cheek that begged to be kissed. He was keenly aware of her whenever she was near, her laughter lighting up the otherwise gloomy estate. The servants respected her, the children adored her, and he strongly suspected that if she were to organize a coup, his own household would follow her without a second thought for him.

Owen was cognizant of his faults, foremost among them a

tendency to pursue his passions with single-minded intensity. Although such drive could be a blessing when it came to his business, it was a curse when it came to his personal life. He could not allow his attraction to his governess to continue. He *would not* allow himself to imagine her hair spread across his sheets, her eyes glazed with passion, her sweet breath escaping on a moan.

Bloody. Hell.

Thoroughbred, Hackney, Dartmoor Pony.

Rather than risk more of her cheeky teasing, which would inevitably tempt him into saying things he should not, he said, "I will speak plainly, Miss Bennett. Does it appear to you that Lady Brackley is attempting to matchmake me with Miss Pithins?"

"I appreciate your candor. Yes, it appears so."

His gut twisted. He *hated* this. Very few in Prussia had known he was the son of a viscount, so he had escaped the machinations of those who would use him and his title for their own gain. He had not been in England a fortnight, and already his stepmother was scheming to manipulate him. "She is wasting her time. I have no interest in marriage at present."

"You and I are alike in that way."

"I know you did not wish to marry Mr. Marthin, but I thought it was the gentleman in question you disagreed with, not the institution itself?"

She seemed surprised that he remembered the name of the man who had wanted to "break" her, when it was branded into his brain. Marthin had already been added to his "do-not-sell-to" list.

Ivy's cheeks reddened. "That is correct. There is someone I would marry, but he does not know I exist."

Owen blinked in surprise. She had set her cap for someone? He was suddenly desperate to know *who* had brought that blush to her cheeks, but it would be inexcusably rude to pry further. "I do not know what to do about Lady Brackley," he said instead, returning to the latest in a series of never-ending problems foisted upon him by the viscountcy. "I will tell her I am uninterested in Miss Pithins, but I do not think her scheming will cease."

"Perhaps you could tell her you have no intention of marrying *anyone*."

"I fear she would take that as a challenge."

"'Tis possible." She chewed on her lip, and Owen averted his eyes.

"It is not your burden, Miss Bennett. I required only your confirmation."

"Nevertheless, I shall think on a solution."

"I will have you know I do not condone murder."

Ivy clutched her hands in front of her chest. "Does Viscount Brackley have a sense of humor? Do the papers know? Shall I alert them?"

Owen scowled. "They would never believe you. Perhaps the dowager feels the need to interfere because she fears I will turn her and the girls out, and I need to redouble my efforts to reassure her that will not happen."

"Perhaps."

"You sound doubtful."

"My lord, you have already made it abundantly clear that you intend to provide for your sisters as well as the dowager. I suspect her scheme has more to do with power than fear for her children." Ivy's skin paled beneath her freckles. "I should not have said that," she whispered. "'Twas not my place to speculate so plainly."

"Do not fret, Miss Bennett. You are safe with me."

Her pupils expanded, and he belatedly realized he had said

the last sentence in the low, masterful way he spoke when he was doing...other things. Owen scrubbed a hand down his face. He ought to be struck across the cheek.

Ivy took a shuddering breath, and he was captivated by the sudden idea that she was affected by him and the way he spoke to her.

Or mayhap she is frightened of you. She *had* just said there was another man she wished to marry.

That was a far less appealing notion.

They resumed walking, and all too soon the rambling manor came into view. The house had once been grand, boasting more than twenty guest rooms along with private quarters for the family and separate lodgings for the staff; a ballroom; and an indoor orangery. Now the gardens and orangery were a mess of browned brambles and weeds, and the windows were dirty and some of the panes broken. The majority of the rooms were sealed to the chill of winter and hosted an assortment of squirrels and mice rather than guests. Even the façade, once a stately gray stone, was streaked with rust.

The stables and carriage house were in equal disrepair. A line appeared between Owen's brows as he once again tried to imagine where his father could have been spending his money if not on the upkeep of the seat of the viscountcy. He had not had a gambling problem as far as Owen could tell, nor did he seem inclined to purchase luxury items and baubles. Owen had seen the books: He knew his father had invested wisely enough that he had not been suffering for funds. So where had it all been *going*?

The girls had reached the house ahead of them, but instead of entering, they had gathered on the steps with the dowager and Miss Pithins to gape at a beautifully lacquered carriage parked in the drive.

Ivy picked up her pace, her eyes widening.

"What is the matter?"

She did not answer, but broke into a skipping trot, and Owen finally understood what had distressed her: plastered across the door of the carriage was her family crest.

"Someone from my family is here. What if my mother is ill?" she asked breathlessly.

They had almost reached the carriage when Owen unthinkingly cupped her elbow. She paused long enough to lift her face to him, her honey eyes filled with concern.

"Whatever is the matter, we will take care of it."

A moment later a harsh voice he had not heard in over a decade said, "Take your bloody hand off my sister."

Chapter 9

Ivy gasped with delight and tugged her arm free of Owen. She ran across the remaining distance and flung herself into Barnes's arms.

Her eldest brother's stiffness slowly receded as she clung to him, until his arm wrapped around her shoulders and he said gruffly in her ear, "I missed you too, Trouble."

Ivy pulled away and studied him. His eyes were a solemn gray as always, and his dark hair was neatly cut. His stature was so imposing that it was nearly identical to Brackley's. "What are you doing here? I thought you were abroad? Is something the matter?"

"Father wrote to me."

That somber statement chased away the small amount of pleasure she had felt at being reunited.

"Who is that?" a girlish voice asked before it was hushed, and only then did Ivy remember they had an audience. She stepped back and wiped her palms on her skirts. The dowager and Miss Pithins were eyeing her brother in a way that made her hackles rise, while the girls curiously studied him on shifting feet, and

Brackley... when her eyes landed on him, she was taken aback by the strange mixture of longing and fury in his eyes.

What *had* happened between them?

Barnes dragged off his hat and bowed to the dowager and Miss Pithins. "My deepest apologies for not introducing myself. I am Mr. Bennett, Miss Bennett's eldest brother."

"We are ever so pleased to meet you," the dowager purred. "Will you be joining us for tea?"

"It pains me to decline, but I have come to speak with my sister about an urgent matter."

"Girls, go inside," the dowager snapped, the sweet tone she had used on Barnes absent. The girls reluctantly shuffled indoors, but neither the dowager nor Miss Pithins joined them.

"Perhaps Miss Bennett and her brother would like some privacy," the viscount said in a deep voice beside her.

Barnes practically snarled at him. "Miss Bennett does not require you to speak for her."

Ivy's eyes widened at the obvious animosity. Heaven knew her brother could be difficult, but he was not typically *that* rude.

Miss Pithins pulled a handkerchief from her dress and pressed it to her lips, obviously thrilled with the unexpected drama.

"You might as well stay, Brackley," Barnes said, making no apology for his aggression. "You ought to know that as of this moment my sister resigns her post."

Ivy's head jerked. "Pardon me?"

Barnes gave a curt nod, affirming that she had heard him correctly. Ivy recognized the stubborn jut of his chin as The Barnes Look. It was the same expression Barnes had worn when he had ordered their father out of the house and informed him that he would live in their London residence, far away from their mother, and would not *ever* return. It was the look he'd had when he had dismissed their brother's tutor for cruelty. If fortified stone were to come up against The Barnes Look, it would crumble. This was the immovable Barnes, the Barnes who brooked no argument.

"Barnes, *no*," Ivy said, despite The Look. "The girls need me."

He tore his eyes from Brackley, the dislike so palpable between them that Ivy could brush it with her fingertips. "I came the moment Father wrote that you were employed here. I would no sooner allow you to work for this dishonorable swine than I would allow you to join a pirate ship."

Ivy swore she could feel Brackley stiffen behind her shoulder. She divided a disdainful look between Barnes and her employer. "Whatever happened between the two of you does not involve me. Now if you will excuse me, I have duties to attend to."

"Did you not hear me, Ivy? You cannot stay here."

Ivy's temper was always slow to heat, her disposition naturally leaning toward forgiveness, but once it did—and lord knew Barnes always had a knack for stoking it—she was as much a force to be reckoned with as her brother. If mulishness ran in the blood, then the Bennetts were half donkey. "You cannot stop me."

"You know I can."

Ivy's fingernails bit into her palms. She *hated* feeling impotent simply because of her sex. Her eldest brother could, in fact, make decisions for her, but if he forced her to leave her position because of a grudge he held against Brackley, she would make him pay dearly. There was no place he would be able to escape her rage, no continent far enough, no civilization remote enough.

He must have caught a glint of the devil in her eye because he added, "I am not here only because you have taken employment with *him*, Trouble. Father has found you another suitor. He wrote that he will not tolerate his daughter, the granddaughter of a marquess, 'masquerading as a governess,' and insists you quit your post at once." His eyes trailed over Brackley, who stood as still as stone. "Considering the circumstances, marriage is the preferable choice."

"Who is it? Who is the suitor?"

"Mr. Ellis Reedly."

Ivy paled. Mr. Reedly was her father's age and a widower three times over. He had pouty lips and lovely locks threaded with gray. Women flocked to him, and used words like "distinguished" and "beautiful" when speaking about him. But Ivy had seen his true personality one too many times and knew he was no better than he had to be. Ivy would *not* become her mother, trapped in a poisonous cage with bars formed of vows.

"No." She felt Brackley's gaze boring into the space between her shoulders as she spoke. "I shan't marry him."

"Reedly is well off and a distinguished fellow."

Tears stung the backs of her eyelids. She wanted to teach her classes at night and the Dove's school during the Season. She wanted to make a difference that went beyond how many children her hips could bear. Marriage to one of her father's monsters would dash all of her hopes and dreams.

"We shall miss you," the dowager said, with as much warmth as a soldier saying goodbye to the pox.

Ivy's throat closed. She could not speak. She could not move. She could barely think.

"Let us take this indoors," Brackley said quietly.

"I would not step foot inside your—"

"Can you not see that your sister is affected and needs a moment? Have some compassion."

Barnes's eyebrows snapped together, and he opened his mouth

to retort, but he must have seen something on Ivy's face that stilled his tongue. Grudgingly he said, "Yes, let us find you a spot of tea, Trouble."

The dowager and Miss Pithins hooked arms to enter the house. Ivy's desperation was so crushing that she barely noticed the dowager calling for Barnes to escort them into the sitting room. The two women and her brother disappeared down the corridor. Ivy knew she must be following because when she looked down, her feet were treading marble tile, and yet she felt as if someone else were maneuvering her body.

"Miss Bennett."

Ivy paused, and when she turned, it was to find Brackley so close that she had to take a step back to meet his eyes.

"Do you wish to marry Reedly?"

"*No.* He is unkind. That is probably why my father likes him."

Brackley pressed a hand to the wall beside her, his gaze raking over her face. "Tell your father no, like you did with Marthin."

Ivy's temper returned, burning through some of the cool numbness. "I said no to Marthin and found a position as a governess instead of as a wife, and that clearly did not deter my father. You do not know him, Lord Brackley. He will not stop until I am unhappily wed." She halted, realizing who she was speaking with and the inappropriateness of it. "It does not matter, my lord. It is not your problem, except I fear you will have to find a new governess."

She stared over his shoulder, blinking back tears of rage.

"Look at me."

When he gave her an order in that low, shivery voice, she had no choice but to obey. Her eyes met his.

"It matters." He opened his mouth as if to say more, and then shut it again. He turned his profile to her, his jaw clenching. "You said there is someone you *do* wish to marry. Why do you not have your father approach him?"

She gave an incredulous laugh. "He is a marquess! I am nobody to him."

"I wonder... if there is a way we can help one another."

"How?"

"Perhaps there is an alternative to marrying Reedly."

She considered what he was saying. "I suppose I could run away." She would hate to never see her brothers again, and what of the girls, and the women in her classes? Which would be worse: to isolate herself from everything and everyone she loved, or to marry Reedly?

"Do not do that." His command was immediate and firm, as if she were a horse to be handled.

"I shall do as I like."

He sighed and pinched the bridge of his nose. "My apologies. I should not talk to a young maiden in that tone. What I meant to say is, *please* do not run away, because I may have a solution that could suit us both. Allow me to court you."

Her jaw dropped.

"Not in truth," he added hurriedly. "It would be a mutually beneficial arrangement. If your father knew I was courting you, it would, at the very least, delay the arrangement with Reedly. Your father sounds like the sort of man who would prefer the chance of having a viscount for a son-in-law over an untitled man. Similarly, the dowager would leave *me* alone and cease her attempts to match me with Miss Pithins."

"But then we would be expected to marry," she said slowly, as if he were very stupid.

"No. After a few months passed, you would end the courtship.

A lady may call off a courtship or engagement, even in instances where a gentleman may not."

"Are you mad?"

"Miss Bennett." His hand dropped from the wall and he shifted closer, until she could smell the horse leather and polish from the stables on his clothes. "Would a courtship not give you several months of reprieve from your father's machinations? Would earning the attentions of a viscount—and then jilting him—not elevate you in society so that you could have your pick of husbands afterward? Would attending all of the most sought-after society crushes not give you the opportunity to finally catch the eye of your marquess?"

Her thoughts raced as she considered the idea. It was bold and dangerous and a little bit exciting to think of pulling the wool over everyone's eyes. Her father would consider it quite a feather in his cap if she were to be courted by a viscount, and it *would* grant her a reprieve from his incessant matchmaking. And it was true that men of the *ton* coveted what others had, so if she were to be seen with the viscount, it could very well bring her to Lord Hartford's notice.

There was also the fact that a faux courtship with Brackley would mean she would have unprecedented access to the man, his associates, and his whereabouts. There would be no more sneaking around and trying to catch glimpses of his comings and goings from the stables. She would have ample opportunity to fulfill her duties to the Dove and, hopefully, clear his name.

Yet there were two obstacles that stood in their way. The first was Barnes, who would challenge the viscount to a duel the moment he heard the news. The second was the girls. If they thought she and Owen were to be married and then they were not, would it crush them?

Owen waited patiently while she considered his proposition. Finally, with a sigh, she shook her head. "I am sorry, my lord, but I cannot do it. What of your sisters? Would they not be devastated when the courtship ended?"

His features softened. "Yes, of course. We will have to keep it from them."

"They will hear about it whether we wish them to or not."

"Then we let them in on the secret."

Ivy brightened. Most adults would not trust children to safeguard such sensitive information, but Ivy happened to know the Brackley girls were *excellent* secret keepers. She was pleased that Owen was inclined to involve them, enough so that he was willing to risk one of the girls slipping up and exposing their charade.

She agreed instantly. "That solves that problem, but there is still the issue of Barnes. I fear, after what I witnessed, that my brother would not take the news well. It is apparent he does not like you."

"Barnes does not dislike me, he *hates* me."

Ivy leaped at the chance to learn more. "What happened at Harrow?"

"It is complicated." Before she could pry further he added, "I must admit, infuriating Barnes is part of the appeal." He eased away from her, and Ivy took her first, deep breath in minutes.

"Well, you are nothing if not honest, my lord." And yet despite Brackley's indifference, she could not lead Barnes to believe she was intent on marrying his mortal enemy. "If we do this, and I am not saying I have agreed to it, we must tell Barnes the truth as well."

Brackley scowled.

"If he knows it is a farce, that it has an end date and that you have no intention of *actually* marrying me or compromising me, he may be more amenable."

"Somehow I doubt that."

Ivy propped her fists on her hips. "Barnes does not get to orchestrate my life. I will *make* him see reason."

"As you wish. Do we have an agreement?"

"What about my position as the governess?"

His eyes flicked to the sconce on the wall and he frowned. "You cannot stay on as the governess if I am courting you, but you cannot simply leave my sisters, either."

Ivy twisted her fingers together as she thought. "I have a good friend, Diane, who is in between governess positions. I could invite her to take the position, and I could stay for a while to ease the transition for your sisters." That way, Ivy would be able to squeeze in a little more time with the girls before she was forced to leave.

Brackley gave a curt nod. "Yes, that should be suitable, assuming your friend is a satisfactory replacement."

Ivy took a deep breath. "Then yes. I will do it."

His green eyes bored into hers. "I am trusting you to quietly end the courtship on a mutually agreed-upon timeline, Miss Bennett."

Ivy laughed and patted the breast of his jacket. "Do not worry, my lord. I will not require you to follow through with our ruse. If I cannot have Lord Hartford as a husband, I do not want anyone."

His gaze sharpened at the name before it dropped to where her fingers remained pressed against his coat. She quickly removed her hand, and he cleared his throat. "You should call me Owen, now that I am courting you. At least in private."

"And you may call me Ivy."

"Ivy."

The way he said her name, as if he were wrapping the sunny syllables in silky shadows, made her shiver. For a fleeting moment, she wondered if she was in over her head, but she quickly dismissed the thought. Brackley—no, *Owen*—had just bought her several months of freedom and the possibility of making herself known to Lord Hartford; she would not waste this opportunity worrying about what could go wrong.

Chapter 10

Owen dragged his palm over his jaw and took a long drink. How could his day have taken such an alarming turn in only a few short hours? He glared at Barnes, who sat amiably on the settee and droned on about the most boring topics known to man. The dowager was rapidly losing interest, splitting her time between throwing triumphant smirks in Ivy's direction, and calculating ones in his. Miss Pithins, however, appeared to be absolutely *enthralled* by the lime content percentage on Barnes's property.

Owen dropped his eyes before his gaze could return to his governess, and drained the rest of his glass while he stared at the piano. Seeing Barnes for the first time in a decade had rattled him more than he cared to admit, so when he had learned that Ivy was to leave her position and marry another man, he had reacted without thought. The despair on her face had angered him more than anything else had in years. He had fondly come to liken Ivy to one of his wild horses, and to see her father try to break her was a goddamned shame. He had spotted a slim opportunity to save them both, and he had taken it.

When she had told him the only man she wished to marry was Lord Hartford, it had done something odd and uncomfortable to his chest. He did not have any direct dealings with Hartford, but he knew the marquess was young and kind. He was the sort of man who drifted through life with a soft smile on his lips, his head above the clouds, and his intellect focused on philosophy and *what ifs*. He was the antithesis of Owen, who was grounded in *doing*, and doing as much as possible with his own hands. Ivy had set her cap for a man who was gentle and pleasant, rather than rough and grumpy, and Owen could hardly blame her. If she were looking for a man who would treat her like porcelain, Hartford was the perfect match.

And yet, he was not convinced Ivy *did* want a husband who treated her like a doll. She was vivacious and clever, and he rather thought she needed a man secure enough to appreciate her spirit in all its facets.

But what did he know about marriage? The only other woman he had broached the topic with had laughed in his face.

He went to take a drink, and was surprised to find his glass empty. The proposition he had found springing from his lips in the corridor had seemed shaky at best, but the more Ivy had argued against it, the more he had found reason to like it. Not least among those reasons was the fact that it would infuriate Barnes. Barnes had destroyed their friendship and all their future plans ten years ago, and it felt good to finally return some of the anger and helplessness Owen had felt at the time. After Barnes had struck him in the face and told Owen not to contact him again, he had left Harrow and never once responded to Owen's letters. He had ignored every visit. He had completely cut Owen out of his life without reason or explanation, so when the offer to visit family in Prussia had come, Owen had taken it, vowing to excise Barnes from his life.

Yet here he was, a decade later, sharing the same air as his former friend and discovering that forgiveness was the farthest thing from his mind. He wanted to hurt Barnes as much as Barnes had hurt him. And if in the process it helped Ivy, then it was all the better.

Owen glanced at Barnes, whose ungloved hands were clasped between his knees. Barnes seemed entirely at ease, but then, as if he could sense Owen's gaze, he lifted his eyes. He never stopped talking about the chemical properties of soil, but if looks could slay, Owen would be lifeless on the ground.

Owen flashed him a satisfied smile, and Barnes practically snarled.

Despite his best efforts to avoid looking at her, Owen's attention shifted from Barnes to Ivy, who was pacing at the back of the room. A tendril of hair had escaped her pins and was curling over her cheek, and her soft maroon gown complemented the enticing flush on her cheeks.

He winced as he realized where his mind had wandered, where his mind *always* seemed to wander with Ivy. The last thing he needed was to lust after the woman he was going to falsely court, when half the purpose of their ruse was to help her catch the eye of the man she *did* wish to marry.

She must have felt his gaze, because she stopped pacing and smiled at him. It was naught but a sweet tilt of her lips accompanied by that crescent-shaped dimple, but it was enough to make his stomach clench.

Miss Pithins finally stood. "My apologies, Mr. Bennett, but I must be on my way. Mama and I are to attend the church fair today."

"It is time for my afternoon rest as well," the dowager added, latching on to the excuse.

Barnes was the perfect gentleman as he escorted the women

from the room and closed the door behind them. He prowled to the decanter and poured himself a drink, glaring at Owen with challenge the entire time. Owen was tempted to cross the remaining space between them and connect his fist with Barnes's jaw and demand to know what it was that had fractured their friendship, but he would not lower himself to begging for information again. Barnes had made up his mind about him over a decade ago, and far be it from Owen to corrupt his former friend's crusade against him.

"Heavens," Ivy said, "she lasted longer during your boring monologue than most."

Barnes's eyes warmed fractionally when they settled on his only sister. "I did not even know what I was saying by the end. But alas, now it is the three of us, so let us wrap this up, Trouble. I want to make it home before nightfall."

Ivy nodded. "I have decided to resign my post, brother. I will write to my governess friend to replace me, and I will await her arrival so that I can ease her into the situation."

Barnes bobbed his head in satisfaction, then frowned as the part about waiting for her friend sank in.

"It will be especially important that I pass on my duties," Ivy continued, hesitating only slightly before adding, "since I am being courted."

Barnes seemed surprised, but pleased with her easy acquiescence. "Then let us write to Father."

"No, you misunderstand." Ivy stepped closer to her brother, her honey eyes pleading. "I am sorry I did not tell you before, but I was too stunned. You see, I cannot marry Mr. Reedly, because I am already being seriously courted by another gentleman."

Barnes's head jerked in confusion. "Who?"

"Someone with a title. You know Father will love that."

Silence.

Barnes's eyes slitted. "*Who?*"

"Lord Brackley."

One moment passed, then two. Barnes looked over at him and must have seen the affirmation on his face. What happened next was so quick that Owen did not have time to think. Barnes set his glass down and charged toward him, shoving him against the wall. "The hell you are! Over my corpse will you *ever* touch my sister!"

Ivy shouted in the background, but Owen was too busy dislodging Barnes's arm from his throat. His former friend was strong, especially when fueled by rage, but Owen had spent a decade honing his body with hard work. He knocked Barnes's arm away and shoved his friend off him.

"You touch me again, and I will lay you flat," he growled. "That was your one free shot."

"*Enough,*" Ivy snapped, inserting herself between them. "Barnes, you dolt, will you let me finish before you turn into a Neanderthal?"

Barnes ignored her, and that ignited Owen's temper further. Ivy deserved her brother's respect. "Pay attention to your sister."

"Lord Brackley, I challenge you to a—"

"It is not real!" Ivy shouted.

Barnes paused his issue to a duel long enough for her words to penetrate his fury. He glared down at her. "What?"

"It is not a real courtship. Step away, Barnes, and listen for once in your life."

With a dagger-filled look, Barnes reluctantly stepped back. His chest was heaving, and his cheeks were red. It took everything Owen had not to provoke the man into a good brawl, but he did not wish to upset Ivy.

Ivy very calmly picked up Barnes's discarded glass and handed it to him. "Drink."

He did.

"Good, now listen carefully, brother. I do not wish to marry Reedly. He is cruel."

At that news Barnes stilled. Barnes was an ass, but he had zero tolerance for bullies. At Harrow he had garnered more than one black eye defending those who were smaller or different.

"Lord Brackley does not wish to marry at present, and we all know that, with his title, there will be more than one mama throwing her daughter at him," Ivy continued. "We have agreed to announce a mutually beneficial, but *false* courtship. Father will leave me be, and it will ease the pressure on Lord Brackley. Once enough time has passed, *I* will call off the courtship, preserving my reputation." Her cheeks pinkened when she added, "And it may give me the opportunity to catch the attention of a suitor I *would* be willing to marry."

Barnes rubbed his hand over the back of his head. "Do you have a particular suitor in mind? Perhaps Father can—"

"Lord Hartford."

Barnes's expression faltered. "The marquess?"

She nodded, and his lips pressed together. He knew as well as Owen that if Ivy's father approached Lord Hartford now, the marquess would turn him down.

"I will remain here at Brackley Estate until the new governess is settled," Ivy continued. "With my friend's presence, along with the dowager's, there will be no question about propriety."

Owen poured another glass of Scotch and tossed back a mouthful. It burned his throat as his eyes landed on Ivy's form, the sweet curve of her bottom just visible beneath her skirts. *Bloody hell.* He averted his gaze before Barnes could catch him. Then he would *really* have a duel on his hands.

Barnes's fists flexed as his eyes darted to Owen. "Are you truly entertaining this absurd scheme?"

Ivy answered for him, which was a good thing, because Owen honestly did not know what to say. "It is not absurd, Barnes. Unconventional and daring, perhaps. Do not ridicule something so precious as my chance to find a happy marriage."

"Not every marriage can be happy, Trouble."

"I will not settle for our mother's life."

Barnes flinched and set his glass on a side table with a clink. He began pacing back and forth, his arms behind his back and his brows drawn in thought. Owen could practically see his former friend's hatred warring with his desire to make his little sister happy. Even in his Harrow days he had had a soft spot for her.

"You intend to use your courtship to entice the marquess?"

Ivy nodded. "He does not know I exist. Arriving at society events on Lord Brackley's arm could change that."

"You do realize," Barnes said at last, addressing Owen, "that under no circumstances would I *ever* allow my sister to actually tie herself to you?"

Owen ground his molars, tempted to ask why that was, but refusing to give Barnes the satisfaction of once again denying him answers.

"Why not?" Ivy asked, having no such reservations. Her eyes traveled between them. "What is your history? Owe—Lord Brackley has not been forthcoming."

Barnes's eyes went flat. "No, he would not be, would he?"

What did *that* mean?

"*If* she does this, and I *strongly* advise against it, she will remain untouched and her virtue intact so that her reputation is not ruined when she ends the courtship." Barnes once again closed the distance between them, his boots silent on the carpet, until they were almost nose to nose. "Do you understand that, Brackley? If you touch her, I will destroy your life."

Barnes had always known how to rile him, but Owen would not allow a reaction this time, not when Barnes was threatening him over something he probably *needed* to be threatened over. With her freckled cheeks, impish eyes, and curvy body, a man would have to be dead not to notice Ivy Bennett, and despite all of his internal admonitions, Owen had noticed her.

If Owen was going to go through with this hoax, he would have to be very, *very* careful. No more admiring her curves. No more innocent touches. No more letting his voice fall into *that tone*. He was not going to marry Ivy Bennett or anyone else, for that matter, at least not for a good long time. All he had to do was keep his hands and thoughts to himself. He could do that, surely?

"Barnes," Ivy said sharply, "I am entirely capable of making decisions about my own body."

"Ivy, if he compromises you, then he has to marry you, and I cannot allow that to happen."

"Have you married every woman *you* have touched?"

"That is different."

"How? Because society says so?"

"No, you do not understand. There are things about him you do not know. Hateful, horrible things."

Her expression faltered for a moment, and something like doubt flashed in her eyes.

Owen could have defended himself—maybe he *should* have since Barnes was lying about him—but he had always balked at being forced into things, so instead he lifted a brow and remained silent in the face of Barnes's accusations. He tilted his amber-filled glass at Ivy. "It is your choice. Back out now if you wish."

She glanced between the two of them, Owen leaning casually against a writing desk and sipping Scotch, and Barnes hovering several feet away, vibrating with anger.

"The plan remains," she said.

Barnes cursed and turned away. "I do not like you staying here."

"With two other women in residence, I will be chaperoned at all times."

"Not good enough. I want you to move home."

"I will in due time, but I cannot leave the girls yet."

"If you insist upon living with this meater, sister, then I have no choice but to move into Brackley Estate until this absurd charade is over."

Owen barked out a laugh. "You are mad if you think I would allow that."

"No, old friend, you are mad if you think I will allow this to happen any other way. I am home for two months before I must depart again, and I shall spend it here, watching your every move, haunting your every thought, my eyes peering into every dark corner. When I leave, Ivy will come with me. You two had best hope your little scheme has had its desired effect by then." He stared them both down. "The countdown to the end of your courtship has begun."

Chapter 11

"Is it true that our brother is courting you?" Ophelia asked three mornings later. Ivy guiltily halted in the act of wrapping a dummy sword handle. The house had been in an uproar from the moment the viscount had stated his "intentions" toward her, and neither she nor Owen had had the time to speak with the girls. The dowager was tight-lipped with anger, and Miss Pithins had not visited again, although her lady's maid had told the Brackley cook's assistant that Miss Pithins had thrown a *very* expensive vase across the room.

The servants were in a tizzy about the impending arrival of Barnes, their first proper overnight guest in years, and there had been a number of awed and accusatory glances thrown in Ivy's direction, as if she had betrayed them by acting as one of them only to turn around and secure the master's affections.

Stomach clenching with shame, Ivy finished her task and brushed a strand of hair from Ophelia's face.

"It is true that your brother is courting me, but I will share a secret with you now, and with your sisters later. Do I have your word that what I say will not leave your lips?"

Ophelia nodded with determined maturity.

"The courtship is not real. Your brother and I are helping each other. I am avoiding marriage to another man, and your brother is avoiding the attention of unmarried ladies, and we are doing that by pretending to have him court me."

Ophelia studied her with eyes that saw more than a ten-year-old's should. "So you are not going to marry?"

"No. In a few months our 'courtship' will end."

"Will you leave us then?"

Ivy nodded sadly. "My father insists that I must leave my governess role here and marry. This pretend courtship is only delaying the inevitable."

"Then why can you not marry my brother for real?"

At the innocent question, butterflies took flight in Ivy's stomach. She could not marry Owen for a number of reasons that included her brother and the fact that Owen appeared unwilling to expose his heart again after Heidi, but for a moment, the thought of being the growly viscount's wife was not entirely horrid.

"Because we are not a fit," she said, even though that did not feel like the right answer. At Ophelia's crushed expression she added, "But I still have several months left with you and your sisters, so we do not have to worry about goodbyes yet. Besides, your new governess will arrive soon, and you will adore her. I promise."

Ophelia seemed unsure, but before Ivy could sing Diane's praises, Opal and Ollie ran over, leaves clinging to the hems of their skirts as they waved swords over their heads.

"I am a pirate!" Ollie growled, pointing her sword at Ivy. "Give me your loot or you shall perish."

Ivy lifted her own sword and gently tapped it against the six-year-old's. "I have no loot, but I enjoy a good fence anyway."

Ollie's eyebrows pinched with menace. "So be it, lass!" She made the first lunge, which Ivy easily parried. She thrust again, and Ivy ducked. While Ollie continued taking swings at her, Ivy gently instructed her on her foot placement and how to anticipate a rival's moves.

"Your swings are wild, Pirate Ollie. Control is key." Ivy shifted her shoulders in time to avoid a jab from Ollie's twin, Opal. "Two on one!" Ivy cried in mock dismay. "You did not say you brought a pirate friend."

Opal tried not to giggle but failed as she and Ollie continued to try to outwit their governess.

Ivy and the girls spent the next hour working through thrusts, parries, and footwork. One day the girls would be able to hold their own with any of their male counterparts.

The girls' cheeks were red with exertion when suddenly Ophelia's head whipped around, and her eyes filled with panic. "Is that our brother cantering toward us?"

"Make haste!" Ivy squeaked, collecting the wooden swords in her arms and frantically whirling around, searching for a place to stash them. They were in a small clearing a good distance from the house and out of eyesight of the manor. There was nothing between them and the trees except for crunchy, fallen leaves. "Help me bury them under the leaves!"

The eight girls hurriedly swept leaves over the pile of swords.

"Grab hands in a circle," Ivy instructed.

They made a ring and held hands, and as Owen drew closer Ivy closed her eyes and intoned, "May the heavens bless upon us this wondrous— Oh, Lord Brackley. What brings you to our daily prayer session?"

On foot the man was taller than most; on horseback he was a giant. Plumes of warm breath puffed from his horse's nostrils and the beast pranced in agitation, ready to continue his run. Owen expertly controlled him with powerful thighs and steady, gloveless hands. He wore a dark navy riding coat, and his hair curled beneath the brim of his hat. His jaw was unshaven again, his green eyes sweeping over the flushed little girls and their wild hair. A blush crawled down the skin of Ivy's chest, and she was thankful for the cloak she wore against the autumn chill. This giant, handsome, rough-and-yet-still-polished viscount was supposed to be courting *her*? What had she been thinking, agreeing to this? No one would believe that someone like *him* was seriously courting someone like *her*.

"Prayer in the fields?"

"It is God's cathedral," she replied solemnly.

Owen swung down from the horse and petted his neck with smooth, firm strokes. Ivy averted her eyes, not understanding why the gesture should make her stomach flutter. "I have always thought so, Miss Bennett." His attention stayed on her for a moment too long, until Olena's horse whinny broke the awkward moment. Owen's brow furrowed as he took in his disheveled, red-cheeked sisters. "Girls, are you feeling well?"

"It was a long walk," Ivy said hurriedly. "They are flushed from the exertion."

All the girls nodded, except for Octavia. The three-year-old turned curious eyes on Ivy, as if wondering why they must keep their fun swordplay a secret.

Owen seemed unconvinced. "Girls, head inside to the kitchen. Tell Cook the viscount said you are each to have a hot chocolate."

The girls squealed with delight and took off for the house, the littlest lagging behind but her legs pumping no less fiercely.

The moment they were out of earshot Owen murmured, "You look as if you are keeping secrets, Miss Bennett."

Ivy ducked her head. "I do not know what you mean, Lord Brackley. And remember, you must call me Ivy now."

"Ivy." He spoke her name in a low way that drew out the syllables and caused a shiver to trip down her arms. "And no more *Lord Brackley*. That is my father's name."

"Yes, my lord."

The look he gave her was half amused, half annoyed. "Do not 'my lord' me, either. If this courtship were real and leading to marriage, I would never stand to hear those words cross my future wife's lips."

Wife. The gravity of what they had done struck her anew with the utterance of that single word.

"This may have been a mistake," she choked out. "I do not think—no one will believe—"

Owen dragged his hat from his head and tossed it on top of his saddle. "No one will believe what?"

"No one will believe you are courting me with honest intentions."

A line appeared between his brows. "Why not?"

She made a distressed sound. Was he really going to make her say it? "You are a handsome, wealthy, and well-respected viscount, and I am...me."

She could not parse the look he gave her, not even when his eyes dropped and insolently traveled from the hem of her dress to the top of her head. Her cheeks were flaming by the time he finished. "Nonsense."

"But—"

"Barnes arrived a half hour ago," he interrupted, cutting off further protests. Ivy groaned. "I suggest we discuss the specifics of our ruse."

"What else is there to say?"

"There are several details that need clarification. First, as of this moment, you are no longer employed by me. It would not do for anyone to think I am courting my governess, not because I am embarrassed by it, but because I find the power imbalance revolting. You and your brother are my guests now. That said, you have my blessing if you wish to continue visiting with the girls.

"Second, we must discuss what the courtship will look like. The dowager is far too perceptive. If she suspects this is not what it seems, she will not hesitate to spread rumors that may impede your chances with Hartford."

"All right." Ivy fiddled with the edge of her cloak. "So we must make it look real. How would you go about wooing a woman you truly wished to wed? Would you bring her flowers? Write her love poems?" She could not help thinking of his Prussian mistress, and wondered what he had done for her.

"I am not the type to write poetry."

"I did not think so."

He tugged at his cravat, looking awkward. "I have not courted a woman in the traditional sense. I suppose I can send you flowers if that is what you wish."

"That is too generous of you, my lord."

His gaze snapped to hers. "Are you mocking me, Ivy?"

"I would not dream of it."

The look he gave her told her he knew better. "We will need to be seen in public. I will need to walk with you. Dance with you.

Look at you as if you are my world." He cleared his throat. "But it is not real. I wish to reiterate that."

Ivy grinned, enjoying his discomfort. "Do not worry, your lordship. You are far too grouchy for me to grow fanciful about."

There was a flash of surprise in his eyes, and something that looked a lot like disbelief. "Did you just call me grouchy?"

"Do you deny it?"

"Most people are not so brave as to say it to my face."

"Alas, I am not most people. I am your *love* interest."

He blanched, and she could not help laughing again. "You cannot act like that in front of others. You must pretend to truly care for me. We shall practice. Compliment me."

His eyes trailed over her body before he jerked his gaze away. "You are not so terrible."

Ivy's lips parted in horror. "*Owen!* Your flattery needs serious improvement. *You are not so terrible,*" she mimicked. "Shameful. Can you not think of one thing you like about me? Here, I shall give you three compliments you can use when we are in front of others." She stuck her tongue between her teeth and thought. "You can tell me I have pretty eyes."

"Honey."

"What?"

"You have eyes the color of warm honey."

She paused, surprised. "Yes, that is poetic. Very good. You can also say I look like…" She searched around for inspiration, her gaze falling on a wild aster. "A delicate flower."

"But you do not."

Ivy fisted her hands on her hips. "My lord—"

"You do not look delicate, or like you will wilt. You look strong and competent, and wise and unyielding. More like an oak than a silly flower."

She went speechless at the unexpected compliment that had more meaning than any flattery she had received in a long time. "That is actually quite nice, but I do not know that *others* will think calling me an oak is a compliment."

"Fine. You are as pretty as a flower."

"Delightful. And finally, you can say I am a docile and virtuous lady with many accomplishments."

He stared at her.

"Well, I am accomplished."

"You are accomplished," he parroted.

"Now, if you can only remember to say those things without appearing ill."

"Therein lies our trouble. This will have to be a carefully orchestrated balancing act. We must appear to be smitten in front of others, but not *too* smitten lest we put Hartford off, or convince Barnes there is something real to it."

"I do not think Barnes would make that mistake, but I shall speak with him again."

"Please do. As for social engagements, I have gone through a pile of invitations and chosen three engagements where we can start making our courtship public, and where Lord Hartford should also be in attendance."

Her heart pounded. Was this truly happening? Was she going to attend a *ton* gathering on the arm of a viscount and with her eye on a marquess? How had her life changed so rapidly? Ivy's palms turned clammy. What had seemed a perfect solution at the time now felt as if it were spiraling out of her grasp.

"The first event is hosted by a business partner of mine. He lives in the country and puts on an annual party before he leaves for London. He has business dealings with Lord Hartford, so I believe the marquess will be in attendance."

Ivy mentally ran through the gowns in her wardrobe. Most of them were out of fashion. Would she have time to order new dresses on her salary? Doubtful. She would need to have her current dresses turned and ribbons and lace added to spruce them up. "When is the party?"

"In a fortnight."

That should be enough time if she delivered the gowns to the modiste shop straightaway.

Owen rubbed the back of his neck. "I secured invitations for Barnes and your governess friend, Miss Diane Wixby, as well." His horse bumped his shoulder, and he petted him reassuringly, his large hand dragging down the horse's nose. "Perhaps it is a blessing your brother is here. I am not a gentleman, no matter what title I have had thrust upon me. It is best to remember that, lest we find ourselves believing this is real."

By *we* he clearly meant *her*. He seemed very concerned about the possibility that she would start to think the courtship was real, no matter that she had repeatedly reassured him she had no designs on his affections. "My lord, I do not harbor secret plans to entrap you in a real marriage. Unless you have forgotten, I wish to wed someone else."

He stared at her with intense, jade-green eyes, until she flushed under his scrutiny. "You react to me."

She pulled her cloak tighter. "What does that mean?"

"It means I know how fanciful young women can be. You and I are not a match, Ivy. You are not someone I would ever truly marry."

His words pricked at her affable manner. She had not thought Owen was the type to feel superior about his position, but it seemed she had been wrong. Was this what Barnes had been trying to warn her about?

"Once again, I must stress that I have no illusions about you," she said coolly. "Do not fear that you will end up wed to me. In fact, I shall take *great* joy in ending the courtship when the time comes. Does that appease you?"

A line appeared between his brows, and his lips parted, but before he could insult her further, she took off at a brisk walk, clutching her cloak at her chest. She was grateful when a few moments later she heard his horse's hooves recede in the distance.

As her doubts about Owen crept in, she thought once again of the Dove and the hysteria in London. She would have to find a way to question Owen about his visits in the city. Perhaps Lord Brackley was not the man she had thought he was after all.

Chapter 12

Barnes appeared to be in a foul mood during drinks before supper that evening, but Owen was not feeling all that chipper himself. After his discussion with Ivy, he had been reassured she felt similarly about the courtship and he did not have to worry she harbored secret ambitions to be a viscountess—and yet he could not shake the feeling that he had said something to upset her. It had to have been when he told her she was not someone he would ever truly marry, but surely she had known that was a compliment? Ivy deserved a man who would whisper sweet things that amounted to more than, "You are all right." She deserved a husband who would reflect her sunshine instead of swallowing it like a black abyss. She deserved a lover who would treat her gently while kissing her on a bed of roses—or some such nonsense like that.

Owen was none of those things. He was surly and had demanding desires. It would be a *shame* if someone like Ivy were bound to him. The only woman he would consider taking for a wife, and only far in the future, would be an equally jaded person who knew exactly what she was getting.

His lips tugged as he thought of his former governess's flushed face when he had ridden upon her and the girls in their "prayer circle." They had looked flustered and guilty as sin. Ivy had been quick to answer his inquiries, but the girls did not have the same practice at subterfuge. They had exchanged obvious glances and had bit back smiles. Something was afoot, and he was determined to discover what it was.

Owen glanced at Barnes, whose face was a mask of granite as he lounged on the settee in the parlor, a tumbler of whiskey clasped in his hand.

"The governess, my lord?" Millie hissed, appearing at his elbow. Fury flashed in her eyes before she banked it into gentle curiosity. Not for the first time, Owen wondered how his father had been so blind when it came to this woman.

"Do you have a question, my lady?"

"I have given you a few days to come to your senses, but it seems you have not. You must excuse my disbelief that you have fallen for the governess, when there are more appropriate options." Her gaze drifted briefly to the window, as if she could see the Pithinses' estate from where she stood. "You could make an advantageous match, one that would benefit your sisters, and yet you pursue the governess?"

"You seem to be quite upset that Miss Bennett held a governess position for a month. You may rest easy, Lady Brackley. The granddaughter of Marquess Rothford is no longer educating the girls. She and her brother are guests now. *My* guests."

The dowager's lip curled, and she lowered her voice. "You can be honest with me, my lord. I am your mother. Have you compromised her?"

Owen became aware of Barnes's undivided interest in their

conversation. "You were my father's wife, *never* my mother." Millie was a year younger than him and did not have a motherly bone in her body, just as his father had not had a fatherly bone in his body. Perhaps they had been an ideal match after all. "Let me be crystal clear: Miss Bennett has not been compromised in *any way*. If she had been, I would be marrying her, not courting her."

Christ, was it hot in the room? Was his cravat too tight?

"He speaks the truth," Barnes said coolly. "Lord Brackley's *interest* in my sister has extended back years. Did he tell you that he and I went to Harrow together? He had his eyes on her even then."

Owen met Barnes's burning gaze and frowned. He did not recall ever talking about Barnes's sister—had not even known her name back then. Why would he have? He would have been eighteen to Ivy's eleven. The mere thought was reprehensible, and yet he did not refute the fabricated statement. The most important thing was keeping Ivy's reputation pristine so that neither of them ended up bound to the other.

Barnes's lip curled in disgust at his silence. "With my presence here, it shall be known far and wide that my sister is chaperoned at every moment. Anyone who dares suggest otherwise would be outed as a fool, as I would make it my personal mission to discredit her."

As far as threats went, it was an effective one, because the dowager paled and pressed a gloved hand to her chest. "You are not suggesting that *I* would engage in such common behavior as gossip, Mr. Bennett?"

Barnes gave her a placating smile. "No, my lady. I know you would not."

Ivy chose that moment to appear in the doorway, a vision in a purple silk taffeta dress that accentuated her narrow waist and ample bottom. Her shoulders were bare, touched only by artfully loose tendrils of hair draping from her pins. Her cheeks were flushed, as if she had been outdoors, and that made the sprinkle of freckles on them stand out more. Her honey-colored eyes scanned the room, and she smiled tentatively, that little crescent-moon dimple popping into relief.

Owen wanted to taste that dimple. He wanted to draw his mouth down her smooth, bare neck before he gently closed his palm over her throat.

Angry at where his thoughts had drifted, he turned his back on her, thanking heaven Barnes had risen to greet her and had missed the flash of lust that had no doubt crossed his face. His unwieldy thoughts were getting out of hand. It seemed that every time he was near Ivy, he found some new point of desire to contend with.

Distance was what he needed. Aside from the social engagements they must attend together, he would have to find a way to be as scarce as possible. They only had nine weeks before Barnes whisked her away. *Surely* he could manage to avoid her for a grand total of sixty-three days?

Barnes poured Ivy a drink, and Owen only remembered the dowager's presence when she gave a low, mocking laugh. "You do not have to court the girl to satiate your *appetite*, my lord. There are others in a better position to appease it while you search for a proper match."

"What do you know of my *appetite*?"

Her dark eyes glittered. "I may have read a letter from Miss Heidi Wagner."

Owen's fingers whitened on his glass. "How do you know Miss Wagner?"

"I do not. A letter of hers arrived, and I thought it was mine. My mistake."

"Yes, I am sure my name on the front was misleading."

She was unapologetic when she said, "She misses you and has changed her mind about marrying the man her father chose. She wishes to travel to England and mend your relationship. When I received the letter, I had still hoped you would find joy in Miss Pithins's company, but as it has become apparent you do not, I suggest you consider Miss Wagner's offer. It sounds as if you once loved this woman, and she is noble-born, if a foreigner. She is the wiser choice, not only for your own social standing, but for that of your sisters."

Her deception and scheming rankled him, and he had the horrifying realization that Heidi and Millie would get along splendidly. It was enough to make him question just what the hell he had been doing with Heidi in the first place.

"It is not too late," Millie added slyly. "Courtships end all the time."

Owen swallowed the amber liquid. He was drinking too much, so he set the glass down and contemplated what to say. As the mother of his sisters, Millie was always going to be in his life, but he would not tolerate her continued interference. "I will see to it that the butler keeps a keener eye on the post from now on." She flushed, but he continued in a steely voice, "Miss Wagner is in my past. Miss Bennett is my future. I do not want to hear anything else about this."

He didn't realize he had spoken so loudly, or that the room had grown quiet, until Millie turned her shoulder and spun away, leaving Barnes staring at him with a stitched brow.

The butler opened the door and intoned, "Miss Diane Wixby."

A woman with shocking red hair whirled into the room like a compact and exuberant cyclone. She wore an outrageously bright traveling gown, and she gave the butler such an impish smile that he visibly faltered and closed the door quickly, as if he feared he might accidentally become the center of her attention.

The woman's gray eyes scanned the gathering, skimming past Barnes and then darting back to him for a moment before she cried, "Ives! I have come as requested, and now that I know Barnes is here to insert his signature awkwardness into every situation, I see why you wrote for me."

Ivy's face split into a grin. "Diane!"

For heaven's sake. This was the new governess? Forget sobering. Owen lifted his drink again when Barnes practically snarled at the new arrival. All Owen wanted was a bit of peace to work with his horses, and now he was courting his former governess in order to help her marry someone else, the man who hated him most in the world was living down the corridor, and with the arrival of her governess friend, whom Barnes clearly despised, Ivy had just thrown a match into their already precarious powder keg.

Chapter 13

Diane hugged Ivy hard enough to crack her spine and let her go just as quickly. "It is good to see you."

Diane was a whirl of bright taffeta and scented lemon, and Ivy was so happy to see her friend that she could not stop smiling, even if the moment Diane had proclaimed Barnes awkward and he had bristled like a cornered dog Ivy had known she had made a grievous miscalculation in asking Diane to come. How could she have forgotten the animosity that had existed between Diane and Barnes their entire lives? Ever since they had been young, Barnes could not stand the wild and mischievous Diane, but Ivy had not considered that his dislike would carry into adulthood. She had been mistaken.

"Thank you for coming."

Ivy wished they could escape and catch up together in a more intimate setting, but at that moment supper was announced. Barnes quickly took Ivy's arm to escort her in, shooting Owen a triumphant look. Ivy sighed.

Supper was no less awkward. Owen frowned silently from the

foot of the table, although occasionally she felt his eyes lingering on her face. Barnes sat opposite her, alternating glowers between Owen and Diane. The majority of the evening's entertainment fell on the dowager. Unfortunately, she seemed to have taken an immediate dislike to Diane, and was doing her best to cut her with every breath she took, but Diane was far too quick-witted and blithely twisted her every word.

"How quickly you arrived to your friend's aid," the dowager said, her fork paused over a slice of lamb. "How was it that you were available? I would think a highly qualified governess would already be engaged."

"The family I was employed by recently moved to a more fashionable area."

The dowager's lips pressed together. "I suppose it is fortunate for you that Miss Bennett is leaving her position, since you have no husband and must work."

Diane nodded. "It is true that I am free to choose my employment, whereas I would be most tethered if I had eight children."

The dowager's retort was cut off by the arrival of the servants, who cleared the dishes and removed the tablecloth for the next course. Before the dowager could start in again, Diane turned to Owen and said, "Have you heard of the recent rash of illness in London, my lord?"

Ivy's eyes widened, and she dropped her hand. Here she had been in Owen's employ for several weeks, skulking around and listening to gossip and searching his chamber to no avail, and within an hour Diane had managed to bring up the very topic Ivy was so keen to learn about.

Owen's gaze lifted from where he had been contemplating the wine in his goblet. "I have not read the papers today."

"It has been in all the papers every day this week. A large number of women have recently become ill, but no one knows why. Some are saying the symptoms are figments of their imagination, and several have been institutionalized for hysteria."

"Good!" The dowager gave a delicate shudder. "I have heard hysteria is catching."

Ivy was studying every minute expression on Owen's face. Frown lines appeared at the corners of his eyes. "That is nonsense. If I had to wager, I would bet the rash of illness is not hysteria at all."

"Then why does it only affect women?" the dowager demanded. "If it were a disease or true illness, would it not infect everyone?"

Owen's large hand wrapped around the stem of his glass. "I do not know why it has only affected women, but I am certain there is a missing variable. Hysteria does not exist."

"How are you so certain?" Barnes challenged.

Owen grunted in return, not bothering to rise to Barnes's needling. That only urged Barnes on.

"Are you speaking from your vast knowledge of women?"

The not-so-subtle cut hung over the table like a storm cloud.

"Have you ever seen a hysterical woman?" Owen countered, his heavy brow raised. "I am talking about a woman who is hysterical for absolutely no reason whatsoever other than her own female madness?"

A muscle flexed in Barnes's jaw.

"Exactly. It is fabricated. Whatever illness has come over those women is real."

"And yet they will be cast into institutions anyway," Ivy said angrily, unable to help interjecting. "Barnes, if I come down with this mysterious illness, will you allow Father to send me away?"

"He will *not*," Owen growled.

Barnes glared at him. "That is not your decision to make."

"I am courting her—"

"But she is not yet—"

Diane clapped loudly, her bright eyes bouncing from Owen to Barnes with undisguised glee. "This is ever so entertaining. I have never known a person able to get a rise out of Barnes so quickly, other than myself. What is your history together?"

The storm cloud grew darker until Barnes stood, threw his napkin on the table, and stomped out of the room.

Ivy released a tense breath. Was every supper to be like this? She did not think she would survive the animosity between Brackley and her brother for the next two months.

"Well," Diane said, lifting her spoon and stabbing her pudding, "that went well."

The following week was, if possible, tenser. Barnes was pasted to Ivy's side. He escorted her and Diane to the schoolroom, trading thinly veiled insults with her friend the entire way, and was leaning against the wall waiting for them when they finished. He followed Ivy into the stables and rode with her on the property. He ate his dinners with her, and once even tagged along with her to the kitchen to fetch tea. The staff had immediately clammed up in his presence, and she had almost missed a vital piece of gossip because of it. Just as she had been leaving with the tray in her arms and Barnes at her back, she had heard Eliza whisper to Thomas, "No, I swear I seen him lingering on the property twice now."

"You sure it was a stranger and not the viscount?"

"Think I know my own master," she had sniffed.

Ivy's brow had furrowed. The maid had seen a stranger on the estate? When? What had he looked like? She needed to find a way to discreetly pump Eliza for the details, and in the meantime, she would have Diane keep a closer eye on the girls.

But if Ivy ever wanted the chance to learn more, she needed to dislodge Barnes. He was so attached to her hip that he was practically her shadow.

After the fourth day of his constant, brotherly, scowling presence looming over her, Ivy halted him in the corridor when he would have followed her into the library. "Barnes, stop."

"Why? Are we going elsewhere?"

"No, *we* are not. Stop following me around like you expect Brackley to jump out from behind a bust and compromise me at any moment."

"The whole purpose of me being here is to protect your reputation, Trouble. And I would not put it past him," he muttered.

Ivy pinched the bridge of her nose and took a deep, calming breath. "Barnes, when was the last time you saw Lord Brackley anywhere near me?"

"He accosted you in the yard yesterday."

She gaped at him. "He stopped me and told me he was having a dress made for me for the party." She had argued with him, explaining that she had a few gowns that would be perfectly suitable with a little added trim, but he had been as unyielding as stone. He had insisted that as long as they were playing their parts, they were going to do it right, which meant he would clothe her in the best dresses for maximum effect. End of discussion.

Barnes grumbled. "He leaves you alone because *I* am always with you."

"No, it is because he has no interest in me. He knows my

intentions regarding Lord Hartford, and he is doing his best to make me an attractive option for the marquess. He is doing me a *favor*, Barnes, and you are treating him like a lecher."

"If you think Brackley does not have any interest in you, then you are as blind as a bat, and it is fortunate I am here." Before she could respond to that ridiculous statement, he added, "Why Hartford, Ivy? You are so intent on him, when I have never known you to be keen on marriage before."

"It has become apparent Father will not rest until I am wed, and if I must marry, I want to choose my husband. Hartford is kind. I once saw a servant spill something on his coat, and he did not strike her."

Barnes's expression was stricken. "Not all men are like Father, Ivy."

"No, I suppose not. But some are. Women become property of their husbands, and I will not marry a man who can hurt me however he pleases. Hartford has proven his kindness, and so he is my choice. Lord Brackley is helping me achieve that goal, so you need to stop treating him so poorly."

His expression darkened further. "I am treating him how he deserves to be treated."

"*What* happened between you two? If it was so terrible, do you not think I deserve to know?"

"It does not bear repeating."

Ivy clenched her teeth. *Men!* "I cannot live like this. I *will* not live like this. You may stay at the estate and chaperone, but you will not act as my jailer."

He glared at her, a muscle twitching in his jaw. "Fine. But the moment I think he has crossed a line, I am throwing you in the carriage and taking you home."

Ivy exhaled. Inhaled. Exhaled. "Barnes, I love you, but I am one more Neanderthal statement away from breaking your nose."

He gave a bark of laughter. "I forget how fearsome you are. Perhaps I do not have to worry so much after all. Unless...you do not fancy *him*, do you?"

Ivy huffed and stepped over the library threshold, where she was progressing through the most interesting book on Genghis Khan's military strategy. "I am not going to dignify that question with a response. And now that you will have free time on your hands, it does not mean you can spend it sparring with Diane," she threw over her shoulder.

Barnes was as good as his word, and although she felt his heavy eyes on her from time to time, he no longer followed her around like a puppy. He had even eased off Diane, only trading verbal insults with her a few times a day rather than at every accidental meeting.

The girls loved Diane, to Ivy's immense relief. Diane was a whirlwind of fun and snappy comebacks, and she was an excellent teacher, too. The worship in Ophelia's eyes told Ivy she had nothing to worry about when she departed, an eventuality that made a lump appear in her throat every time she thought of it.

Suppers were horribly awkward, although none so explosive as the first. Still, each night Ivy could not wait until they ended. Owen would sit at the foot of the table, eating in silence with his head down, while the dowager grilled Diane about the girls' progress and made snippy comments about Diane's lineage. Barnes divided his time between throwing loathing looks at Owen and defending Diane to the dowager. The first night he had done it, Ivy and Diane had been stunned into speechlessness. The dowager had made a comment on Diane's needlework being inferior, as was "expected from a poor country governess." Barnes had, with a furrowed brow, said, "What good are neat stitches if the woman who wields the needle is graceless?"

After that, every time the dowager began to pick at Diane, Barnes would throw out an insult just disguised enough that she could never take true offense, perplexing Ivy to no end.

Everything had seemed to settle into an awkward, uncomfortable rhythm, when Ivy's dress arrived via courier. Barnes was in the foyer when it was carried inside in a white box, and his lips turned down.

"It is Father's job to buy your clothing," he said sternly. Owen happened to be walking into the foyer at the moment, his head down as he read a letter, but when he lifted his face and saw the man holding the box, he nodded and instructed the maid to take it to Ivy's chamber.

"You do not buy her clothes," Barnes hissed at him. "She is not poor. She was not a governess because she had no means."

Owen stared calmly at him, lowering the letter so that it dangled at his side. "If I am not mistaken, your father is already funding the travels of your brothers. Would he be willing to spend a similar sum on clothing Ivy at the height of fashion?" At Barnes's angry silence he added, "If she wants to catch Hartford's eye, she needs to dress in the latest and the best."

"Are you sure it is not *you* who is embarrassed by her clothing?"

"Miss Bennett could wear rags and I would not care."

"Buying her a wardrobe is going above and beyond. What is your real motive?"

Owen sighed and started to walk away while Ivy glared daggers at her brother. When Owen was at the door, he paused and said to them, "Everyone needs to be ready to depart by noon tomorrow."

Ivy's heart pirouetted. Tomorrow she would enter society on the arm of Viscount Brackley. Tomorrow, she would lay eyes on Lord Hartford for the first time since the country ball two years ago.

Chapter 14

"You have not looked in my direction once."

The deep voice came only inches from her ear. Ivy startled, her skin breaking out in gooseflesh when she felt the viscount's body heat at her back. He circled her and held out a glass of punch, his gaze skating over her tight expression before dropping to the gown he had bought her.

It was one of the most exquisite pieces of clothing Ivy had ever worn. When she had opened the box, she had gasped with delight. The warm amber was the color of clover honey and perfectly matched her eyes. The skirts were wide, the bodice narrowed to a point at her waist, the neckline beautifully curved to show off the slightest swell of her breasts. She had been wearing a cloak when they had left the house, and upon their arrival Owen had immediately been swept into conversation with his business partner and their host, Mr. Donnelley. This was the first time he had seen her in the gown.

"I have looked in your direction," she lied. In fact, she had been avoiding seeking him out, stupidly afraid that if she did, she would somehow give away their charade. "You have been too busy to notice."

"I would have noticed." He was staring at the gown with a tight expression on his face. "You look... nice."

"The quality of your compliments renders me speechless."

The corner of his lip tugged, as if he were *almost* going to smile. "Beautiful. You look beautiful, Ivy."

Her heart gave one tiny, extra beat, but it was only because he was an adept pupil, not because of the way he had said her name, as if *she* were beautiful and not simply the dress. "Much better, my lord. Now, why does it matter whether or not I gaze at you from across the room?"

"Because you are supposed to be wildly infatuated with me."

"Is that how one shows wild infatuation in polite society? By making eyes? Perhaps it is *you* who should be pretending to be infatuated with *me*."

"In that case, I am failing as well. We have not convinced anyone I am courting you. We entered separately, and we have been apart the entire night. You may not have noticed, but now that gossip of our courtship has made the rounds, everyone is watching us, including Lord Hartford. We need to persuade him that you fancy me, and that I find you so desirable I cannot keep away from you."

"Lord Hartford has not noticed me." Ivy could see him now across the parlor, speaking with a cluster of men in black frock coats and shiny shoes. His chocolate eyes sparkled with laughter, and his gloved hands gestured as he spoke. He was not quite as she had remembered. When she had last seen him some years ago, she had thought him tall and handsome, but now that he was sharing a room with Owen, it was clear he was of average height, with narrow shoulders and a slight stoop. Nevertheless, he was smiling kindly and genuinely, and despite the decided lack of emotion she felt looking at him, she knew she would be safe and respected as his wife.

Unfortunately, he did not yet know she existed.

"He has," Owen said shortly. "*Everyone* has, and what they have seen so far is a woman stiffly removed from the man who is supposedly courting her."

"You give my presence too much credit. They are all looking at you. This is your first social engagement as the new viscount." Still, her eyes swept the room, and she swallowed. The luxurious rooms that had been opened for the evening party were lit with hundreds of candles glowing against the crimson flocked wallpaper. Women circulated the space, reticules dangling from their gloved wrists and curls hanging over their ears. The men were outfitted in evening coats, and there was the low murmur of voices as a hired harpist played prettily in the corner. During Ivy's short perusal, a number of eyes had turned discreetly toward her before the owners had spoken to their companions in low tones.

For the first time, Ivy was the center of gossip, and it was not a nice feeling.

"I see what you mean." Suddenly anxious to persuade society Owen truly was enamored with her, she awkwardly patted his arm. "My, my, how...ah...tall you are tonight."

He sighed.

"I do not know how to do this!"

He tapped his finger on his glass, appearing as irritated and frustrated as she felt. Finally, he said, "I can teach you."

"Teach me what?"

"Teach you how to seduce." His jaw clenched as he looked at something over her shoulder. "I can carry us both through this, but I do not wish to make you uncomfortable."

"How would you make me uncomfortable?"

"Real seduction is visceral. If I do it properly, your heart should race." His eyes fell to her chest, as if he could see where the traitorous organ had skipped a beat. "Your fingers should tingle, and your entire body should feel too hot and too tight. It can be uncomfortable and confusing, especially when it is only a lesson."

Her blood turned slow and honeyed in her veins even as his words stirred her temper. "Owen, I can handle a few simple lessons on seduction. Do not flatter yourself about my reaction."

His gaze returned to her, so heated and possessive that she took a half-step back. "Are you certain? I may not have the flowery language of flirtation, but I know how to make a woman...feel."

"I certainly *feel* like you are adept at complimenting yourself."

His lips curved into a full smile, and Ivy felt as if she had just accomplished the impossible. She had made the grouchy, unapproachable Viscount Brackley smile, no matter how reluctant it was.

His smile faded. "If at any point it feels like too much, tell me."

"All right."

"Promise me."

"I promise I will tell you if your seduction is simply *too good*," she said, barely refraining from laughing.

But he was not laughing. His eyes traced over her skin, and her merriment slipped away at the scorching heat of it. "We will start simply. The first lesson," he said in a deep voice that sent chills up her spine, "is that when you are mad with desire for a person, every near-touch can be a prelude to lovemaking." His breath ghosted over her cheek, and his fingers almost brushed her waist as he crowded into her space. Absolutely nothing he was doing was inappropriate, and yet she felt her body inexplicably swaying closer, as if she were a sunflower swiveling toward the sun.

"My heat, my breath, my eyes on your skin," he continued, allowing his gaze to roam over her until it felt like an actual touch. They dropped lower, to her neck, where her pulse beat rapidly. His tongue darted out to wet his lower lip, and she wondered what it would feel like if he pressed those lips to her skin. "They can make you react as surely as my hands or mouth. I need you to blush now, Ivy, as if I am whispering sweet lovers' words to you."

"I cannot blush on demand."

He smiled wickedly. "Lord Hartford is watching. No, do not look," he added quickly when she reflexively turned to check. "Remember, you are too caught up in me to care that anyone else is here."

She nodded. "Right. Mayhap if I hold my breath, my cheeks will redden?"

He leaned so close that the front of his coat brushed the swell of her breasts. "Did you know, Ivy, that you have a beautiful throat? It is so smooth and delicate. I want to wrap my hand around it and squeeze a little. I want to see if being dominated by me makes you we—weak."

He had cut himself off, and she was not certain what he had been about to say, but even so, no one had *ever* talked to her like that, not even the crass footman she had kissed when she was sixteen years of age. Involuntarily, she imagined how it would feel to have Owen's huge palm cupping the side of her neck and his intense jade eyes focused on her while he showed her all the things she had only heard about while skulking in the shadows around her brothers.

Her cheeks flushed scarlet, and her breath came out in a sharp burst of something that was curiously, horrifyingly close to arousal.

"There we go, Sunshine. That blush is perfect." He backed away, his inscrutable expression evidence that he was entirely unaffected by their little exchange, and the knowledge only made her flush harder. How mortifying! Had he been right, after all? This would not do. "That is a good start, my *smitten* girl. I will find you later to introduce you to Lord Hartford and teach you lesson number two."

Bloody *hell*. Owen left the room and stepped outside to breathe in the crisp October air. The half-bare branches bobbed in the breeze, and he prayed the stinging temperature would douse his desire.

Ivy had been fumbling in there. At his estate she was bubbly, bossy, and competent. She was here, too, except for when it came to him. He did not know if it was because of Barnes's watchful eye, the presence of her precious Lord Hartford, or because a good number of the *ton* were intently scrutinizing them, but she had frozen. She had been unable to even look at him, and when he had approached, she had stiffened like a woman who had no interest in being courted by him, perhaps even *disliked* him.

The only way he had figured he could get her to resemble more of a lovestruck woman than a board of lumber was to teach her about seduction. He had thought to impart a few bits of wisdom about body language and the power of words.

He had known his words would affect her. He had spoken them so that they would, but what he had not known was how her reaction would affect *him*. Her response had been stunning. Beautiful. So bloody perfect that even now, he was uncomfortable in his trousers.

Owen preferred a specific type of intimacy, and that required a certain type of partner. Ivy was not that type. She was strong, confident, and so sweet that everyone who met her gravitated toward her light. She was the sort of woman who desired men like Lord Hartford: kind, soft, and gentle.

Except when he had spoken to her in *that way*, her pupils had dilated, her plush lips had parted as she had exhaled, and her cheeks had flushed...suggesting that perhaps sweet Ivy did not quite know what she desired after all. And how could she? Ladies were not given the opportunity to learn about their own bodies before they were shepherded into marriage.

Lust twisted in his belly at the thought of being the one to help her learn what she liked.

Furious with himself, Owen pressed the heel of his palm into his chest. This faux courtship had been a terrible idea, but he was stuck now. Rumors were circulating, and with his little performance inside, he had all but verified he was after her hand. He could not retreat now.

He exhaled evenly and straightened his coat. He could remain impartial to Ivy. Unaffected. It was not as if he were *ever* going to touch her for real. This was all pretend. He could do this.

The moment he re-entered the room, his eyes narrowed. She was surrounded by men. Until their exchange, she had not been approached. Now he could barely see the top of her head past the shoulders of gentlemen vying for her attention.

That was the purpose of their ruse, he thought, even as his jaw flexed. One single, smitten interaction with a viscount, and suddenly every man wanted to know what was so special about her. He *hated* that. If they needed a viscount to show interest first, then none of them deserved her.

He should go back outdoors. He should let her discover who was available to her...but of all the men encircling her, none was Lord

Hartford. He had promised her an introduction to Hartford, had he not? And Owen was a man of his word.

He strode toward her, several men moving hastily aside at his approach, until he could see her face. She was frazzled and smiling so hard her cheeks looked ready to crack.

"Miss Bennett." He offered his arm. "Would you take a turn about the room with me?"

Ivy hooked her gloved hand through the crook of his arm, murmured an excuse to the horde of men who were very fortunate this courtship was not real, and tucked herself tightly to his side as he navigated her to freedom.

She took a deep breath and let it out slowly through her lips. "Thank you. I do not know what happened."

"They want to know what makes you special."

"How very disappointed they will be to discover the answer."

"Do not be absurd."

She peered up at him with those honey eyes of hers, but the emotion in them was concealed. "Your compliments are starting to improve. You must be careful, lest I get silly, girlish notions in my head and start to believe this is real."

He sighed. He supposed he had acted pompous enough to deserve that.

"Let us promenade for a few minutes, and then I shall introduce you to Lord Hartford." After another moment he cleared his throat. "I am sorry about what I said to you before, when I was trying to make you blush. I went too far."

She arched a brow, and he could not help noticing how the yellow gleam of candlelight made her skin glow, as if she were lit from within. "Do not fret, your lordship. I found the lesson fascinating. I am eager to discover if I will find success using it."

He stopped abruptly, and she took another step before being tugged to standing. "What do you mean?"

"I mean I look forward to practicing your last lesson with Lord Hartford. It had not occurred to me before tonight how woefully inadequate I am in the art of seduction. What is the next lesson?"

He gazed down at her eager expression and felt the most incomprehensible mixture of disbelief and annoyance. He wanted to explain in no uncertain terms that he was *not* teaching her how to seduce another man, that the lessons were meant to convince the *ton* he was courting her, and nothing else. But why? Since this was a platonic arrangement between them, he should be happy to help her enhance her skills.

Ignoring the sour feeling in his gut, he said, "I am pleased I could help."

She gestured for him to lower his head, and when he did, her warm breath, sweet with punch, skated across his cheek as she whispered, "Do you think if I spoke to Lord Hartford like this, it would be a successful deployment of lesson one?" Her eyes met his before tracing over his cheekbones as if she were planning where to press her lips.

Owen thought of her soft breath on Lord Hartford, and ground his teeth together. "Yes."

"You do not look as if you are affected. You look pained."

"Because your brother is here," he lied. He had no idea where Barnes or Miss Wixby were.

She nodded in understanding as they resumed walking and asked again, "What is lesson number two?"

It took him a moment to force himself to speak. "The art of conversation."

"I know how to converse."

"Not this way, you do not. It is a way of speaking that suggests meaning beyond the words. A double entendre."

She peered up at him with fascination. "Can you give me an example?"

They had reached the end of the room, where his business partner had displayed several ostentatious marble busts of war generals. They turned, and when they did, he surveyed the room. The music flowed, as did the conversation, but he was keenly aware that eyes were on them, and that even Lord Hartford was having a difficult time looking away from her.

"Your gown is beautiful tonight," he murmured. "I especially like the cut of the neckline."

She glanced down at her gown, and seeing the soft swell of her breasts over the neckline, scoffed. "That was terrible."

"I am under pressure."

"What would I use for a gentleman? I like your trousers..." She trailed off, and then a devilish gleam entered her eye. "Were they made for three legs?"

Owen stopped abruptly, his mouth going slack with shock, and Ivy let out a peal of laughter that drew even more looks.

"You minx! How do you—"

"Six brothers, my lord," she reminded him.

"You most certainly cannot say that to a gentleman," he warned, growing hot beneath his cravat.

"Oh, I know. Do not fret." She waved away his concern, but her cheeks were glowing, and she looked entirely too pleased with herself for shocking him. Before he could speak again, Barnes appeared at their side.

"Sister," he said, his smile not reaching his eyes, "you have done a splendid job convincing the aristocracy that you are being courted by this lout. Shall we go remind everyone that I am your chaperone? That I am watching at all times?"

"You do not have to worry," Owen said coldly, lowering his voice so that he could not be overheard by anyone beyond their trio. "I would not touch your sister if she were the last lady in England. She is related to *you*, after all."

Something flickered across Ivy's face before she smoothed it away. "I cannot, Barnes. Lord Brackley was about to introduce me to Lord Hartford."

"I too have been looking forward to meeting the man. I shall come with you," Barnes replied.

Owen glared at him, but they moved as one toward the marquess.

Lord Hartford was entertaining a number of women by the fireplace, but when they approached, he stepped forward and held out his hand to Owen. "Lord Brackley. Welcome to the House of Lords."

Although Hartford was shaking his hand, his eyes were all for Ivy. She was flushing, and it irritated Owen that she had had to threaten to hold her breath to flush around him, but merely being in Lord Hartford's presence was enough to get her blood flowing. He did not see what was so special about the marquess. Yes, he was incredibly wealthy and had land holdings across the country. Yes, he was respectable in the sense that he did not gamble or frequent brothels, at least as far as Owen knew—and he had certainly dug into his past when Ivy had shared his name. Hartford was a member of White's, attended every parliamentary session, and not a single man had a poor thing to say about him. He had inherited his title four years prior, and although he was frequently seen riding in Hyde Park with one lady or another, he had yet to propose to any of them.

But was he the right man for Ivy? Owen was not yet convinced.

"Lord Hartford, have you met my close friends, Miss Ivy Bennett, and her brother, Mr. Bennett?"

Hartford smiled at Ivy, a small dimple appearing in each of his cheeks. "It is my pleasure, Miss Bennett." He released Owen's hand and took hers, bowing over it and kissing her glove.

Barnes beamed at Hartford, while Owen wanted to rip his hand away. He took a deep breath. He did not know what had activated this possessive streak, but it would only do him a disservice. Ivy was not his. He did not even *want* her. The only explanation was that something about Hartford was putting him on edge.

"Where have you been hiding this orchid, Mr. Bennett? 'Tis unfair that Lord Brackley should discover her before the rest of us have had the opportunity to gaze upon her petals."

What the hell did he mean by *that*? That better have been a very poor attempt at lyrical flattery rather than an example of lesson number two.

Barnes gave an uncomfortable chuckle, and Owen knew he was as disturbed by Hartford's petal flattery as he was. "I have not been hiding her, but my lovely sister is too modest to make herself the center of attention. It is no wonder she went unnoticed."

"I do not understand how that is possible." Hartford continued to hold her hand and smile at her. "If I had set eyes on her before, I would have remembered."

It was on the tip of Owen's tongue to tell him he *had* seen Ivy at a party before, but that would only embarrass everyone involved.

At last Hartford released her hand and addressed her directly instead of talking *about* her. "Do you care for poetry, Miss Bennett?"

"Oh, yes, your lordship."

That was news to Owen, but then it was not as if he had sat down with her and discussed her likes and dislikes. He frowned, wishing he knew more of the tiny details about her. Perhaps they should arrange a meeting where he could get to know her better—for the purpose of their ruse.

Hartford's eyes were so focused on Ivy that Owen was beginning to fear he was a soul-sucker. Who stared at another person like that?

Barnes nudged him hard while Ivy and Lord Hartford fell into discussion about Alfred, Lord Tennyson. "Stop it," he hissed. "You look like you are about to knock his teeth out."

"There is something wrong with him," Owen muttered back. "No one likes poetry that much."

"Maybe not uneducated oafs," Barnes retorted. "I think he is a good match for Ivy."

"I do not understand what she sees in him."

A flicker of regret passed over Barnes's eyes at that, and Owen pounced. "What do you know?"

"None of your concern, Brackley."

"It *is* my concern, and if you do not tell me this minute, I will interrupt them and—"

"He is kind."

Owen's brows drew together. "What do you mean, 'he is kind'?"

Barnes shrugged. "You may recall some of the things I told you about my father when we were boys at Harrow."

Owen remembered once sitting in a tree with Barnes and trading stories about their horrible fathers. Neither of them had ever gone into specifics, but they had found camaraderie in the unspoken.

He frowned in Ivy's direction, wondering what her father had done to make *kindness* her only requirement for a suitor. And if that was Hartford's only draw, did that mean she was not in love with the lord?

Barnes gave a mocking snort. "You do not have to look as if you want to avenge her. Our father has been taken care of. He lives in London now, and he has not seen her for years."

"Did he hurt her?"

Barnes hesitated. "I do not think so, but I cannot be certain. He hurt other people in our family until I was big enough to stop it. Ivy saw that, and it changed her. Apparently, she spotted Lord Hartford displaying kindness to a servant a few years ago, and she set her sights on him then. If Father is determined to force her into marriage—and he is, because he does not believe a woman should go without a master—then she is equally determined to find someone who will be safe."

Someone who would *be* safe, or someone who could *keep* her safe? Was she still afraid of her father even though Barnes had sent him to live in London? Hartford's temperament was too gentle, too easygoing. What if Ivy's father wanted to see her again? Once Hartford was her husband, he would have the power to arrange meetings on her behalf, and Owen suspected he would acquiesce to her father to keep the peace, leaving Ivy vulnerable. And after she was married, Barnes could no longer protect her.

"Hartford is *too* nice."

Barnes opened his mouth to make another sarcastic comment, but he let it die on his tongue, because he knew it, too.

Chapter 15

Two nights later, Ivy was still replaying Owen's words in her mind as she headed from the kitchen to the library, where she met Diane most nights to play chess and gossip about the day. *"I would not touch your sister if she were the last lady in England. She is related to you, after all."* She had been deeply offended at first, but after some contemplation, had realized the insult was meant more for Barnes than her, and now she was using it as a reminder that this situation with Owen was a ruse, and nothing more.

Besides, right now she was feeling she could forgive Owen anything. Not only had he convinced the *ton* he was courting her, but he had also introduced her to Lord Hartford, and she had had a long and pleasant conversation with the marquess. Before the party, Hartford had not known she existed, but the day after, he had known her well enough to have a book of poems by Robert Browning delivered to her. Owen had taken one look at the small, leather-bound poetry book and snarled about men who lacked self-preservation before stomping away.

Ivy could not be happier; their plan was working. At the party,

Brackley had been the attentive, smitten lover, so it should not have bothered her that after the party he had chosen to ride home on horseback, or that he had not spoken to her since. She suspected he was avoiding her, and when she did spot him from afar, he looked so thunderous and cranky that she did not feel all that compelled to seek him out anyway.

No matter the reason for his poor disposition, it was very obvious that the flushing and chills she had experienced in his presence at the party had been one-sided. *I would not touch your sister if she were the last lady in England.* Owen may not find her attractive, but Lord Hartford had at least seemed pleased by her. He had compared her to two different flowers and a type of rare vase during their conversation, and although she had found the compliments strange, she knew she should be flattered. Being called a rose was preferable to being growled at.

Ivy's thoughts drifted from Hartford to what she had just learned while in the kitchen. Ostensibly, she had been there for tea, but in reality, she had been hoping to catch the maid, Eliza. She had been relieved when she had spotted the sassy maid dropping off the dowager's tea tray. Ivy knew she would not have much time, so she had quickly dived in, pretending she had spotted a man near the stables that she did not recognize, and asking if Eliza knew him.

"No!" the maid had cried, "but is he tall with a hat that keeps his face in shadow?"

"Precisely so," Ivy had lied.

Eliza had nodded. "I have seen him twice now, though never so close as the stables. Both times he was in a clearing near the east fields, where you kin have a good view of the house." She had blushed furiously, likely praying Ivy was not going to ask *why* she had been in the east fields, but Ivy already knew it was because she was meeting Thomas, and had no opinion about the maid's activities one way or another.

"Did he flee when he saw you?"

"Aye." Eliza had nodded. "I told the butler, and he said he would let the master know."

Ivy wondered if he had done so. "Perhaps you had better find a different place to... to read your Bible."

Eliza had scrunched her nose for a moment, and when she realized what Ivy was pretending to assume, she had nodded enthusiastically. "Yes, madam. Of course. I like to read in the sun, but I shall find another place."

Who was the stranger? Did he have anything to do with the accusations being made about Lord Brackley? Ivy did not know, but whatever the man's reason for trespassing and spying, she most certainly had to tell the Dove about it.

Ivy's foot lifted over the library threshold, but before she could call out for her friend, she spotted two silhouettes in front of the blazing fireplace: Diane and Barnes.

Spots of color splotched Diane's cheeks, and she looked angry enough to spit as she faced Barnes, who was standing unnervingly close and looking down at her as if he wished to spank the sass out of her.

There was something intimately explosive about the tension that made Ivy falter. She knew her brother and Diane did not get along—hated each other, in fact—so why did she feel as if she was about to intrude on a lovers' spat?

She slowly backed out of the room and bumped into a broad chest. She would have squeaked in surprise if a rough hand had not quickly clamped over her mouth, while another snaked around her waist to hold her steady. She knew by the scents of leather and polish that it was Owen.

"I would not go in there," he murmured, his breath coasting across her cheek. He withdrew his palm from her mouth, but kept his arm wrapped around her waist, his forearm flexing under her breasts.

"I was not going to," she whispered.

"I have been looking for you. I thought I might find you here. Someone has been reading through my books on historical war figures."

Oh, heavens. "How—how can you tell?"

"They have been returned out of order. I only noticed because the section is near that on horses."

"Barnes must be interested," she lied.

"Mmm." The low hum made her stomach dip. "Barnes was never much for history, if I recall."

"Why were you looking for me?"

"To apologize."

"To apologize? For what?" Why did her voice sound so breathless? And how could he be both soft and hard against her, his broad chest so warm and enticing that she had the wild thought that she would like to turn around and bury her face in it while he held her? The unbidden fantasy was so alarming that she said somewhat abruptly, "You are still holding me."

"I know. Apologies are not easy for me to face." Yet he inserted an inch of space between them, his arm loosening and his palm sliding down her ribs until his fingers were splayed across her belly. Ivy's skin felt like it was on fire.

"If you cannot face me, hurry on with it." She intended to sound teasing, but her heart was pounding, and she was afraid her voice came out higher than usual. The feel of his chin by her temple and his hand spanning her waist were forcing her stomach into acrobatics.

"I am sorry for losing my temper with Barnes at the party, and I am sorry for saying I would not touch you if you were the last woman in England. I meant to insult him, but I used you to do it, and that was untenable. It will not happen again." He paused, and she felt the barest rasp of his unshaven cheek against her temple. "And I *would* touch you. If you were the last woman in England, that is."

Ivy let out a soft snort.

Owen sighed. "That came out wrong. I should think it is obvious by now."

"What is obvious?"

His hand on her belly dropped lower as he shifted, and if she did not have her corset on, his index finger would have been resting on her navel. Ivy swallowed.

"It should be obvious that I would touch you," he said softly, stirring the fine hairs on the nape of her neck.

The words hung between them, and she did not know what to think. Did he mean them in a kindly way, simply letting her know he did not find her repulsive? Or did he mean he *wanted* to touch her? Instead of asking, fearing either answer, she said, "Barnes can drive any reasonable person to madness. I should know."

His chin bumped her shoulder with a nod, and his warm palm slid off her completely, his heat abandoning her as he stepped into the shadows of the corridor. "I have received an invitation for an evening musicale at the Fleetwood estate in two days."

"Fleetwood?" Her frazzled brain was unable to make connections as she turned to face him.

His lips lifted with a hint of a smile, as if he knew she was momentarily incapable of thinking straight. "Baron Fleetwood. It is my understanding that your uncle, the future Marquess Rothford, will also be in attendance, along with Lord Hartford."

Ivy's skin flushed with both dread and anticipation. If her uncle was going to attend, did that mean her father would as well? It was quite a trip from London, so she did not think so.

But the reminder of her father was enough to shore up her determination and settle the flutters in her stomach. She *had* to succeed with Hartford. There was no other choice.

"You will still teach me how to seduce Hartford?"

The chill in the hallway intensified. Several seconds passed before he said, "We will have lesson number three at the musicale."

"Thank you."

But he was already gone.

"Do you think he will choke?" Diane asked Ivy. She nodded to Barnes, who was deep in conversation with several gentlemen at the Fleetwood musicale two days later. Ivy did not know why Owen was securing invitations for Diane, but she suspected it was to put Ivy at ease, which was strangely sweet.

"I hate to disappoint you," Ivy said, "but he is not eating, therefore I do not think so."

"I meant, do you think he will choke on all the false words coming out of his mouth? He despises Lord Pithins. It was only a few days ago he said the man was as dry as plaster."

At that moment Barnes tilted his head back and laughed as if Lord Pithins were the most amusing man in the room. Barnes was handsomely dressed, with the light from the chandelier catching in his dark hair and his eyes creasing with cheer. Ivy's brother was beyond irritating, but she did love him, and she was proud of the person he had become. She could not understand why Diane felt so dissimilarly. "Why do you dislike my brother so much?"

"It is *he* who dislikes *me*. He has ever since we were children." Diane lifted a bare shoulder. She was wearing a canary-yellow dress that should have clashed with her red hair, but instead made her stand out like a brilliant cetirizine stone. She was a vision in the candle flames. "I decided long ago that if he did not like me, I would not like *him*, and that I would do it better."

Ivy sighed. She did not know what had put the bee in Barnes's bonnet when it came to Diane, but he appeared to have unexplained grievances with half the people in his life.

"Who is that other gentleman with Barnes and Lord Pithins?"

Diane peered past her shoulder. "I am not sure, but he looks as if he is trying to talk Barnes into a particularly profitable scheme, because his eyes are glinting like little greedy beetles."

Ivy snorted at the oddly apt description, and made a mental note to ask the Dove for the names of the men whose homes Lord Brackley had visited before their wives and daughters became ill. If she was going to be out in society anyway, it would not hurt to use her God-given ears to listen.

She peered into the crush of guests mingling along the outskirts of the room. None seemed very eager to take their seats and lose the opportunity to socialize. The Fleetwoods would be returning to London imminently, and this was their last social hurrah in the country before the official start of the Season. They had twin daughters expected to debut, and Ivy had heard the girls were quite musically talented. She did not think it was a coincidence that their mother was putting on a musicale and inviting all of the eligible bachelors in the area to attend—including Lord Hartford.

Ivy spotted Hartford chatting with a gray-haired mama and her lovely daughter. The girl did not appear to be much older than sixteen, her cheeks flushed with youth and her eyes sparkling with rapture. Ivy's heart sank. She had serious competition from ladies with generous dowries and surnames that could be traced back a thousand years. Ladies with classically high foreheads and bodies that were more soft than athletic. Ladies who did not already have three failed Seasons behind them. How had she ever thought she had a chance with Lord Hartford? She was a fool.

"If you will excuse me, Miss Wixby, I require a moment with Miss Bennett."

"I have need of refreshment." Diane winked at Ivy and flounced off, Barnes's eyes flickering toward her as she exited the room.

"Are you ready for your next lesson?" Owen asked gruffly. A frown line was etched into his forehead, as if the offer were painful.

"Oh, what is the point?" Ivy moaned. "Look at Lord Hartford. He has beautiful, wealthy women falling at his feet. What chance do I have?"

"None of them compare to you," he said dismissively. "He needs to be reminded why you are more desirable than the others. That is where tonight's lesson comes in. We are going to make him jealous."

"How?"

The hint of a smile touched his lips, which only served to make him appear roguish. Hartford was not the only highly sought-after bachelor in the room. Owen was outfitted in a black, tailored evening coat that emphasized his broad shoulders, and dark trousers that hugged his heavily muscled legs. His dress was impeccable, from the snow-white cravat knotted around the tanned column of his throat to the tips of his leather Hessians—she supposed he would have to be pried out of his boots and held under threat of death to wear the more fashionable heeled shoes. Yet despite his clothing, it seemed difficult to remember he was a gentleman. He was larger than life. Raw. Untamed. It was as if he did not belong in the confines of the drawing room, but out on the moors riding until his hair was even more unruly than it already was.

His jade-green eyes were piercing, and when his lips threatened to smile as they did now, he was so devastatingly attractive that Ivy's own heart fluttered. She could not imagine how ladies who *actually* wanted to marry him felt. They probably melted into puddles.

"You will see." He kissed the back of her glove and tucked her hand into the crook of his arm. "That mama has hogged Hartford's attention for long enough, do you not think?"

"I think it is too late to interrupt; the musicale will soon begin."

A gleam entered his eye. "I know."

She allowed him to guide her across the room anyway, keenly aware of the way he possessively angled his body toward her, and the heated looks he kept dropping on her mouth. He was putting on an extraordinary show, and she worried for a moment that perhaps it was *too* good. What if Hartford did not think he had a chance against Brackley? If Owen were truly courting her, Hartford would be a fool to think he could compete.

Before they reached him, Hartford caught sight of her, his eyes tracing over her cheeks and dipping to where her arm was tucked in the crook of Owen's. She smiled warmly at him, and a responding smile curled across his lips. He excused himself from the mama and her beautiful daughter and strode across the rug to meet them.

"Miss Bennett," he said, taking her free hand and bending over it, a lock of chocolate hair falling into his eye as he planted his lips on the fabric. "I had hoped you would be here this evening. You are a vision."

She was wearing a powder-blue gown with a daring neckline and a skirt so silken it swished against her petticoat with even the slightest movement. It was stunning. All of the frocks Owen had ordered for her were. The man had excellent taste.

"She is." Owen's eyes swept over her so thoroughly that her pulse jumped at the base of her throat. "Is your uncle going to be in attendance tonight, Miss Bennett?"

"I…believe so?" she answered, unsure where he was going with the question.

Owen smiled like a cat with a canary. "I would like to meet him."

Oh, heavens.

Owen waited patiently for her response while her thoughts scrambled to get in order. "My lord, you do flatter me, only the Season has not yet begun, and we still have much to learn about one another before we take that step."

Hartford's eyes twinkled at her coy delay. "Miss Bennett speaks wisely. Marriage is no simple matter, and the bride and groom should be compatible. For example, should not a husband and wife share similar tastes in art, poetry, and music?"

"Yes, indeed." Ivy fluttered her eyelashes. "Is it not lovely that you and I both enjoy the words of Mr. Browning?"

Lord Hartford nodded in agreement, even as his gaze dropped to where her other arm was still caught in the crook of Owen's. She freed herself, and Owen scowled in displeasure.

At that moment the lady of the house called the guests to their seats, and Hartford took advantage. "May I escort you, madam? I am eager to learn your thoughts on the musical arrangements."

"I would enjoy that." She almost looked at Owen to make sure he was coming with them before remembering she was supposed to be enchanting Hartford, not sticking to Owen like a barnacle.

"I am *eager* to hear your thoughts as well," Owen said, although he sounded more sarcastic than adoring.

Hartford's fingers flexed on her arm, but he gave Owen a genial smile. "Why of course, Lord Brackley."

Ivy ignored the curious gazes as she was escorted by the viscount on one side and the marquess on the other. When they sat on either side of her, she turned slightly in Hartford's direction so they could chat. To her left, Owen's broad shoulders and size took up so much space that he invaded some of hers.

"I hear the youngest twin, Miss Alma, plays the piano beautifully. Do you play any instruments, Miss Bennett?"

Ivy plastered on a smile. "I play the piano as well, but I am sure I am not as lovely at it as Miss Alma. My talents lie elsewhere."

Owen stilled at her side. He was so close that the sleeve of his coat kept brushing her bare arm, and his leg was pressed into her skirts. The poor man could not be comfortable. She knew he detested being cooped up, and now he was stuck in a tiny chair in a sea of society faces while being forced to listen to music for the next several hours, all so that she might enchant another man into becoming her husband.

She noted a number of feminine glances being cast in Brackley's direction, and she frowned. Yes, Owen was sacrificing for her, but he was using his pursuit of her as a shield, too. She must remember that he was also benefiting from their arrangement, and that he was not helping her catch Hartford's attention out of the goodness of his heart.

Hartford gave her an encouraging smile. "And what are your talents? I am sure you possess many."

"I speak French, I am adept with a needle, and I can dance well." *I can knock a man twice my size senseless, and I am a skilled swordswoman.*

"Do not forget your talent with children." Owen's deep voice rumbled above her ear. "You are extraordinary with my young sisters."

Hartford glowed. "My own mother was a near angel, and I have always thought very highly of women who possess natural maternal instincts. I would not wish for my wife to always pawn my heirs off to the nanny."

Ivy swallowed and was thankful she was wearing gloves to conceal her suddenly perspiring palms. *His heirs.* She had been so intent on marrying him that she had forgotten what that entailed. Thanks to her brothers, she had a general idea of what procreation required. She darted a quick look at Hartford's soft, pillowy lips. Would she enjoy kissing him? She thought it might be pleasant, if a little uninspiring.

She was saved from having to reply by the opening chords of the piano, and over the next hour lost herself to the truly beautiful music. The expression on Hartford's face was one of rapture, and she could not help noticing that his gaze was drawn quite often to the eldest twin, Miss Florence. Her cheeks were rosy and her eyes were closed in ecstasy as her fingers deftly strummed the harp strings.

"You are losing him," Brackley murmured in her ear. "He looks as if he is about to sink to his knees and ask the girl to marry him."

She gave an exasperated grunt. "What do you suggest I do? Rush up there, shove Miss Florence aside, and demonstrate my own mediocre harp skills instead?"

"Take his mind off her. Say something scandalous."

"Such as?"

"Compliment Miss Florence so that you do not sound jealous, and then tell him you have never been kissed, but you imagine it would make you feel as beautiful as this music. Get his mind off the girl and on the idea of giving you your first kiss."

"But he would not be my first kiss."

Owen's eyes darkened. "Some other man has had the pleasure?"

"'Twas a long time ago."

"Then lie," he snarled, so low that only she could hear. "I have not given up my entire afternoon to watch him fall in love with a harpist."

"Fine!" She pasted a smile on her face and leaned closer to Hartford. He was so enraptured by Miss Florence that he did not notice.

She nudged him gently with her arm, and when his eyes dropped to hers, she knew his mind was far away. She lifted her mouth, and he tilted his head to the side. She whispered Owen's words softly, her bottom lip brushing his earlobe, and she could feel when his attention slipped from the harpist and sharpened on her.

Blushing, Ivy sat back, aware that it had not been the most appropriate thing to share, but it appeared Owen was right. Hartford was staring at her with a mixture of shock and keen interest, the harpist entirely forgotten.

"You are a virtuous young lady, to have never had your lips touched," he said quietly, his eyes on said lips. Ivy unconsciously dragged her tongue across her bottom lip, and Hartford leaned closer. "Many a young woman has given a kiss to a hopeful suitor."

"I have not yet been so enticed," she replied demurely. "I fear I shall have to wait for my future husband to visit upon me that particular pleasure."

Owen coughed into his handkerchief.

Ivy ignored him. "Do you think me foolish for being so loyal to my future betrothed, Lord Hartford?"

"Never! I admire a woman who is so discerning and dedicated to her future husband. I can only hope my wife will possess similar virtue."

"Oh, I am sure she will! You are a man worthy of dedication."

Hartford was beaming at her when intermission was announced. He was quickly swept away by a gentleman from his club chattering about an incredible investment opportunity in a textile mill.

"He is a man worthy of dedication?" Owen asked as they meandered toward where Barnes and Diane stood with acquaintances.

"What about it?"

"I doubt you would dedicate your life to a man."

"How would you know? Perhaps I would be the most doting little mouse of a wife you have ever seen."

Owen scoffed. "You would not be."

"You are so certain you know what kind of wife I would be?" She faced him, her fists on her hips, her reticule and fan dangling from her left wrist.

"Yes."

"Please, enlighten me."

He lowered his head and curved his body toward her, creating an intimate cocoon of conversation. "You would be a hellion. You would put on a pleasant face for your husband while gaining the loyalty of all the servants and children in the house and then running roughshod over every single limitation. You would promise to do as he wished, all while doing just as *you* pleased. And you would get away with it, because you are so damned charming with your little half-moon dimple and that sassy mouth."

Ivy exhaled with both exasperation for the unflattering—and truthful—estimation of her character, and confusion over how he could know her so well. And what did he mean when he called her dimple charming and her mouth sassy? Was he saying her husband would find them so? "That is not a flattering picture you have painted of me."

"I disagree."

"Lord Brackley." An acidic voice interrupted their low conversation, and Ivy sprang back, only just becoming aware of how close they had gravitated during their discussion. A gloved hand snuck between them, and Owen shook it while he sized up their intruder. "I am Lord Mawe, Earl of Wynster."

Barnes immediately appeared at Ivy's side, inserting himself between her and Lord Mawe, their uncle and the heir to their grandfather's title.

Their uncle possessed similar features to their father, with narrow shoulders, thinning hair that was more white than blond, and a pointed nose. Ivy's limited recollections of her uncle were that he was as mean and shrewd as her father, too. She had only met her grandfather, the marquess, once, but she remembered him to be wizened and eternally unhappy. She supposed her uncle and father had come by their nasty demeanors fairly.

Owen dropped his hand after the briefest handshake, as if her uncle's touch disgusted him. "Lord Mawe."

"I hear my niece and nephew are staying as guests at Brackley Estate," her uncle said, his voice oily and calculating. "I did not know you were so well acquainted."

"Barnes and I attended Harrow together."

"I was an Eton boy myself, although I suppose my nephew was too stupid to attend, even with his grandfather's connections."

Ivy's eyes widened at the blatant insult to her brother and the passive insult to Owen. Both men took it in stride, her brother smiling as if he found it amusing, while Owen's face remained flat and bored.

"Eton men certainly have a reputation," Owen commented.

Her uncle frowned, unsure if he was being insulted or not. "Is it true you are courting my niece?"

Owen's eyes flicked to her and then Barnes, the tiniest line between his brows easing when he noted how close her brother stood to her—his body an immovable mountain between Ivy and the horrid little man related to them by blood. "Yes."

"Have you spoken with my brother?"

"It has not progressed to that point," Owen said firmly. "Miss Bennett will have her choice of suitors this Season, but I have expressed my interest in joining the queue of men vying for her hand."

Her uncle snorted and craned his neck around her brother. "Move, boy," he snapped. "I want to take a better look at her. Her father always said she was short and ugly and would need a firm hand to guide her."

Barnes did not move, but he did spare their uncle a disdainful glance.

Their uncle snarled and maneuvered himself instead, Barnes shifting so that although her uncle could see her, he would have a difficult time reaching her. Ivy stifled a smile. She could take care of herself, but she loved her brother for wanting to protect her all the same.

"I have not seen the chit since she was a child, but she is not as ugly as my brother made her out to be," Mawe said, continuing to talk about her as if she were not present, "although I suspect she is as headstrong as reported. If you do marry her, Brackley, I suggest you do not spare the rod. A woman appreciates a man who lets her know her place. Boundaries, I always say. Beat her once or twice, and she will never dare test them. You will have a pleasant marriage without all of the yapping and demands."

A muscle jumped in Owen's jaw, and he glared at her uncle as if he could skewer him with his eyes, yet her uncle appeared unaware of his quietly building fury. Owen loved his sisters, and Ivy had witnessed how kind and gentle he was with him. He would *never* tolerate abusing a woman or a child. Heavens, she did not think he would even tolerate harm to a creature if the whispers she had heard about his horse-breeding ethics were true.

Her uncle's cold gaze ran over her flushed cheeks. Ivy was sorely tempted to knock his front tooth out and teach *him* a thing or two about physical pain.

Lord Mawe sniffed and continued, despite the fact that, like Owen, Barnes was coiled stiff with rage. "My brother did not keep his own wife in line, and look at—"

"That is enough now," Barnes snapped.

"Pardon me, boy?"

Barnes took her uncle roughly by the arm and said, "Have you met Miss Diane Wixby?" before steering him away with a conniving smile. Diane would rip him to shreds. Ivy almost wanted to follow so she could watch.

Owen stared after her uncle for a long time, his knuckles white as he fought off some silent impulse. When he turned back to her, his eyes were as frosted as a glacier. "Are you attached to your uncle? Or may I kill him?"

Ivy let out a shaky laugh. "He is a terrible human being, but no worse than my father."

Owen flinched at that.

"My uncle is a reminder of why we are here: for the alternative."

"Hartford is not the only alternative. Not all men are like your father and uncle. *Most* men are not."

"Then let us hope I find one of them for a husband."

Chapter 16

The rest of the musicale was uneventful. Owen continued to lavish her with attention, which only egged Hartford into a silent competition to see who could flirt with her more, but after the meeting with her uncle, some of Owen's flippancy had vanished. He no longer seemed as irritated about his role in their charade. It was as if he finally understood what was at stake for her and was taking their objective seriously.

Ivy glanced at the clock on the library mantel where she was reading with Diane. It had been two days since the musicale. Hartford had formally called upon her the morning after and stayed with her for over an hour, chattering about poetic meter while her mind had drifted to what Owen was doing at the moment. Probably on a horse. Most certainly scowling. Ivy had then spent hours regaling the girls, who were now all in on the ruse, with every detail of the party.

Jolting at the late time, she made her excuses to Diane and hurried to her chamber. She wriggled into a pair of breeches before letting the fabric of her dress fall over them again, then crushed her riding hat to her head, snatched a pair of gloves from beside her bed, and snuck out to the stables.

The sun was descending behind the horizon, and the air was laced with wood and coal smoke. Wind rippled across the dry grass and plastered her skirt to her legs. She clutched her hat to her head and entered the barn, where the stud groom she had befriended, Bernard, stood with her saddled mare.

"Bernard, you waited for me!"

"You are later than usual, Miss Bennett."

"I lost track of time."

Bernard handed her the reins to Tansy the Temperamental. The mare had been the least-loved beast in the stables when Ivy had arrived, thanks to a penchant for snacking on sleeves and nipping at hats, so of course Ivy had taken an instant liking to her. After a weeks-long campaign that involved feeding the mare sugar cubes every day and cooing her praise, Ivy was now the only person the mare tolerated.

Ivy adored Bernard equally. His hair was as gray as Tansy's mane, and his knuckles were thick with arthritis, but it was clear he treasured the horses, living and breathing to take care of them each day. What was more: He had never once asked Ivy where she went every Tuesday evening or looked askance at her for riding astride.

Ivy stroked Tansy's neck, and the mare nickered and butted Ivy's shoulder. She slipped a sugar cube from her pocket and discreetly fed it to her. "I will take care of her as usual when I return. There is no need for you to get out of your warm bed at such a late hour."

When Ivy would have pulled herself into the saddle, the groom stopped her. He chewed on his lip for a moment and, apparently deciding it was worth the risk, dropped his hand and said, "Mayhap the young miss might consider that should the master discover she is traveling alone in the dark, he would be verra displeased."

Bernard turned his head out of respect when Ivy threw her leg over the saddle. Once she had readjusted her skirt, she grasped the reins. Owen had caught her leaving her class once before when he was visiting an acquaintance, but as far as she knew, his being in town was a rare occurrence. "I do not think I have to worry, Bernard, although I appreciate your concern. I am sure his lordship is in his study by now, drinking himself surlier over my brother."

"Miss Bennett," Bernard whispered, his lips barely moving.

"Or mayhap he is planning his audition for the circus, where he will growl with the best of the beasts."

"Miss Bennett..."

Ivy snapped her fingers. "I have it! The viscount is surely writing to an American orphanage, offering to scare the children on all hallows eve with his legendary frown—"

"MISS BENNETT!" Bernard roared, his eyes as wide as saucers.

"Heavens, Bernard. No need to shout."

Bernard swallowed heavily, and that was when Ivy noticed his eyes were not focused on her at all, but rather on something over her shoulder.

Oh, no.

"Wrong on all accounts, Miss Bennett," a cool voice said. Ivy's stomach dropped straight to her toes, and she closed her eyes. "The viscount is, in fact, spending his evening hours in his stables."

It took Ivy a moment before she worked up the nerve to turn her head, and when she did, she blushed at the inscrutable green gaze of the viscount.

"Yes, of course you are, my lord."

Owen was leaning against a rough-hewn post, his arms crossed.

His shirt sleeves were rolled halfway up his forearms, revealing the powerful muscles of a man used to taming wild animals. His chestnut hair was tousled, and once again he had not allowed his valet to shave him, leaving his square jaw shaded with growth. Ivy could not help observing how well his trousers fit him, or how his boots were scuffed and there was dirt on the side of his thigh. She should have known he would escape the confines of the house the moment he had the opportunity. He was not a lord who enjoyed sitting about smoking and clutching crystal glasses.

"What brings you to the stables at eight o'clock in the evening?" His gaze fell to her legs, and Ivy was acutely aware of the fact that once again she had been caught riding astride.

"I am exercising Tansy. I have missed her company the past few days."

His gaze bore into hers. "You intend to exercise a horse after dark, when she might misstep and throw you?"

"That will not happen." She fondly petted Tansy's neck. "The lady is quite surefooted."

"I agree that it will not happen."

Ivy's smile faltered. "If you are about to tell me where I may and may not travel, then we had better call off this faux—"

"Bernard, would you leave us?" Owen cut in sharply.

Bernard tugged on his cap and disappeared with a look of relief on his face.

Owen dropped his arms and strode forward, sliding his hand down Tansy's neck. Instead of nipping at him, the traitor nickered in delight and lowered her head for more. He continued onward, dragging his palm over the horse's withers and stopping at the saddle, just inches from Ivy's knee. His voice was gravelly when he said, "You were saying?"

Ivy swallowed hard. What *had* she been saying? Oh, yes, she had been close to revealing their farce in front of Bernard. It was clear the viscount knew she was lying about exercising Tansy, and so rather than doubling down, she decided to tell him part of the truth in hope that her candor would soften his attitude. "I am visiting my modiste friend in town. I have a standing appointment to see her on this day."

"Although I am occupied tonight writing to the circus about joining the lion exhibit"—Ivy suppressed a grimace—"the letter can wait while I escort you."

Her lips parted in surprise. He was not going to fight her about riding into town at night? She thought for sure he had been about to forbid her from going, and she had been prepared to let him know she would not tolerate such restriction.

"You are not going to tell me I cannot go?"

His hand slipped forward until only centimeters separated his fingers from her knee. "Why would I tell you what you can and cannot do?"

"Because you are domineering."

"Perhaps in some areas of my life."

"I do not need an escort. I am capable of taking care of myself."

"Nevertheless, I shall escort you tonight, and every week from herein out."

"I—"

"Ivy, if you think I would let the woman I am courting ride alone on a dangerous road, then you do not know me at all."

"But the courtship is not real," she argued, lowering her voice. "You do not have to pretend to care about me."

His expression was blank when he removed his hand and turned his back on her. "I am saddling Saxony. I will meet you outside."

True to his word, he joined her outside the stable a few minutes later, and they took off toward the road. The stars and moon were bright, which made for surer footing for the horses. Ivy tugged her navy cloak tight and slid a glance in Owen's direction. He was frowning, as usual, and appeared deep in thought as the moon slicked over his hat and the gleaming flanks of his horse.

The minutes passed in silence save for the sound of the horse's hooves and snorts, when Owen finally spoke. "Are you ready to tell me who you are really meeting tonight?"

Ivy stiffened, and wariness flashed in her eyes. Now he was certain there was more to this "visit" with her modiste friend. Why else would she sneak out of the house every Tuesday night? Why not take the carriage out in the open? Could she be meeting a gentleman? Had his original assumption the first time he had met her on the road been accurate after all?

Something hot and potent stirred in his belly. He was intensely driven, whether it involved breeding the best horses or pleasing the woman in his life. He did not juggle tasks well and he never had, which meant he was unshakably faithful in his chosen pursuits. His bullheaded attention—and possession—had become a legendary part of his reputation, which meant if he and Ivy were going to successfully trick the *ton* into believing this was a real courtship, she had to know she could not keep an outside lover. He told himself it was only because if it were discovered, it would expose their ruse and ruin her reputation, and not because that "something" in the pit of his stomach was jealousy.

"I am going to the modiste shop," she answered carefully.

Owen nudged Saxony in front of Tansy, forcing the spirited mare to a standstill. He had not been surprised to discover Ivy had befriended the most unlikeable mare in the stable; Ivy's sunshine could coax gentleness out of even the grouchiest beast. Her honey eyes, clearly visible in the moonlight, widened in question.

"If you have a lover," he growled, "get rid of him. If you cannot part with him, then we end this charade now."

Her lower lip dropped, revealing a neat row of teeth. "You think I have a lover?"

"I do not know, but I *do* know you are lying about visiting your friend."

She pulled that swollen lip between her teeth and gently bit, making his groin stir.

"I do not have a lover." She looked up at him from beneath her lashes. "Do you?"

"No."

"Will you take one during our ruse?"

"No." Was that relief on her face, or was he imagining it? "So, Ivy, darling, where are we going?"

"As I said, I am going to the modiste shop." She looked at the saddle, the horse's mane, and the sky. She looked everywhere but at him.

"To see your friend, the modiste."

She did not reply.

"I would like to meet her. I want to set up an account for you and the girls."

Panic flitted across Ivy's expression. "You should wait until business hours. Besides, I do not need an account there."

"You do need an account, but if I cannot open one tonight, then I shall simply introduce myself to her."

"No! She does not see patrons outside of hours."

He stared her down. She was not telling the whole truth, and obviously had no intention of doing so. It only stoked his curiosity further. What on *earth* could she be up to? She had the same air of fidgeting secrecy as his sisters whenever he came upon them when they were not expecting him.

He was about to prod further when a form materialized in the road ahead of them. A black horse and a rider wearing a dark cloak stood horizontally, blocking the dirt road ahead. A flash of moonlight winked on the depthless eye of a pistol pointed directly at them.

Owen tugged on Tansy's reins, drawing Ivy closer to him.

"What—"

"Highwayman," he said quietly, his entire body tensing. Saxony sensed his shift and tossed his head. Ivy's eyes widened with fear when she realized they were sighted by the cold, faceless pistol.

"When he is distracted taking our coins," Owen continued in a low, hurried voice, "I want you to gallop back to the manor. I will buy you time. Do not stop under any circumstances or for anyone."

"No."

"I am not asking you, Ivy." He did not give a damn about losing the sizable amount of coin in his pocket, but he was terrified for Ivy's safety.

The highwayman lifted the pistol higher, and in a flat and polished voice that made true fear slide down Owen's spine he said, "Throw your purses ahead of you. If either of you moves, I will shoot. I am an excellent marksman. You do not want to test me."

Something about the man's tone—so void and emotionless it was almost inhuman—chilled Owen to the bone. He knew with some baser instinct that the man blocking the road would not hesitate to put a bullet in their flesh.

This was no rough-and-tumble highwayman out on his luck. The man's cultured accent and inflection spoke of someone who knew exactly what he was doing—and who his targets were.

Owen contemplated possibilities as he slowly withdrew his wallet and coin purse from his coat. Ivy extracted her own coin purse and, without awaiting further instruction, tossed it ahead of her. It landed in the dirt with a clink of metal. Owen followed suit, his eyes never leaving the highwayman.

"Dismount," the man instructed.

Owen ground his teeth together, his natural disinclination to obey orders chafing at his skin, and dismounted. He needed Ivy out of there. *Now.* He lifted his hand to smack her horse's flank and send them sprinting in the opposite direction, but the highwayman said sharply, "If that horse moves so much as a foot, I will lame the beast."

"No!" Ivy cried, quickly slipping off Tansy to stand by Owen's side. Although she was shivering with fear, her eyes were bright and angry. She was small and slight beside him, and something fiercely protective stirred in Owen's chest. If it meant taking a bullet to the heart, he would not allow any harm to come to her.

"Take the money and begone," Owen ordered.

The highwayman gave a low, humorless laugh as he dismounted, the pistol never once wavering, and leisurely strolled forward. Something about the way the man moved was familiar, and it gave Owen the uneasy sense that he knew him from somewhere.

The man scooped up the coin purses and wallet. A black band of fabric was tied around his head, with two neatly cut eye holes. It concealed most of his face, but again his mouth had a shape that was vaguely familiar to Owen.

"Now that you are a viscount, I wager everyone scrapes and

bows to you, and yet your flesh will be shredded by a bullet the same as any other. How does it feel, *your lordship*, to be humbled by a highwayman?"

"Do I know you?"

The question seemed to sour the highwayman's gloating. "No one knows me." He turned the pistol on Ivy, and Owen's heart leaped into his throat. "Who is she?"

"A maid."

"You are lying." He studied Ivy with such thorough perusal that Owen's entire body went white hot with rage. "This is the governess the gossip rags are talking about. The one you are courting."

Whoever this man was, he knew too much about Owen's life for this to be a random robbery. He had to have been waiting for Owen specifically. How many nights had he haunted this road, biding his time, hoping Owen would pass? Was he someone Owen had denied a horse? Owen was very discerning about who he sold his animals to. He had turned down men who had wealth pouring out of their pockets for being cruel to their animals. He was sure there were any number of people still bitter about it.

Whatever the man's vendetta, it had everything to do with Owen and nothing to do with Ivy.

"No, she is not," Owen refuted, flexing his hands. He wanted to tear this scoundrel limb from limb.

The man *tsk*ed and waved the pistol. He stood too far for Owen to make a lunge, keeping them both at his whim and mercy. "Your lying is beginning to upset me, Viscount." The highwayman's eyes crawled over Ivy. "She is pretty, but she is no Heidi."

Owen felt as if he had been struck through by an axe. "Did Heidi send you?"

The man smirked. "I see Harrow did not make you any smarter

than the boys who were not allowed to attend." His voice was so bitter that Owen knew he had been denied entrance.

"What do you want? We gave you all our money."

"I want justice."

"Did I wrong you in some way?"

"I want justice for *your* mother."

The heat coursing through Owen's body cooled to slush at the mention of his mother. His mentally fragile mother had died of gastric fever when he was twelve. For a moment, the memory of her lying in her casket flashed in front of his eyes: the high-necked, white-lace gown wrapped around her cold body, her hair spread out as if she were floating underwater. He swallowed hard. "What injustice was done to my mother?"

The highwayman's eyes flared with a maniacal rage. "Do not *dare* play innocent."

Ivy must have moved in some manner, because the man's attention shifted to her.

"Did you say you were too stupid to attend Harrow?" Owen taunted, desperate to draw the highwayman's eyes back to him, but it did not work, because the other man was already entranced by Ivy's soft mouth.

"Have you kissed the governess yet?"

Ivy gasped. "I am a respectable young woman!"

"So he has not. I shall take the first kiss then, and you, *Lord* Brackley, will forever know that it was not you who first kissed your wife, but *me*. Come here, Miss Bennett."

Ivy planted her feet, and Owen knew it was now or never. He would shove her behind her horse and charge the highwayman. With any luck he would tackle the man to the ground, and Ivy could take off on one of the horses.

Owen had barely shifted to put his plan into action when a shot cracked through the air and smoke billowed from the end of the pistol. Simultaneously a searing, blinding pain sliced through his left shoulder. He blinked down at the ragged hole in his coat, watching numbly as a hot wash of blood began spilling down his chest.

Ivy lunged for him as he staggered backward, but the highwayman said sharply, "If you do not come here and kiss me this instant, wench, I shall finish him off." As if to prove his point, he pointed the gun at Owen again.

Ivy's eyes searched Owen's, and she said in a low, soothing voice, "It will be all right, Owen."

He pressed his palm to the wound on his shoulder and nearly blacked out from the pain before he blinked and regathered his senses. He staggered forward, but he was so weak that she was able to stop him with a simple touch to his arm. "No."

He tried not to sink to his knees. He was losing too much blood and too fast, but he did not care. He could not allow this man to hurt Ivy. He could not—

While his sluggish thoughts tried to keep up, Ivy hurried toward the highwayman with her arms open wide, as if she planned to throw herself into his embrace. The man lowered the pistol in surprise, seeming unsure about her intentions. When she was a foot away, she struck so fast that Owen was certain he was hallucinating. A swift punch to the highwayman's nose was accompanied by the sound of cartilage cracking; and then the man screamed as her sharp boot connected with his groin.

Owen dropped slowly to his knees, black spots dancing in his vision as Ivy disarmed the thief and turned the gun on him. Owen was dreaming. There was no way his former governess had just done what he thought he had seen. Ivy's voice sounded far away as she instructed the groaning highwayman to put his wrists together behind his back.

Owen was so cold. He had never felt this cold before, as if he would never be warm again. Had the temperature dropped?

He must have made a noise, because Ivy spun to look at him, and when she did, the highwayman, still retching, crawled atop his horse and took off.

Ivy barely seemed to notice; she was already running toward him, her small, warm hands pressing his chest, and her face close to his as she reassured him that she was going to get help. "You must stay awake, Owen."

"I cannot," he murmured, his eyelids closing.

"Then climb atop your horse. That is all I need from you. Then you can rest."

With Herculean effort, he staggered to his feet, blind now and relying solely on touch. He was aware that he was going to pass out any moment, but he needed to get on his horse. He was too heavy for Ivy to lift, and if he was left here while she went for help, he would bleed out. The bullet had clearly hit an artery.

Ivy guided his hands to Saxony's saddle, and then his blessed horse bent on one knee, lowering himself so that Owen could sling himself over his back. He had barely landed in the saddle when he slumped over and slipped into blackness.

Chapter 17

Ivy had a notoriously cool head on her shoulders when it came to blood and injuries. When she was a child, her brothers had suffered all manner of scrapes, bloodied noses, and even broken bones. Once, her third eldest brother had fallen on a hunting trip and snapped his arm bone clear through. She prided herself on being immune to the sight of blood at this point in her life.

But this... this was different. The amount of blood that soaked Owen's coat made her skin buzz. His face was pale and clammy, and she knew without a doubt that he was dying. She ripped off her cloak and swung onto Saxony. The beautiful horse seemed to sense it was an emergency, because he stood statue-still while she awkwardly wedged herself between the stallion's neck and Owen's heavy body. She twisted and tucked her balled-up cloak into Owen's coat, praying it would stanch some of the bleeding. When she faced forward again, his full weight fell over her back, but she barely felt the burden. The closest doctor was half an hour east, and she did not think he had that much time.

She did not allow herself second thoughts as she took off for town, pushing Saxony as fast as she dared. She grabbed one of Owen's lifeless hands and pulled it across her belly to ensure he did not tip off. His chin bounced against her shoulder, and even through her cloak she began to feel the stickiness of his blood.

She pulled a heavily breathing Saxony to a halt in front of the modiste shop and raced upstairs, praying with every fiber of her being that the Dove had come tonight. She burst into the studio, wild and blood-soaked, her eyes falling with relief on the one woman she needed. Ivy did not know why she was so certain the Dove would know what to do—but in her bones she knew the Dove was Owen's only hope.

The Dove assessed Ivy's disheveled, bloodied state. "Where?"

"Outside. Brackley's been shot."

The Dove went into action with a competence that made Ivy want to weep with gratitude. "Molly, you are a nurse. I need you to go downstairs to the modiste shop and gather as much cotton fabric as you can and tear it into strips. Find needles and other sharp implements that you can sterilize over a flame or with alcohol. We may need to dig the bullet out." She turned to the youngest of the group, Mable, whose eyes were wide at the blood coating Ivy. "I need you to find where the modiste makes tea and start boiling water." The Dove set her lips as she focused on Ivy, Bertha, Tulle, and Tabitha. "I have seen the viscount. He is a large man and will be heavy. I need all of you to help carry him in."

Ivy's feet were in action the moment the Dove finished speaking. She was keenly aware that with every passing moment, Owen plodded closer to death. She raced down the stairwell, her soles barely touching the treads, and burst onto the street where Owen still lay slumped over the still horse. She choked back a sob, praying he was not dead.

The Dove snapped out instructions about where each woman should stand, and on the count of three they slid him off the horse, staggering under his muscled weight. They carried him toward the door of the modiste shop, and Ivy thought it was in his best interest that he was unconscious.

Mable was already holding the door open for them. "The water is on, and I have lit some lamps."

"Over here!" Molly instructed with the same calm efficiency as the Dove. The stout older woman had already fashioned a bed of sorts by clearing off a sewing table and laying cushions on it.

The women grunted as they heaved Brackley onto the table. In the light of the candles his face was ghostly pale, his shirtsleeves and coat so saturated with blood that Ivy did not know how he was going to survive. She leaned over his face and exhaled with relief when she felt the faintest puff of breath on her cheek.

"Scissors," the Dove said with authority. Tulle, the young newlywed who had whitened during the lesson on strangulation, was standing by the sewing implements soaking in a bowl of brandy. Despite her hesitant nature, she immediately jumped into action as the Dove's assistant. The Dove snipped away Owen's expensive coat and shirtsleeves, peeling the fabric back to reveal a raw wound gone black with clots. Blood coated his broad chest and had dried in rusty rivulets down a stomach delineated with muscles and lightly dusted with hair.

Ivy pressed her knuckles to the side of his rib cage and blanched at the cool feel of his skin.

The Dove began cleaning the wound with a wad of cotton dunked in hot water and shouted, "I need more brandy, or any other liquor that might be available!"

"Already ahead of you," Molly said, bustling forward with a

bottle of gin. "Found this hidden beneath the counter." She had taken over organizing the other women, setting Tabitha, the widow, to sterilizing the tools with alcohol, and her cousin Bertha to ripping strips of muslin. The Dove grasped the bottle of gin and poured it over the cleaned wound. She leaned closer to study the ragged flesh, but still she did not lift her veil. Without the clots, the bullet wound had begun to freely bleed again, although it looked much smaller and less gruesome than before.

"I believe the bullet is still in him," she said, straightening. "We will need to extract it before we can sanitize and stitch the area. Ivy, I need you to apply as much pressure as possible to stop the bleeding while I prepare." She laid several layers of muslin over the wound and Ivy stacked both her hands on top of it. "Press *hard*, Ivy. He is unconscious and you cannot hurt him, but if you do not apply enough pressure he may die."

Ivy leaned her full weight on him, feeling his flesh depress.

"Good."

Ivy was vaguely aware of the women bustling around her, of the dancing shadows and the pungent smell of gin, but all she could focus on was Owen's face. His lashes were dark against his deathly white cheeks. One lock of hair curled over his forehead, and his lips were partially opened as he struggled to breathe. She hated this for him, not only because he might die, but because he would abhor being as vulnerable as he was in that moment. He was a vibrant, active man who, if he were conscious, would despise lying here at the mercy of others.

She pressed harder, blood oozing through the cotton and wetting her fingers. "Do not dare die, Owen," she whispered fiercely. "There are better ways to get out of this courtship."

The Dove appeared at her elbow with a tray of sterilized sewing and dining implements. "It is best that he is unconscious for this. Ivy, are you able to hold the lamp over the wound with a firm hand?" Ivy nodded. "Excellent. Molly, I will need you to insert the sugar nips and separate the wound while I remove the bullet."

Ivy forced her hand not to tremble as she left her compress and took the lantern Tulle silently handed to her. She would *not* fail Owen now. Forcing her breathing even, she held the lamp over the splotched white cotton while the Dove and Molly bent over his chest and peeled back the fabric. They murmured to one another as if they had previously done a thousand surgeries in the middle of a modiste shop. Ivy blessed their competence and synchronicity as they expertly probed the wound.

"It appears to have nicked the brachial artery," the Dove said.

Molly peered closer. "But it is not severed, thank heaven."

"Indeed. I am not delicate enough of a seamstress to sew arterial walls together." The Dove reached for the tweezers while Molly lifted the slender nips and inserted them into the wound with a wet sound that Ivy forced herself to block out. Blood had never bothered her before, so she did not understand why hearing the work on Owen's wound should make her want to scream.

It seemed like forever, but it could not have been more than half a minute before Ivy heard the clatter of metal and the rolling of the bullet. Then the Dove and Molly were moving quickly, the bleeding having turned ferocious again. They disinfected the site and the Dove began sewing the skin together with silk thread, unflinching as she pierced the viscount's skin over and over.

Ivy shifted her gaze to the net concealing the Dove's face. This woman had obvious experience with traumatic injuries. She was clever, excelled at defense, was the spymaster of an entire network of governesses, and had known exactly what to do to save Owen's life.

Who could she be?

"We need to get him to Brackley Estate and fetch the doctor," the Dove said, straightening. She had knotted the thread and snipped it away, leaving a neat row of white stitches holding the puckered, raw skin together. "However, before any of us leaves the safety of this building, I must speak with Ivy about what happened." She gestured with her chin to Molly. "Molly, will you bandage the wound? Ivy, come into the back with me."

"Will he survive?" Ivy asked, trailing after her in a daze.

"I have done all I can. If his body can fight off any infection that occurs, he should make it. The artery nick will heal itself in time. If the bullet had been a fraction of an inch to the side... I would have different news for you."

Ivy numbly followed the Dove into the small kitchen, where the woman washed her hands with a pitcher of cool water. After wiping them on a towel, she turned to Ivy, who was still standing with a white-knuckled grip on the lamp. "You are covered in blood. Come wash yourself."

Ivy rinsed her hands, watching the water turn pink with Owen's blood. Her dress was stuck to her back with blood, the material stiffening and pulling on her skin.

When she finished, the Dove's competence morphed into a steely flatness that sent fear skittering down Ivy's spine. "Now tell me everything."

Ivy recounted the run-in with the highwayman, and when she finished, the Dove said, "It sounds as if Lord Brackley was specifically targeted." Her stance was preternaturally still, and a whisper of danger brushed against Ivy's skin. She would not cross this woman—ever. "He intended to make it appear as a robbery, but based on your account, he had an ulterior motive."

"You believe his true intention was to murder Brackley?"

"To humiliate the viscount, at the very least."

Ivy was appalled to discover her lower lip was trembling. She clamped her teeth over it. "Do you think he is the same man who has been lurking at the estate?" She had already written to the Dove about the curious interloper Eliza had spotted.

"It is possible." She seemed thoughtful, her only tell a slight press of her lips. "Why does this man suspect Brackley of wronging his own mother, and why does he care? Does he have anything to do with the mysterious disease in London? These are questions we must find the answers to."

"How?"

"I have a number of plans in motion and a brilliant mathematician searching for patterns related to the hysteria. If this highwayman *did* intend to murder Lord Brackley, his lordship is in peril. Would you feel comfortable staying in your position, not only to continue probing into his past deeds and now his relationship with his mother, but to keep him safe until we have gathered all the facts?"

Ivy nodded. "There is something else I must tell you. Owen—Lord Brackley—is courting me."

The Dove did not appear to be surprised, and Ivy realized with a flush that of course the Dove would have already heard the gossip. She was a *spymaster*.

"It is not real," Ivy hurriedly added, and launched into the details of their scheme.

"This works to our advantage," the Dove said when Ivy had finished. "As the woman he is courting, you will be expected to be near his bedside during his recovery. He will be bored and stationary, and he may be willing to talk more than usual. Probe into his business. Ask about his contacts in London. Find out where he was over the past year. There *must* be a connection somewhere, and I will not rest until we find it. Above all else, stay alert."

The Dove's words slipped into her ears without really sinking in. She turned her eyes downward and distantly noted that she had missed a streak of blood on her wrist.

"It has been a trying night for you."

Ivy lifted her chin. "Indeed, but it is not over yet. Someone must fetch the doctor, and I must ride back to Brackley Estate and send the carriage to collect his lordship."

The faintest hint of a smile touched the Dove's lips. "Women always do what needs to be done."

When they returned to the main part of the shop, Owen's face was pale, his breathing shallow as his chest rose and fell. Ivy stopped at his side and comforted herself by observing his inhalations for half a minute.

"You will take care of him while I am gone?" she said to Molly.

"Like he was my own brother."

"Thank you," Ivy whispered. "I am leaving to fetch the carriage from Brackley Hall."

"Who is riding to the doctor's house?" Tabitha asked.

The Dove pulled her gloves on. "I will, after I escort Ivy to the estate."

Tabitha shook her head. She was too young to be a widow, Ivy thought, but her face was set when she said, "Nay. That will take too long. I shall ride to the doctor."

The Dove hesitated.

"Go with Tabitha," Ivy said. "If the highwayman is still on the road, he will not be lingering near Brackley Estate. I will be fine."

The Dove gave a brusque nod. With one last look at Owen, Ivy followed the two women from the modiste shop. Tansy stood by Saxony, having followed them on their mad gallop to the modiste. Ivy petted her neck and pressed her forehead to her warmth. "Sorry, my girl, but I need maximum speed right now. I shall be back for you."

Tansy nickered as if she understood, and Ivy mounted Saxony. Saxony was a large horse, and because his owner was the top horse breeder in Europe, he was also fast.

Ivy leaned forward and gripped the reins, praying she could control him. He had been a perfect gentleman when they had galloped to the dress shop, but then he had still had his owner on his back. "Let us fly, Saxony."

Chapter 18

Owen woke with a hammer banging inside his skull and cotton stuffed in his mouth. A cup was pressed to his lips before he could so much as stir. He drank down the cool liquid and peeled open one eye. "Ivy?" he croaked.

She sat beside him, the sun streaming through the window and lightening her brown hair into a golden hue. She smiled, her crescent dimple making an appearance, and he wondered if he was dreaming. There was no other explanation for Ivy Bennett being in what he now recognized was his bedchamber.

"Lord Brackley." She pressed the back of her hand to his forehead. "You are still feverish, but not as hot as before."

"Am I ill?" He tried to sit, but a blinding pain in his shoulder set his teeth on edge. He hissed as he scooted backward. Slowly he opened the partially buttoned nightshirt and stared down at his shoulder. A white bandage was wrapped over his shoulder and under his arm, but beyond its clean edges he saw purple and green bruising. All at once his memory of the robbery flooded back. He had been shot by a man who had seemed so familiar that

Owen swore he knew him from somewhere. Owen had sunk to the ground as Ivy had walked toward the scoundrel, who had been demanding a kiss.

He had been entirely unable to protect her.

He gripped her wrist with his good hand. "Did he hurt you?"

"No."

"How…" Another memory surfaced, this one hazier, as if viewed in a dream. Ivy, striking the man in the face, kicking him in the groin, and disarming him as easily as if she were a seasoned London brawler. "You disarmed him."

"You were bleeding out, my lord. Your memories are faulty. Once you collapsed, the highwayman rode away. Perhaps he was frightened by what he had done."

"Owen," he corrected, still keeping her wrist trapped. His thumb was pressed against her heartbeat, and her steady pulse calmed him, reassured him that she had come away from the incident unscathed. It had been his job to protect her, and he had failed miserably. He thought of the thousand things that could have happened to her, and his stomach churned.

"You are turning pale." She pulled her wrist away and reached for a tin pail, but he stopped her by snatching her hand again and drawing in deep, slow breaths through his nose. He needed to feel her skin right now, just until his brain caught up with what his eyes were showing him: that she was healthy and unharmed by his side.

Had he been so close to death that he had hallucinated what he had seen? He must have. It was unlikely his former governess had disarmed a man twice her size. "Tell me everything."

Was it his imagination, or did her pulse kick beneath his thumb?

"After you were shot, the thief took off. He was too rattled to even snatch our purses."

"I am not sure the coins were ever his intent." He squinted against the blinding pain in his head. Everything about the interaction had seemed personal, as if to punish *him*.

"You were able to climb on Saxony, and I took you to the nearest place I could, which was my friend's modiste shop," Ivy continued. "We left it quite a mess, I am sorry to say."

"I will send her funds to cover it. What happened there?"

"I left you at the shop and rode back to Brackley Estate to fetch the carriage. The doctor arrived not long after."

He ran his gaze over her pink cheeks and the honey-brown eyes that could not quite meet his own. "How did I manage not to bleed out before the doctor arrived?"

"Pressure?"

"Say it without the question at the end the next time you lie, Ivy."

"Pressure."

"Hmm." When she tugged again, he released her wrist and studied her in the slanting light. She had shadows beneath her eyes, and her usual cheer was strained. "How long have I been unconscious?"

"Three days. You were quite feverish. We did not know…" Her voice broke.

Owen gave her a wan smile. "It will take more than a bullet to keep me down, although I am confident the reason I am alive right now is because of you and not my hardy constitution."

She refilled his water and passed it to him before ringing the bell for the maid. Once she had instructed the maid to bring broth and tea, she turned back to him, and he glimpsed the slightest tremble in her lower lip.

"I am sorry you had to witness what you did," he said gently.

"Try not to die on me, Owen, even if it *would* save me from having to end our courtship."

A few minutes later the maid arrived with tea, broth, and an unwelcome visitor.

"I see you are still alive," Barnes said, pulling out a chair. He did not appear to be happy about it.

"I do not have the spirit for you, Barnes."

Ivy tried to lift the broth to his lips, but he took it from her and did it with his own good hand. He was not an invalid yet.

Barnes frowned at Ivy's attempt to nurse him. "You need to regain your spirit in that case, so that I may call you out for almost getting my sister killed."

"Barnes!" Ivy twisted in her chair, her voice heavy with censure. "The viscount woke up not half an hour ago, and you are already threatening him with a duel? Are you addled? He could not have stopped that highwayman from pulling the trigger any more than I could have. If you have no kind words to say, please leave."

A flicker of something crossed Barnes's face—regret, perhaps?—but then it was gone, his mask of disdain firmly in place once again. "Mayhap I'll stay a bit and hear about the attempted robbery from the viscount himself."

Ivy glared at him. "You would not be trying to avoid Diane, would you?"

"She is with the girls, so no, dear sister, I am not avoiding anyone."

Owen sipped the broth and sighed as the salty warmth slid down his throat. "How are the girls?"

"Diane fully took over my governess duties while I nursed you, but I am still helping when I can." Ivy glanced at the clock over the mantel and startled. "Oh! I promised her I would help with outdoor prayer." She stood and ran her eyes over him. "Will you be all right for an hour or two?"

"Of course."

She nodded, and when she passed by Barnes she said sternly, "Behave."

The door snicked shut behind her, and still Barnes did not move from his sprawled place in the chair at the foot of the bed. Owen drank the broth, his eyes meeting Barnes's over the rim. Neither of them looked away.

"Tell me what happened," Barnes ordered.

Owen was tempted to tell Barnes to bugger off, but if it had been *his* sister held at gunpoint, he would demand to know every last detail, so he told him all he could recollect. When he finished, Barnes steepled his fingers beneath his chin. "Perhaps you took up with this man's sister, and he wants revenge."

"If I did not have a bullet in my shoulder, I would knock you out for the mere suggestion."

"You do not have a bullet in your shoulder."

Owen lifted a brow. "The doctor was able to extract it?"

"Not quite. When the footmen and I arrived at the modiste shop, the bullet was in a tray and your wound was stitched."

Owen leaned against the pillow, reeling from dual shocks. First, that Barnes had come to fetch him. And second, that the wound had already been cleaned and stitched before he had arrived home. That explained how he had not bled out, but it did not answer who had done it. "The modiste?" he asked, although he did not fully believe it.

"That is what Ivy says." Barnes continued to stare at him. "The highwayman could have injured her, Owen. I know you do not give a damn about her well-being, but Ivy is the baby of the family. She is tough and she is clever, but she still needs protection. When you started this charade with her, it was with the expectation that you would see to her safety. He could have assaulted her. Kidnapped her. Killed her."

Owen's stomach was in knots at the recitation of every last one of his nightmares.

"She should not have been out late at night. She should not have been with you. But she *was* with you, and you failed to protect her." Barnes arched a brow at Owen's silence. "No excuses to make?"

"No."

Barnes leaned forward, his eyes glittering dangerously. "Make a mistake like this again, and I will kill you myself."

With his promise still ringing in the air, he left the room.

Owen fell asleep, and when he woke again it was to find far more welcome visitors.

"Brother!" Ophelia, the eldest of his sisters, cried. She and her sisters leaped from the floor, where they had been quietly playing with dolls, and crowded around him. Over their silky heads he glimpsed Ivy and Diane, and flashed them a grateful smile. Even though his entire body ached and his shoulder felt as if someone were spearing it with a heated blade, some of the itchiness in his soul eased at the sight of the girls.

"Did you get shot?" six-year-old Ollie asked plainly, and Owen was proud of himself for knowing both her name and her age.

"I did. But as you can see, I am perfectly fine now because Miss Bennett saved my life."

A few of the older girls still seemed close to tears, but the younger ones shivered with excitement, and the look they gave Ivy bordered on hero-worship.

Owen reached for a glass of water, going clammy when it felt like the stitches were being torn out of his skin. He was grateful when Opal jumped to help him. "Is he going to come back?" she asked.

"Who?"

"The highwayman."

The girls stilled, awaiting his answer. Before he could respond, Oriana, who was five, squinted her eyes and said, "Let him try to hurt our brother again! Thanks to Miss Bennett, we will be re—" Odette gave her a swift kick, and Oriana immediately shut her mouth.

"Thanks to Miss Bennett you will be what?" Owen prodded, his eyes narrowing on Oriana. When her lips remained stubbornly pressed together, he glanced at the other seven girls, each one looking guiltier than the last. *"Oriana?"*

"Nothing," she blurted. "I only meant that because Miss Bennett saved your life, then you will be safe so long as she is here."

They were keeping secrets. Although Diane's expression appeared thoughtful and Ivy's entirely blank, he knew without a doubt that he was missing something. His brow furrowed, and he opened his mouth to *demand* answers, when Ivy said, "Girls, I think your brother needs to rest. We will return tomorrow."

They all scrambled to pet his arm and say their goodbyes. The littlest one climbed onto the bed, jostling his tender body, and gave him a sticky kiss on his cheek. He snatched her with his good arm before she could get away, and squeezed her in an awkward hug, unfamiliar with casual affection. But he must have done it right, because she gave him a toothy grin before slipping off the bed.

"You are safe, girls. You do not need to worry for me or yourselves. No one will separate us," he vowed, and watched as some of the tension eased from their shoulders. They trusted him, he realized with awe. He had done nothing to earn their love and devotion, and yet they freely gave it to him. In that moment, he knew he would do anything to be worthy of them.

When his valet arrived later, Owen instructed him to dispatch an urgent missive to a private detective he had heard of. The man was richer than Satan, but took on work in order to stay sane. As if that were not enough to endear him to Owen, the detective constable had also unveiled the identity of the Evangelist some months ago, and had since started his own private detective agency with his wife.

"Send this letter to Mr. Zachariah Denholm," Owen instructed, handing over the sheet of stationery. He *would* uphold his promise to his sisters, which meant he needed to know who that bloody highwayman was, and what he knew about his mother.

Chapter 19

"Are you going to tell me what really happened that night?" Diane asked as the wind blew a red curl across her forehead. She stood beside Ivy, watching as the eldest set of twins practiced their fencing footwork without swords.

It had cooled considerably overnight, the wind heightening until Ivy's cheeks were chapped. Winter was well on its way, but that did not mean the girls had to be imprisoned indoors when a warm cloak would do. Fortunately, Diane was Ivy's closest friend and knew all about her lessons with the girls, and had wholeheartedly agreed to continue their defensive education.

"I told you: The viscount was shot by a highwayman."

"And he arrived home fully sewn." At Ivy's look she grinned. "I have ears. You are not the only person who enjoys a bit of gossip."

Ivy's brows drew together and she called, "Odette, you must remain on the balls of your feet. Imagine you are as light as a hummingbird, buzzing and darting and striking with speed."

Odette flashed her a smile with a missing a tooth and bounced on her toes.

Diane, fortunately, moved to the next topic. "I am so happy here. The girls are full of fire and vinegar, and I love them already."

The girls began giggling and playing a game, lessons officially over for the moment. "I am happy you are here, too, Diane," Ivy said, her heart twisting at the reminder that *her* time with the Brackleys was temporary.

"I will be even happier when Barnes leaves," Diane added, laughing as Ollie spun so fast that she fell into a pile of leaves. "He is a bore. I do not know how you tolerate him lording over you."

"It is not as if I have a choice."

"Oh! I know that. I apologize."

"No, it is fine. I know how my brother is."

"Handsome, charming, and shouldering the burden of unwieldy siblings?" The deep, cantankerous voice came from just behind them, and Ivy flinched, thanking the heavens the girls were playing now instead of engaging in their other studies.

"Ah, here you are," Diane said brightly. "Did you sense happiness and come to destroy it?"

Barnes's scowl deepened. "A sharp tongue befits no one, Miss Wixby."

"You mean it befits no woman."

"Did I say that? Or are you once again putting words into my mouth?"

"I would like to stuff a sock in your mouth," she muttered.

"What was that?" Barnes's steely voice dripped with disdain. Other than Owen and their father, Ivy had never seen him dislike someone as much as he did Diane.

"Can I help you, brother?" Ivy interrupted before either of them could draw blood.

"Brackley wants to see you," he said, still staring at Diane. She stared right back, as defiant as always.

Ivy doled out hugs as the little ones asked for them and brushed back wild hair from the older girls' faces. "Behave for Miss Wixby."

"I do not think she would give us any other choice," Ophelia said, but even though her teeth were showing, her lower lip trembled.

Ivy briefly cupped the oldest girl's cheek. "You saw that he is awake," she said firmly. "Awake and roaring down the house, and you may visit again soon."

Ophelia nodded and gave her a quick, hard squeeze. "Thank you, Miss Bennett," she whispered.

Ivy joined Barnes as he escorted her back to the main house. "You are too attached," he said once they were out of earshot. "You are leaving. You should be putting distance between yourself and the girls, not acting as if you are their mother."

"Has anyone ever told you how insufferable you are?"

"Yes. Ivy, I have been thinking: What were you doing on the road with Brackley, unchaperoned, in the middle of the night?"

"It was eight o'clock in the evening, first of all," she said, although she knew the time was not the real issue, "and I was visiting my modiste friend. Owen caught me leaving the stables and insisted on escorting me."

"He should have forbidden you from leaving. Then none of this would have happened."

Ivy looked up at her brother, so tall and handsome and utterly unyielding. "Forbid me? Barnes, when did you become such a barbarian?"

A muscle flexed in his jaw, and he had the grace to look ashamed. "I am sorry. It is not you, Trouble, but Brackley I do not trust."

"Again, the highwayman was responsible, not Owen. I know you want to think the worst of him, but—"

"I think the worst of him for a *reason*, Ivy. I wish you would trust my judgment for once."

"Then tell me!" she shouted. "Tell me why you hate him so much."

He turned his face away, but not before she caught the flash of pain, and on its heels, disgust. "All you need to know is that he is wildly unworthy of your kindness."

Ivy sighed at her stubborn brother's refusal to tell her what Owen had done to turn him, one of the most loyal people she knew, so thoroughly and irrevocably against him.

Barnes's fists clenched. "Forty-six days, Ivy. Forty-six days until you never see that lout again."

Owen was lounging in a chair, the drapes opened and the sun gleaming on the mahogany grain of the table beside him. His hair was wet and curling slightly over his ears, meaning he had somehow threatened or bullied his valet into letting him bathe. His shirt was open at the collar, and he wore trousers and boots. If it were not for his pallor, or the skin pulled slightly too tight over his cheekbones from missing several days of meals, she would not have known he was ill at all.

"What are you doing out of bed?" Ivy chided, sitting when he gestured with his good arm to the chair on the opposite side of the small table. The room smelled of his signature scent mixed with the hydrangeas that had been delivered that morning. A glass of water stood beside the book he had set down upon her entry, the pages splayed open to mark his place. Curious to see what type of literature he enjoyed, she read the upside-down gold lettering and bit back a sigh. It was a reference book on horse breeds.

"I could not stay abed one more moment." His eyes traced her wind-flushed cheeks. "Did you enjoy outdoor prayer with the girls?"

"Yes. 'Tis getting quite chilly now, and the trees are mostly bare." She laughed at his poorly concealed jealousy. "You will be out of doors soon enough. The doctor is visiting again tomorrow, and I am sure he will give you a time when you may leave your sickbed—one that you will completely ignore."

"I am not a fool. I will heed his advice within reason. I wish to regain full function of my arm."

"Are you in pain?"

"Yes. I was shot."

She could not help smiling at his put-out look, as if it galled him to say the very words. "Has the nurse given you laudanum?"

"She has offered, but I will be fine with a few nips of brandy to stave off the worst of it."

She could not blame him for refusing after having witnessed the effects of opium on the dowager viscountess. The dowager seemed to have stopped relying on the opium since the viscount had come, but Ivy would never forget her corpse-like existence before he had arrived.

"My recovery should not impact our plans to attend the opening ball of the London Season, but I fear we will be absent from social events until then. I apologize. I know it is not ideal."

"That is not—that is fine, Lord Brackley." He had been shot by a man out for revenge, and his concern was that she was missing out on social events?

"Will you come closer?" Although it was phrased as a question, his tone held a hint of command, and she found herself standing before she had fully made the decision to do so.

Ivy rounded the table and closed the short distance between them. When she stood before him, Owen reached for her hand, the warmth of his fingers contrasting against the chill of her own. His gaze was hooded when he said, "What have I told you about calling me Lord Brackley?"

"*Owen.*"

"Better." His thumb swept over her knuckle, leaving heated prickles in its wake. "I wanted you to have as much exposure to Lord Hartford as you wished, although considering the books and flowers he has sent, I believe you have already succeeded in catching his interest."

Ivy gave him a questioning look. "Flowers?"

"Ostensibly they are for me, but since I have not exchanged more than a few words with the man, I suspect they are truly for you." He nodded toward a bouquet of pink dahlias standing beside the vase of hydrangeas. They were stunning, but rather than feeling excited that she had piqued Lord Hartford's interest, Ivy's chest felt curiously empty. She waited for a delayed glow, but nothing came. She had already known there would be no violent twists and that her heart would not jump or wring the way it did in Owen's presence, but she had thought she would at least feel *something*. The lack of emotion was worrisome.

Owen made a grumbling noise and cast a dark look at the flowers. "Take them when you leave."

"Mayhap he was genuinely worried about you."

"He was not."

"Mayhap he wants a horse?"

"He does not. He wants *you*." He tugged her closer, until she took a step between his open thighs. It was inappropriate, and she should remove her hand from his palm and retreat. They were discussing how to make Hartford her husband—which meant she should not be holding Owen's hand.

She stayed in place.

"Have you eaten?" she asked.

"If you call sipping broth eating. They refuse to give me anything else, as if it is my stomach injured and not my shoulder."

"I shall sneak you something." She gently patted his cheek with her free hand, as she would one of the girls, but she knew it was a mistake the moment her palm touched the rough rasp of his skin. Before she could yank her hand away, he caught her wrist and held it in place.

Ivy's pulse fluttered.

"I cannot stop seeing you walking toward the highwayman and knowing I could do nothing to stop it. It will haunt me for years to come." Slowly, so slowly that she could have stopped him if she wanted to, he turned his face until his mouth brushed against the center of her palm. It was not a kiss, but it was alarmingly close.

"I am fine," she said softly, chastising herself for her reaction to him. The viscount had made it clear that this was a ruse only and that he was unaffected by her, and yet her body did not seem to understand. It was embarrassing to have such a visceral response to a man who would only kiss her if she were the last woman in England. Owen was a tactile person, and this exchange was nothing more than him reassuring himself that she was alive and well and that he did not fail someone under his protection.

He opened his mouth to speak, but instead released both her hands. Ivy let out a breath and quickly stepped back. Owen dragged his palm down his face. "I cannot stay in this room. I will go mad. Promise me you will visit again, and that you will soon send the girls."

"I will." She inserted more space between them, even as she thought of the Dove and the mission she had been given. News of the hysteria had crowded the papers that morning. She had to find a way to help, and soon. "I will visit you daily—for a trade."

His eyes narrowed. "What is your price?"

"I will visit in exchange for your honest answer to three questions each day."

He drummed his fingers on the arm of his chair. "My life is not so interesting. You are squandering an opportunity. I am so desperate for relief from this interminable boredom that the world is yours for the taking."

"That is my price."

"You must stay for a minimum of an hour."

"I can accept that."

He nodded. "Then it is a done deal."

She backed so far from him that she bumped into the door. "I will see you tomorrow, Owen."

He traced a finger over his lip and smirked. "Tomorrow, Sunshine."

Once the doctor left, Owen returned to his work, squinting at endless numbers and lines of correspondence until his head ached and he was so surly his lips were in a permanent snarl.

Ivy did not arrive until the afternoon, slipping into his room in her navy gown with little sprigs of leaves embroidered on the hem. Sunlight seemed to slide in with her as she cheerfully bounded over to him and sat in the chair on the opposite side of the table. Her honeyed eyes were twinkling, as if she knew he was in horrid temper and it amused her.

She tossed a stack of gossip rags on the table. "I know you only read boring horse facts, but I thought you might enjoy a change of pace."

"I could not enjoy anything less."

Her twinkle intensified. "Not even when the gossip is about you?"

"Especially then."

"*I shall read it then.*" She reached for the top paper, the *Tatler*, and his bad mood soured further. Either not understanding his expression, or not caring, she snapped the paper open and began to read aloud:

"*One would have to be hidden beneath a rock not to have heard about the juiciest morsel of gossip to start the Season: the newly returned, reclusive, and highly anticipated bachelor, the Viscount Brackley, is courting the granddaughter of the Marquess Rothford. The newly titled viscount has only recently returned to England, and is already pursuing the young lady who had been acting as his governess. That is correct, dear readers and disappointed ladies across the* ton. *It seems that while tending to the viscount's eight sisters, the lovely Miss Bennett caught the lord's eye. They were spotted most recently at a country party hosted by Mr. Donnelley, and again at a musicale hosted by Lord and Lady Fleetwood.*

Chapter 20

Owen spent the next morning with his correspondence and ledgers. The only upside to his infirmity was that he was forced to do the tedious bookkeeping he had been putting off for too long. He paused his work only for the doctor to visit, examine his wound, and proclaim him the luckiest man he knew.

"It seems you owe the seamstress your life." The doctor, a man in his fifth decade with thinning gray hair, shook his head in amazement. "Imagine a woman being able to do that! I can hardly believe it. Of course, *I* would have cauterized the wound rather than stitched it, but what can you expect from a woman?"

"You are a fool."

The doctor, taken aback by his rancor, finished the visit by ordering him to stay in bed and rest for six weeks.

"Absolutely not!" Owen roared. "What is the bare minimum?"

The doctor stammered, "My lord, you need to heal. At the very least you must refrain from using the arm for a fortnight, but it really should rest for four to six weeks."

"Two weeks it is."

According to attendees, they appeared to be smitten with one another. But this writer would be remiss not to share that several other gentlemen also appeared quite interested in the young lady, who has already had three Seasons. Will the viscount win her hand? Or do the ladies of the ton *still have a chance?"*

Owen was appalled. "Do they have nothing better to do than speculate about our arrangement?"

She gestured to the pile of gossip rags. "No. We are mentioned in all of them."

"You never told me how your father handled the news of the courtship. Did it cause problems with Reedly?"

"Father wrote to Reedly," she answered cautiously.

"And?"

"And?" Her eyes were far too innocent. Ivy was always sparkling with cheer and mischief; she was never the docile woman that peered at him now.

"And *what* are you not telling me?"

She folded the corner of the paper and then unfolded it again. "I have no idea what you mean, my lord."

He reached over and lightly grasped her wrist. "How many times have I told you not to call me *my lord*."

She licked her lips, her pupils expanding. "Owen."

"Good." He stroked his thumb over her delicate skin, his blood singing when he found her pulse beating wildly. "Now what are you not telling me?"

She tugged her hand away. "Reedly was unhappy, but expressed continued interest in matrimony should the courtship fizzle. It seems I will need a marriage prospect lined up rather quickly when our charade is over, lest I end up right back where I started."

The news was like a serrated knife cleaving him in two. One

half of him wanted Lord Hartford for Ivy, if only for her own happiness. The other half bristled at the news, like he was some wild beast with his hackles raised. How was it that so many men should have the gall to express interest in her when she was supposed to be *his*? Did they not have even an ounce of self-preservation in their bodies?

He knew the answer. How could they *not* desire her? She was clever and amusing and so bright and cheerful that he found his thoughts returning to her near constantly throughout the day. There was the way she moved under her gown, graceful and athletic, and those plush lips of hers that made him fantasize about pulling her into his lap and kissing them swollen. He could picture himself now, sweeping his hand down her back and cupping her bottom, then lifting her against him and—

Blast! Blast.

He swallowed. "Then we will do our best to see that Lord Hartford proposes." The words tasted sour coming from his lips, and he could not look at her as he said them. If he did, she would know how badly he wanted to pull her to him and do all the things he had dreamed about doing last night. Ever since he had been shot, she had dominated not only his waking hours, but also his unconscious hours, disturbing his sleep and leaving him frustrated and aroused each morning. But what he did with Ivy in his dreams started and stopped there. Under no circumstances could he allow himself to act on this inconvenient attraction. She deserved more than Owen Brackley and his world of bedroom sinning.

"Good," she said, clearing her throat. "I should probably—"

"Your questions." He should not have reminded her, but he did not want her to leave yet. She was the bright spot in his days, and he did not want to ruin that by making her uncomfortable. That meant no more putting his hands on her. No more inserting a commanding tone into his requests and feeling a deep burn of pleasure when she complied. This was a blossoming friendship, and nothing more. It could *never* be anything more.

"Oh!" Her awkwardness instantly disappeared. "I almost forgot. How good of you to remind me."

"Yes, I am a saint."

"You are many things, but I doubt a saint is one of them."

The smile he gave her made her cheeks redden, but she did not back down. "My question is about Heidi."

His smile melted, and he could not conceal the unpleasant shock of hearing Heidi's name leave her lips, although he should not have been surprised considering how loud Millie had been when she had discussed his former lover in the sitting room.

"If you thought I would ask silly questions about your favorite color, I fear you will be disappointed. If you wish to back out—"

"No. I made a deal, and I will not back out," he said, offended. "What sort of man do you think I am?"

The corner of her mouth turned up, and he realized that was exactly what she had been expecting to hear, the little schemer.

"You must tell me the truth. What we have between us is a business dealing, and these questions will supplement our knowledge of one another to validate our ruse. Do we have an understanding?"

Her words stung like ever so many bees, but she was right. Just because *he* was losing control of his attraction to her, that did not change the nature of their arrangement. "What is your question?"

"Do you still love her?"

She had prepared him for a question about Heidi, but he had not expected her to ask something so simple and yet so monumental with five simple words.

His throat turned dry, and he took a swig of water, shifting in a way that made his arm burn. He had cared for Heidi, but he had not loved her. He had been content knowing she was at ease with his demanding desires, and that he did not have to hide that part of himself. He had thought that was enough for a union at the time, but now he was grateful that Heidi had only been occupying her time with their affair while she had looked for a Prussian-born husband. Owen had been too single-minded and focused on her to see the wider picture of who she truly was. His pride had been hurt when she had turned him down, but now he shivered to think that he had asked someone with a similar temperament to Millie to marry him.

"No." The word rang firmly in the room. Ivy waited patiently, her eyes tracing over his stony expression. She was waiting...for what? An explanation? "I never loved her," he added.

She lifted a brow. "But you had an affair with her?"

Owen's jaw flexed. He did not know if Ivy was innocent or not, but either way this was not a proper topic for him to discuss with Barnes's little sister—or *any* woman who was not his lover. But she sat there, her honey eyes wide and curious, and he had promised he would answer her questions in good faith. "Yes."

"Do you have affairs with many women?"

He had been taking another drink of water when she asked, and he choked, coughing until his shoulder seared. "I do not think that is an appropriate question."

Ivy sighed and slumped in her chair. "You are like my brothers." The disappointment was clear on her face. "The things they say when they think I am not listening are raw and crude, but when they speak to me, they treat me like a stupid doll. Why is it that your sex thinks my sex is so delicate?"

"It is more that it is improper to discuss such things among mixed company."

"I did not take you for a rule-follower."

He pressed his finger to a bead of water on the side of his glass and smudged it, tracing his finger up the cool surface. Ivy's eyes were fixated on his hand.

"If I told you about *my* affairs," she taunted softly, "would you feel more comfortable telling me about yours?"

His heart stopped.

Chapter 21

Owen was lounging in the chair like any leisurely lord, his shirt open at the neck and his hair mussed, one big, calloused finger sliding up and down the side of his glass in a way that made her warm and itchy. She was grateful he was not still in love with Heidi—only because it would make their ruse more complicated if he were—but she did not like that he would not let her in deeper, that he was still treating her as her brothers did.

So she said something that she thought would shock him into considering her an equal. She had not counted on his reaction.

Owen's finger stilled and his eyes cut to hers, suddenly so blazing that her cheeks felt scorched. The atmosphere in the room thickened, and his voice lowered, brushing against her nerves like black satin. "I knew you had kissed a man before, but have you also had love affairs, Sunshine?"

The question sounded dangerous, as if there was a right and wrong answer, but she did not know which. She swallowed and lifted her chin. He did not need to know she had only experienced a few tepid meetings of lips. All that mattered was that she broke down this barrier of civility between them. She did not know why she felt the need to throw herself against it, only that she sensed it was the key to getting to know the *real* Owen. "If I share, will you?"

"This is not a school game." He stood, and she knew by the look on his face that whatever pain he felt from the motion was the farthest thing from his mind. She started to rise as well, but he shook his head, rounded the table, and crouched in front of her, bringing his face eye level with hers.

"Wha—what are you doing? You will hurt yourself." Her face flushed at the image he made. His muscled body was so large and hot that she could feel the heat radiating from him as he practically knelt at her feet, and his green eyes were so piercing that she physically could not look away.

"We need to get one thing straight before we continue with this charade. You are a good girl, and I am a bad man. We will not be discussing affairs, relationships, or lovers again."

She could smell the tea on his breath, pleasant and light, and her eyes fell to his mouth. He was so close that she could lift her hand and trace those firm, scowling lips if she wanted to. What would he do if she touched him like that?

"Do. Not. Even. Think about it."

"What?"

"Whatever just made your eyes go hazy. Remember, you want Lord Hartford as your husband, not me. Does your brother know about these men?"

"The men I have kissed? Probably as much as I know about the women *he* has kissed."

His hand wrapped around the leather ankle of her boot, and even through the material she felt the heat of his palm and the gentle yet firm feeling of being trapped by someone much larger.

"Do not talk to me about the *men* you have kissed. Not unless you want every single one of them to be erased from your memory."

She did not know what possessed her to blurt, "I wonder if Lord Hartford is up to the task."

"Now that is just mean, darling." His thumb slipped beneath the hem of her gown to stroke over the leather. "No one kisses what is mine, not even Hartford—not until he has asked for your hand. And until he does, and as long as we are in this ruse together, you *are* mine."

"Does that mean you are mine as well?"

The question was so soft she was not sure he heard it, until he leaned forward a fraction and breathed, "Entirely."

Before she could think of a response, there was a knock at the door. Her eyes met his unamused gaze. He had crouched at her feet in order to make his point, like she was an unruly child, and his hand was still underneath her dress and wrapped around her ankle. It looked entirely, completely scandalous, and it would *definitely* count as a compromising situation if they were caught.

"Give me a moment!" he shouted as he stood, his jaw clenching from the pain in his shoulder. He rounded the table and sat again, lifting one of the gossip rags and setting it on his lap as if to appear he was reading it.

A moment later the door swung open and Barnes appeared. "I hope you are decent because I do not want to see your bare ar—Ivy! Why is the door closed? I assumed you had left already." He looked suspiciously between them.

Ivy tucked a strand of hair behind her ear, and as casually as she could manage said, "The wind shut it. What are you doing here?"

He held up a letter with an all-too-familiar crest. "Father wants to meet with Brackley."

Anger caused a flush to rise beneath her skin. Her father wished to meet the viscount, but he had not once expressed a desire to see her after he had been removed from the house. "That is a waste of time, as this courtship is a façade."

"I know, and I shall put him off for as long as I can, but you know father. He is nasty in his persistence." He narrowed his gaze on Owen. "Do you know that Ivy has a very small dowry? She would not be able to contribute much to an estate."

Ivy's cheeks heated further, but for a different reason.

Owen's expression went flat. "Careful, or one might think you are disparaging your sister."

"*Pardon* me?"

"Your sister has far more to contribute to a marriage than a dowry, which no matter how large it was, would never equate her worth."

Ivy was not sure if she was more stunned by the compliment or Barnes's lack of rejoinder. Instead of his usual cut, Barnes looked at Owen with a strange expression on his face.

"I tire." Owen stared pointedly at Barnes, who gave a jerky nod and held out his hand for her.

Since she needed fresh air anyway, she took it. Before she left the room, she glanced down at the gossip rags and said, "Enjoy your gossip, *my lord*."

The look he gave her at deliberately using his proper form of address was dark and filled with promise.

◈

Over the next two days, Ivy asked Owen unassuming questions so that she would not spark his suspicion.

"When did you know you wanted to work with horses?" was met with, "Always." And then after some glaring on her part he grudgingly told her how his love for the beasts had angered his father on more than one occasion.

"He wanted his heir to be an aristocrat in every sense of the word: a lord who would show up in ballrooms with exquisitely tailored clothing and glossy compliments on his tongue; a lord who would be invited to all the most prestigious events and bring honor to the title. He did not care about the details of financing that lifestyle, or anything else that remotely smelled like work."

His gruff admission had held more than a tint of bitterness, so Ivy had steered to the topic of his sisters soon visiting.

The next afternoon, after the girls had left Owen exhausted and slumped in his chair, his eyes half open in the slanting sunlight, Ivy had asked him about his time at Harrow.

"It was fine," he had said, and no matter how much she had cajoled, he had had nothing more to say on the topic.

So much for determining what had caused the rift between him and Barnes.

The day after that Ivy slipped into Owen's chamber and found him pacing in front of the lit fireplace, the warm glow giving his pristine shirtsleeves an orange hue. There had been a frost on the ground that morning, and the crackling flames were welcome in the drafty, ill-kept house. His short hair was curly and tousled as if he had been outdoors, even though she knew he had not, and he was driving everyone mad with his bad temper over it. His boots squeaked on the hardwood as he paced back and forth, back and forth.

"You should not be standing," she admonished as she closed the door behind her.

"There you are!" he snapped, spinning around. His eyes were restless and hungry. "I have been cooped up indoors all day with nary a person of interest to visit."

"You have seen the nurse, the valet, and your business manager—and those are only the people I know of."

"Exactly."

"I am not your personal entertainment," she said, staying by the door. He seemed in a dangerous, reckless mood that afternoon.

It was the wrong thing to say, because his eyes flared and made a languorous perusal of her, from the tips of her boots to the top of her head. Ivy's breath left her lungs with a stutter of air. "If the circumstances were different, you would keep me entertained quite nicely."

Ivy shook off the touch of his voice, determined not to let him know how he affected her. "But circumstances are not different."

"They are not," he agreed. He made a noise of frustration and threw himself into the chair. "I cannot take this confinement any longer. I have to leave this room."

"Let me distract you." She edged toward the seat beside him. "With a question."

He flapped his hand. "Fine."

"When you were in Prussia, how often did you visit England?" She asked the question as casually as she could manage, trying to arrange her features into a bored, uncaring expression even as her heart flailed against her rib cage.

"On occasion."

That was not going to be enough to satisfy the Dove, so she pressed. "You never visited Brackley Estate?"

"And voluntarily see my father? No. Whenever I returned for business, it was mostly contained to London."

"When was the last time you went to London?"

He gave her strange look. "Two years ago. Donnelley deals with most of our English business, and that freed me to focus on the horses. Very occasionally I was needed in person. Two years ago, we had a particularly large request from the Duke of Houndsbury, who wished to outfit his entire stables with the best horseflesh money could buy, and he would only deal with me directly. *Why exactly are you asking, Sunshine?*"

Her escaped heart settled back into place. He had not been to England in over *two years*. Which, unless he was lying, meant he could not have visited the houses of the afflicted women. And yet how could so many governesses have mistakenly identified the man who *had* visited as being Lord Brackley? It simply did not make sense.

"No reason," Ivy said, jumping to her feet. She was eager to write to the Dove. Until the highwayman was caught, the Dove had asked Ivy to cancel her weekly classes out of concern for the safety of the women, who were all traveling in secret at night. Ivy had intended to do so anyway, so she had readily agreed. But that also meant that she would not see the Dove in person any time soon and must reach out by post instead. "I have to go."

She would have rushed past him, but his hand shot out and caught her wrist, gently encircling it with his large fingers. The heat of his bare skin on hers sent sparks leaping across her arm and into her stomach. "Your skin is so hot. Are you feverish?" she asked, turning to him. "Is the wound infected?"

He released her, his fingertips sliding off her skin as if he were reluctant to let her go. "No. The doctor has said I am healing quite nicely, although I think the nurse knows more than he does. He prods and grumbles about how *he* would have cauterized the wound instead of sewing it, and that it is obvious an uneducated female took care of it. Meanwhile, the nurse washes her hands and uses carbolic acid and alcohol and nods with satisfaction at the neat row of stitches. I am blessed the seamstress got her hands on me before that blasted doctor. Speaking of your seamstress friend, has she received my letter of gratitude along with the funds to repair her shop?"

Ivy averted her eyes and nodded. She had visited the modiste in person and explained what had happened, leaving out several important facts. She had made it sound as if the shop were simply the closest stop to where the shooting had taken place, and that Ivy alone had taken care of Owen.

The seamstress had been close to tears, but the amount of money Owen had sent her to replace the used items had quickly fortified her.

"She was pleased with your generosity. Diane is scheduled to take the girls two at a time over the next several weeks to update their wardrobes."

His gaze stayed on her face, and although his expression was mostly shuttered, there was a hint of desperation in his eyes. "Do not leave yet."

"If you are bored, you could read a book." But she relented and took a seat. The letter to the Dove could wait another hour.

"I have read a book. Many books."

"The gossip rags?"

A muscle twitched in his cheek. "There is far too much being printed about us, and about the highway robbery, and nearly all of it is hogwash. As for the rest of the gossip, I am not well acquainted with half the people they are talking about, so why should I care if they were spotted walking together?"

She tried not to smile at the fact that he *had* read the gossip rags she had left behind. "Caring about the people is certainly a key component. Perhaps you would find more relevant gossip entertaining. I have loads of it collected from around the estate."

"No, I do not—"

"For example, the dowager apparently threw not one, but *two* teacups against the wall, and Clara, one of the maids, had to pick all the shards out of the carpet. Then the silver candlesticks went missing from the ladies' parlor, and the housekeeper turned the servants' quarters upside down looking for them, but one of the maids swore they were there when she last dusted. The dowager tried to blame Diane, but Diane marched the head housekeeper straight to her chamber and insisted she search it to clear her name, even though the head housekeeper was horrified to do so. Diane thinks Miss Pithins is the culprit.

"And Cook ordered two fat pigs from Farmer Bailey in town, but when they arrived, they were the runts of the litter and Cook had paid a good price for them, and so now she is not talking to Farmer Bailey and instead has purchased a pig from Farmer Taylor, who everyone knows is Farmer Bailey's *archnemesis*. Supposedly Taylor's grandfather stole from Bailey's grandfather even though no one really remembers anymore what it was he was supposed to have stolen, but there has been bad blood between the families ever since. Well, just yesterday the largest hog you have ever seen showed up outside the kitchen—*alive*—and Cook thinks it was Bailey trying to make amends while still being cheeky about it. So now there is a hog in one of the horse stalls, and one of the girls has named him Mr. Porkster and put a funny paper hat on him, and Cook is growing fearful that she will not be allowed to slaughter him when the time comes because the girls are becoming attached."

Ivy paused to drag in a breath, but did not start up again when she caught the expression on Owen's face. His head was tilted, and he was assessing her like she was a complete stranger.

"What?" she demanded.

"How is it that you know more about my estate than I do?"

"I listen."

"A woman who listens is a dangerous creature," he murmured. "You could ruin empires with those ears."

Now *that* was a compliment. "Was that not all far more interesting than the gossip rags?"

"It was," he admitted with a pained expression. "Mayhap I would not mind if you shared more. On occasion."

Ivy grinned at him. Anyone who pretended not to like gossip was a liar, and she had never taken the viscount for a liar.

"You are not visiting your modiste friend at night anymore, are you?"

"Do you think Barnes would allow it?"

"I do not think Barnes could stop you."

Her skin itched with the uncanny feeling that this man knew her better than her own brother did. "No, I do not wish to run into the highwayman again. I can only hope he is caught soon."

"Good. I would not like to think of you riding the roads at dark. Now it is my turn to ask you a question."

Her brow furrowed. "That is not part of our bargain."

"I would like to amend our bargain." Before she could protest, he said, "It is important that we appear to have some knowledge of one another when we arrive in London, is it not? I have written to the Marchioness of Southampshire and accepted her invitation to the opening ball of the Season, and I have had word that Hartford will be in attendance."

She swallowed down her nerves. She had been raised among genteel society, but she had never been invited to the major crushes reserved for the diamonds of the *ton*, and now she was to arrive at the opening ball, with the entire city speculating about the viscount courting her. She was to dance and make conversation as if she were not being scrutinized like a bug under a magnifying glass. Mayhap, if the hysteria had not resolved by then, it would not be as heavily attended. "What do you wish to know?"

"What was it like growing up with six brothers?"

"It was fun and often frustrating." She smiled fondly as she thought of her older brothers, who were, for the most part, sweet and kind humans. The most overbearing one was Barnes, but as the eldest she supposed that was to be expected. "They treated me like a baby, fighting my battles in public, all while terrorizing me in private. Once, Silas, one of my middle brothers, put a frog in my bed. We had a lot of fun growing up, but then my father thought I was not acting as a young girl should, and he began to penalize my brothers when they played with me." Her heart sank at the memory. "He ostracized me. Over time, they were afraid to play with me, or talk to me, or engage with me because they were punished severely when they did."

Owen's face hardened. "Barnes abandoned you, too?"

"Barnes does not listen to anyone. It was one of the many issues he had with my father." Owen did not pry further, giving her the space to share more if she wanted. Normally Ivy kept mute on that part of her childhood, but sometimes she wondered if secrets were like wounds and needed air to heal, lest they fester.

Besides, if anyone understood a strained relationship with one's father, it was Owen.

Ivy absently wrapped a section of hair around her finger,

winding and unwinding it. "When I was young, my father was very severe with all of us, including my mother. There were times when I fought back, but I did not have the skill. It ended poorly for me."

Owen's jaw was so tight she would not have been surprised to hear a tooth crack.

"Then Barnes left for Harrow, and Ezra became the oldest at home. He went from being silly and kind to dark and silent. I think he inherited the pressure Barnes lived under—and the horror—of seeing his father hurt those he loved and not being able to do anything about it.

"I remember the day Ezra snapped." Ivy took a soft breath. "My mother walked into the breakfast room with a black eye, and Ezra just... he could not bear it any longer. He lunged at my father, and he was still young enough that my father had the upper hand. My father was hitting him over and over, and my mother was shrieking. It is only through sheer luck that Barnes was scheduled to arrive from Harrow that day. When he walked in—"

She drifted off, remembering how she had pressed her ten-year-old body against the breakfast room wall, her eyes wide and her hands shaking while her father bloodied Ezra's face and her mother screamed for *Ezra* to stop—not their father. Her other brothers had been out of the house, and Ivy had been terrified that her father was going to kill Ezra. She had grabbed her father's right arm, hanging on to it with all her might until he shook her off and she went flying into the sideboard, a dish of rashers crashing on top of her. That was what Barnes had walked in on.

As irritating, uptight, and overbearing as Barnes was, Ivy would never forget the sense of relief that had settled over her when he had burst through the door. He had been very, *very* angry. Not their father's kind of angry, where he became red-faced and mean with spittle flying from his lips. No, Barnes had been so angry that he had been pure, Arctic ice.

"Barnes pulled my father off Ezra and shoved him against the wall and said something so low I could not hear it, but my father paled to the pallor of a ghost. That night he packed his belongings and moved to the London house. He has not been back once, but he still reigns over us by letter, and punishes with the purse strings."

She shivered at the expression on Owen's face, and in that moment, she knew he could be just as icy and violent as Barnes. "He will not hurt you again, Sunshine. *Ever.*"

No, he would not. She had made certain of that. If she ever ran into her father again and he dared lay a hand on her, he would be in for a nasty surprise. Ivy would never be afraid of Mr. Hollister Bennett again.

"Not physically, but he can hurt me in other ways, such as forcing me into marriage. I think he has deliberately chosen horrid suitors to punish me. You have eight young sisters, Owen. I hope you remember how their lives and future happiness rest entirely in your hands when it comes time for them to marry."

"I do not intend to sell my sisters like cattle. They will stay here."

She laughed. "Will you keep them old maids?"

"If that is what they wish."

"You are a good brother."

He glanced away. "Hardly. I did not bother to visit them once before my father died. I did not think of them at all, except to bemoan that none of them was a boy."

"Why should their sex matter?"

He lifted the teapot and poured another splash into his cup. "I had an arrangement with my father." He threw the tea back like it was alcohol, and set the cup on the saucer with a click of porcelain. "If he sired another male heir who could legally inherit the estate, I would renounce the title."

Ivy gasped. "Can that even be done?"

He met her eyes. "We would have found a way. But in the end, it did not matter. He had eight more children, and all of them ineligible to inherit by British law."

"Do you hate being a viscount so much? It comes with such tremendous privilege and wealth."

"I had more wealth before the viscountcy," he muttered. "It also comes with tremendous responsibility. More than that, I had wished to sever any and all association with my father."

"Was he that much of a monster?"

"Yes."

At the flat, singular word, chills raced up Ivy's arms. "It seems we were both unfortunate with the men who sired us."

He smiled softly. "Is that the origin of our love story? Bonding over our fathers?"

Her heart thrashed confusingly in her chest for the space of three beats before she realized he was talking about their *supposed* love story for their *supposed* courtship. *Of course* he was.

"We were fortunate at the previous parties that we were not asked to delve too deeply into how we met. We had best align our stories now," he said.

"I have the perfect answer to that question. Our courtship started the moment you laid eyes on me. The sun burst from between the clouds and shone down, illuminating me like the divine. You later told me you thought you were looking at an angel descended from heaven. After that moment, you knew you could not take one more breath without me by your side."

The look he gave her was so incredulous that she almost let her face twitch.

"It is a good thing we are going over it now," he said dryly. "I fear by the time you told that story across the ballroom, you would have embellished it to the point where I fell to my knees and sobbed into your skirts at the sight of your beauty."

"That is not bad."

"The story is we met when Barnes and I were at Harrow. You and I have corresponded over the years, and when I arrived and met you after all this time, I knew I had to court you."

"I suppose that is more believable than my story," she said grudgingly.

"Do not mistake me: your story was perfectly believable, Ivy. You are sunshine itself, and no one would doubt that you could bring a man to his knees, but I prefer to keep the *ton*'s interest in you at a reasonable level. We want to entice Lord Hartford, but we do not want him making any rash declarations of love yet."

"I disagree. That would be spectacular. Then I could jilt you for him. It would solve all of our problems."

Owen's thunderous expression said otherwise.

Chapter 22

Owen stayed in his chamber, restless but willing to tolerate his cage only because the first time he had tried to escape, he had nearly collapsed with dizziness. His account books had never been so in shape, his correspondence so current.

The only bright spots in his otherwise mundane days were when Ivy and the girls visited. The eldest of his sisters, Ophelia, had taken to visiting him on her own, slipping in just before supper in the nursery and staying until one of the nannies came to fetch her. She was always bright and babbling, talking nonstop about what she did that day, but there was an undercurrent to her childish words—as if she were masking a worry she could not, or did not dare, express.

He had been laid up for exactly eight days and sixteen hours when she slipped into his room and shut the door so quietly behind her that if he had not already been sitting up and reading, she would have startled him.

"Ophelia," he rumbled.

She began to wander restlessly around his chamber. She usually liked to examine his stacks of books and tell him all about what she was currently reading, but today there was a little line between her brows and a pinch to her lips. No ten-year-old should look so serious, Owen thought when she finally came to stand before him. She clasped her hands and took a deep breath. "Brother, I wish to talk...I wish to talk about our father."

Owen felt his expression harden. "What is there to say? You are old enough to remember him."

She nodded and cast her face down. "Yes."

"Was he good to you?"

Silence was her answer, and the absence of words pierced through his ribs and straight into his heart. He had been so damned busy divesting himself from any responsibilities that had to do with his life in England that he had left his little sisters to the mercy of a loathsome man.

He thought of Barnes and what Ivy had told him, and how his former friend had protected *his* siblings. If Owen had ever given any thought to his sisters at all, perhaps he would have considered what their lives might have been like here. But he had not; he had been far too focused on his own escape and building his own life. Burning with shame, Owen knew that at the very least, he owed Ophelia this discussion. "What do you want to talk about? Nothing is forbidden."

She lifted her face. "You will not think poorly of me?"

"I could never. I *will* never."

She was quiet for another moment, but he did not rush her. Finally she blurted, "I hated Father and I am relieved he is dead!" Then she burst into tears.

Owen pulled her to him with his good arm and awkwardly petted her silky head while she soaked through his shirtsleeves with her tears. When her shoulders eventually stopped shaking—he had not known so many tears could physically reside in such a small body—she pulled a handkerchief from her pocket and blew her nose loudly. Her eyes were swollen and red, her cheeks shiny with wetness.

She sniffled. "I apologize."

"There is no need to apologize, Ophelia."

"I am a bad daughter."

"Then I am even worse, because I hated Father, too, and the night I got word he died, I opened my finest bottle of wine in celebration."

Her eyes widened in shock. "You did?"

"Take a seat, Ophelia."

She pulled the chair from the other side of the table and dragged it around, so that when she sat, her little dress-draped knees were almost touching his.

"Children are raised to respect and honor their parents," he said slowly, "and for so many lucky children, that is not a duty but a natural consequence of their love. But sometimes the people who created us are not good people. Sometimes they hurt us, and it is not fair that we should feel shame over the relief of being released from that torture. Do you understand what I am saying? You must never feel badly for no longer being trapped with a person who hurts you." His jaw clenched. "Did he...did he *hurt* you, Ophelia?"

She shook her head no, a strand of hair sticking to her wet cheek. "He did not strike me, if that is what you mean."

"Ah." The tiniest bit of pressure eased from his chest. If his father had taken his hand to this vulnerable girl in front of him, he would have dug up his body and killed him again. "He tortured you with his words, then."

She nodded.

"He did the same to me. He was merciless and he was cruel, and the wounds of the mind are not easily healed. Even now, his words haunt me. Diminish me. Enrage me."

"Me as well. Sometimes I lie in bed and think that all the things he said about me are true, and that it would be better for everyone if I ran away."

Owen took her hand in his. "You must *never* run away. You are extremely important to this family, and you are needed and loved. The next time you are lying in bed and his words haunt you, I want you to ask yourself: Are these my words, or my father's words? And if they are Father's, you may dismiss them out of hand. *Nothing* he ever said to you was true."

"How do you know?"

"It took me a very long time to learn that I was not the man he had made me believe I was. Was he cruel to your sisters?"

"Not as much as me. Mostly he ignored them. He hated us all because we were girls, but me the most."

Because Owen had fled the country, leaving her to bear the brunt of his father's cruelty, Owen thought with disgust. If anyone should be ashamed enough to run away, it was he. Except he would not abandon these girls ever again. "The youngest girls are lucky that they will have no memory of him, but you and I...we will have to work for a long time to banish his voice until it is so small that when it resurfaces, we can easily stomp it out. We do not owe him a lifetime of controlling us even in death, do we?"

"No, I suppose not."

"I want you to make me a promise. Whenever these feelings come over you, I want you to come to me and talk about it. I will be here, and if I am away on business, I want you to write to me. I will help you see the real Ophelia. The brave, clever, and kind girl that I see every single day."

Ophelia burst into tears again, and when she finished, he handed her his own handkerchief just as the supper bell rang. She squeaked in alarm and dashed out of the room, leaving his heart a little more shredded than when she had first entered. He would have to talk to Olivia and Odette—the eight-year-old twins—and gently probe about their feelings. His father had been cruel and insidious, planting thoughts in malleable minds and letting those seeds of doubt and despair flourish, occasionally watering them with more of his poison.

Owen had worked hard to bury his feelings, but after his visit with Ophelia, he felt the strangest touch of lightness beneath his crushing guilt, and he wondered if forcing those dark thoughts into a solitary closet in his soul over the years had only aided in their growth. Perhaps air and light were more effective in banishing evil than burying it.

The next morning Ivy blew into his room in a whirlwind of cool fall air and her signature scent of lilac and mint. She dropped a stack of gossip rags on the table next to him and chattered about the preparations that were being made for their departure for London in two days, all the while making sure to keep a proper distance between them. Ever since he had lost his mind and crouched at her feet and held her ankle, she had been carefully distant.

Owen wanted to blame his behavior on fever, but he had not felt feverish when he had brought his face to hers, the desire to ruck up her skirt and smooth his palms over her skin so intense that he had nearly done it.

In truth, he was grateful she was being so cautious around him. It would not do to compromise her. Society was beginning to see her in a new light, and she had already made quite an impression on Hartford. *That* was the plan, not the two of them ending up in his bed.

He told himself that multiple times a day: when she came in smelling fresh and laughing, a bloom of color in his otherwise dreary world; when she gossiped about the household or made snappy, insightful comments that left him dazzled by her intelligence; or whenever she bent near to arrange his reading material or gently ask about his wound. And every day he found it just a little bit harder to cling to his reasons. A little bit more difficult to remember exactly *why* he was trying so hard to keep his hands off her.

Except for the days when Barnes made his unwelcome presence known, and then Owen was nothing *but* reminded.

Ivy took a breath after telling him about the newest maid's penchant for stockings—she had thirty-three pairs and spent all of her money on them, and hell if Owen knew why he found it so interesting except that Ivy had a way of holding his attention over even the most absurd things—when she halted abruptly as something out the window caught her eye. "Oh, I did not realize the hour. I am late for—"

"Let me guess: outdoor prayer meeting."

"Indeed." She flashed him that dimpled grin and bounded out the door.

Owen had had enough of being suffocated in his room. His shoulder was healing well, he did not have a fever, and in two days he would be traveling to London. It was time he pushed past any dizziness and nausea and began to regain his strength.

He acquitted the room like a burglar afraid of being caught, and when he did not feel like vomiting or blacking out, he slowly made his way to the rear door. The minute he exited and breathed in the fresh air, he felt his vigor returning. Feeling steadier and surer than he had since the shooting, he crossed the leaf-strewn lawn to the stables and entered. He went straight to Saxony, and the horse nickered and pushed his nose into Owen's palm. The tension seeped out of his shoulders as he breathed in the comforting scents of hay and leather that had come to dominate his life. He swung open the stall door and pressed his forehead to his horse's neck and just existed for several moments, all of the disquiet in him settling as Saxony's heat warmed his palms.

"Missed you, rascal," he mumbled.

"He missed you, too, your lordship."

Owen turned to find Bernard tugging on his cap, his weathered face split into a grin. "I ought've known no bullet could keep you down, my lord."

"It nearly did. A seamstress saved me." And Ivy, who had not lost her wits while being robbed and watching the life bleed out of him, but instead had coolly directed him to the horse and taken him to the nearest place she could find help. There were very few of Owen's friends or even acquaintances who would have had the presence of mind to act so quickly.

Bernard nodded to Saxony. "I've been lettin' him out in the fields to run, but I don't have a rider strong enough to control him. Don't know how the little lass did it that night. He's restless an' eager to ride."

Thankfully, Owen was equally eager. It chapped him to let

Bernard saddle his horse, but he was aware of his current limitations, and when Saxony was ready, prancing and excited, he swung into the saddle.

The minute he was crunching over the leaves, he relaxed into the cadence of his horse and breathed deeply. Aside from a constant twinge in his shoulder and unusual tiredness, he felt more like himself than he had in a fortnight.

He and Saxony traversed the estate, waving to workers and examining the stonework that was being fixed on the south side of the main building. Everywhere he went, people greeted him kindly, and damned if Ivy's gossip was not coming in handy. Because of her, he knew the apprentice stone mason was only fourteen and had lost his father that winter, and when Owen patted the lad on the shoulder with a heavy hand and slipped him a shilling, the boy looked as if he was going to burst into tears.

He asked the grounds caretaker about his daughter, who had just had a baby named Arabella, which had caused a ruckus because that was the father's mother's name and the caretaker's wife had cried for three straight days over it.

He could see the surprise on the faces of the people he spoke with, and a flash of something that looked almost like respect. He had run from his responsibilities when it came to his sisters, and they had suffered for it. He could imagine how his father had treated the people he employed, and Owen knew he would have work to do there as well.

Duty coiled around his chest and tightened, but for once it did not feel as if his lungs were suffocating. It felt…bearable. Not pleasant, but not nearly as bad as it had his entire life.

He was riding back to the stables from the east woods, having detoured to examine a field he was considering turning into a paddock, when he heard childish laughter. His brows drew together as he and Saxony turned toward the noise. As far as he knew, prayer was not typically a time when children laughed.

He weaved through the trees, following the sounds of clashing wood, whooping, and then—Ivy's voice, calling out instructions he could not decipher. Another ten feet and he caught a flash of a white dress and a flare of sandy hair.

More curious than ever, he and Saxony slowed to a creep, until at last the scene was clear in front of him: two of his sisters—the eight-year-old twins—were *sword-fighting* with wooden swords. He watched in absolute amazement as Odette expertly dodged a strike and spun with technique that would have made his old fencing master proud. They parried, feinted, and thrust, and the entire time Ivy, with her hair messy and her dress clinging to her legs with the press of the wind, called out pointers and tips. His other sisters watched from the side along with Miss Wixby, the new governess.

They were so engrossed in the performance before them that they did not notice him until he was almost on top of them. "What the bloody *hell* is going on here?"

Chapter 23

Ivy watched Odette and Opal fence and called out pointers, but her mind was in London with the Dove. She had written to her explaining that in the past two years, Owen had only visited England once to broker a deal with the Duke of Houndsbury. The Dove had written back that she would corroborate Owen's story with other sources, and expressed equal confusion over the number of reports that had claimed to spot him in London on multiple other occasions.

> *Whether he is responsible for the hysteria or not, I still have reason to believe there is a connection to Lord Brackley that we have yet to uncover. Keep a close eye on the viscount, and be extraordinarily careful, Miss Bennett. Until we know what his part is in all this, we must continue to tread lightly.*
>
> *~The Dove*

Ivy was worrying her lip when a cold voice cut through the air. "What the bloody *hell* is going on here?"

Odette and Opal froze, their jaws unhinging, and everyone turned in dreamlike horror to find the viscount atop his horse, his jaw shadowed and tense, his eyes taking in the scene with a flat expression.

Oh, *no*.

"I...I..." Ivy glanced at the girls, who were staring at her with wide, blue eyes. For once, even Diane was subdued as she reached for Ivy's hand and squeezed.

"Miss Wixby, please collect the wooden swords and take the girls inside. I need to have a word with Miss Bennett."

Diane opened her mouth to protest, but Ivy shook her head. The girls hurried to collect the swords and the real fencing foil Ivy had discovered in a dusty closet. Then, with guilty and worried looks, they followed Diane out of the woods like a line of chastened ducklings.

Owen swung down from his horse and stalked toward her, his advance slow and silky. Ivy held her ground even though it felt like a large, wild cat was approaching her. "Prayer circle?" His voice was deep and soft.

He came so close that she had to tilt her chin to keep eye contact. There was no point in answering: He already knew she had lied to him.

"Tell me one thing, Miss Bennett."

It did not seem a good sign that he was back to calling her Miss Bennett.

"The night the highwayman shot me and I swore I saw you knock him to the ground, you told me I was feverish and hallucinating. But I was not hallucinating, was I?"

"No," she said through numb lips. Oh, heavens, she was in deep trouble. Little girls were supposed to be taught decorum and how to pour tea and balance guest lists. Their governesses were most certainly *not* allowed to teach them the best way to strike a person in the face, *especially* when said little girls were sisters of a viscount. Ivy's father had made the difference between the sexes clear when he had forbidden her brothers from playing with her. She knew she had been taking a risk teaching the girls self-defense, but she had not truly thought she would be caught.

Her arrogance, in hindsight, made her burn with misery. She should have been more careful, more mindful of Owen's habits. She knew he liked to be outdoors and that it was a possibility he would one day run across them, only she had still thought he was in his sickroom. She did not believe for a moment he would punish the girls, but it was possible he would call off their charade or dismiss Diane.

Ivy's actions did not affect only her. She had positioned her charges and her dearest friend directly in the viscount's warpath with her actions.

Owen prowled around her, his eyes burning into the side of her face, until he stood at her back, and her pulse was in her throat. "What have you been teaching them?"

Ivy did not turn around. It was easier to admit to her sins this way. "Fencing and self-defense maneuvers."

She could have sworn she felt his breath stir the hair on her nape, but she stared ahead at a half-bare maple and tried to slow her heartbeat.

"Why?"

"They need to know how to defend themselves, my lord. Men

like to tell women it is unnecessary, but it is so often men that women need protection from."

That was *definitely* his breath she felt on her skin now. Goose bumps raced across her shoulders, which the gaping shawl had exposed to the air. She had meant to snatch her cloak before she went outdoors, but she had spotted little Ollie tugging a wooden sword across the grass through Owen's window, and had hurried out to help her conceal it before she could be caught.

"What did I tell you about calling me 'my lord'?"

"You just called me Miss Bennett."

"Hmm."

The wind buffeted around them in cool contrast to his heat at her back. She sensed something dangerous in him, something raw and not quite bridled. She had sensed it a few times before, but never in the wilds of the woods, with the October wind tunneling through trees and leaves whipping around their ankles. Here, it felt right. Something tense and delicious pulled her taut despite her worry.

"Are you angry?"

"That you lied to me about what happened with the highwayman? Yes."

She shivered. "No, are you angry about what I have been teaching your sisters."

He stepped closer, his coat brushing the back of her shawl. "Am I angry that you have been teaching my defenseless sisters how to protect themselves from cads and thugs?"

She peered over her shoulder and up at him. He was staring down at her, the green of his eyes almost swallowed by his pupils. "No, Ivy," he said softly. "I am not angry about that."

Some of the tension eased from her body, even as she frowned a little, because he was most certainly riled. Was he truly so upset that she had lied about what happened with the highwayman?

"Do you know how that memory has haunted me?" he asked, as if reading her mind. His hand drifted down, skimming her hip. Accidentally? On purpose? "I watched you disarm the highwayman, so adept and sharp and skilled, like a warrior princess, and I *burned* for that version of you. My only comfort was that it was a hallucination. Although I lusted for that woman, she was but a figment of my imagination. A *fantasy*. Now that I know it was not a hallucination, I find myself in the untenable situation of realizing I was not lusting after a figment of my imagination, but you. The *real* you. That is a problem, would you not say?"

Before she could reply, her heart hammering in her chest and her mouth dry, he added, "I am not angry about the lessons, Ivy. I *am* angry to discover how much I have desired a version of you that appears to be all too real. This is a pretend arrangement, darling, and there are certain lines that must not be crossed, even in my fantasies and dreams."

"Right," she breathed, facing the maple again and swaying back just enough to feel him against her shoulder blades. He had fantasized about her? About the *real* her, not the version she presented to society? It seemed so unfathomable, so unlikely, and yet he had freely admitted to it. Her blood roared through her veins and her skin prickled.

He had called her *darling*.

"Right," he repeated. "The way I see it, we have two choices. The first choice is I climb back onto my horse and we keep this faux courtship entirely proper. I take you to London and present you to Lord Hartford, and we remain courteous and distant. I wrestle my desires back into the depths of my soul."

"What is the second choice?"

"The second choice is you let me kiss you, my own Athena." His voice lowered, and he bent his head so that his lips brushed her ear. "One time. You let me put a taste to the vision in my head. You let me command you, you who commands so many of my dreams and waking hours."

Her knees went uncharacteristically weak. How was it possible that he desired her? He had made it abundantly clear that this was nothing more than a charade.

But then Ivy recalled the way he had crouched at her feet in his sickroom, and how he had held her waist outside the library. She remembered the countless times she had felt the heat of his gaze and heard the slight possessiveness of his words, and she wondered if perhaps the viscount had been saying one thing all along, while his actions had been saying something else.

He pulled back a few inches. "It is entirely your decision."

She knew what she *should* choose and that he would not fault her for it, but when she opened her mouth she blurted, "I choose both."

"Both?"

"Both. I want to continue the charade *and* have you kiss me. You can make kissing lesson number four. The truth is that I have not had as many love affairs as I implied earlier."

"Not as many?"

She huffed. "I have kissed but a few men, and I want to learn how to do it better. You could teach me."

Her first kiss had been with a boy whose lips were stiff and unyielding, his tongue poking through her tight mouth like a worm. She had written to Diane about it, and Diane had written back that it was not supposed to be like that, but Ivy's second experience had been similar, albeit much wetter.

She instinctively knew that a kiss with the magnetic man behind her would be different. There was a dark edge to him that promised sin and skill. Would the firm, yet gentle way he handled his horses translate into how he would handle her? A shiver tripped down her spine at the thought.

Owen's calloused palm closed around the side of her neck, and he said softly in her ear, "For the second time, I must ask that you do not talk about kissing other men in front of me."

"Why not? You cannot fault me for a few stolen kisses." She frowned. "Or mayhap you are one of those men who does?"

"No, I do not fault you, but that does not erase my irrational jealousy."

"Jealousy?"

"I am courting you, am I not?" His thumb dragged up the back of her neck.

"False courting."

"Mine, all the same."

He released her throat and rounded to her front, the emerald of his eyes so dark they were almost black. "Lesson number four? Are you certain you want me to teach you how to kiss, so that you can please another man?" The toe of his Hessian slid beneath the hem of her dress, and he rested his palm lightly on her waist. Even through her shawl, the heat of him branded her. He smelled of soap and leather, and she breathed in deeply.

"Yes."

The thumb of his other hand smoothed between her brows. "Why the frown, Sunshine?"

"No reason," she said brightly, even as her skin tingled at the intimate contact. She could not remember the last time a man had touched her face.

He began to withdraw. "Let us not—"

"No!" She snatched his wrist, and his eyebrow lifted in challenge, as if he were not used to being told what to do. "I am not frowning because I am unready. It is that I cannot help worrying that it will be like the other times after all."

His expression darkened, and his hand returned to cup the back of her neck, his long fingers delving into her hair and subsequently loosening the locks from their pins. She almost purred. He tilted her head so that she was looking up at him. "Why are you afraid kissing me will be like the *other times*?"

"They were unpleasant kisses."

"Why is that?" His thumb traveled across her jawbone, and she swallowed hard. Her heart was pounding like a bird trying to free itself from a cage.

"I am beginning to think it was because I did not desire them."

"And now?"

"Now I do not think that will be an issue."

Satisfaction burned in his gaze, and he bent his head. Ivy caught her breath, waiting for the most intense kiss of her life, and was disappointed when he only ghosted his lips across hers. Even though it was the barest touch, it still put her other kisses to shame. His lips were warm and smooth in contrast to the roughness of his unshaven face. His breath smelled of mint and tea, and she clung to his good shoulder, wishing she could taste more of him.

She got her wish when he did it again, this time lingering slightly at the corner of her mouth and pressing a dry kiss to it. He drifted to the other corner and left another kiss. "This smiling mouth is a gift," he murmured with something that sounded like regret as he began to pull away. "I should not sully it."

Ivy acted on instinct. She threw her arms around his neck and pulled his head down, planting her lips squarely on his. She did not really know what to do once she had mashed her mouth to his, so she held him there, hoping he would take over.

The wait felt interminable even though it was probably only half a moment. He did not react at first, his mouth partially parted beneath hers in surprise, and then it was as if a flame had been set to tinder. All of his reverent hesitance vanished in an instant. His hand in her hair tightened while the other came to the side of her neck. He angled her mouth and he kissed her.

Really kissed her.

Plundered, even.

His lips moved over hers with such surety and skill that she parted her own instinctually. He took immediate and full advantage, sliding his tongue into her mouth and curling it in a way that sent a flush racing across her skin. He pulled her closer, until she could feel every line of his broad chest, and continued to devour her, licking, sucking, and nipping until her entire body was trembling and she ached with need.

She pushed her hips against him, instinctively seeking something more.

He rumbled in her mouth and shifted so that his thigh pressed between her legs, providing pressure she had not even known she desired. It was entirely wicked, and yet she could not bring herself to put distance between them. The best kiss of her life had rapidly turned into something very illicit. She was supposed to slap a man who took such liberties. She was supposed to shove him away and remind him that she was a proper woman and must not be compromised.

Ivy did none of those things. She moaned as her fingers twined with his curly hair, and it felt like silk on her fingertips.

He broke contact, both of them breathing heavily, his mouth hovering over hers as he continued to cradle her head in his large hands. "We need to stop."

"Lesson number five. Teach me lesson number five."

"What is lesson number five?"

"I...I do not know," she admitted, frustrated by her ignorance, but there *had* to be more to learn. When it came to men and their desires, she knew more than most women simply from overhearing her brothers talk. But although she had heard crass jokes and rude references, she had heard very little about the woman's part in it all.

Owen had been in the process of extracting his thigh, but at her frustrated admission he paused, visibly warring with himself as both desire and reluctance battled on his face. Then he pressed his leg back between hers, and she melted into him. "Lesson number five is that a woman's pleasure enhances a man's."

"I have not heard that before. Do all men know that?"

"No."

"Women are not taught it, either."

"Hence lesson number five."

Ivy's fingers slid down the sides of his face, brushing against the rough growth of beard. "Teach me."

His wide hands grasped her hips. With aching care, so that she could stop him if she wished, he tugged her closer, until his thigh was fully between hers, wrapped in her skirt as he pushed upward and nudged her center down with his hands.

Ivy's cheeks heated, and a soft gasp escaped her lips.

"Tell me to stop."

"No."

He manually shifted her hips, grinding her against him, and Ivy's fingers clutched his shoulders hard enough that later she would marvel that he had not flinched from the pressure on his sore side. How was this possible? She had never guessed that a woman could feel like this with a man. Whatever he was doing to her was sinful and wrong, and she would scream if anyone stopped him.

Owen leaned forward, his lips at her ear as he lifted his thigh and simultaneously pushed on her hips. A noise escaped Ivy that should have embarrassed her, but she was drowning in sensation and did not care. "What you need, Sunshine, is for pressure to build between your legs. That empty achiness you feel right now can be partially sated with just the right amount of friction. Help me. Grind down on me."

Ivy rocked her hips, and he groaned with approval. "Good lass. Have you touched yourself in this way before? Lying in bed at night?"

Writhing against him, knowing that she should feel ashamed and yet finding it impossible to do so when he was tempting her on with his strong hands and filthy words, Ivy nodded.

He ran his nose down the side of her neck. "Did you find release?"

She shook her head no. She did not know what he meant.

"I will show you how to find it. After today, when you touch yourself, I want you to think of this moment and know that you have the power to take yourself to the crescendo. Do not ever feel guilty about finding your own pleasure." He shifted, doing something that made her forehead fall to his shoulder. "And when you are recovering, satisfied and tingling, I want you to know that I am *pleased* with you."

She barely knew what he was saying anymore. Her skin felt too tight, her lungs unable to fully expand, and something deep in her core was heating and heating until it felt like she might burst.

His voice lowered to an impossible level. "Women who walk around like rays of sunshine deserve to see rainbows." On the word "rainbows" he ground her hard against him while simultaneously biting the junction between her neck and shoulder. Ivy cried out against his hair as she experienced a stunning climax of pleasure, sparks of color indeed flashing behind her eyelids.

She clung to him, trembling and confused and oh, so sated, until at last she felt as if the bones in her body were liquefying. He held her tight, supporting her when she did not know if she could stand on her own two legs.

"Beautiful," he murmured, stroking one hand down her back while the other kept her upright. "So perfect."

Ivy did not know what to think, much less say. She knew she should probably be embarrassed or ashamed, but he was still lavishing her with praise so she could not find it within her to self-flagellate.

"What just happened is normal, Ivy. It is how men feel when they copulate, and it is how a woman should feel, too. A woman's pleasure enhances a man's, and if it does not, then he is not worthy. Lesson number five is that *your* pleasure should become your lover's pleasure."

Ivy could have happily snuggled into his chest for the next hour, listening to him calmly and factually state information about culturally taboo topics, but at that moment she heard the far-off call of Barnes shouting her name. She lifted her head, the satisfied flush on her cheeks draining with horror.

"Owen, if he catches us alone together—" She did not have to finish the statement. A normal brother would insist Owen marry her after coming across the compromising situation, which would be bad enough, but Barnes was not normal. If he saw her mussed and alone with Owen, his hatred for Owen would have him recklessly calling for a duel, no matter how illegal.

Owen's fingers flexed on her arms, and he stared down at her with a dark expression she could not decipher. Then he nudged her away, releasing her to the cold autumn wind. "Go," he ordered. "I shall ride toward him. Take the roundabout way to the house."

She nodded and snatched fistfuls of her skirt, about to run, when he said, "Ivy, we are not finished. We need to talk about this."

Ivy waved him off with a flick of her wrist, far more concerned with her brother catching her than with the heavy promise in Owen's voice.

Chapter 24

Owen did not have a chance to speak with Ivy before it seemed half the house was packed into the carriages and headed to London. His sisters had been so dismayed to be left behind that Owen had found himself agreeing to open the London town house for the Season. Once it was ready, he would send for them.

The prospect of spending months in a city bustling with people and noise was enough to put him in a terrible mood, but what had really made him grumble and glower at every person who had crossed his path was that he had not been able to find a moment alone with Ivy since their tryst in the meadow. Every minute had been spent preparing the estate to function in his absence, even as his every thought had been consumed by the memory of their kiss. He could not stop picturing the way her plush mouth had opened beneath his, or how their tongues had tangled so perfectly. The kiss had felt fluid, as if they had been doing it their entire lives, rather than the awkward first kiss of two people who had yet to learn each other.

She had smelled so sweet that even walking into a room and

breathing in her lingering scent now made him hard. Her hips had been soft and athletic between his palms, her pulse rapid beneath his fingertips. Absolutely everything about her was perfection.

And then she had let him bring her to crisis, and it had been the single most exultant moment of his life. The way she had let him work her body, the flush across her cheekbones, the dark shadow of her lashes over her skin as her lips parted and her lungs heaved—it was fodder for his every fantasy. She had melted under his praise, until she had been as pliable in his hands as wax. When she had reached her peak and shattered in his arms—he never could have imagined how possessive he would feel watching her, knowing that it was *he* who had brought her there.

He had given Ivy her first taste of true pleasure, and the hidden, dominant part of him was convinced that now meant she was *his*, even as Owen forced himself to replay her reaction when she had thought they were about to be caught and she would be forced to marry him.

Ivy did not want to marry *him*. She had wanted practice so that she would one day be able to satisfy Lord Hartford.

Bloody hell.

Owen scrubbed his hand down his face, swaying with the gait of his horse as they ambled beside the carriages. When he had discovered what she was teaching his sisters, that she was indeed the wildly capable and fierce female who had taken down the highwayman while he lay bleeding to death, he had been so awed that he had not been thinking properly. He was far from angry about her unsanctioned lessons. In fact, he was *thrilled*. The savage satisfaction he felt at the thought of one of the little girls kneeing a lad who had become too bold was undeniable. It was a shame not *every* girl received such tutelage.

He had not lied about his fantasies about warrior princess Ivy. The dreams had started when he was still bordering on fever and severely wounded: in them, she would incapacitate their attacker, and then she would run to him and begin kissing him all over. The first time he had had the dream he had felt uncomfortable, like he had gone to a place he should not have, but then it had happened again, and soon he had begun to fantasize about warrior Ivy when he was conscious. He had told himself it was acceptable because it was not the *real* Ivy he had been lusting over.

Then he had discovered she truly *was* the woman of his dreams, and his entire world had stopped spinning. He had acted without thought to consequence, and although it had been reckless and stupid, he could not bring himself to regret it.

It was painfully clear to him now that he wanted her beyond all reason, and it was equally clear that if Ivy was going to escape their arrangement with her reputation intact, he would need to put as much distance between them as possible in London. What took place in the field could not happen again, and he needed to tell her that.

Owen ignored the sinking pit in his stomach and attributed it to his dread at having to live in London. It had nothing to do with the spunky ray of sunshine that had wriggled her way beneath his skin.

No, it had nothing to do with her at all.

Owen probably should have ridden in the carriage, but he could not stand to be in confined quarters with either Ivy or Barnes, although for entirely different reasons, so he had made his excuses and chosen to ride instead. When they reached the inn after hours of traveling, he barely glanced at Barnes before escaping to his chamber.

The next day was a continuation of the first. He studiously avoided Ivy in her brother's presence, while being keenly aware of her the entire time. He needed to find time alone with her to talk, but with Barnes hovering like an old mother hen, he found his temper growing shorter with each passing hour.

When they reached the Brackley town house, Owen was dismayed to discover it was falling apart as surely as the country estate. The skeleton staff had done the best they could to prepare for their arrival, but they could not fix the water stains on the wallpaper, the out-of-date furniture, or the crumbling mortar between bricks.

Barnes studied the foyer with lifted brows.

"Do not even say it," Owen snapped, walking past. "Fale!" he roared. The butler hurried forward, dotting his hairless brow with a handkerchief. "Hire some goddamned staff, will you? This place is falling apart. We need several ladies' maids, a full kitchen staff, and whoever else you think will be necessary to competently run a household of twelve."

"Twelve, my lord?" the butler gasped.

"My sisters will be arriving for the Season whenever this heaping pile of bricks is ready. On that note, hire a mason, a carpenter, and a roofer." He paused as Ivy drew even with him, her little navy hat squashed atop her head. She took in the chandelier overhead that had not been dropped and dusted in what looked like a solid decade. The marble flooring was chipped, the mahogany railing scratched. For a brief moment he felt embarrassed that he had brought her to a house that was a short cry from ruins.

"Fale," he continued, nodding to Barnes and Ivy, "meet my guests, Mr. and Miss Bennett."

The butler's eyes widened even further, and he dropped into a hasty bow.

"What do you think, darling?" Owen asked Ivy sarcastically.

"I think it has a lot of potential."

"Do you, now?"

She nodded, that blasted dimple appearing in her cheek. "It only needs a little care."

He studied her for a moment. Without taking his eyes off her he said to Fale, "Although Miss Bennett is my guest, I am also courting her under the chaperonage of her brother, which means that whatever she wants, she is to have. Do you understand? If she wants to redecorate the house entirely in pink, I expect the wallpaper to arrive the next morning. If she wants quail eggs for breakfast every Tuesday, find them." He finally tore his gaze from her smooth cheeks and touched them on his panicked butler. "And give yourself a raise, Fale. You are going to need it."

Owen stormed off toward the study, leaving the servants to lead Ivy upstairs to her chamber, which was to be in the opposite wing from his for propriety's sake.

Barnes easily caught up with him. "Why are you giving her so much power?" he asked, keeping stride. "In a month she will be gone."

He did not know how to answer.

Barnes stared at the side of his head as if he were trying to figure out a mathematics problem. "She has terrible taste. Her chamber at home is entirely yellow. It is her favorite color. Your house will look like the outside of a canary when she is finished."

Owen could not help smiling. Yellow was a perfect fit for the ray of sunshine being led up his staircase. "The house could use brightening."

Barnes hurried in front of him, forcing Owen to a stop. They stared at each other, a mere foot separating them. "I hope you are not developing feelings for my sister," Barnes said coldly. "She is not yours to have, and never will be."

A muscle twitched in Owen's jaw. "You should be thanking me, Bennett. When I am finished parading her around town, she will have Hartford prostrating himself at her feet." He leaned forward and snarled, "Now get out of my way."

"You are acting nastier than usual, Brackley."

"Only to you." He shouldered past Barnes, wishing instead he could knock out his former friend. Barnes was right; he was in a foul mood, and for the life of him he did not understand why. All he knew was that the next day he and Ivy were going to present themselves to the *ton* with the sole purpose of making her more enticing to Hartford, and something about the fact now made him sick.

Chapter 25

At supper Barnes suggested the three of them walk the fashionable hour in Hyde Park. "It is important to set the tone." Barnes blotted his napkin against his lips. "The news of your run-in with the highwayman has eclipsed talk of the hysteria for the moment, and all eyes will be on you. We must make it plain, on your very first appearance, that I am here strictly chaperoning. We do not want Hartford to doubt Ivy's reputation for a moment."

"Joy," Owen muttered into his glass, low enough that only Ivy could hear it.

"His lordship is weary from travel," she said, making an excuse for him. Although a number of people had left the city for fear of catching hysteria, the lure of the social season was too strong for the majority. "We can present ourselves another day."

"*Owen*," he growled. He took another swig of brandy and slammed the glass on the table. "And your brother is right." He pushed back from the table with a loud scrape, making the footman jump. "Be ready in an hour." He strode from the room without a backward glance.

"Who put the bee in his bonnet?" Barnes asked, relaxing once Owen was gone. "He has been more ogreish than usual."

Ivy frowned down at her plate and slid a piece of fish across it with her fork. "Perhaps the city does not agree with him." *Perhaps he is angry about what happened in the field.*

Ivy had thought of little else. She knew she would never have another kiss that passionate, that skilled, that *heady* again. She had thoroughly enjoyed the kiss. She had enjoyed *everything* they had done.

When she had lain in bed the night after, she had begun to feel ashamed for finding pleasure with a man who was not her husband, but Owen had not seemed to judge her for it. In fact, he had told her he was pleased with her. That she was beautiful. Perfect.

Just the memory of his praise made her flush. Ivy was a resilient and independent woman, but the way he had taken control of her body had been exhilarating in a way she never could have imagined or known she wanted. Because she had *liked* ceding control. She had *liked* hearing him praise her while he brought her to crisis.

And then Barnes had nearly caught them, and the regret that had flashed across Owen's face had been so intense that it had made her stomach clench. He would be miserable if he were forced to marry her—that was if Barnes did not incite him into a duel first—and she would forever feel like a burden. Ivy did not expect a love match, but she did hope her future husband would at least find the marriage mutually beneficial. That was one of the reasons she had wished to wed Lord Hartford. She would never feel anything but warm, friendly affection for Hartford, and she suspected he felt similarly about her, but at least she could offer him companionship.

When it came to Owen, there was nothing she could offer a man determined to avoid the altar.

As for their lessons, in the beginning she had convinced herself she was trying to learn to be a better lover for Hartford, but now she could not imagine doing what she had done in the field with anyone other than Owen. The thought of kissing Hartford with such passion, or allowing herself to become uninhibited enough to reach crisis the way she had with Owen, was unthinkable.

Panic began to settle into her bones. Perhaps Hartford would not wish to engage in such activities with her. Perhaps he would not desire an heir.

No, of course he would. She was being absurd. But now that she had foolishly had a taste of passion with Owen, she was not sure she would be able to stand any other touch. She had urged Owen on despite all his warnings and hesitancy, and now she was afraid he had ruined her, because she no longer wanted a gentle marriage with Hartford.

She wanted Owen.

Ivy mentally chastised herself. It did not *matter* that she wanted Owen; she could not have him. He had made his objections to marriage quite clear, and Barnes would never allow a union between them anyway. She had a brief window of opportunity to find a marriage match that was satisfactory, which meant she must push Owen from her mind and forge ahead with her plan lest she end up married to that monster Reedly.

"I need to dress," she said, pushing away from the table.

Barnes lifted a forkful of fish. "Choose your gown wisely. This is your first foray into society. And, Ivy, I must warn you...do not be surprised if you run into Father." The atmosphere between them darkened. "He lives in London, and he is basking in the social currency your courtship has been building him. I would not put it past him to approach you in public. Mayhap not tonight, since I doubt news of our arrival has spread, but soon."

Ivy stiffened. "I look forward to dashing his hopes when I end the courtship."

Barnes nodded. "You and me both."

In her chamber, Ivy dressed with care, knowing that how she presented herself reflected not only on her but also on Owen. She chose a dark maroon velvet walking dress, complete with a pair of gloves and a little matching hat. She laced herself into a sturdy pair of boots with a heel, pinned her curls firmly in place, and nodded in satisfaction at her reflection. She looked fresh and proper, the material of her gown so clearly vibrant that it had to be new. The outfit was in high fashion, and it felt like armor that would protect her from the discerning eyes of the *ton*.

When she descended the stairs, her gloved fingers trailing the scratched banister, Barnes nodded in approval and turned away, while Owen's gaze swallowed her. He extended his arm, and she put her fingertips lightly on his black frock coat, and they exited the house with Barnes trailing a respectable distance behind.

The moment her feet landed on the Mayfair streets, colors, scents, and sounds burst around her. It was a two-mile walk to Hyde Park, and she took in every lavish moment with awe. Ivy had been to London before, but never to the fashionable heart of it. Women everywhere were eager to be seen, wearing feathered hats and bold colors, the latest of which was a garishly bright "parrot green" that almost hurt her eyes. Carriages drove past, dust flying in the air to mingle with the ever-present cloud of coal smoke, the horses' coats glistening in the early evening light. A girl was selling flowers on the corner, while a boy covered in black soot dodged past. For a woman who had spent the majority of her life on quiet, romantic country lanes, it was a shock to Ivy's senses.

While she walked silently beside Owen, she imagined what it would be like to teach self-defense at the Dove's school for governess spies. Was Perdita's nearby? What sort of women attended? How long could she expect to be employed there?

"We shall be on the front page of the papers tomorrow," Owen muttered. Ivy snapped out of her daydream to realize that as they had neared Hyde Park, they had attracted more and more attention. Folks were trying not to openly gawk, but the furtive glances were obvious all the same. Barnes had drawn closer, tipping his hat and calling out gallantly to those he knew, making his presence known.

When they reached the footpath that wound near the carriage way, Ivy's fingers were nearly cramped with how hard she was gripping Owen's arm. She deliberately relaxed them.

"Sorry," she whispered. "I knew to expect scrutiny, but I did not understand the level of—"

"Lord Brackley, is that you?" An older woman in an impeccable ensemble and mink muff lifted her glittering gaze to Owen.

"My lady." He swept her a bow, while Ivy panicked that she did not remember who the woman was. She should have refreshed herself on the names and titles of the peerage.

The woman gazed past him, her birdlike eyes landing on Ivy. "Is this the governess everyone is talking about?" Her sniff said everything she thought about *that*.

Owen stiffened under Ivy's touch. From the corner of her eye, she noticed Barnes react in a similar manner. "Lady Ruth, this is Miss Ivy Bennett, the granddaughter of the Marquess of Rothford, and, should my courtship prove fruitful, the future viscountess." He inclined his head to Barnes. "Her brother, Mr. Bennett."

Lady Ruth harrumphed, dismissing Barnes with barely an acknowledgment, her eagle eyes returning to Ivy. They swept over her hair and gown with such vulgar assessment that Ivy was appalled. And here she had thought the ladies of the *ton* had manners!

The lady's lip curled when she could find no fault with Ivy's dress. Dismissing Ivy as she had Barnes, she turned a rusty smile on Owen. "My daughter, Lady Cora, has returned from the country to attend the opening ball of the Season. She is the loveliest harpist; 'tis like standing in the presence of an angel when she plays. Will you be in attendance, my lord?"

"Miss Bennett, Mr. Bennett, and I have accepted our invitations."

"Excellent." With one last disdainful look at Ivy she added, "I do hope you will save *Lady* Cora a dance. I know your father would have approved of *her*."

Once the odious woman had swept away, Ivy whispered, "Lady Ruth?"

"Countess of Glenwood," Owen explained, his tone hard.

"How do you remember all of their names after being gone for so long?" If Lady Ruth was any indication of what was to come, Ivy wished the fashionable hours over already.

His lips tilted downward. "I was forced to memorize them as a boy, and it seems they have stuck despite my best attempts to forget them. There will be younger people I do not know."

"I know most of them," Barnes said, appearing at his side. "I will supply their names when appropriate."

Owen cut him a disbelieving glance. "You would help me?"

"Not you; Ivy. I do not like how Lady Ruth spoke to her."

"Lady Ruth and the others will remember their manners when

I am finished here. In fact, I believe I owe Lord Glenwood a visit. He recently put in a request for a pair of Cleveland Bays."

For the first time since Owen and her brother had reunited, Barnes nodded at him with something akin to respect.

"What am I missing?" Ivy asked.

"Do not worry yourself," Barnes said dismissively.

"Do not treat me like that. I am not a child."

Owen's thumb swept over her arm. "I intend to visit Lord Glenwood and make it clear that if his wife continues to cut you, he will not have his horses."

Ivy's eyes widened. "Owen, you do not have to risk your business for me."

"'Tis good for the men of the *ton* to be reminded that even though I now hold the title of viscount, I am not a man to be crossed. An insult to you is an insult to me."

Barnes's eyes narrowed, but he remained silent for once.

Over the next hour they were stopped so often that Ivy felt as if they were standing in place. Viscount after duke after earl gave Owen their condolences on his father's passing and welcomed him to his seat in the Lords. They asked after his horse breeding and other business.

The third time one of the gentlemen mentioned his "other business," Owen scowled and said sharply, "What other business?"

The man, Lord Wittle, was bone-thin with a bulging cyst on his neck that was hard to ignore. His hair was oily, and no manner of powder was helping dull the shine. He shifted uncomfortably at Owen's blunt question and glanced at Ivy. "Ah, I see how it is, Lord Brackley. My apologies." He scurried off before Owen could question him further.

Owen stared after him, his expression thunderous. "What am I missing?"

Barnes tilted his head, thoughtful. "Mayhap visit White's. If anyone will tell you, it will be those old gossips."

The exclusive men's club was supposed to be for serious discussion and leisure, but Ivy was unsurprised to hear that it was essentially a gossip club for the male sex.

"My father's club?" Owen scoffed. "I think not."

Ivy spotted Lord Hartford at the same time that he saw her. He quickly made his way over and dismounted from his horse, giving her such a boyishly happy smile that Ivy could not help but return it.

"You are the talk of the town," he said, kissing the back of her glove, his silky locks falling over his forehead. "You cannot know how relieved I am to find a kindred spirit in this horrid city. Smoke and waste do not inspire the poet's soul, do they?"

"I knew you appreciated a beautiful turn of phrase, but are you a poet yourself, my lord?"

"I confess that I am." He dropped his chin shyly. "Would you care to hear some of my poetry?"

"Indeed I would."

He ducked his head, pleased. "It is only fitting that their verses should first touch the ears of the muse who inspired them."

It took a moment for his words to sink in, and when they did, she blinked at him in astonishment. He meant her! *She* was his muse, which could mean only one thing: Their plan was working. She should have been elated. What did it matter that the kind man beside her had not seen her until Owen had? Unless she wanted a lifetime of misery with her father's suitor of choice, Hartford was her only option. And he really was a sweet man.

She should have been flooded with happiness, so why was a pit opening in her stomach?

Ivy forced a smile to her lips. She needed to focus on the gentleman who might be her future husband, not the man who had kissed her into a quivering mess in a meadow.

She drifted closer to Hartford as they began to walk, lightly touching her fingertips to his arm as she skirted the tiniest, almost invisible patch of mud. "I do not want to slip," she murmured.

He protectively tucked her hand into the crook of his elbow and guided her around the "puddle."

Ivy glanced up at Lord Hartford and thought of all of Owen's subtle reactions to her over the past weeks. How his eyes darkened when she licked or bit her lips, how he glared when she brushed her hair aside and exposed her neck, how his fists clenched when she leaned close enough for him to catch her scent. Even though she had not understood what his reactions meant at the time, after their kiss, she had become attuned to the realization that he was attracted to her, and that those little movements drew his interest. Would they draw Hartford's?

Ivy's tongue darted out and wetted her lower lip, but Lord Hartford's gaze did not drop to her mouth. In fact, he was discreetly eyeing a young gentleman striding past in a pair of tight breeches, a giggling woman on his arm. The gentleman had beautiful golden locks and the bone structure of a Grecian statue, and Ivy watched with interest as his gaze snagged on Hartford's. For one heavy, heated moment their eyes lingered, and then Hartford deliberately turned away. His mouth was no longer smiling, and there was something akin to sorrow, or perhaps jealousy, in the lines of his face.

Ivy glanced over her shoulder at the blond gentleman, and saw his hands clutched behind his back, his knuckles white.

"You have not told me how the viscount came to court you," Hartford said abruptly.

"He attended Harrow with my brother. We have been writing letters to each other for some years now with the intention that he would court me when he returned home. I had taken a governess position at the manor in the meantime."

His lips curved into a smile, and she caught sight of two women across the path flutter their fans when they witnessed it. Hartford did not so much as spare them a glance. "Do you and Lord Brackley share an interest in poetry?"

"No, I do not think he enjoys poetry." He was far more interested in horses, nonfiction, and now, because of her, gossip. In fact, his favorite book was a copy of the Arabic *Book of Horses* by Imru'al-Qays, which he had read so many times the spine was falling apart.

"That is a pity. I strongly believe a husband and wife should share common interests."

Ivy felt as if they were having the same conversation over and over again, with nothing of substance being shared between them, and she wondered if he was speaking by rote. She wondered if his attention was in fact still on the blond gentleman who had passed them, and if it was, what that could mean.

Hartford's horse snuffled at his shoulder as he led the beast alongside them. While Hartford's soft lips moved, she tried to envision them on her mouth, tried to imagine feeling the same passion that Owen inspired in her, but she was almost certain that while kissing Hartford would be pleasant and nice, it would be nothing like kissing Owen, which was like setting a match to a tinderbox.

Owen and Barnes followed them at a respectable distance, but

Ivy swore she could feel the heat of Owen's eyes burning into her back.

"Common interests are lovely, but they are not all that matters," she said.

"Indeed. One must also consider comportment and lineage."

"Yes." She nodded enthusiastically, even though that had not been what she had meant. What mattered most in a relationship, Ivy thought, was respect. The respect in the marriage between her parents had been entirely one-sided; her father had not had the slightest breath of respect for her mother. A man who respected his wife would take into account her feelings and treat her as an equal, much how Owen did when he spoke plainly to her about topics that were considered too delicate for young women. She glanced up at Lord Hartford, trying to fathom if he would speak honestly with her, but he must have mistaken her searching gaze for one of rapture, because he smiled down at her.

"I find my poet's heart stutters in your presence," he said softly. "Your beauty outstrips even that of the fairest lily of the valley."

Ivy thought of how Owen had told her she was "all right," and for some strange reason, found she preferred Owen's grudging admission to Hartford's flowery flattery.

Stop it, she scolded herself. Owen was not her future. Hartford could be, though.

Before she could reply, Owen approached. She sensed him before she saw him, felt his heat at her side, smelled the scent of his shaving cream and the horse leather that seemed to cling to him no matter where he went. His shadow fell across them, and he glared at Hartford like he wished to skewer him through with his riding crop.

"Lord Hartford," he said coolly.

Lord Hartford smiled congenially, and there was no more talk of poetry. He spoke with Owen and her brother for a few minutes about horses, and then made his excuses. Before he swung into his saddle, he turned to Barnes and said plainly, "You should know that I have honorable intentions toward your sister." To his credit, he did not shrink under the death stare Owen gave him.

Barnes smiled so widely his teeth showed. "I am pleased to hear that, Lord Hartford."

Hartford gave Ivy an indulgent look. "Will you save me a dance at the ball, Miss Bennett?" When she nodded, he climbed into his saddle, touched the brim of his hat, and took off.

The air was growing chill as the sun began to sink under the horizon. Carriages were pulling out of the park, and Ivy was ready to leave and return to the house, where she could have a few moments alone with her thoughts.

"Hartford appears smitten," Barnes commented as they headed back down the footpath. "I do believe that was a declaration of his intention to court you."

Owen's expression was thunderous.

They had exited the park when two gentlemen in elegant clothing and top hats stopped them. One of them was tall and dark and devilishly handsome; the other was attractive as well, but there was something conniving and malicious in his gaze. He smirked at Owen.

"Lord Brackley." He tilted his head in a small bow. "I thought you were out of town?"

"We just arrived." Owen's tone was less than patient, and Ivy could tell his limit for civil discourse was nearly at an end.

"Can I expect to see you at the club tonight?"

Owen's brows drew together. "And who the devil are you?"

Barnes made a noise in his throat that sounded suspiciously like aborted laughter. He cleared it and said, "Lord Brackley, this is Mr. Quinn, proprietor of Red's tavern in Bethnal Green, and Mr. Jasper Jones, owner of Rockford and Turner's golden hell."

The tavern owner's face had turned to stone at Owen's insult, but Mr. Jasper Jones's eyes had sharpened as if he had found the exchange absorbingly interesting.

"Your lordship," Mr. Quinn said stiffly, "my apologies. I understand we are in mixed company." He looked pointedly at Ivy. "Perhaps we might have a private discussion this evening?"

"Why?"

Mr. Quinn's cheeks reddened. "To discuss business."

"I have no business with you."

Mr. Jones, who had no right being so handsome, watched the exchange with a flat expression, but Ivy could see the clever calculation in his eyes. Goose bumps lifted on her arms, and she had the distinct feeling that Mr. Jones was a dangerous creature.

Mr. Quinn's eyes glittered. "Quite right, *my lord*." He bowed stiffly and turned away, his companion joining him after one last thoughtful glance at Lord Brackley.

"That was odd," Barnes commented as they continued toward the town house. "He certainly seemed to know *you*."

"There were several veiled references to *something* tonight," Ivy said. There had been an undertone from several of the men that had felt...ominous.

When she and Owen pulled ahead of Barnes, she said quietly, "I think you should arrange a meeting with Mr. Jasper Jones."

"The owner of the gambling hell?" When Ivy nodded, he said, "Why the devil would I do that?"

She hesitated. She could not tell him about the niggling feeling she had that their odd reception today was related to the Dove's investigation of him, so she said, "He appeared to be a clever man. If anyone knows what Mr. Quinn meant, it would be him."

"I do not care what Mr. Quinn meant."

She sighed. It appeared she was going to have to take matters into her own hands.

Chapter 26

Socializing at the park had been tedious at best, soul-crushing at its worst. The only thing that had kept Owen somewhat civil with the various lords and ladies of the *ton* was the fact that he needed to elevate Ivy's standing.

Thankfully, they had exchanged enough banal pleasantries with enough gossips that confirmation of their courtship would spread across London by morning. He still intended to visit the houses of those who had snubbed Ivy, however. That type of behavior would not be tolerated. Ivy was sunshine and cheer, and he would not stand for anyone to treat her as less.

Owen had just sat behind his desk with a tumbler of brandy when his butler announced the arrival of a guest.

"No," Owen snapped. "Tell him to bugger off." He was *done* playing nice for the day.

Fale's eyes widened in alarm, but before he could stammer, a gentleman slid past the butler and said, "He will see me."

Owen stood and assessed Mr. Jasper Jones. Even *he* had heard of Rockford & Turner's. It was the most exclusive gambling hell in

London, which meant Mr. Jones was wealthy beyond reason and knew everyone's secrets.

"You may leave," Owen said to the butler.

Fale sighed with relief, and the door snicked shut behind him.

Owen sat back down and inclined his head to the crystal decanter. "Drink?"

"No." Mr. Jones stuck his hands in his pockets and assessed the stuffy, dusty décor of Owen's father's study. "I should be at Rockford and Turner's."

"Then why are you here?" If he sounded ungracious as hell, it was because he was.

Mr. Jones tilted his head. "Because you asked me here."

Owen's glass paused halfway to his mouth. "No, I did not."

Jones pulled a missive from his pocket and tossed it on the desk. Owen turned it over and read the request written in the neat, loopy handwriting he had seen many times before on the chalkboard. It appeared Ivy had found a way to *make* him do her bidding, and heaven knew why it delighted him so much that she had the nerve to stand against him. It was the rare person who did.

"You have a problem, my lord. I assume that is why I am here." Jones's eyes traveled over him, taking in every last detail. "However, my information is not free. There is something you have that I desire, and there is something *I* have that you need."

"Stop speaking in riddles, or get out."

Mr. Jones's smile widened, and he took a seat across from Owen, sinking into the cracked leather with the grace of a panther. "I am married now."

"My felicitations."

"My wife is brilliant," Jones continued matter-of-factly, and with more than a hint of pride. "She is brilliant at *many* things, and one of them is finding patterns. I, too, have an interest in patterns."

"I do not."

"You should." Jones splayed his fingers on his knee, and Owen spotted the flash of a dark ring on his finger. "I believe someone is impersonating you."

Owen's body temperature plunged, freezing him in place. "*Who?*"

"As I said, my information is not free."

Owen snarled. "How much do you want?"

"I do not want your money. I have enough of my own. How did you enjoy your re-entrance into society today?"

Owen's temper, already frayed by hours of socializing, unraveled further with the digression. "I did not."

Jones smirked. "I could tell. My wife is one of the kindest, most intelligent people I know, and yet she does not have many society friends."

"Probably *because* she is kind and intelligent. Those vipers care for little more than appearances and frivolity."

For some reason, Owen's ire seemed to please Jones. "If you will have the lady you are courting, Miss Bennett, extend an invitation to my wife for tea, I will tell you all I know and suspect."

"*That* is your price? An invitation for your wife to attend tea?"

"That is my price."

Jones had to know he could ask Owen for almost anything, and yet all he desired was a kindness toward his wife? Was it possible the devil of London's underbelly had come under thrall of his own partner? Owen nearly shuddered at the thought of a woman having that much power over him.

"I will ask Miss Bennett, but I shall not force her."

"I respect you more for that. Then we have a bargain. I have been keeping an eye on your business dealings over the past year."

Owen's jaw worked, but he remained quiet. This dangerous man had an ear to the underground, and Owen wanted information more than he wanted to howl at the fact that *anyone* was keeping tabs on him. He thought of the side-eyed looks and insinuations during the evening promenade, and realized Ivy's instincts about the situation were right. He had brushed off the odd interactions, but perhaps there was more to it.

I believe someone is impersonating you.

"My horse breeding business," Owen confirmed.

"No."

"What business could you mean, then?"

"Exactly. You are an anomaly, Lord Brackley. You left England, and the only time anyone heard from you was when you returned to strike a deal with this duke or that marquess. Then a year ago, men began talking in my gambling hell. They were investing in *the* Lord Brackley's newest business venture, and if it were half as good as his horse breeding business, they were soon to be flush with money."

Owen's skin prickled as the comments about his "other" business began to make a little more sense. "I have no other business, and I sure as hell would not ask any of those layabouts to invest in one if I did."

"And yet your business has been profiting in spades. Men who owed me money have paid their debts, and the *ton* considers you a new-age Midas. The *ton*, your lordship."

The emphasis halted Owen's next comment. "Speak plainly."

"I do not hear gossip only pertaining to the *ton*. Did you know that I once was a fishmonger's son?"

"I have heard."

"I have not forgotten how it felt to starve and be taken advantage of by money-hungry men who cared nothing for the well-being of those more vulnerable, so long as their pockets were lined." He stared hard at Owen, and a frisson of danger raced down Owen's back. He sized up the man in front of him. He was a physical match for Jasper, but he did not think he could fight as dirty as the gambling hell owner. He did not think he would know *how*.

"Your point?"

"Your profitable business venture is a factory. It has failed to meet every minimum safety standard there is. Lord Brackley overpromises and underpays his employees, luring them with healthy wages and then entrapping them by overcharging them for their board, so that they are eternally indebted to him."

Owen pushed to his feet and roared, "The *hell* I do!"

Jasper did not flinch, but he assessed Owen with cold, hard eyes, until finally he gave a single nod. "I realized today, when I met you, that something was wrong with the picture. You did not strike me as the sort of man to play oily games, and when you did not know what my dishonorable acquaintance was talking about, it occurred to me that there may be more at play than what meets the eye. It seems the pattern does not create the picture I thought it did."

Owen's fists were clenched when he slowly sat back down. If someone was using his name to secure investors and oppress workers, he would not rest until he had ferreted him out. This was no longer his father's viscountcy. Owen had been bequeathed it whether he wanted it or not, and he would be damned if he let anyone think he was a continuation of his amoral father.

His voice was menacing when he said, "Tell me everything you know."

An hour later Owen sat in the kitchen, backlit by a dying fire and playing with a set of Chinese Baoding balls he had found in his father's study, the two metal balls clicking together rhythmically as he rotated them in his palm.

What he had learned from Jasper Jones had equally enraged and flummoxed him. Who could have tricked so many gentlemen of the *ton* into believing they were investing with the real Viscount Brackley? Was he so nondescript that any man could claim his visage and name?

Jones had given him the name of one of his club members who had invested with the imposter Viscount Brackley, and Owen's first order of business tomorrow was to visit the man before the ball and discover what he knew.

He was deep in thought when a figure appeared in the open kitchen doorway, a slender silhouette wearing a silky purple dressing gown. *Ivy.* Her loose hair curled over her shoulders, and her honey-colored eyes were warm in the banked light of the fire.

She halted when she caught sight of him. He must have made quite the picture, his hair mussed and the cuffs undone on sleeves that were rolled halfway up his forearms. A glass of cold milk sat untouched before him, along with a hard-crusted roll and the case to the Baoding balls.

"Oh... Owen. I did not know you were here." She paused, hovering by the fireplace, neither leaving nor coming closer.

"Midnight snack, Ivy?"

She lifted a shoulder and padded toward the table, her bare feet soundless on the floor. "Barnes is snoring loud enough to wake the dead, and I was feeling restless. I can leave you alone, if you prefer your solitude."

Owen eyed the matching purple silk rope tied around her waist. She followed the direction of his gaze. "This is one of the many items included in the wardrobe you bought."

It was not appropriate for her to be alone with him in the house kitchen, wearing nothing but a dressing gown, but he was incapable of suggesting she remove herself. The neckline of the robe gaped enough for him to catch sight of the pristine white cotton of her nightgown. Had she removed her chemise and corset? Was she entirely bare beneath the fabric?

He was grateful for the table covering his lap when his thoughts veered toward the inappropriate. He pushed the roll toward her. "Hungry?"

She sat across from him and tore a hunk off the bread and popped it between her lips. He stared at her mouth as she delicately chewed and swallowed.

"Owen?" The way she spoke his name suggested she had said it more than once.

"Yes?"

"I have something I must confess."

His eyes lifted to hers, and whatever she saw in them made her lips part and her legs shift beneath the table. "You do not need to confess to me, Sunshine. I am a sinner, not a saint."

Her cheeks flushed at the words, and he tried not to think about that flush creeping down her chest, or how rosy her skin would look in the aftermath of pleasure. The balls clicked in his hand, and he also tried not to think about how he could use them to enhance her pleasure. He was supposed to talk to her about what had happened in the field. He was supposed to reassure her that it would not happen again, and that he was going to act the ultimate gentleman, and yet all he could picture was slowly untying her dressing robe until the silk panels parted, lifting the hem of her nightdress and...

"But I do," she said, her voice breaking into his wicked fantasy.

"You do not have to fret, Ivy. I already know that you arranged the meeting with Mr. Jones, and I am not angry."

She perked up. "What did you learn?"

His lips twitched at her eagerness. "Many concerning things that I need time to think about."

She was clearly displeased with his answer, but to his surprise did not push the issue. "The meeting with Mr. Jones is not what I must confess to. I spent the entire carriage ride to London thinking, and I came to the conclusion that I must tell you the truth for your own safety."

The haze of his lust slowly began to dissipate. "The truth about what?"

She exhaled, the little puff of air lifting one of the strands of hair on her forehead. "IteachdefenseclassestowomenandIhavebeen spyingonyou."

The words came out in such a jumbled rush that he could not separate them. "Say it again. Slower. I will not bite." The comment slipped out before he could stop it, and something hot uncoiled in his belly at the memory of nipping the skin on her perfect, smooth neck.

She took a deep breath. "I teach secret self-defense classes to women over the modiste's shop. And I have been spying on you."

Owen sat back, his head spinning. He felt as if his arrival in London had somehow dislodged secrets left and right. "Spying on me," he repeated. Anger began to form in the pit of his stomach as he thought of the impostor who had borrowed money in his name and then dragged his reputation through the dirt. Was she spying for *him*? Betrayal, thick and sour, coated his tongue. "For who?"

She traced her fingertip along the wood grain of the table. "A woman."

"You will have to elaborate," he said coolly.

"I only know her as the Dove. She gathers information from governesses across the country to help right wrongs done to those who do not have the power to right things themselves. She holds the *ton* accountable for their crimes."

"And what crime have I committed?"

"None." She lifted her head. "She thought you were entangled with the hysteria sweeping the city, as you were seen in a number of the households with affected women."

That he had not expected. "Impossible."

She nodded. "I know that now. When you told me your most recent trip to London had been two years ago to meet with the Duke of Houndsbury, I passed along the information. But she still thinks your name is in some way tied to it—and she is worried about your safety."

Her confession eased some of the anger coalescing in his heart. He was not pleased to learn that his privacy had been violated, but at least she was not working for the impostor. It also allowed one more piece of the puzzle to tumble into place.

"It must be the man impersonating me."

"The man impersonating you?"

Owen told her about what he had learned from Jasper, and watched as she began to vibrate with excitement.

"Of course!" She jumped from her seat, the neckline of her dressing gown widening to reveal more of that maddeningly proper nightgown. "When you were abroad and your father was ill, someone took it upon himself to pretend to be you. Using your name, he visited numerous gentlemen of the *ton* and convinced them to invest in his factory. *That* is why the governesses swore they saw you visiting houses across London!" She took a step toward the kitchen door. "I must write to the Dove at once. I—"

He moved so quickly that she let out a squeak when he rounded the table and advanced on her. "Your letter can wait. We are not done talking, Sunshine."

She swallowed.

"You teach self-defense classes. That is where you go each week, not to visit your modiste friend."

"Oh yes, there was that part of my confession."

"You teach grown women the skills you teach my sisters?"

She nodded.

"Are you even friends with the modiste?"

She shook her head.

He leaned forward and pierced her with his eyes, connections falling into place one by one. "Did the modiste sew my wound, Ivy?"

"Not exactly."

"How *exactly* did I come to have a bullet removed from my shoulder, then?"

"The Dove."

He paused at that, resting his hand over her head on the wall. So this mysterious Dove had asked Ivy to spy on him, and then had saved his life. He did not know if he was angry about her interference or grateful for her stitching skills.

His jaw worked as he tried to get a grip on this odd sense of betrayal, when Ivy gently cupped his cheek. Her fingers were cool and soft, and he could not make himself shake them off. "I am sorry, Owen. I did not know you well when I agreed to pass along information about you. I thought you might truly be involved. I did what I thought was right at the time."

"And once you discovered I was innocent?"

"Then I became committed to *proving* your innocence. And I was worried about your safety."

He let his hand fall. "My *safety*?"

"You were shot by a man who clearly has a vendetta against you." She worried her lip between her teeth. "You know what I am capable of. I thought I could clear your name and protect you while we finished out our ruse."

He scraped his palm over his jaw, assessing the fierce woman standing in front of him. Her chin was held high in defiance of his ire. Ivy Bennett did what she thought was right, whether that meant risking her job as a governess to teach little girls to defend themselves, riding the streets at night to teach older women the same, or spying on her employer to help solve the mystery of hysteria that was injuring so many women. He could be angry that she had violated his privacy—and he was—while still understanding that she had done it with the best of intentions.

"Any other confessions, Sunshine?"

She licked her lips, and at the look in his eye, took a step back, pressing herself against the wall. "No."

"Good. Because *I* have one."

Chapter 27

A weight was lifted from Ivy's shoulders now that she had told Owen everything, even as a different sort of tension wound around her chest. Owen towered over her, his hair tousled and his sleeves rolled to his elbows. His eyes were dark and dangerous, and that sense of wild abandon had once again come over him.

She knew he was hurt that she had spied on him, and he had every right to be, but the way he was looking at her seemed to hold more heat than injury.

"What is your confession?" It was a dangerous question. If she had more sense, she would scurry to her room. She knew he would let her go. But Ivy had never once passed up a chance for a good piece of gossip or a shocking confession.

His eyes fell to her lips, scorching a path along her skin. "I cannot stop thinking about our kiss in the meadow."

Her fingertips tingled. "Oh?"

"I cannot stop remembering how perfect you were. How soft your lips were. How sweet your gasps were when you came apart."

Ivy's cheeks flushed, and her breathing accelerated. "We were almost caught."

"Which is why it cannot happen again."

She nodded in agreement, even as disappointment slithered through her. What he had done, what they had shared—she would be lying if she said she did not want to experience it again.

"We are in agreement, then."

She nodded again, expecting him to back away and take with him his delicious warmth and the tension that thickened the air between them. But he remained in place, a muscle twitching in his jaw.

"What are you wearing underneath your nightgown?"

It was an obscenely inappropriate question, and she did not know if he had asked it to shock her into fleeing, or if he truly wanted to know. Before she could reply, he said, "Do *not* answer that. Leave now. Please."

"No. I came to the kitchen for a snack, and I have only had a bite of bread." She edged around him, feeling his eyes on her as she walked to where the roll lay discarded. When she reached the table, she peeked over her shoulder at him. He was as stiff as stone, his knuckles white, and she realized two things: First, no matter what he said, Lord Owen Brackley wanted her, and second, he would not do anything about it. He was too honorable, too worried about tarnishing her reputation to make another mistake like they had in the meadow.

And yet it was nearly midnight, and they were alone in the kitchen. Ivy knew how crucial a woman's reputation was, but how would anyone *know* if she and Owen were not entirely proper? If neither of them told, why could they not indulge? Why could this not be their very own secret?

When they had kissed in the meadow, he had made her feel both pleasured and treasured. If she was lucky, she would find a marriage match, preferably with Lord Hartford, but she knew without a doubt that neither Hartford nor any other man could ever make her feel the way Owen did. Why should she not experience passion with him one more time?

The clock ticked over the stove. One second passed, then another.

"If you want to know what is underneath my nightgown, you shall have to find out for yourself."

His pupils fattened. "You do not know what you are asking."

"Do not speak to me as if I am naïve and stupid."

"That is not what I meant. You do not know *who* you are tempting. You do not know what kind of lover I am."

Her pulse skipped a beat. "What kind of lover are you?"

He took a single step forward and halted, his iron will a nearly visible force holding him back. "A demanding one." His voice roughened. "A commanding one."

She had a memory of them standing outside the schoolroom while he asked her if she was adept at taking orders in a voice that had made her stomach twist with desire. "You like to give orders."

His eyes burned, but he said nothing.

She considered what that might be like. She thought of how his hands had known exactly what to do with her in the meadow to make her reach her peak. She did not think she would mind following his orders if it was her choice to do so.

"I can listen," she said, losing her breath a little at the look in his eye.

"Can you?" He advanced another step. "What of your reputation? I cannot take your virtue."

"That decision should be my choice, too," she argued as he closed a little more distance.

"Mmm." His gaze raked across her dressing robe. "You are certain you know what you want?"

"Yes. No. I mean, I cannot be certain if I have never experienced it."

His grin was sinful. "Does the governess require more schooling?"

"Mayhap she does."

He had reached her now, and he dipped his head to whisper in her ear, "Another lesson, then? Turn around, Sunshine."

With the order, his tone shifted from teasing and heated to commanding, and Ivy did not know why the primal direction had her skin flushing, only that it did something to her insides. Something she liked.

She turned to face the kitchen table, her heart pounding in her chest like a bird fighting to take flight.

"Put your palms flat on the table, and do not move them unless I tell you to."

Ivy obeyed, but could not help asking, "What if I do?"

She felt his heat at her back as his hand brushed the hair from her neck. He dropped a kiss to the sensitive skin, his lips hot and dry. Chills raced down her arms. "Test me and find out."

She liked that, too, because she knew despite the promise in his voice, she was safe with him.

His hands trailed up her back to her neck, to the lapels of the dressing robe, and he slowly dragged the robe down her shoulders until it draped at her wrists, but she did not move her hands to remove it completely.

"So lovely, so good at listening," he praised, sweeping her hair across her back so that he could kiss the other side of her neck. The heat of him was an inferno, his chest hard and firm. She felt enveloped by him. Cherished by him. Desired by him.

She felt *powerful*, which was strange considering he was the one giving orders.

His fingers crept around her neck, stroking her throat as they drifted to the laces on the high-necked collar of her nightgown. He deftly undid them, until the fabric gaped open. He dipped his hand inside, tracing both collarbones with his finger, and chills sprang up on her skin. She pressed back, and he squeezed her hip with his other hand, stilling her.

"You have been driving me to madness," he growled against her neck. "So soft and capable and sunny. I am going to take my time wringing out every ounce of pleasure you have to give me."

Ivy involuntarily moaned, and he chuckled softly. He cupped her chin and turned her head to the side so that he could meet her eyes. "If you want me to stop at any time, tell me to stop. I will. Do you understand?"

"Do not stop."

"You do not want me to stop now, but I might go too far or too fast for you, and I would be devastated if you did not halt me."

She nodded, his assurance easing tension she had not even been aware of. He was so much more experienced than she was, and she was worried she could not be what he needed.

"You are safe with me," he murmured, releasing her chin. "I will never be angry with you. I will never be unhappy so long as you are honest with me."

"All right," she said softly.

He must have been satisfied, because he spread the neck of the nightgown wide and dragged it down her shoulders with such aching slowness that by the time her breasts spilled over the collar she was panting. She expected him to take it off entirely, but he left it in the crook of her elbows, pinning her arms to her sides, her breasts bare to the cool night air and the dying orange glow of the kitchen fire.

"Are you all right with this?" he asked, brushing his lips across her shoulder.

"Yes."

"It appears the answer to my question is nothing."

"W-what?" Her mind was already going fuzzy from the erotic feeling of being bare-breasted in the kitchen, her nipples puckering in the cool air.

"The answer to my question about what is underneath your nightgown. Turn around."

She did, the dressing robe falling off her hands and leaving her with the nightgown tight around her arms. His eyes fell to her chest, and the expression on his face was *worshipful*.

"You are stunning." He pressed a kiss to the corner of her lips. "I knew you would be." He kissed the other corner, and then finally the center of her mouth, just a warm, brief touch that left her longing for more. Before she could protest, he ran his lips down the side of her neck, dragging his tongue along a pathway of nerves that made her skin buzz. His hands closed around her upper arms, and still he did not touch her breasts—he did not even allow the front of his shirt to accidentally graze them.

Ivy felt as if the delay was only making her heavier, more aroused. His touches were teasing, alternating between giving her flashes of what she wanted and then retreating.

Slowly, he slid his palms to where the fabric bound her arms to her sides, and slipped his hands inside her nightgown to cup her rib cage. He was so large that his fingers met at her back, his thumbs resting just beneath the heavy globes of her breasts.

Ivy's heart was pounding in her ears. She lifted her eyes to his, and he smiled before crushing his mouth to hers. The pressure of his mouth, the skill, the coaxing of his tongue—it was a balm to all of the light half-touches she had received thus far. He forced her mouth wider, even as his thumbs brushed upward once, grazing the undersides of her breasts.

Ivy moaned into his mouth and tried to press closer, but he withdrew, leaving her lips wet and swollen. "Not yet, my love."

Ivy's brows drew together.

"You do not like to be teased?" he asked.

"I do not know. It is frustrating."

He nodded in understanding. "I can stop, if you want. I can be more direct. But if you wish to try it, I promise it will be rewarding in the end."

She thought about it and said, "Do not stop."

He kissed her lips lightly. "Thank you for being honest." Then he kissed the top of her breast and she gasped. "Your desires are important." He dragged his scruff across her skin to the other breast, and then down, closer, closer, and then gently bit her where the skin changed color—but not at the tip of her breast. She writhed in frustration as he repeated the action with the other breast, then began circling her with his tongue, expertly avoiding the exact place she wanted his mouth.

Her hands flexed helplessly at her side and her teeth sank hard into her lip, and just when she thought she could take no more, he sucked one tip into his mouth. Pleasure streaked from her breast to her core, and her knees wobbled. She gasped as he suckled her, palming her free breast with his other hand, pinching and shaping and handling her with alternating touches of aggression and tenderness that overwhelmed her with an onslaught of sensation.

He released her nipple with a pop and shifted to the other breast. Her legs were shaking so hard that she was afraid she might embarrass herself by collapsing, but then his arm snaked around her waist and held her tight. He lifted his head, a curl falling across his forehead, his lips wet and his eyes feverish.

"You are unsteady."

"I—"

"I do not want you to fall," he interrupted, a wicked glint in his eye. He lifted her by the waist and she gave a little squawk of surprise as he plunked her bottom on top of the table. Sitting like this, her face was even with his, and she grinned.

"This must be what it is like to be your height."

He returned her smile, and then pressed his palm to her belly and gently nudged her backward, so that she was looking up at the ceiling and her bottom was on the edge of the table. She was about to ask what he was doing, when his hands wrapped around her bare ankles and dragged upward, bringing her nightgown with them. She was equal parts horrified and thrilled when he flipped the hem over her knees, tracing his knuckles over her calf and up to her knee, then back down to her ankle and up again.

"Your legs," he groaned. "It is clear you partake in exercise." As he spoke, his hand drifted higher up the inside of her thigh, and back down again. "Do you spend a lot of time in the saddle as well?"

"I—" She choked on her response when his hand drifted higher again. Why was he distracting her with talk of riding? This time his fingers slid all the way up her inner thigh, and when she glanced down, she was grateful her gown was still covering her most intimate part.

"Answer me, Sunshine."

"What was the question?"

"Do you like to ride?" He smirked when he asked it, but she did not have a chance to ask him if there was secondary meaning to the question, because his fingertips brushed the curls at the apex of her thighs and she jolted.

"Do you want me to stop?" he asked, the smirk disappearing.

"No!"

He lightly traced his fingers through her folds. Ivy thought she was going to die, either from pleasure or humiliation, she was not sure. Was she supposed to be that wet? It was not as if anyone had ever talked to her about such things. Then she thought of someone she *could* ask. Someone who did not balk at answering intimate questions. "Is it normal to be...like this?"

"Yes," Owen answered matter-of-factly, knowing exactly what she meant. There was no shock, no censure, no amusement in his tone. "It means I am doing my job. It is a man's duty to pleasure his partner so that her body produces lubrication." It was almost clinical the way he spoke, in sharp contrast to the sweep of his fingers gliding through her. "It helps facilitate mating. It is important biologically. And it makes men bloody wild," he added, briefly grazing the nub at the top of her thighs, the one that she touched when alone in bed.

She gasped. "Then it is all right?"

"It is more than all right. Your body is responding perfectly, love." He traced his fingertips over that spot again, this time with slightly more pressure.

"Owen!" she cried, wriggling against the binds of her nightgown.

He paused, his fingertips pressed against her and yet unmoving. "Yes, Sunshine?"

"Why did you stop?"

He withdrew his touch, and she groaned in frustration, but a moment later she felt him at her entrance, and then the slightest twinge of discomfort when he slowly pressed a large finger inside her. The rasp of his finger against her sensitive tissues was enough to send her hips bucking up from the table. She had never been penetrated before, and when his finger slid out and then in again, she lost all rational thought. The house could have burned down around her and she would not have been able to focus on anything other than the feeling of Owen inside of her, and the way he was staring down at her face, his cheeks flushed, as if she were the goddess of all humanity.

He continued his slow assault on her senses, and then his thumb found that spot again and she was spinning up, up, and—

Owen withdrew, and Ivy clenched her fists, fighting back a howl of anger. She was so desperate for relief that when he lifted her nightgown around her waist she did not even care. His palms pressed on both of her inner thighs, spreading her wide like a banquet displayed on the table, and the look on his face was one of such worship that she could not find it within her to be embarrassed at what he must be seeing.

"I want to taste you."

"You... is that done?"

"Yes."

She knew she was going to say yes. Besides frustrating her, Owen had not disappointed her body yet. And the way he had answered her earlier question, so patiently, so comfortably... If she was going to allow anyone to be so intimate with her, it would be this man.

"All right," she breathed.

He gave her another moment to change her mind, and then he buried his face between her thighs. His tongue slid across her with a long, firm stroke, and Ivy came up off the table in shock. With one hand on her belly, he pressed her back down, and then he was feasting on her. Licking and swirling, rubbing and lapping, until she was pushing up against his face and whimpering without any thought to what was coming from her mouth. He slid his finger back inside her and gently sucked that sensitive bundle of nerves into his mouth. She was on the edge when he said severely, "Climax."

The command sent her shattering into a thousand pieces. Ivy cried out as she writhed against him, her thighs clenching until she went entirely lax on the table.

She was still seeing stars when he wiped the back of his hand over his mouth and left her so he could stand by the door. All remained silent, and she was just beginning to feel self-conscious, still splayed out on the table and unable to move her arms, when he returned and grinned down at her.

"Bloody perfect, Ivy. I knew you were going to be brilliant."

She warmed at his praise, even as he traced a finger over her wet heat. "That was a good start."

"*Start?*"

He slid a single finger into her, and then, since her release had made her so wet and pliable, he easily added a second, stretching and scissoring against her swollen tissues. "We can stop whenever you desire."

"I do not understand. How often is one supposed to…" Her question trailed off on a moan as he slowly began curling his fingers.

"It depends," he answered honestly. "Once is usually considered sufficient."

"So then why…"

He flushed then, even as his thumb very carefully touched her swollen bud. "I have always had different desires than my peers. Combined with giving orders, it greatly pleases me to bring my partner to her crest over and over again, until she physically no longer can."

Ivy gaped at him.

"But we do not have to do that," he added quickly, withdrawing from her. "That was perfect as it was."

"No, wait." Did he truly think she would not want to experience that again? "It is that it does not seem fair. That you are left without pleasure."

"Trust me," he said, his eyes darkening, "I receive plenty from it."

"You did not hear anyone?"

"The house is silent."

"Release my arms."

He obliged, pulling her gown down so that it pooled around her waist. She sat up and knew she looked like a trembling, wanton mess. "I would like to do it again," she said shyly. "If you truly want to."

He grabbed her face and kissed her deeply as he dragged her off the table, until her feet touched the ground. Then he said, "Sit down on the chair and part your legs."

She complied, making sure her gown covered her bottom even as he immediately rucked it up over her legs and knelt between her thighs. "Remember our deal when I was ill?"

She nodded.

"Let us make another one. I will give you anything you want if you find your peak three times tonight."

"*Three?*"

He frowned. "I thought I would make it an easy number, since it is your first time."

She stared at him. "And if I do not?"

"Then I shall be disappointed in myself, but never you."

"How is that a deal that benefits you?"

But he was already ducking between her legs, and suddenly it no longer mattered.

Chapter 28

He had brought her to crisis four times. The last time he had pulled her into his study and lain on his sofa and had her straddle his face. After that, she had become a quivering mess and he had not wanted to push her too far. He had stroked her arms and back and hair, and snuggled her close, until she had dozed.

When the clock struck three in the morning, he had gently woken her so that she could return to her room.

"You are still a virgin," he had told her, his hands in his pockets, afraid that if he did not remind her, she would find a way to regret their tryst in the morning.

Or maybe he was saying it for himself, to make himself feel better about debauching her when she was going to marry someone else.

Ivy had winked at him. Winked! "For today."

He had gone straight to his chamber and stroked himself to visions of her, reaching his climax in a matter of moments after a long night of giving her pleasure.

When he awoke a few hours later, he hoped he might find his

need for Ivy Bennett satiated, but was unsurprised to discover that now that he had tasted her, felt her break apart under his tongue, kiss him with plump and swollen lips, he could think of little else.

He had fed the beast inside of him, and now it wanted more.

Owen struggled with obsessive thoughts. It had made him a top-notch horse breeder and businessman, and it made him a devoted lover. But when it came to trying to forget something he desperately desired, it was his greatest flaw.

He thanked Fale for the letter he handed him as he crossed the foyer after breakfast, and nearly ran into Ivy on his way out the door. She was returning from a morning stroll with Barnes, her cheeks flushed and her hair perfectly coiffed underneath her little navy hat. The hat was so simple compared to the garish green and feathered monstrosities that were currently all the rage, and the simplicity somehow made her seem fresh and innocent.

Barely innocent, now.

She sparkled up at him. "Good morning, Owen."

Barnes scowled. "Lord Brackley," he corrected.

"Good morning, Ivy," Owen replied, just to see that muscle clench in Barnes's jaw when he deliberately called her by her given name. "Where have you two been?"

"Partaking the morning air," Ivy answered. "Are you leaving?"

Barnes caught sight of the butler and hurried over to speak to him about the mail. Owen lowered his voice and invaded her space. When her breath stuttered, he felt a swell of possessive satisfaction and knew he was in serious trouble. "How do you feel this morning?"

She gave him a secretive look. "I feel well. How about you?"

Hungry for more of her and disappointed in himself for it. He was playing with fire when it came to Ivy, and he was worried that when the flames died down, he would be the one left blackened by them. "I am fine. I am about to leave to visit the man Jones told me about yesterday, the one who has supposedly invested in my business."

"All right, let us be off."

"You are not coming with me."

"If you have forgotten, your life may be in danger."

He gave her a cool look. "You seem to think I am incapable of taking care of myself because I took a bullet, but let me be clear: I am no shrinking violet when it comes to a fight."

"Fine. Then you will need my charms when you visit with the investor. You are too forthright, too cranky. You will put him off. If we make it a social call, it will cast a layer of civility over it. That always puts the *ton* at ease, and he may be willing to tell you more."

She was right, but it did not sit well with him to further drag her into whatever scheme this impostor had put into motion.

She must have sensed his hesitation, because she added serenely, "You do not have to take me with you." His shoulders lowered an inch in relief. "I want to explore the city anyway. I shall slip away from Barnes and do a bit of prowling. I have always wanted to visit the docks."

"The hell you will!" he nearly roared. He did not care how clever and capable she was, there were places no one should travel alone, man or woman, and the London docks was one of them. She blinked innocently up at him, and he pinched the bridge of his nose.

"We made a deal last night, did we not?" she added. "This is what I want."

"Tell Barnes you are lying down to rest, and meet me on the corner of the street in ten minutes."

She flashed him a grin and brushed past him closely enough that he felt the drag of her shoulder across his chest, and the simple touch made him far too aware of the fit of his trousers.

Christ, what had he gotten himself into?

Ten minutes later on the dot, she appeared on the street, as fresh and spritely as a nymph. He quickly folded the letter Fale had handed him and tucked it into his breast pocket, but not before Ivy spotted it.

"Does that have to do with the case?"

"The case?"

When she peered up at him in exasperation, he ran a finger underneath his cravat. "Ah, no. It is a letter. From Lady Wagner."

Ivy's lips formed an O of understanding. "Your former lover."

"A bit quieter, if you will please," he muttered. The last thing he needed was someone overhearing Ivy discuss his former lover. The letter was another plea for him to reconsider marriage, even though he had already responded to her last letter and clearly reiterated that their relationship was over. He had tried to be gentle with her, even though Heidi was a shrewd and calculating woman who did not typically respond to anything but command, but the next time he wrote he would have to make sure she understood. When they had been together, he had been entrenched in their relationship, but it had not been love, or even healthy. Now that he knew what it was like to bask in Ivy's sunshine and sweetness, he could never return to his prior soulless relationships.

They began walking toward Lord Quincy's house. It was an almost sunny autumn day in London, and those were rare enough that he did not despise being in the city as much as usual. "Does she still wish to marry you, as the countess said?" Ivy asked.

He flicked his eyes toward her, but her expression was warm and curious rather than judgmental. He frowned. Did she not care in the slightest that his persistent former lover continued to write to him? "Yes."

"I think you should accept. You can avoid marriage for a good while, but you will not be able to ignore your duty to sire a male heir forever."

The back of Owen's neck prickled, and he spun around, scanning the bustling streets crowded with color, parasols, and top hats. Horses clopped by, their hooves ringing on the cobblestone, and the scents of dung and coffee mingled in the air. He did not see anyone, and yet he could not shake the feeling that they were being watched.

"I will *not* accept," he said, returning his attention to her, his tone surly. Did she not feel one iota of claim over him? He had been inside her *body*. He had tasted her. Felt her pulse around him. Knew her more intimately than any other person on this earth. Did that mean nothing to her?

She was quiet for several moments before she launched into a steady, entertaining stream of gossip that eventually eased his ire and dragged more than one bark of laughter from him, causing heads to turn.

They crossed an intersection behind a street sweeper, and Owen tipped him before offering his arm to help Ivy over a pothole. "Your defense classes," he finally said, once she had talked herself out, "how did you come to be doing that?"

"'Twas fate. I was passing through Richmond on my way to meet a friend, and I spotted the sign in the modiste's shop advertising the above space for rent. It was not too far from my house, and I had a small sum saved from my pin money, so I stopped and inquired. When I discovered the owner was willing to lower the rent because it had sat vacant for so long, I knew it was destiny.

"I had enough funds to secure it for six months, which I did using the false name of a male solicitor. I always knew I wanted to teach other women how to defend themselves, but I did not know how to go about it. If women had leisure clubs like men, it would have been far easier. I also did not know how to get the word out safely and secretively.

"For two more months it sat vacant while I tried to figure out how to accomplish what I wanted. That was when Diane stepped in. She knew someone she thought would be amenable to lessons and willing to pay a small stipend. Once Tabi—once that first woman showed up, everything fell into place. When she landed her first hit, her face lit up, and I knew it was what I was meant to be doing. After that, word of mouth spread, and women came to me by referral, including the Dove.

"That was when my father promised me to the first ogre—Marthin—and I knew my only hope of escaping was to become a governess. It so happened that the governess position was open at Brackley Manor, and again it felt like fate was on my side."

When Owen realized he was a shoulder ahead, having become lost in her story, he slowed his stride to match hers. "Where did you learn to defend yourself?"

"My brothers. They did not know it, but I was always watching, always learning. I could provoke the youngest into dueling with me, until my father cut off my communication with them."

Fury burned in his gut. After all he had heard, Ivy's father was a man whose jaw he would dearly like to dislocate. "Do you feel so strongly about teaching women to defend themselves because of your mother?"

She chewed on her lip for a moment, and Owen was sorely tempted to soothe the bite of her teeth with his thumb. "Yes. My mother lived in miserable fear of my father. We all did. Once, after I had had a particularly... *fraught* interaction with my father, I vowed that I would never follow in my mother's footsteps. *No woman should be consigned to that sort of hell,* and I knew I could help others if given the chance."

His admiration for the spritely, compact woman beside him knew no bounds. She was everything good in this world: selfless, determined, and giving. She fought her way figuratively and literally out of constraints designed to imprison her, and she made her own way with a ferociousness that it would have done many men well to possess.

And still, even as fearsome as she was, when she let her guard down, she was beautifully open. And soft. And sweet.

Owen suddenly had the discomfiting realization that he would do absolutely anything in his power to keep her safe and happy. If for some reason Lord Hartford was too stupid to ask for her hand in marriage, he would do it himself. If the choice was to remain a bachelor while Ivy suffered under her father's rule—well, that was simply no choice at all.

And in that brief moment where he allowed himself to imagine a scenario where she was his wife, something lightened in his chest.

She was smiling up at him, her eyes warm with feeling, and because he was drowning in them, he almost missed the carriage barreling straight toward them.

The horse's black coat was gleaming, his mouth frothing as he careened wildly through the intersection. He dragged behind him a gig with its hood up, concealing the driver in shadow. People cried out in alarm, and Owen reacted out of pure instinct, shoving Ivy roughly to the ground and throwing himself over her, landing heavily on her chest.

Ivy cried out as her back hit the cobblestones and Owen's body forced the air from her lungs. He caged his arms over her head and tensed his body, bracing for impact. When the carriage ran over him, it would kill him, but would Ivy survive? That was all that mattered.

He vaguely registered the screams of passersby, the snuffing of the horse right above his head, and the hooves pounding so close that one struck the extra fabric of his frock coat splayed on the road. There were shouts of outrage as the carriage wheel roared inches past him. From the corner of his eye, he witnessed the carriage take a sharp, *controlled* turn, and race off without stopping to see if anyone was hurt.

Owen's heart hammered against his rib cage and energy coursed through his muscles as he lifted his head to look down at Ivy. Her light brown lashes fanned across her bloodless cheeks, and his heart ceased to beat.

"Ivy, *Ivy*!" He roughly gripped her chin, and her eyes opened, her pupils swallowing her irises. "My God, Ivy, are you all right? Are you hurt anywhere?"

"I—I am fine, I think. Are you?"

He could not answer her question. His blood was slush, his hands still flexing with the panic of seeing the carriage race full speed at her. If he had not looked up in time, if they had landed even two inches more to the right, if she had been alone...

He grasped her face between his palms and pressed his lips to her forehead, then both of her cheeks, trying to reassure himself that she was still breathing and alive. "You are all right? You are all right?" he murmured the question over and over between featherlight kisses on her face, even as she stroked his shoulders in reassurance.

"I am fine, Owen. I am—Owen, we are—" Her eyes widened and he whipped his head upward. Had the carriage come back? If the driver knew what was good for him, he would run that horse far and hard.

There was no carriage, but there *was* a small crowd gathered around them. It was comprised of the grim faces of men who had witnessed the near-accident, women pressing sachets to their noses, and the shrewd and disapproving eyes of a number of gentry watching as he *kissed Ivy's face in public* while still pressing her into the cobblestones.

"My God, Owen." She tried to shove him off, and he obliged, rolling to the side and reaching down to help her up.

"Are you all right, madame?" A man in a top hat stepped forward, his mouth grooved with concern.

Ivy nodded, and the gentleman's companion, a woman dressed in finery, fussed over her, exclaiming with dismay as she helped brush off her dress.

"Did you see the carriage driver?" Owen asked the man while he readjusted his cravat, trying not to flinch at the streak of heat in his shoulder.

The man shook his head. "He sat in shadow." He hesitated and then said in a low voice, "I do not want to frighten the women, but I do not think that was an accident."

Owen's hand froze as he tried to recall the image of the carriage roaring toward them. Black gloves on reins, steady hands. There had been no shouts from the carriage driver, no warnings, no panic. He thought of the sharp turn it had made afterward, and the fact that the driver had not stopped to make sure he and Ivy were alive.

"What did you see?"

The man described the gig and the same gloves Owen had spotted, then commented on the expert control of the driver after he had nearly run them over. It was exactly as Owen had feared.

He looked past the man to Ivy, who was in the center of a gaggle of women fretting over her, her hands still finely trembling from the close call. Once again, Ivy had almost died because of him. It had not been an accident, but another attempt on *his* life.

Ivy must have felt the heaviness of his gaze, because she lifted her chin and gave him a tight smile. Always so brave, this woman he was faux courting.

His chest tightened as all of a sudden the stunning consequence of his actions slammed into him. Any gentleman would have saved Ivy, but Owen had gone beyond that. Instead of helping her to her feet when the danger had passed, he had cradled her head and kissed her over and over in full view of everyone on the street.

He had well and thoroughly compromised her.

There was no longer anything fake about their courtship. Ivy Bennett may have wanted Lord Hartford, but it was Lord Brackley who would be her husband.

Chapter 29

Owen had wanted to take her home after the carriage incident, but she had refused. After an hour of mindless chatter over tea with Lord and Lady Quincy, she wished she had conceded, especially when, after Owen brought up business, the men had retired to Lord Quincy's study, leaving her with the lady of the house, who sniffed approximately thirty times a minute and ran a handkerchief underneath her nose until her upper lip was raw. There was a cloying scent in the room that was starting to give Ivy a headache, and she would not have been surprised to discover that the lady was allergic to her own perfume.

When Owen came to collect her, his lips were flat and his eyes cold.

"What did you learn?" she asked as he took her arm and positioned himself between her and the street.

"I have learned that the impostor looks like me, or has disguised himself well enough to pass as me."

She gasped. How was that possible?

Owen's eyes darted down the street and probed into every

passing carriage. "Before today, Lord Quincy had not glimpsed me in over a decade, so when the impostor appeared on his doorstep with the business proposition, he looked enough like me to convince Quincy it *was* me. Jones left me a list of other men he knows have invested with the false Brackley, and all of them are passing acquaintances at most, leading me to believe the impostor purposely avoided anyone who knew me well."

"Did Lord Quincy give you the details of the investment?"

"He said 'Lord Brackley' had an idea for a new textile mill that would quadruple his investment within the year, so he did not ask too many questions." Owen snarled at that. "It appears 'Brackley' upheld his promise: A mere six months later, Quincy's first dividend check arrived, and it was twice his investment."

"Considering the factory's conditions, I am unsurprised."

"The impostor started a business by trading on *my* reputation, and tied my name to an abomination."

Ivy tugged gently on her arm. "You are holding me too tightly, Owen."

He immediately relaxed his grip. "Sorry, love."

Her heart beat faster. He had used the term of endearment before, but she knew it could not mean anything. "I have been thinking that perhaps the carriage accident was not an accident."

"I agree."

His immediate response surprised her. "You do?"

"It was another attempt on my life, and *you* almost died for a *second* time because of some madman's agenda against me. That is why when we arrive at the town house, I am sending both you and Barnes home."

She stopped, and he stilled with her, obviously having anticipated her reaction. "You cannot send me back to my mother's house now." Her skin crinkled with dread. "You cannot strip away my chance with Lord Hartford when he has only just declared his intentions. Please, Owen. What is the point in saving my life only to let my father destroy it?"

He stared down at her, his brows furrowed. "When I said *home*, I meant Brackley Estate. Hartford will not be courting you." The distress on her face must have been apparent, because his tone gentled. "Ivy, I kissed you on the street in front of a good number of people. You are thoroughly compromised. I ruined any chance you had with Hartford today, and I am sorry for that. I know you wanted him, but it is *me* you shall have to marry unless you wish to live your life as an outcast."

At the plain recitation of her circumstances, Ivy finally acknowledged what she had avoided admitting to herself all morning: The Viscount Brackley had compromised her.

She had barely seen the carriage before Owen had shoved her to the ground and slammed his heavy body over hers, protecting her with his life. And when it had been over, he had cradled her face as if she were the most cherished person on the planet, brushing his lips across her cheeks like he had needed to taste her warmth to know she was still alive.

It had made her chest ache in a way she did not fully understand, and when she had realized they had an audience and what it all meant, she had forced the entire incident from her mind out of sheer panic.

But now that he was acknowledging it, Ivy too had to face that it was real, which meant she also had to admit to herself that she felt nothing but relief.

She *liked* Owen. She liked how he talked to her and how he kissed her. She liked that beneath the grumpiness, he was caring and thoughtful, and how he tried to act as if he were not thoroughly entertained by the gossip she shared, even as his lips curved into a half smile. She liked how he handled his horses, with love and respect and calm command. Her cheeks heated as she thought of how he had handled her similarly in the kitchen. And his study.

She had set her sights on Lord Hartford because he was a rare example of kindness, but that was before she came to know Owen. Owen was *nothing* like her father. Owen would, quite literally, take a carriage wheel to his back before he ever hurt her or allowed her to be hurt. When he had discovered what she was teaching his sisters, he had been *proud*. Never once had he made her feel bad for who she was, or scoffed at her dreams, or demanded she act more ladylike. He had growled his way into her life, and had accepted her for exactly who she was.

The mere thought of talking poetry with Lord Hartford day in and day out, and having to hide her lessons again, had begun to make her skin itch. She had been loath to acknowledge it because she had not felt she had a choice. In truth, there was only one man who made her burn with desire, who made her laugh, who made her so frustrated she wanted to scream, and it was Lord Brackley.

But a quick glance at his face told her he did not feel the same. Just because Owen was unlike anyone she had ever met, it did not mean he felt similarly about *her*. He had had lovers before, including a woman still willing to move from Prussia because she realized she had made a grave error in letting him go. He was a powerful viscount with a reputation for fearsome deals and quality horseflesh. Until today, he had had so many options, so many women available to him who would have been perfect, who would have elevated his station if he had decided to marry in the future.

Time and again he had made it clear how much he did not wish to marry at present, and now he was being forced into marriage with her. She would be the yoke around his neck, the reminder that the worst had happened: He had compromised a woman and had been forced to take vows.

Ivy flinched at the thought of being an obligation to the man she had grown to care for. "Perhaps we can find a way out of it."

"Ivy, darling, I kissed you repeatedly in front of at least three dozen people."

"Only on the face. You were shaken up. You did not know what you were doing."

The look he gave her was unreadable. "If you do not marry me, it will ruin you. Plain and simple."

She tugged her lip between her teeth, her thoughts bouncing to what a ruined life might mean to her, and if it was preferable to being Owen's eternal albatross.

"Do not tell me you would rather be ostracized from society than marry me?" His voice sounded confused and...hurt?

"I do not wish to live as your obligation."

He towered over her, the brim of his hat blocking out the weakening sunlight as clouds moved in, his expression thunderous. "How could you think that? I am the one who stole your chance to marry Lord Hartford. I am the one who thoughtlessly, foolishly compromised you. If anything, *I* am the obligation."

"Yes, but it turns out, I rather enjoy your company."

"Tell me more about that," he murmured silkily, cupping her elbow. "What about my company do you *enjoy*?"

Ivy had never flushed so much in her life as she did in Owen's presence. It was rather humiliating. "I enjoy your kindness and that you listen to me, *really* listen to me, and that you were not angry when you discovered what I have been teaching your sisters. I enjoy that you are good to your siblings, and that you have even tolerated Barnes when he has acted abominably toward you."

The heated expression on his face faltered, and he stared down at her with wonder. "You were not talking about what we did in the kitchen?"

"Do not mistake me, I enjoyed that very much, but that was not what I meant."

He continued to stare at her, his lips parted and his hand firmly wrapped around her arm as if he were processing some emotion and needed to ground himself with touch. "You enjoy me?" A little line appeared between his brows. "You enjoy me for more than how I can make you feel?"

She sensed the answer was important to him, and when she recalled the letter from his former lover, she thought she understood why. His father had hated him, and his best friend had abandoned him. His lover had not thought him good enough to marry, until she had realized she missed their physical relationship. Had anyone ever told Owen Brackley that he was a good man? That he had value beyond the horses he could provide men, and the pleasure he could provide women? He had grown up without approval and had made himself into a man who did not require it. But did not everyone deserve to know they were valued?

Ivy lifted her arm, and he automatically released it. She brushed her fingertips across his cheek, and his eyelashes fluttered as he leaned ever so slightly into her touch. "I thought you must know all the wonderful things about yourself, but perhaps you do not. Perhaps no one has ever told you that you are a good friend, even when that friendship is not deserved. That you are solid and dependable, and everyone at your estate respects you because of it. They know that if they need something, you will provide it, and that you will carry some of their weight on your shoulders to make their loads lighter. You give your sisters the love and acceptance they so desperately crave, and you are a constant beam of affection in their lives when no other adult has been. Perhaps no one has ever told you that we can all see through the grumpy exterior to the generous-hearted man inside, the man who helped his governess by pretending to court her, and who makes everyone feel safe to be exactly who they are."

His emerald eyes burned as his fingers lightly encircled her wrist. "Ivy Bennett, I do not deserve you."

"That is what I am saying, Owen. You deserve everything you want."

"And what of *your* desires?" he asked. "You set your sights on Lord Hartford, and I have taken that option from you."

Ivy pulled her lip between her teeth. "I never wanted *Hartford*, Owen. I wanted kindness and safety. Never once have I wanted to kiss Hartford, or do with him what we did together. He is sweet and handsome, but I cannot think of him as anything other than a friend. While you...well, you are all of those things and more."

He leaned forward, his breathing erratic, his magnetism drawing her like a moth to a candle, when someone bumped into her, knocking her into his arms.

Owen snarled after the adolescent, holding her close to him as if he could be her armor. "Are you all right?"

Ivy nodded and he released her. She felt the absence of him as one might feel the absence of sunlight during the day hours. "Let us go," he said gruffly. "You and Barnes need to pack."

"Owen, I am not leaving."

"You are. Nothing has changed in that regard."

Maddening! And after all the nice things she had said. She set her jaw. "I am not."

"If something happens to you because of me, I shall never forgive myself."

"If something should happen to you because I am not here, I shall never forgive *myself*."

They stared at each other, neither acquiescing. "I could make you."

"You could try."

"Do you understand how I felt when that carriage was careening toward us? I could think of nothing but you. If something were to happen to you, that generous heart you claim I have?" He thumped his chest. "It would blacken into coal. You have very quickly become my conscience and my light. Do not damn me to a lifetime of knowing I could not save the one person—" He cut himself off.

Ivy's heart twisted behind her rib cage, slow and sinuous. Was she falling in love with this passionate, kindhearted grump?

"Owen, I was given a mission. Although I have cleared your name, I have not helped the 'hysterical' women. Worse, there is a man posing as you who is possibly involved. I cannot leave now. You will simply have to support my decision, and trust that I can take care of myself."

His jaw clenched as he wrestled with his need to control the situation. Finally, he clasped her elbow and drew her close, dipping his head so that his lips brushed her ear. "You are going to drive me to madness, Lady Brackley."

She had won this battle, but there was one more to conquer when they arrived home. If gossip traveled as fast as she suspected, Barnes would already know she had been compromised and would have to marry the one person he hated almost as much as their father.

Chapter 30

Owen should have been dreading the confrontation with Barnes, but, strangely, he was looking forward to it. There was no choice but to marry Ivy, and despite Barnes's grudge, even he would be able to understand that. Owen could have lived the rest of his life without being tied to his former best friend, but what was done was done. He had let Barnes's sulking go on long enough. Ivy was going to be his wife, and Barnes could either accept it or get out of Owen's house.

He did not have long to wait. The moment he and Ivy walked through the door, Fale said shakily, "My lord, Mr. Bennett wishes to see you alone in the drawing room."

Ivy smiled, thanked the butler, and stormed ahead to the drawing room.

"Miss Bennett," the butler called, about to hurry after her, but with one sharp look from Owen he halted.

"That is the mistress of the house," Owen said quietly, "and she may do as she pleases. Always."

Fale snapped a smart bow. "Yes, my lord."

Owen grimly followed Ivy to the sitting room. The moment they stepped through the door, Barnes halted his pacing by the heavy velvet drapes. His face was a mask of cold fury as his eyes skated over Ivy and landed directly on Owen.

"Is it true?" His voice was as icy as his expression. "Did you compromise my sister after I warned you not to? After I gave up my life these past weeks to play chaperone so that she would come out of this unscathed?"

"Yes." There was no point in making excuses. There were no excuses to be made. He had not needed to kiss her, but he could not have stopped himself even if were to happen all again.

Barnes's dark eyes glittered as he drew himself to his full height, which was very near Owen's. "In that case, I challenge you to a duel, Lord Owen Brackley."

Silence fell around them, and for the briefest moment Owen almost laughed at the absurdity of it. Who would have thought a decade ago that he might die at the end of his dearest friend's pistol?

The silence was interrupted by a very fierce *"No."*

"This does not concern you, Ivy. Go upstairs."

Owen's temper sparked at Barnes's command. "Do not speak to her like that," he warned, and Barnes's brows lifted in surprise. "She may be your sister, but she is going to be *my* wife, and any man who talks to her like that will have to answer to me, family or not."

If possible, the tension in the room thickened further.

Heat was rising in Ivy's cheeks. Owen very rarely saw her angry; she typically took Barnes's heavy-handedness with more grace than he did, but for the first time he was getting a glimpse of his future wife in a temper, and it was a glorious, terrifying sight to behold. "Barnes, I will not be told to run upstairs as if I am a little girl who still needs to be protected by her older brother. I *want* to marry Owen. Furthermore, there will be no duel. I will not have my brother and husband illegally shooting at each other in a field like two idiots."

Barnes's jaw was immovable. "I would rather die than let you tie yourself to him."

"What is your *PROBLEM*?" Owen roared, finally, *finally* loosening the grip on his pride. He had prostrated himself once before, determined to get to the bottom of Barnes's sudden disgust for him, and when Barnes had refused to toss him even a crumb, he had vowed that he would never humble himself by asking again. But it seemed there was one person he was willing to debase himself for: Ivy. If making peace with Barnes was what it took to make her happy, then he would tear his pride down brick by brick.

Owen strode toward Barnes, intent on shoving him against the wall and demanding answers, and only Ivy's worried face halted him a few feet away. "What did I do to make you turn on me? We had plans to open our own horse breeding business. We were *days* away from starting the life we had always dreamed of, when you punched me in the face and told me never to speak to you again. Then you left Harrow and refused to see me again. And I still have no *bloody* idea why."

Barnes's cheeks were hot and his body tensed for a fight. "You are a rotter!" he spat. "How dare you pretend not to know?"

Owen wanted so badly to return the favor from a decade ago and punch Barnes in the jaw. He wanted to take out all of his rage and frustration on this stupid, infuriating man in front of him, except Ivy was here. So with the most restraint he had ever exercised in his life, he gave a low scoff and said, "I will not keep asking only to give you the joy of denying me answers. If you cannot accept our marriage, then you can bugger off." He turned away.

"Meet me at dawn, or I will spread word that you are a coward."

Owen halted, his arm outstretched for Ivy, but she bounded out of his grasp and walked up to her brother. Even though she was a full head and a half shorter than him, she was so fierce that Barnes took an involuntary step back.

"Barnes," she said, her voice trembling as if she did not trust herself to speak, "you may know what Owen did, but I do not. If you want me to speak to you ever again, you will tell me right now. No duel would ever convince me. Only the truth."

Barnes's eyes were glittering with rage and something that looked a lot like fear. Fear for Ivy? Did he truly think Owen would ever harm her? "You need to trust me, Ivy."

"I have always trusted you, Barnes, but I am no longer a child. If you will not treat me as your equal, then I am afraid our familial relationship ends here."

"Fine!" he shouted. "You want to know how terrible he is? I'll tell you. Do you know that you are not the first woman he has compromised, Ivy, but you *are* the first he has had the decency to offer marriage?"

Ivy's lips parted.

"It is true that I had planned to start a horse breeding business with him. We were so close we were like brothers. Then mere days before graduation, my friend James and I were returning home from a walk at dusk when I spotted him on the street outside Moretons. He was kissing a young woman where he believed no one could see them, but when he lifted his head, I realized it was not a young woman but a—" Barnes's lip curled. "A *girl*. She could not have been older than fourteen."

"That *never* happened." Owen's voice was so icy the temperature in the room dropped. Barnes could shoot a bloody hole through his chest before he allowed him to lie about something so reprehensible to Ivy, who was the only person in the world whose opinion Owen actually cared for.

"I was *there*," Barnes snarled. "I recognized your coat: that ridiculous peacock blue coat that you wore simply because your father hated it. And *still* I did not believe my own eyes, not even when James confirmed what I was seeing. I could not believe you would do something so dishonorable, not until you left the note."

"The note?" Ivy asked faintly.

"The note," Barnes repeated, "written in his hand, where he apologized for what I had witnessed. Where he told me he could not help himself because the girl had looked so much like *my* sister, whom he had been obsessed with for years."

Her eyebrows lifted and she silently mouthed, *Me?*

"Owen and I were eighteen at the time, and you were *eleven*, Ivy. Eleven! And the perversions he admitted to in that note." Barnes's jaw clenched. "Lewd things that no man should say about a woman, much less a child."

Owen was stunned into silence while Ivy tugged her lower lip between her teeth. Did she *believe* Barnes? In that moment he stood on the precipice of true, life-altering loss. He had not been sad when his father died, or all that heartbroken when it had ended with Heidi. It had not even been terribly awful to leave his life in London behind all those years ago. But if he lost Ivy, lost her cheer and goodness, it would shatter him.

Her eyes traced over his face, and she sighed and turned away.

Owen's soul began to fracture.

"Barnes," she said severely, "did it not occur to you that such an act was extremely out of character for your dearest friend?"

Owen's eyes widened with surprise.

"Ivy, I saw his coat. I read the note written in his hand," Barnes said, all of his anger gone. Now he just looked defeated and bitterly disappointed.

She waved her palm as if the proof were nothing but circumstantial. "I have known Owen a much shorter amount of time than you, and even *I* know his character would not allow for such a thing. Did it not seem odd to you that he decided to compromise a young girl outside of your boarding house? That it happened at dusk, when you could not see his face well but could clearly recognize his coat? That he did it knowing you were on a walk with your friend and would soon return? That he left you a note debasing the one person you felt most protective over?"

"Ivy—" Barnes began.

"No." She held up her hand, halting her much larger brother's speech with a single gesture. "Perhaps you should know what is going on, Barnes. Perhaps," she said, turning to Owen, "that was your impostor's first foray at impersonation."

Instantly all the puzzle pieces snapped into a horrifyingly clear picture. "My God," Owen whispered. She was *right*. There was no other explanation for what had happened. It had seemed impossible that there even *was* an explanation, and yet she had found it, and within minutes of learning what had happened. She had heard Barnes's story and immediately peeled back the layers, because she had believed in Owen. Owen's soul returned to his body, once again whole and eternally devoted to this woman. Never in his life had someone believed in him so unconditionally. Her faith made him want to be a better man, made him want to be everything she would ever need.

"Impostor?" Barnes asked, a tiny spark of interest in his voice. "What do you mean?"

"How is it possible?" Owen asked. "Who could—"

"Excuse me," Barnes cut in, "I believe I am owed an explanation."

"Just *'trust me,'*" Ivy said, throwing Barnes's words back in his face, and Owen felt savage satisfaction at her bite.

Barnes looked wound so tight that Owen was afraid he would snap, but then Barnes took a deep breath and said, "I am sorry, Ivy. I should not have treated you like a child. You have taken care of yourself for a long time, and you deserve better."

"Thank you," she said, once again Owen's cheerful and loving Ivy. She did not hold grudges, not like her brother. Not like Owen. "Now take a seat, and let me tell you how Owen and I almost died today."

❖

Barnes paced in front of the chipped fireplace mantel, practically vibrating with angry energy. The clock, which had not been wound when they first arrived but was now ticking merrily along, chimed the late afternoon hour. Soon they would have to prepare for the opening ball of the Season, which was to take place that evening.

"You are telling me," Barnes said, "that this impostor severed our relationship a decade ago, ensuring we would not enter into business together. He knew where you lived, who your friends were, how to snatch your coat, and how to forge your handwriting."

The extent of the intrusion into Owen's life made him feel ill. "Yes."

"Why?" Barnes asked.

"I do not know."

"Perhaps he intended another outcome," Ivy suggested. "He could not possibly have known his actions would drive Owen to Prussia."

"Did you have any issues with fraud in Prussia?" Barnes asked.

"Not that I am aware of."

"Which would suggest the impostor stayed in England," Ivy said, her honey eyes alight with intelligence as she pieced it together. "Perhaps he was satisfied with the results of his treachery."

Barnes frowned. "If he was content for a decade, then what changed a year ago when he started sourcing funds for the factory?"

"My father grew ill," Owen said softly.

Ivy nodded. "The impostor must have known your father was ill and that you would soon return to London. He began to impersonate you once again, using your name and visage to collect investors for his factory."

"How does that make sense?" Barnes argued. "Would this man not do better to impersonate Owen when he was away, rather than when he returned to London and could reveal his scheme?"

They were silent, because no one had a good answer to that.

Barnes plunked on the settee and slumped, letting his head rest against the cushion. "I do not know if this is the wildest fabrication I have ever heard, or if it is an equally wild truth." He met Owen's eyes and, for the first time in more than ten years, did not look as if he hated him. "You—or he—remained in shadow where I could not see him well. I may have been blind with rage, but he *did* look like you, Owen. At least somewhat. I would not have mistaken a stranger for you."

Ivy clucked her tongue. "That is what Lord Quincy said when we visited him this morning. Is it possible this man is using prosthetics to alter his face?"

Owen poured a glass of brandy for Barnes, who accepted, and then poured another glass for Ivy, much to Barnes's disapproval, but she declined anyway, so he took a sip, relishing the liquid burn.

"Perhaps. Whoever he is, he has known me for over a decade. He looks enough like me, or has altered his appearance enough, that he is easily mistaken for me. He knew that Barnes and I were friends all those years ago, and he wanted to punish me by separating us. He knew I was returning to London."

"He has been watching you." A gleam entered her eye. "Just like the highwayman was watching for you on the road. The highwayman knew about your days at Harrow, and about your mother. You think it is him."

"Yes," he said simply. "Whoever the impostor is, he has targeted me specifically. Hates *me* specifically." He ran his finger around the rim of the crystal glass, and was still frowning when the butler arrived in the doorway with a strained expression on his face.

"Announcing Mr. and Mrs. Denholm."

Owen eagerly set the glass on the newly polished table and stood, just as London's most notorious detective, Zachariah Denholm, and his equally intrepid wife, Emily Denholm, swept into the room. It had been just over a week since Owen had sent the missive requesting their services, and he knew they would not be visiting now if they had not discovered something of interest.

"Of course the impostor hates you," Emily said, inserting herself into the conversation as if she had been there from the start rather than having heard more down the corridor than she should have. Her dark, curly hair was tumbling from her pins, and the way her husband was looking at her, one would have thought he was a lovestruck youth rather than an iceman with a fearsome reputation. "He is your brother."

Chapter 31

Ivy did not know where to look first: at the beautiful woman, who had a grim tilt to her lips and was wearing a fashionable navy afternoon dress, or at the tall, blond-haired and blue-eyed man beside her, who was so chilly that Ivy swore the air cooled upon his entrance.

"Please meet Mr. Zachariah Denholm and Mrs. Emily Denholm," Owen said, rising to shake Mr. Denholm's hand. "They run a private detective agency, and I have asked them to look into the matter of the highwayman."

"Call me Zach," the man said as he and his wife sat. Ivy tugged on the silk rope in the corner to order refreshments for their guests before taking a seat beside Owen, her brother in an adjacent chair. Ivy curiously studied the woman across from her. She had never before heard of a lady detective, and she was very much intrigued.

"Zach is the man who caught the Evangelist a few months ago," Owen explained.

"With the help of my wife," Zach murmured, the corner of his mouth lifting and his blue eyes warming a fraction.

His wife smiled back at him with such radiance that Ivy's heart twinged. They were so clearly in love. After a moment Emily turned away from her husband, and the happiness faded.

"Lord Brackley, we have discovered concerning information regarding your highwayman," she said, her fingers winding together in her lap. "He is not a disgruntled client of yours, nor an acquaintance who holds a grudge, but a bitter half-brother."

Owen's body language had been stiff from the moment the detectives entered, even though his tone had been genial. At hearing the word "brother" again, he said in a deceptively mild voice, "Please explain."

Zach leaned his elbow on the arm of the settee. "Your impostor, as you call him, is named Oscar Forsythe, and he was born four years after you."

Owen's jaw clenched, but other than that, he had almost no reaction. "Did my mother know?"

"I should say so. It was she who birthed him."

That got a reaction out of all of them. It was common for noblemen to stray and sire byblows, but it was not so often done in the reverse and the child kept secret.

Emily took up the dangling thread of the story. "From what we have gathered, your mother had an affair with a marquess in London." Her cheeks whitened, but she continued. "You likely do not remember because you were quite young, but it appears your mother and father had a period of estrangement at that time, and he never even knew she gave birth. She left the child under the tutelage of a caregiver in the city, and visited from time to time. We tracked the caregiver down, and she told us tales of your brother. She said he was volatile and mentally unwell, and that he would sulk for days after your mother visited. He was manipulative to the point that she still feels ill talking about him."

Ivy edged closer to Owen, so that her skirt brushed his trousers. She wanted to hold his hand, but all she could do was watch as a muscle feathered in his cheek and he absorbed the information.

"When the boy was eight," Emily continued, sweeping a stray curl behind her ear, "your father arrived at the caregiver's house. He had discovered money was being sent to the address, and he wanted to know why. When he learned of the existence of your brother—his wife's illegitimate child—the funds ceased."

"He had a lot of nerve," Owen said flatly. "I do not remember a time when he did not blatantly flaunt his mistresses."

Emily and Zach exchanged a speaking glance, and silence swelled in the room. It was broken by the maid entering with tiny sandwiches and tea. While Ivy poured the tea and offered lumps of sugar, Owen sat with his brow furrowed and his finger tapping on his knee. When the maid left, he said, "Did you say the boy was eight when my father visited him? That would mean I was twelve."

Emily nodded, and Zach watched with sharp eyes as he lifted his teacup to his lips.

"My mother died when I was twelve," Owen said slowly.

Several moments passed before the weight of what he was implying crashed into Ivy's chest. Did he think...

Owen looked directly at Zach. "You believe my father killed her."

"We do not have proof," Zach replied. He set the teacup in the saucer with a soft click. "The caregiver's memory is not sharp, but she believes your father arrived in the spring. Your mother died several months later."

"In the last summer of her life, my mother became unsound

in mind," Owen said. "She was often confused. Her complexion changed, and white lines appeared in her nails. She complained of a sore throat and chest pain, and then in October she began to exhibit symptoms of gastric fever. One morning I awoke and my father told me she had passed in the middle of the night." His lips thinned when he looked up from his hands. "She did not have gastric fever. He was poisoning her."

Chills raced up Ivy's arms. From what little Owen had told her about his father, she already knew he had been a monster, but she never could have imagined just *how* monstrous. This was what the Dove had meant when she said powerful men got away with powerful misdeeds. Even murder.

Neither Zach nor Emily refuted his claim.

"What happened to my brother—Oscar—after she died?"

"We do not know," Zach answered. "We believe he stayed in London, watching you."

"He ruined my friendship with Barnes." Owen nodded to Barnes, who was sitting in his chair and listening with unwavering attention. "I was meant to stay in London, but I spent the past decade abroad instead because of him."

Zach appeared unsurprised. "The more threads we pulled on, the more we unraveled. We have reason to suspect your brother was also blackmailing your father over your mother's death."

Ivy thought of the disrepair that Brackley Estate had been in before Owen had arrived, and his obvious shock at finding it so. That, she supposed, was where the viscount's money had been going.

"Earlier this year, Oscar opened a factory using his blackmail gains and the investors he acquired while pretending to be you."

"That part I figured out," Owen said. His emerald eyes took on a distant look. "He has become bold in his confidence in how much he looks like me. What is his ultimate plan? Does he believe he can kill me and take my place as viscount without anyone being the wiser?"

Ivy paled, but his hypothesis would explain the attempts on Owen's life. "He thinks you are complicit in your mother's death," she said. "Do you remember him saying he wanted justice for her?"

"I am not surprised he blames you," Emily interjected. "Based on the caretaker's description of Oscar, he is mentally unwell. That is to be expected, when one comes from bad stock."

Owen's head jerked upward, and he said stiffly, "My mother had her failings, but she was a fine woman."

"Oh!" Emily seemed taken aback. "My lord, I did not mean your mother."

Her statement hung in the air, as heavy as the sweet scents of lemon cakes and tea wafting from the tray. "Are you saying that you know the name of the marquess my mother had the affair with?"

Zach reached over and squeezed his wife's hand in support. She cleared her throat, her cheeks still bloodless. "Yes. It seems the marquess was busy siring bastards across London at the time." She nervously licked her bottom lip. "During our investigation into your brother, a number of connections came to light. When Oscar left the caregiver's home, he also left behind several belongings. One was a miniature portrait of a man presumed to be his father. You may know him as the Silk Stalker."

Ivy gasped. The Silk Stalker had terrorized noble-blooded ladies across London six years previously, and had strangled eight women with a silk cravat before he was revealed to be a marquess. She had read gossip about the Silk Stalker's bastard daughter becoming involved with a detective constable; it had caused *quite* the scandal, since that same constable had been tasked with catching another of London's lady killers at the time. Ivy had not matched the Denholms sitting before her with the gossip until now.

And Emily was saying the Silk Stalker, *her father*, also sired Oscar Forsythe.

Emily nodded as recognition sank in across the room. "It seems I have a newly discovered half-brother as well, Lord Brackley. One who appears intent on destroying you."

Once the Denholms had taken their leave, Owen asked for a few moments to gather his thoughts. Ivy slowly took the stairs to the second floor, trying to recall all the gossip she had read about Emily Denholm earlier that summer. She thought she remembered that Emily had been a governess. Was it possible she had worked for the Dove, too?

Ivy heard footsteps on the runner and whirled around to find Barnes behind her, his hands in his pockets and a strange look on his face.

"That was unexpected," she said lamely. "I suppose you are delighted to discover that you are not alone in your hatred of Owen."

"I am stupid, Ivy."

Ivy's brows winged upward. Barnes rarely admitted to his faults, much less stupidity.

"I was stupid not to question what I saw that evening ten years ago. I was so certain of the evidence that I did not once consider it could have been falsified." Barnes inhaled deeply, his dark eyes fixed on a portrait over her shoulder. "Despite what you have every right to believe, I am not delighted to discover there is a madman after Owen, especially now that you are to marry him."

"I would have thought you would find Owen's murder a rather convenient end to our betrothal."

He shook his head. "I have seen how he looks at you, Ivy. I saw it the moment I arrived at the house. Why do you think I insisted on staying? Owen Brackley is in love with you. Even though it has been a decade, his personality has not changed. He is singular in his focus. If he loves something or someone, he loves them with his whole heart, and he cannot hide it. I could not wish anything better for you."

"You have misread the situation, Barnes. He does not love me. We are marrying because he compromised me, and that is all."

To her annoyance, Barnes smirked. "Trouble, that man was never going to let you go."

Chapter 32

Owen glanced at his pocket watch. It was late, and he knew Ivy was dressing for the ball, but what he had to say to her could not wait.

He bounded up the stairs to her chamber and rapped on the door. When the lady's maid opened it, he said, "Do not take offense, but please get out."

The maid giggled and slipped out of the room. Owen shut the door softly behind him and prowled through the chamber to the attached room, where Ivy stood in the center, a gorgeous, dark-red ball gown halfway buttoned up her back, tendrils of hair falling across her shoulders. She was smoothing the fabric over her hips and did not see his reflection in the looking glass.

"Anne, do you think the necklace is too heavy?" she asked, lifting her fingertips to touch the teardrop ruby in filigreed silver that he had had delivered from the Brackley safe.

Owen came up behind her and brushed the shell of her ear with his lips. "I would like to see the necklace without the dress."

Ivy gasped and whirled around, clutching the loose bodice to her chemise-covered breasts. "Owen! What are you doing here?"

He raised a finger and twirled it around, and she slowly gave him her back again. Her eyes met his in the ornate stand-up looking glass, and he watched them go unfocused when he traced a fingertip down her spine. He began to unbutton the gown, his eyebrows raised in a question. Ivy nodded, and he finished the task, letting the silky fabric pool at her feet. He hooked his fingers into the petticoat and began to work on the clasps. "I sent the maid away."

He released the last clasp on the petticoat and let it drop, leaving Ivy in her stockings, chemise, and corset. She took a shallow breath. "Why?"

He pressed a kiss to the side of her neck, inhaling her scent. "It occurs to me that I have not made my intentions clear. You suggested I marry Lady Wagner today after I received her letter, and it has been bothering me." When she would have spoken, he slowly shook his head, his cock twitching when he watched her bite her lip in the looking glass. "Barnes found me after the Denholms left, and he not so subtly suggested that I quit being stupid and share my feelings with you."

"I will murder him."

"No, he was right. It has taken me far too long to admit them to myself, so there is no wonder you are unsure. Let me be very, very clear: I want *you* for my wife, Ivy. For far too long I have left you with the misconception that I abhor marriage, and I cannot let you go another night believing I am not fully invested in this. I *thought* I did not want to marry after Heidi, but then you burst into my life like a ray of sunshine in a dark room, and I realized it was never about marriage, but about the woman. There is no one else I want to be with. Not now. Not ever. But it seems I need to convince you of that, because I can see on your face that you do not believe me."

He tugged on the laces of her corset, and she trembled slightly. That made him pause. "If you are not ready for more, Sunshine, we will wait. I will never push you for more than you want to give."

"I want more."

"Are you certain? We can—"

She glanced over her shoulder, her eyes hot with need. "Show me how badly you want me. Convince me to marry you, not because you have to, but because you want to."

Feral possession roared in his veins, and his fingers returned to her stays. Within moments the boning of the corset collapsed and he withdrew it from her body and threw it aside. Slowly, he lifted the hem of the chemise and pulled it over her head, leaving her standing in a pool of fabric while wearing nothing but stockings and garters.

His mouth turned into a desert. Her legs were firm from exercise, as was her shapely bottom. Her waist was nipped in, her shoulders and arms strong and lean. He pressed his fully clothed front to her naked back and lightly wrapped his hand around her throat.

He licked a spot on her jaw. "What will it take to convince you to marry me?" He slid his free hand around her waist, feeling her soft, bare skin on his rough fingertips. She arched into him, practically purring. "Do I need to worship your body?" He kissed her temple. "With my hands?" He released her throat and slowly, torturously slid his palm down until he was cupping her small breast, his thumb strumming the peak. Ivy moaned and dropped her head back, allowing him full access to her rosy nipples. "Or do you need me to taste you again?"

His other hand joined the first, and he played with her breasts, palming them and massaging them, lightly stroking over her nipples until she was urgently pressing her backside into him. "Or mayhap what my little ray of sunshine needs is to be fucked." He licked up the side of her neck and did not miss the way her thighs pressed together at his vulgar use of language. "Well?" he asked. "What will it take to convince you?"

"All of it," she gasped.

He huffed a laugh into her hair, his whole body tight with anticipation and his erection testing the constraints of his trousers. "That is right, love. You deserve it all. You deserve *everything*."

He spun her around and took her mouth, groaning when she opened immediately for him and touched her tongue to his. She was a fast learner, her breath sweet and her lips pliant beneath his. He could kiss her forever and still not feel like he had had enough. He sucked her lower lip between his teeth and bit gently before stroking into her mouth again. Her hands clutched his shoulders, her bare body pressed into his shirt, the warmth of her soaking through to him.

"You taste so sweet," he murmured, lifting his head to stare into her passion-hazed eyes. "You taste perfect for me."

"You are still dressed."

"I am. Step out of your gown." She lifted her feet out of the pooled fabric and he walked her backward toward the wall, kissing her again, unable to keep his mouth off her. When her shoulder blades touched the wallpaper, he did not stop, pushing her against it and covering her with his body until she was squirming and tugging on his hair with her fingers. "More?"

"More, more," she chanted, and he wedged his thigh between her legs, forcing them apart.

"I need you to stay very still," he commanded. "Can you do that?"

She nodded, and he began kissing down the column of her throat, nipping and sucking, licking and teasing. He kissed down to her wrist and turned her palm to plant another kiss before sucking one of her fingers into his mouth.

"Oh my..." she gasped as he released her finger, dragging his curled tongue over the length. He repeated the process with the other arm before returning to her chest.

"You have the most perfect breasts," he said in amazement. She was not overly large, but she fit perfectly in his hands, and he could not help thinking about where else they would fit perfectly together. He bent his head and took one nipple in his mouth, and she arched into him, her fingers delving into his hair to hold him there. He lavished both breasts with his lips and tongue and teeth, sucking and tugging until her lower body was writhing against his.

He lifted his head. "I thought I asked you to stay still."

Her eyes flickered, and he realized the playful admonishment had hurt her feelings rather than enflamed her. He cupped her face and made her look at him. "I am sorry, Sunshine. Remember, if I ever do or say anything you do not like, you have to tell me. Promise me."

"I promise."

He waited.

She cleared her throat. "I did not like that."

He smiled as he pushed a strand of hair behind her ear. She trusted him, which was the only way for them to do this together. She trusted him enough to tell him, in the midst of being in a vulnerable position, that she did not like something he had done. "Thank you for telling me, love."

He should have known better, anyway. He had seen how she reacted to his praise, felt how wet she had become when he commanded her and then lavished her with words of affection. She would not like admonishment, or to feel that she had done something wrong. "In that case," he amended, "I want you to move however much you want. Do whatever you want, touch me however you want. You cannot do anything wrong. You are perfect."

Her crescent dimple flashed.

"And thank you for not knocking me in the chin," he added, making her snort.

"Do you think I would win if we sparred?" she asked seriously.

He considered it, his hand drifting to her hip, and then lower. "Perhaps. We will have to try some time. In the nude, of course."

She laughed again, but the sound faded into a moan when he slid his finger inside her. "You are so hot," he hissed, "and wet and tight." He curled his finger, and then added a second digit, making her squirm. Perspiration beaded on her forehead and collarbones as he worked her upward, moving in and out of her, but it was not until he rubbed his thumb against the bundle of her nerves that she cried out.

"Owen, Owen, I am going to—"

He removed his thumb, and she looked at him in dismay.

"Tell me you know I want to marry you."

She gaped at him. "Are you jesting?"

"No."

She squirmed on his fingers and clenched around him. He was so hard he was afraid he might find release in his trousers just from touching her.

"Owen, this is not the time."

"This is the perfect time."

She glowered.

"Clearly I am not working hard enough"—he lightly dragged his thumb across her and she whimpered—"if my future wife has any doubt about how much I want her."

And still she remained silent, impaled on his fingers, trembling with arousal.

"What else can I do to make you believe?" He applied pressure, and her breathing accelerated. "Bloody hell, Sunshine, look at you. You are glowing, all swollen and flushed and spread on my fingers. I want you to come apart for me."

She looked down at him with fevered eyes and blown pupils. "Would you have let me marry Hartford without saying anything?"

He knelt and kissed her thigh, running a lazy circle over her skin with his tongue. "I wanted you to be happy, but I am a selfish man, Ivy. Ever since we kissed in the meadow, you have been mine. I tried to be a better person, tried to let you go, but if I am being honest? No. I would not have."

She had grown wetter as he spoke, undulating against him. At his declaration, her eyes met his, and she said, "I believe you."

His heart soared even as possession streaked through his body, demanding he claim her fully. He stroked her again and again, and she came apart, crying out his name as she trembled through her release. He pinned her to the wall with one arm, while gentling the thrusts with his fingers.

"That is my girl," he said hoarsely.

Ivy sagged against the wallpaper, a faint smile on her lips. Her hairstyle was ruined, the loosened locks framing her freckled cheeks. He reluctantly withdrew from her wet heat and stroked his hands up her sides in long, soothing sweeps.

At last she pushed him away, her body still dewy and flushed, and her eyes dropped to his trousers. "I have overheard enough to know that a man enjoys being touched there as well." She reached forward, and he sucked in a breath when her fingers lifted his shirt and brushed against the skin of his stomach.

"You do not have to do that."

"I know. You do not make me do anything I do not want to do." She unbuttoned his trousers, and when they gaped open and his member sprang free, her eyes widened. "Oh, my."

He was worried that meant she was frightened of his length and girth, but he should not have been. Ivy Bennett was frightened of very little. She reached down and boldly wrapped her hand around him, and he hissed between his teeth. He pressed one palm to the wall and dropped his head to watch her explore his length.

"I have not done this before," she admitted, trailing her fingers up and down. "Does it feel good?"

"It feels incredible." He gritted his molars when she brushed her fingertips over the head, and the pads came away wet. A little line appeared between her brows as she studied them.

"It happens before the man's own release. It shows he is excited."

She beamed up at him. "I like when you explain things to me."

His heart squeezed. Ivy's approval meant more to him than anyone else's. For a long time, he had relied on no one and had cared about nothing but making sure his clients were happy. Now he finally had someone in his life who meant more than a thousand satisfied clients. She had very quickly become everything he had not known he was missing.

She began stroking him in earnest, and he knew he had to stop her before he found his pleasure in her hand.

He wrapped his palm around her wrist, stilling her movements. "If you want more, you will have to stop. But I am also happy to wait to consummate the marriage until after the vows have been said. I am happy to wait for as long as you need."

She looked up him and her lips curved. "You would do that?"

"I will do anything for you. Absolutely bloody anything. You want me to steal the queen's crown? I will find a way. You want me to breed you the finest horse on the Continent? Consider it done. You want my mouth between your legs every night for the next fifty years? It will be my pleasure."

She flushed and gave him a soft squeeze that nearly had his eyes rolling.

"I want to feel you inside me."

He nuzzled her neck, and experienced the most stunning moment of clarity in his entire life.

Good God. I am in love with her.

Chapter 33

Ivy did not know how it had happened, but Owen had wormed his way beneath her skin until she could not fathom an existence without him. The way he spoke to her, the way he touched her with equal parts reverence and mastery—it was all she had not known she needed. She had never wanted to marry because she had not wanted to suffer as her mother had. Under her father's pressure, she had chosen Hartford as the best option. He was kind and considerate, but he was nothing like Owen Brackley. Hartford would never challenge her, never make her the center of his world, never look at her as if she set the stars in the sky.

Ivy licked her lips. Barnes thought Owen was in love with her. Even though Owen had not said the words, he had made it plain tonight that he liked her enough to marry her. That had to be enough, even if it was not everything, because it had become clear over the past few days that she *did* love him.

"What do you know about the act of lovemaking?" he asked, running his nose up and down her neck, one palm pressed to the wall by her head, the other still clasping her wrist.

"I read a woman's book that said a lady should never let a man kiss her on the mouth, or under her dress. That she should only permit the act twice a week, and for as briefly as possible."

He did not laugh. "Anything else?"

"Well, unlike the book I read, my older brothers do not talk about it as a chore."

"Do you want me to explain what will happen?"

Ivy would have been humiliated to have this discussion with anyone else—even Diane—but with Owen it felt natural and safe. "Yes."

And so, in frank terms, he described exactly what would happen. When he told her he would withdraw to prevent pregnancy and she tilted her head in confusion, he continued his explanation about how babes were made.

"My brothers know all this?" she exclaimed, incensed. "Do all men?"

"Men talk to one another. They see drawings and cartoons, and even photographs."

Ivy was white with outrage. Meanwhile, women like herself were kept abominably insulated, told nothing except to bear it on their wedding day. They were told it was vulgar and sinful to enjoy sex, but it seemed men did not receive the same message. "Will you show me?"

His eyes were piercing. "Show you what?"

"All of it. The cartoons and the books."

"I will have to acquire some, but yes."

God, she loved him. Ivy took his hand and walked toward the bed, towing him behind her. When she looked over her shoulder, his gaze was riveted on her behind, and his member was so stiff it looked painful. She spun around and looped her arms over his neck, and then he was kissing her again. He lifted her as if she weighed nothing, wincing slightly as he laid her on the bed.

"Your shoulder—"

"Is fine," he said, standing to divest himself of his clothing. Before she could admire the contours of his chest and shoulders, he was back on her, his mouth drifting over her rib cage. He dipped his tongue into her navel and she squealed, her fingers spearing into his soft hair. His fingers walked up the inside of her thigh and slid inside her again until she was shifting her hips against him. Then he added a third finger, gently stretching her.

"Do not worry, I will fit," he reassured her, somehow reading her unspoken thoughts. He removed his fingers and kissed his way back up her body, taking her mouth and plundering with his tongue. She was so focused on kissing him that when he slid his member through her sensitive tissues, it shocked her and she gasped. He notched himself at her entrance and slowly began to penetrate her. After an inch or so he removed himself, and then entered again, slightly deeper. Each time, just as it began to burn, he pulled back out. Over and over, his teeth gritted and sweat beading on his brow, he repeated the act until at last he was fully seated inside her.

Ivy struggled to take an entire breath, feeling full to the point that she was uncomfortable.

"Are you all right?" Owen rasped, brushing a kiss over her jaw.

"I think so."

He gripped her hip in his wide palm and lifted, shifting the angle so that when he pulled out and entered her again, the pleasure made sparks flare behind her eyelids.

"Open your eyes."

She obeyed, and when he pushed inside her, her vision blurred. "Is that a good unfocused look, or a painful one?"

"Good," she gasped.

Owen continued to pump into her with maddening slowness, until she was fully adjusted and aching for *more*.

He read her body faster than she knew her own mind, because he picked up speed and then reached between their bodies to touch her where they met. After that Ivy could not recall any specific moment. They bled together in a hazy, pleasure-fueled dream of kisses, slick skin, and soft bites. By the time she had peaked twice more, Ivy's limbs were trembling and she was so overstimulated that she did not think she could take much more. Owen kissed her, long and lingering, and then pulled out and spilled onto her belly.

After several moments he rolled over, pulling her into his side even though she was sticky with his release. Ivy curiously touched the substance with her finger, and Owen's eyes darkened dangerously. "Now, that is a sight I like far too much. How do you feel?"

"I feel happy." She was a bit sore, but otherwise the experience had been wholly pleasurable, and she knew that was because it had been with him.

Owen dropped a kiss to her hair. "I am going to apply for a special license. I want to marry you as soon as possible."

"Then the *ton* will really talk."

"They will not talk too much, or else they shall find themselves blacklisted from England's finest horses."

Ivy pressed her hand to his chest, marveling at how warm his skin was and at his crisp and wiry chest hair. She walked her fingers to the puckered and pink skin of the healing bullet wound. "What are you going to do about your brother? About the factory?"

"I am going to visit the factory tomorrow. It is mine in name, after all, and I believe everyone who works there has earned a paid holiday."

"Oscar will be livid."

He nuzzled into her neck. "Then he will come find me."

"I do not like it." It was dangerous. Oscar had already proven he was eager to kill Owen. What if he took another shot at Owen from afar? Owen could not be prepared at all times. She would have to be extra vigilant if she wanted him to survive long enough to become her husband.

Ivy had been to country balls before, but she had never attended such a crush as the opening ball of the Season. The ballroom was bursting with gleaming jewels, scents of pomade and perfume, and flashes of colorful fabrics and feathers. Music from the recessed orchestra swirled around her, as heady as the chatter and energy in the air. Although the crowd was perhaps thinner than typical due to the hysteria, there were still a number of the *ton* ready to see and be seen once again.

Ivy's eyes dragged across the Italian-inspired frescos on the ceiling before dropping back to the throng of nobility. With her gloved fingertips resting on Owen's forearm, they greeted their host and hostess, the Marquess and Marchioness of Southampshire. The marchioness had welcomed Ivy with a touch of frost to her voice, but after her husband had taken a good look at Owen's dark expression, his own welcome had been jovial.

"Punch, love?" Owen asked outside the refreshment room. They were to be announced into the ballroom soon, and Ivy knew every pair of eyes would be on them.

"No." Two women with outrageously tall feathers in their hats swept past with their chins held high, giving her the cut, presumably for the compromising situation she had found herself in the day before.

"I am keeping a list of everyone who slights you."

"You cannot refuse to sell horses to everyone who is cold to me,

Owen. You will have no clientele left. Besides, I am capable of holding my own."

"I most certainly *can* stop selling to everyone who is cold to you, and I will. I do not care if it runs my business into the ground, which it will not." He was so confident that she shook her head in amazement.

"Why would you do that?"

They squeezed their way through two groups of gentlemen talking back-to-back. "Because when we marry, you become mine, and I become yours. That means your problems are my problems, whether you want them to be or not. I will be your bedrock, supporting you while you are building your business giving self-defense lessons."

Ivy came to a halt. "My business?"

He rubbed the back of his neck, looking a bit sheepish. "Only if you want. I am planning to buy a saddlery on Thackery Street. When I visited, there was a spacious second floor being used for storage. I thought it might be a good place for your lessons. It is discreet, but large enough to accommodate a good number of women."

When she continued to gape at him, he said, "If you do not like it, we will find a different location. Or not, if you abhor the idea."

Her heart felt stuck in her throat. "When did you visit the building?"

"First thing this morning."

"We were not betrothed then."

He took her arm and guided her forward. She did not think he was going to answer, but after a few moments he leaned down and said, "I was going to give it to you regardless."

Ivy experienced a whole-body flush. Even when he had still thought she was set on marrying another man, he had planned to gift her the space for her lessons so she could continue teaching, even if Hartford did not approve.

"It will not be much of a business," she said around the lump in her throat. "I do not charge much. Many women only have pin money, and they cannot risk spending large sums and having their husbands discover what they are spending it on."

"That makes sense." His voice was dark with understanding, and she realized he was probably thinking of his mother, who had died when her own expenditure gave away her secret. "I do not think you understand how successful my business has been. You, Lady Brackley, will be wealthy enough to support any endeavor or cause you so wish."

She had never had a chance against this man. Not because he had a fortune, or because he made her body feel extraordinary, but because he respected her enough to want to support her dreams rather than control or crush them. Because he was generous with those he cared for. Because, even when he had done his best to outrun his past, when his father had died, he had still come home to take care of his sisters.

Owen Brackley was more than she could have ever wished for.

All heads turned in their direction when they were announced and descended the grand staircase, Barnes close behind. "Every man here is jealous of me."

"And every woman is wondering how I tricked the most handsome viscount of the *ton* into kissing me on the street."

"'Twas not hard. I have been wanting to taste you since the moment I caught you leaving the modiste's that first night."

Ivy whipped her chin up. "You have not!"

"I may have wanted to taste you in other places as well."

"You rake!"

He threw his head back and laughed. He was unfairly attractive, with his short, curly brown hair, broad shoulders, and muscled thighs, but when he laughed and the skin crinkled around his eyes, he became devastatingly handsome.

They made their rounds, and despite having been absent for a decade, Owen seemed to know every man in the stuffy ballroom. He was chatting with a gentleman with thinning hair and a monocle, who had introduced himself as Mr. Wright Davies, deputy commissioner of the Metropolitan Police, when Barnes appeared at her side.

"Do not react," he said quietly at her ear, "but Father is on his way over here."

Although Ivy's composure did not slip, her insides coiled into something tight and bitter. She had not seen her father since the day Barnes had thrown him out of the house, but she would never forget the way he had ostracized her. How he had hurt her mother, terrified her brothers, and how even now, from afar, he continued to control her life.

Ivy was not inclined to murderous impulses, but in that moment, she thought she could kill a man.

Barnes's heavy hand came down on her shoulder. "We will get through this."

Owen was still talking to the commissioner, even as his eyes bounced from Ivy to their father making his way through the crowd toward her.

Ivy studied the man who had seemed larger than life when she was a child. He had ruled with an iron fist, and she had thought him so large, so nasty, so capable of violence. Now, more than a decade later, she was surprised to discover that he resembled nothing of the man in her memories. This man was frailer and slimmer, with thin lips and even thinner hair. He had the same honey-colored eyes as hers, and they were the only thing that were as mean now as they had been during her childhood. Her glance fell to his hands—hands that had caused so much pain—and she thought she was going to burst into flame.

Owen appeared at her back just as her father reached them. Her father nodded to Barnes, his calculating gaze dismissing his eldest as quickly as he acknowledged him. Barnes's responding smirk was lazy and knowing. Their father hated Barnes. Barnes had sent him away from his own home, wife, and family, and he would never forgive him for it.

"Ivy," her father said, his eyes crawling over her gorgeous deep-red gown and the expensive ruby at her throat. She had remembered his voice as seeming to have a cold echo. When she had heard it as a child, she had tried to slip away before he noticed her and found a way to insult her. But now it was frailer, like his body.

I despise you. "Father," she said curtly.

"Lord Brackley, meet Mr. Bennett," Barnes said, his tone bored.

"The man who has stolen my daughter's heart," her father purred. Ivy wanted to stomp on his foot. How dare he speak as if he knew anything about her? How dare he mention her heart? "I heard that you exchanged letters with my daughter for many years before courting her. In my time, a gentleman asked a father for permission before proposing marriage to his daughter. Yet I hear there is to be a wedding."

Owen slid his palm into hers, surprising her, and squeezed. His expression when he stared at her father, however, was one that would have given her chills if it had been turned on her. There was nothing friendly or warm on his face. It pleased her to see that he towered over her father. Both he and Barnes did. Oh, how the tide had turned in a few short years. Where her father had once been intimidating, now two of his children would gladly knock his teeth out while the viscount held him in place for the beating.

The atmosphere between the four of them was thick with tension, and Ivy understood why the rest of the guests were giving them a wide berth.

When Owen purposely did not reply, her father's brow furrowed, but he forged ahead. "We have not yet discussed Ivy's dowry."

"I will not be accepting one."

Her father seemed momentarily stunned, and she had no doubt he had planned to use the dowry negotiations as an excuse to hold a private audience with the viscount and worm other favors out of him. "Surely you want what is owed to you, my lord?"

"I am not cattle," Ivy interrupted hotly.

Her father's lip curled, and his eyes flickered toward her only long enough to dismiss her as if she were nothing but an annoying gnat.

The disrespect did not go unnoticed by Owen. A muscle flexed in his jaw, and Barnes looked positively delighted by the scene unfolding before him.

"A man of your social standing must want a dowry—"

Owen snarled. "Do not presume to know what a man of my social standing desires."

"Excuse me, Father, but I spoke to you, and you have yet to acknowledge what I said," Ivy interrupted. A bubble of elation lifted in her chest as soon as the words were out. She had not dared to speak back to him in her youth, but now she was a grown woman who had promised herself she would never cower before this rotten man again.

Her father turned up his nose as if a steaming pile of horse manure had spoken to him. "How dare you address me with such disrespect, you worthless woman."

Owen surged forward, but Ivy rested a hand on his sleeve and said calmly, "I dare to address you because I am more than your equal. I am smarter than you, kinder than you, and when I am married, I will hold a higher title than you."

Her father's eyes flashed with disdain. "I did a poor job raising you if you think it is appropriate to speak to your betters in such a manner. I should not have spared the rod so often."

Ivy scoffed. "You never spared the rod, you sadistic fool. Do not fret, this will be our last interaction." Now that she was finally confronting the monster from her childhood, it felt as if the oppressive years of worry and fear were peeling away from her, freeing her from the last vestiges of her childhood prison. "After tonight, you will never contact me again. You will not contact Lord Brackley. You will not use his name to advance your own agenda, or to ask others to extend you courtesies. You will cease to exist in my life from herein out." She stepped forward, her face even with his, and said fiercely, "I am not a scared little girl anymore, Father. I will not spare the rod should you cross me."

The outrage on his face was priceless, and Ivy would prize it until the day she died.

"You may keep the dowry for yourself, Mr. Bennett," Owen added, an expression of absolute adoration on his face when he looked down at her. "Consider it a gift from us, in exchange for your permanent absence from our lives."

It took her father several moments to rally, and when he did, he straightened to his fullest height, his anger so close to the surface that his nostrils flared. "I see now why your father never approved of you, Brackley. Blood cannot make a gentleman."

"Thank you," Owen said sincerely. "It is a high compliment to know I did not become the sort of man of whom my father would have approved. But I must warn you, I *can* be monstrous when I choose. I have been so uncivil, so cutthroat, so vicious to some men, that they have never recovered." He rubbed his thumb over the back of Ivy's hand and said casually, "I do not care for word games and innuendos, so I will make myself plain: You heard my betrothed, and you will respect her wishes. It is not only her you must fear. She need only give me the word, and I will happily destroy every last shred of your dignity. I will ruin you so thoroughly that your only respite will be found six feet under the soil."

Ivy's grin was so savage that her father took a startled step backward.

"Now leave," Owen ordered.

"You are going to let your sister marry this disrespectful ingrate?" her father hissed at Barnes.

Barnes lifted his glass in salute and gave their father such a devilishly satisfied smile that his spine snapped straight.

"You will regret this," he warned Ivy, his cruel lips twisting.

"No, see that right there? That is exactly what I told you not to do," Owen chided, as if her father were a stupid child. "You owe a rather large sum to Rockford and Turner's, if I am not mistaken. You will now be removed from the club and blacklisted, and before tomorrow night the entire *ton* will know you are a gluttonous spendthrift."

Her father's mouth gaped open like a fish. "You cannot—"

"I can, and I will. Consider it your final warning. Next time, I will destroy even the scraps of you that Ivy leaves behind."

With that, Owen squeezed her hand and smiled warmly. "I feel like celebrating, Sunshine. Would you like to dance?"

Chapter 34

Owen glared across the dance floor until Barnes said, "At ease, Brackley. You compromised her, remember? She will not jilt you for him now."

The "him" in question was Lord Hartford, who was smiling benevolently at Ivy as they danced. She and Owen had already turned heads with their first dance together, when they had flowed together like liquid. Owen had never cared much for dancing, preferring instead to match his skill with a horse's, but as in everything else, Ivy had simply fit him, and he had found himself wanting to continue the dance even after the song had ended.

Of course Hartford had immediately swooped in, and now Owen was considering whether or not he should ruin Hartford, too.

"He is a better match," Owen said sourly. "It is no wonder she wanted him."

"You, my dear friend, are an imbecile."

Owen finally tore his glare from Hartford so that he could cast it on Barnes. "Is there a reason you are standing here?"

Barnes smirked. "You cut my father off at his knees, and I must say, it was the high point of my year. Do you truly intend to ruin his credit?"

"Yes."

"Good. He only respects brute strength and cutthroat cunning. If you follow through, he will not bother Ivy again. Thank you for supporting her."

"You are welcome, but your sister did not need me. She can protect herself."

Barnes lifted a brow, and Owen inwardly cursed. He did not think Barnes would be appalled by Ivy's unusual skills per se, but it was Ivy's secret to share, not his.

"What did you say to him?" Owen asked.

"What did I say to whom?"

Owen's eyes were back on his future wife. "To your father, to make him leave the house all those years ago and never return."

"Ivy told you about that?" Barnes rubbed the back of his neck with his free hand and gazed into the distance. "I lost my composure that day. I told him if he did not pack up and leave, I would strangle him in his sleep. It was not an empty threat."

Owen cast an approving look at his former friend, although perhaps no longer former. "I wish I had done the same to my father."

They drank in silence.

Ivy spent the entire dance with Lord Hartford wishing she were in Owen's arms, but she patiently exchanged pleasantries about poetry while the notes of the song drifted over them. Although Hartford upheld his end of the polite conversation, he appeared distracted, his eyes continually drifting to the blond-haired gentleman who had passed them in Hyde Park. The gentleman was dancing with a flushing girl who could not be more than sixteen, and yet he appeared as unhappy as Hartford.

As the violin approached the last portion of the song, Ivy dared to say, "You know of my betrothal to Lord Brackley?"

Hartford nodded, his hand flexing in hers when the chit dancing with the blond man batted her eyelashes and swayed closer.

"I regret that I did not meet you before Lord Brackley, but I hope we can remain friends in the future."

"I hope so too, Lord Hartford." Ivy glanced at the blond gentleman. "Sometimes the heart wants what the heart wants."

She had his attention then. He gave her a wary look from those chocolate eyes.

"I love Lord Brackley, and I think even if I were not supposed to, I would continue to love him." This time she pointedly stared at the blond gentleman, who was scowling at them across the floor. Hartford caught her indiscreet look and paled. "I believe everyone deserves love. And"—she was taking a huge gamble, but if she was reading the situation correctly, it was the right thing to do—"I hope you are able to pursue your own happiness. If you ever have need of a friend, or a sympathetic ear, please think of me."

Hartford gazed at her, his suspicion and fear clearing as he regarded her with genuine warmth, and she realized then how false all of his other admiring looks toward her had been. "It is difficult for people like me and Hans. The masks we must wear are stifling."

She squeezed his arm. "'Tis unfair. If I can help in any way..."

"Would you like to come to tea next week? I think you and I could be good friends."

Ivy beamed. "I would love to."

Hartford kissed the back of her glove, and she was about to turn and look for Owen when a gasp went through the crowd and several women began to scream.

Ivy lifted her wine-red skirts and plunged into the crush, nudging her way through the men and women who had formed a loose ring around something taking place along the outskirts of the parquet floor. When Ivy broke through, she saw why everyone was keeping their distance, and why no one was helping the poor woman who was drifting alongside the wall, occasionally banging on the panels and whimpering that she wanted to be let out as if she had no awareness of there being a door. She was wearing a bright-green dress and matching hat, the feather drooping grotesquely over her face as tears streaked down her cheeks.

As Ivy hurried toward her, she noticed that the woman was breathing heavily, as if she could not quite fill her lungs.

"You must not go near her!" someone in the crowd cried at Ivy. "The hysteria is catching!"

The room was a cacophony of frightened voices and men angrily demanding that the woman be carried out by the servants and brought to an asylum.

Ivy ignored everyone and approached the woman. She did not know her name, but Owen did. He was behind Ivy within moments, resting a heavy hand on the back of her neck. "Mrs. Iverson," he said to the confused woman. "Let us help you. Is your husband here?"

She pressed a trembling hand to her cheek. "My husband?"

Owen nodded, but she seemed befuddled by the question, so he scanned the crowd himself until his eyes landed on a balding man cowering with the spectators.

"Come collect your wife," Owen ordered, his tone so authoritative that Ivy would have jumped to do his bidding if she were the man. But the woman's husband simply shook his head and shrank back to the approving murmurs of several men saying, "Quite right. I would not touch a hysterical woman, either."

"You are a coward," Owen said scornfully. He turned to Mrs. Iverson. "Can you walk?"

But her confusion persisted, because she began scratching at the wall, frantically begging to be let out, so Owen scooped her into his arms. There were gasps of horror, and another two women fainted.

He was carrying Mrs. Iverson to the exit, when a woman with blond hair burst into the ballroom. She was dressed in a muted shade of green, unlike Mrs. Iverson's vibrant gown, and her blond hair was an artful masterpiece of disarray. She wore gold spectacles, and when she spotted Owen and the dazed Mrs. Iverson, she walked so quickly toward them that a less generous person would have called it a run. Following closely behind her was Mr. Jasper Jones.

"Lord Brackley," the woman in spectacles cried, "you mustn't touch her dress!"

"Who are you?" Owen growled, but then he spotted the man behind her, and his expression gentled. "You must be Mrs. Jones."

"Frankie," she said, pushing at the bridge of her spectacles even though they had not been sliding down her face, "and I have finally discovered the common denominator among all of the women who have been sent to the sanitorium."

Mrs. Jones had the attention of those near them now. She did not seem to notice, nor care, that there were a number of skeptical eyes turned toward her.

"It is her dress," she blurted. Her blue eyes scanned poor Mrs.

Iverson and she added, "And her hat. It is the new green dye that has swept across London, the shade they are calling 'parrot green.' The bright green dye is made with arsenic. That is poisonous enough on its own, but a particular factory has been selling the fabric on the cheap. They claim their parrot-green dye is 'brighter' and 'bolder' than all other shades, and they are not wrong. It is so laced with arsenic that within months of wear the fabric becomes nearly lethal."

"Preposterous!" a gentleman shouted at their side, his jaw quivering with outrage. "If you mean Brackley's factory, I am an investor, and what you spew is utter nonsense."

"Careful," Mr. Jones warned silkily. "That is my wife you are disparaging."

Ivy's head felt light. Oscar Forsythe had opened a factory under Owen's name, where he treated his workers horribly and produced garishly green textiles on the cheap. He was poisoning the women of London, who were far more likely to wear the bright green dyes than men.

Oscar had visited the houses of noblemen and secured their investment, and in return those men must have received the very first bolts of parrot-green fabric. They would have had the material turned into gowns and garments for their wives and daughters, which explained why many of their families were the first to succumb to "hysteria." But rather than look for a sensible reason for the sudden rash of mental confusion, memory loss, and lethargy, London had instead consigned the women to sanitoriums out of fear and ignorance.

Had any of the women in the sanitoriums progressed to the more obvious signs of poisoning that would clear up the misconception of hysteria, such as white lines on their nails, sore throats, and vomiting? Or had they been parted from their poisonously fashionable gowns before they could reach that stage?

Owen glanced down at the woman panting in his arms, his expression stricken. "'Tis not my factory," he mumbled. When his eyes met Ivy's, she could read the horror in them.

Shouting broke out, and there were angry glares sent toward Mrs. Jones before the onlookers parted, allowing for a middle-aged woman wearing a necklace worth more money than Ivy would ever see to walk toward their huddle. Ivy's eyebrows flew upward when Owen inclined his head, even as he held Mrs. Iverson. Owen was a viscount, which meant whoever the woman was, she was higher ranking than he.

Everyone gasped when the woman reached them, gently removed the green hat from Mrs. Iverson's head, and threw it to the floor.

"This young lady needs to be removed from her poison clothing," she ordered. Her tone brooked no argument. She surveyed the crowd. "I highly suggest any other young ladies in possession of this color clothing and its accessories do the same."

While a mere moment ago the crowd had been ready to tear Mrs. Jones apart for daring to suggest such a thing, they immediately bowed to this lady's will, and there was a near stampede as people ran for the doors so that they might dash home and warn their loved ones about the poisonous garments.

The lady gave Owen a sharp look. "Carry this woman to the powder room, and we shall take care of her from there. If it is indeed your factory, you have some explaining to do, Lord Brackley."

Owen did not make excuses. He strode to the nearest powder room and gently set the heaving Mrs. Iverson onto a settee before leaving Ivy, the lady, and Mrs. Jones to take care of her.

"It is good we have our ballroom gloves on," Mrs. Jones said. "Miss Bennett, hold her up while I unbutton her. Lady Houndsbury, thank you for your support."

Lady Houndsbury waved her hand as if it were nothing, even though it had been everything. "I have not believed in all of this hysteria nonsense. I should have known you would find the truth, Mrs. Jones. The duke still wishes you would take employment with him."

The duke... meaning this woman was a duchess. Ivy's eyes widened in awe while she held Mrs. Iverson still and Mrs. Jones made quick work of the gown's buttons. Ivy did not think she had ever spoken to a duchess before.

"Is there an antidote for arsenic, Mrs. Jones?" Ivy asked. To her astonishment, the duchess leaned forward to help peel the gown from Mrs. Iverson. The poor woman's shoulders were beginning to redden where the gown had touched her bare, perspiring skin.

"Call me Frankie," Mrs. Jones said, "and no, unfortunately." Her face was grim as the three of them worked in tandem to relieve Mrs. Iverson of her garment. Once it was off, Ivy rushed to wet a towel and wipe across the tender skin of her shoulders. "She will survive, and her confusion will abate if she is removed from exposure. I know of a women's clinic not too far from here where she can recover. Jasper and I will take her."

Ivy nodded. "I will fetch a dressing gown from the hostess, along with your husband."

When she returned with the hostess's worst dressing down, as the lady did not dare part with something so nice for a "contaminated" woman, Mrs. Iverson was lying on the settee, her knees curled to her chest as she breathed heavily and the duchess stroked her hair. Ivy quickly helped her dress and then called out the door for Mr. Jones. He strode in and effortlessly lifted Mrs. Iverson into his arms before spinning on his heel and carrying her back out, Frankie close to his side.

As she passed Ivy, Frankie gave her arm a friendly squeeze. "Do not worry," she whispered, "I will report my findings to the Dove."

Ivy gawked after her as it slowly dawned that she was *the* Mrs. Francis Jones, the woman who had helped expose the Dowry Thieves only months ago.

Ivy plunked onto the settee and stared at the discarded green gown on the floor. The candles flickered in the retiring room, the looking glasses reflecting the light to create an ethereal glow. "It is not Lord Brackley's fault."

The duchess's face firmed. "Love can blind, child. Some men are not who they seem."

Ivy shook her head, and could not believe she was disagreeing with a duchess. "No, Your Grace, you misunderstand. Lord Brackley is exactly as he seems. It is his brother who plays games."

The duchess cocked her head, her intelligent gray eyes sparking with interest. "I did not know the viscount had a brother."

"Neither did he."

"Do tell me more, Miss Bennett."

Chapter 35

Owen's head throbbed the next morning as he stood on a box before a sea of factory workers, their scabbed and dirty faces looking wearily up at him. They had come to work, even as the newsies waved the morning paper announcing one of the biggest scandals in London history. The entire city was in a frenzy over the front-page article explaining that the "hysteria" was in fact arsenic poisoning caused by the parrot green–shaded textiles produced by Lord Brackley's factory.

Owen scanned the workers' expressions. Most of them were young, too young to be on a factory floor. Their clothes were dirty, their skin abscessed from handling the arsenic. Many of them were coughing, and a few had the same glazed-eyed look of confusion as Mrs. Iverson, while others appeared close to vomiting. These women and children, for the most part, had been allowing themselves to be poisoned because they had had no other choice. Because a greedy man had chosen riches and satisfying his investors over their health. Because they were desperate, and they were considered disposable.

"I do not believe it was profit your brother was after when he started the factory," the Dove had said the night before, having arrived at Owen's townhouse with both Mr. and Mrs. Jones well past the midnight hour. She had stood in shadow, her half-veil concealing her eyes, and a frisson of danger had swept up Owen's spine. "I have interviewed the doctor who tended to your mother the night she died. He is retired now, but it was his private opinion that your mother perished from ingesting increasingly large doses of arsenic. For some reason, your brother blames *you* for her death, and has therefore set out to poison your name and reputation by using the same substance that poisoned your mother."

"He has failed," Owen had said harshly. "I am sharing his name and his role in the factory with the London papers tomorrow. He deserves to be incarcerated like the women he poisoned."

"If that is what you wish to do," the Dove had murmured, "but might I suggest that he would consider that a success? He wishes for you to attempt to exonerate yourself. He trusts that it will make you appear a fool, since many will not believe that you suddenly have a convenient half-brother to take the blame. At the same time, his need for you to know that it was *he* who outwitted you, *he* who ruined you, and *he* who avenged your mother's death, will be satisfied. However, if you are willing to take the blame for the factory, I believe we can draw him out. I know his kind." Her lips had thinned. "If you do not follow his script, he will feel that his vendetta is incomplete."

"I will do anything to end this."

So here he stood, his head splitting just from the fumes of the place, and said, "You are all wondering, so I will be blunt. The newspaper articles are right. I am closing the factory, effective immediately."

A little boy's lower lip trembled. A girl cast her face down, her scabbed fingers twisting together, and even though the factory smelled and the ventilation was horrid with the high windows closed, Owen knew this job was all that stood between many of them and starvation. "I am so sorry." He could barely speak past the lump in his throat.

"You ent the man who hired us," a woman called from a few rows deep.

"No," he said hoarsely, "but I am taking ownership of the factory today. Have there been any deaths here?"

Several heads dropped. "Ten people so far, my lord," a young woman said, her voice wavering.

Ten people had died, and the factory not yet a year old. Owen felt as if he had been delivered a blow. He would find his monstrous half-sibling and make him pay for the lives he had ruined if it was the last thing he ever did.

"You will all be released with four months of wages and free visits to the clinic until the toxin clears from your body. The family members of those deceased will receive further compensation."

The workers stared at him for a moment and then glanced warily amongst themselves.

"Do ye jest?" a child asked. He could not have been more than nine.

"No." Owen gestured forward the three solicitors he had brought with him. "Please line up. They will take down your name, and you will be paid one month's wage now, and on the first of the following three months. You simply need to arrive outside the building."

On the way out the door he stopped to speak to the factory manager. "Clear out the office space and send me all records, books, and correspondence within. Once the workers have left, seal off this building."

Ivy was waiting for Owen outside the factory, and when he appeared he looked haggard and heartbroken. She hurried forward and took his arm. "Are you all right?"

He jerked when he saw her, his face flashing with panic. "What are you doing here? You are not supposed to be here. You are supposed to be home, *safe*."

"Someone needs to keep *you* safe."

"Ivy, I beg of you. Please go home. I cannot lose you, and I cannot concentrate with you here."

"We are safer together."

He waited for her to leave, but she only stood there, staring back. "You are not leaving unless I throw you over my shoulder and carry you, are you?"

"What a scandal that would make!"

Owen gave her a desperate look. "As you are giving me no choice but to acquiesce, I will remind you that if you die, all that is good in me will die, too."

The stark words were like a hot spear to her heart. Did he truly feel like that? She glanced behind him to the dirty factory. "How was it?"

"It is miserable in there. My brother must truly hate me in order to injure so many innocent people."

"His mind is not sound, Owen. He was the bastard child of a union between a murderous marquess and a viscount's wife. Both of his parents were noble, and yet he ended up in poverty with nothing and no one to love him. That, combined with a sickness he inherited from his father, made him do this. Not you. Never you."

Owen paused on the cobblestone street, gently tugging her to the side to allow other pedestrians to pass. He scrubbed a hand over his unshaven jaw. "I know we must remain in public today in hopes he will approach me, but I wish you would go home."

"No."

He sighed and brought her so close that if they were not already betrothed, it would have been scandalous. "I have something I must tell you, and it cannot wait any longer."

"If you ask me to go home one more time, I vow to—"

"I love you."

Ivy's words failed, her lips parting and her breath coming out on a short exhale.

"I have loved you for longer than I could even admit to myself. You are good and kind, clever and courageous. You are the sunshine to my storm clouds. Everyone on the estate adores you, including my sisters. Do you want to know what Octavia said to me that first day in the schoolroom, when I asked each of the girls how their governess made them feel?"

Ivy nodded.

"She told me she felt loved, Ivy. That little girl's mother will never love her, her father was incapable of the emotion, and I was not there for the first three years of her life. But *you* were there, and in a matter of weeks you made her feel wanted when no one else in her life had. You loved those girls, and they felt it. *I* feel it." He cupped her chin, his gloves cool against her warm skin. "You are everything to me. To us. I vow that until my dying breath, I will love and cherish you, Ivy Bennett."

Ivy pressed her fingers to her mouth before she dropped her

hand and squealed, "I love you, too!" She threw her arms around his neck and did not care who saw. "*You* are who I want, Owen. Only you."

He kissed her, a fast, hot touch on her lips, and then dragged his mouth to her ear. "I want you to tell me that you love me again tonight when I have you pressed against the wall and your legs spread."

Ivy made a low noise in her throat, instantly warming at the sensuous, dark promise in his voice. "I will tell you tonight. And tomorrow night. And every night. I will never stop loving you."

"Even when I am grumpy?"

"Especially then," she said, skating a quick kiss over his jaw. His hand flexed on her arm and his eyes darkened.

"Mayhap we can go home now and—"

"I think not," a flat voice said.

Owen went unnaturally still, and it took Ivy a moment to spot the muzzle of a pistol nudging his side.

"Is this a robbery in broad daylight?" Owen drawled, not letting on that he knew his assailant.

Ivy's eyes flickered over the man. Although the brim of his top hat was pulled low and he had grown a beard, she would never forget the flat, emotionless voice from the night he had shot Owen.

It was easy to see how Oscar had fooled so many people. Up close, he would never pull the wool over the eyes of someone who knew the viscount intimately, but from a distance their features and mannerisms were similar enough, even if his nose was a bit narrower and his eyebrows thinner. In the daylight, she could see that he even had Owen's eye color, albeit a lighter shade of green.

"Or are you the man who has tried to kill me multiple times?" Owen continued. He widened his eyes at her, and in them she saw a desperate plea for her to run, but they were partners now. She was not going anywhere.

"Tried to kill you?" Oscar's tone was patronizing as he arched a brow. "Do you believe I am so incompetent that I would have missed twice if I had not intended to?"

"The gun wound nearly finished me."

The strangest sense of ludicrousness overcame Ivy as the two brothers conversed on the street in full view of people walking by as if they were old friends, and not as if one of them was holding a pistol on the other. "That was an error," Oscar admitted. "I meant to wound you, but I grew so angry that I nearly made my mark."

"Who are you?" Owen asked, seemingly unaffected by the cold metal pressed into his side.

"*I* am the son who loved our mother, while *you* are the son who murdered her."

"I am my mother's only son." Owen smiled tauntingly at his brother.

Oscar's hand trembled with rage, and Ivy broke out in a cold sweat, silently begging Owen not to antagonize him too far. "You may be her only recognized son, but my blood is purer than yours. Her affair with a marquess produced me, while your father was only a viscount. She was taken from me because you and your pathetic father were jealous of her love for me."

"That is not true."

"He *told* me! He told me it was your idea to poison her. He said that you hated her as much as he did for her betrayal. She gave you life, and you mixed arsenic in her tea as your gratitude."

"My *father* said that?" Owen did not have to fake his fury. "You met him?"

Oscar's lips pressed into a cruel smile. "I spent many years watching you live the life I should have had, and when all your privileged plans dissolved and you fled the country, my focus returned to my mother. I was desperate to learn more about her, to supplement my fading memory. I wanted to know what her life had been like before she succumbed to gastric fever. I decided I was done skulking in the shadows, and introduced myself to your father. I had hoped for a miniature of her, for *any* token by which I might remember her, but he dismissed me with scorn. He bragged to me about her death and about how he slowly poisoned her for her unfaithfulness, that the poison was *your* idea. He delighted in the fact that I could not do anything with the truth because I was nothing but a 'penniless bastard.'

"He underestimated me. Mayhap he would not have taunted me had he known my true lineage. I had a grave robber dig Mother up, and a doctor examine her remains for poison."

Ivy blanched. He had exhumed his mother's body?

"From that moment on, I blackmailed your father until his grand estate was crumbling around his feet. I sent him unpleasant gifts. I broke in and tampered with the rare Scotch that only he, the greedy fool, was allowed to drink. And then, after many years of being terrorized, he died."

Ivy swallowed. "You poisoned him, too."

Oscar's eyes flicked to her, as if only then remembering her presence. "The soon-to-be viscountess. I have a score to settle with you, too."

"Why did you wait so long to kill him?" Owen demanded, drawing his brother's attention back to him.

Oscar's smile was so calculating that Ivy knew she was witnessing pure evil. "He died of incremental arsenic poisoning and suffered greatly every day. It was a fitting and just death. Once he was gone, I knew you would soon return to the country. I had destroyed your friendship out of jealousy, but that was not enough punishment once I learned what you had done. I needed to ruin you so that you would be as much an outcast as I."

Oscar's blink was reptilian. "Although I had the funds from your father, it was important to take on investors in order to make the *ton* complicit in your arsenic scheme. That way, when it was revealed that you were poisoning their wives and daughters, they would turn on you out of shame. Even the best horseflesh cannot be sold to a man whose daughter you sent to the sanitorium. I wanted to poison your life as thoroughly as you poisoned mine and Mother's."

Owen turned to face Oscar, surprising his brother, who reacted by pressing the muzzle into Owen's now exposed front. "I did not kill our mother," Owen said softly. "I loved her, and I was devastated when she died."

Doubt flickered in Oscar's eyes for a single moment, but it was just as quickly extinguished. He could not believe Owen without reconciling that he had hurt so many people under a misconception. His sickness and self-preservation would not allow it. "You lie," he hissed. "You are going to walk quietly into the alleyway." Oscar pointed his chin to an alleyway ten feet ahead. It was narrow and dark, and once inside and concealed by the shadow of the buildings, they would not be noticed by any passersby. This was not Mayfair, but the industrial part of London, where a few scuffles were better left unnoticed. "There you will swallow the arsenic I have in my pocket, and you will die in agony, watching while I sully your woman. I had planned to leave you alive to endure the full effects of your ostracization. I wanted you to break under the humiliation and know that while you suffered, your brother was long gone and laughing with his pockets full. But this morning's papers said nothing about you claiming innocence. There were no foolish and convenient accusations of a secret half-brother ruining your life, and I was left to wonder if you were really so *stupid* as to have not figured out who I was. Did you truly think all this was nothing more than a terrible case of mistaken identity? The idea that you did not know it was *me* who had destroyed your life in *her* honor was unacceptable."

Ivy considered her options while Oscar talked. She could attempt to disarm him here, but he might shoot Owen first, and there were too many people on the street. So despite the threatening looks Owen sent her, she followed the brothers to the entrance of the alleyway. Owen opened his mouth, no doubt to tell her to run, but before he could, Oscar said, "If she runs, I shoot her."

Their uncanny ability to think alike would have been disconcerting if Ivy had not known that Owen stood for the opposite of everything his twisted brother did.

Left with no choice, Ivy followed them into a narrow alleyway that stank of rubbish and human refuse. Something scurried past her skirts, and she breathed through her mouth, calming her nerves. The cobblestones were uneven, and several had partially lifted, making the alleyway a pathway of pitted earth designed to twist an ankle. As they edged into the shadow, a plan formed in Ivy's mind.

The deputy police commissioner, Wright Davies, was supposed to have been tailing Owen throughout the day, but it seemed he had been held up, and none of them had expected Oscar to approach Owen so quickly after leaving the factory.

That meant that she and Owen were alone, and it was up to them to save themselves.

When they reached a cluster of barrels, Oscar motioned for her to stand beside Owen. As soon as she did, Owen stepped in front of her, shielding her with his body as he stared down the eye of his brother's pistol.

"You do not have to do this, Oscar. We can still be brothers. You have been acting under a misconception, but now that you know I loved our mother as much as you, that it was my father who poisoned her and who poisoned *you* against me, we can create something new. We do not have to let him continue to destroy our lives."

It was not true, and even Ivy knew it. Oscar's mind was too warped.

Oscar cocked his head. "Tell me, brother, how can a shadow take form? Because that is what I am. A ghost. From the moment I first took breath, I was a secret. My mother was the only person in the world who loved me, and yet her *other* family would not allow her that joy. Mayhap if she had sung me to sleep every night like she did *you*, or brushed her hand over my hair each morning, or looked upon me with love every afternoon, then I would exist, too."

"We did not know about you," Owen argued. "I could not have—"

But it was the wrong thing to say, because Oscar's face flattened until his expression was nothing but a mask. "You know now, brother. When you see our mother, tell her I miss her dearly."

Before Oscar could fulfill his deadly promise, Ivy wriggled so that her head was poking out from behind Owen. "Did you vomit blood?"

Oscar blinked and tore his gaze from Owen's face. "What?"

"Did you vomit blood, after I beat the daylights out of you on the road?"

Owen squeezed her arm, silently begging her to shut her mouth.

"You little viper," Oscar said, the corner of his mouth lifting. The smile was so like Owen's that her skin crawled. Except even when Owen's was sardonic and grudging, it was always genuine, whereas Oscar's smile was a parody of the action. "You are a formidable woman, but even you cannot best poison. I believe I have a debt to repay you."

He held the pistol with a steady hand as the other slid inside his coat and pulled out a small brown bottle, no doubt filled with potent, arsenic-laced liquid. "Come here, wench."

"No." Owen's voice was so hot with fury that Ivy knew if he had the chance, he would rip his brother apart with his bare hands.

Ivy tugged on his sleeve until his eyes met hers. "I love you," she said softly. "Do you trust me?"

His throat bobbed. "I love you, too, Ivy."

"But do you trust me?"

His jaw flexed, and he gave her a curt nod.

"Be ready," she murmured, just as Oscar fluttered his lashes and said, "A touching scene, to be sure. Come here *now*. I have not before made a concentration so toxic. I suspect death will be swift, but not without pain."

Ivy slid around Owen. He grabbed her arm at the last moment, but at her gentle smile, peeled his fingers off and watched as she walked toward Oscar. Oscar stopped her with the pistol pointed at her belly, and held out the vial. "Swallow half."

Ivy figured a normal person would be trembling and crying and begging for her life, so she shivered theatrically and said, "No, please, anything but that." She heard Owen shift at her back and prayed he would hold off, that he would trust her to be all right.

Oscar's pale green eyes swept dispassionately over her face. "Take the vial."

Trembling, Ivy took a step closer so that she could reach for the vial. She squeaked as her foot caught on one of the loose cobblestones and she pitched forward, her shoulder slamming into Oscar's belly. As she made contact, she whipped her arm stiff, knocking the hand holding the pistol to the side just as it fired. The shot went wide, and before Oscar could aim again, Owen was on top of him. The vial and the pistol went skidding into the refuse scattered along the side of the alley, and while the two evenly matched men traded blows that made bone and cartilage crunch, Ivy sprang to her feet and scrounged for the revolving gun.

When she found it, she swung around and aimed it at them, but they were a blur of movement and she did not have a clear shot. She did not want to hurt Owen, and she had never shot a revolving gun before.

Her eyes tracked them, and she winced when Owen took a hard strike to the jaw, only to return it a moment later with a punishing blow that broke Oscar's nose. Blood dripped from Oscar's upper lip as he staggered menacingly toward Owen, the opening to the alleyway at his back. Oscar's hair was mussed and his eyes were wild, his teeth pink from the blood streaming from his nose. "You cannot best me, brother. You never have, and you never will."

Ivy lifted the pistol. Oscar was far enough away that she had one chance to take aim. Her hand was trembling as she started to pull the trigger, but before it fully depressed Owen tackled his brother. If she had taken the shot, he would be dead.

"Oh, heavens," she muttered with frustration, tossing the weapon aside.

The men rolled, and Oscar ground his palm up and into Owen's still-healing shoulder wound. Owen made a noise of agony, and in an instant Oscar was on top of him, raining down punishing hits.

Every ounce of protectiveness inside Ivy roared to life. Without a second thought she leaped onto Oscar's back and wrapped the crook of her arm fully around his throat and squeezed, compressing the flow of blood to his brain.

He tried to shake her off, his hands lifting to rip her arms apart, but Owen snatched his wrists before he could, and Ivy pressed harder, using every bit of strength in her body. A few moments later Oscar slumped over Owen, unconscious.

Owen was breathing hard as he rolled Oscar's body off him, scrambled to his feet, and yanked Ivy into his arms. Blood dripped from his face, and he was sweaty and filthy and his clothes torn, but he was alive.

He tilted her face and pressed frantic kisses to her forehead, her nose, and her lips in an act that she was becoming familiar with after danger had passed. "Are you hurt? Are you well?"

"I am perfectly fine. Are you?"

"As long as you are safe, I will always be fine."

"I see you have taken care of our brother without me," a woman's soft voice said, and Ivy jerked out of Owen's arms. Standing in the mouth of the alleyway, a pair of wrist-irons dangling from her fingertips, stood the detective, Mrs. Emily Denholm. By the time a panting Deputy Commissioner Wright Davies arrived several minutes later, Oscar was already shackled and propped against the brick wall, his breathing steady even though he had not yet returned to consciousness.

Once the commissioner had caught his breath, he stared down at Oscar and shook his head in amazement. "The resemblance is uncanny, my lord. The papers will be in a proper frenzy over this one."

Chapter 36

Ivy jounced in the carriage, her palm finding Owen's knee across from her as she steadied herself. The curtains were pulled aside even though the temperature was chilly enough that she needed a warm cloak, but both of them wanted the fresh air.

Beside her, on the velvet cushion, lay that morning's newspaper. The writer had detailed Mr. Oscar Forsythe's treachery in depth, and there would be many a nobleman at their breakfast table feeling quite foolish for having fallen victim to the scheme. When the deputy commissioner had searched Oscar's home, he had found various concoctions of poisons, as well as evidence that Oscar had discovered the perfect level of arsenic for his fabric by experimenting on streetwalkers and orphans, resulting in a number of deaths. Davies had also found a tattered shawl on Oscar's bed that had once belonged to the late Lady Brackley. Owen had not said anything, but Ivy was afraid they both suspected it was the shawl she had been buried in. Oscar Forsythe would soon stand trial, and there was little doubt he would be executed.

Ivy nodded to the paper. "Do you think the public will stop wearing clothing dyed with arsenic?"

Owen made a noise of disgust. "I am certain no one will touch parrot green again, but as for the rest of the green dyes? They care too much for the color and fashion. It is in gowns, in wallpaper, and in gloves. Someday they will realize that even the smaller doses are toxic. I grieve for the number of people who will have to succumb to ill health in order for things to change."

Sadly, Ivy agreed with him. "I received a message from the Dove before we left."

Owen arched a brow and waited.

"She congratulated us on exposing Oscar. She wants me to start teaching her governesses defensive techniques next month."

She waited to see what he would say. They had received a special license and were on their way to Brackley Estate to exchange their vows with the girls at their sides. Soon she would be the Viscountess Brackley, but she knew Owen did not enjoy the city, and would likely not want to return to London for the eight weeks she would be teaching.

He smiled at her—a full-fledged smile—not the reluctant one she usually coaxed out of him. "I am proud of you, Sunshine. The Dove is fortunate to have you."

"Will you miss me?"

"I suppose I would if I were not coming with you."

"But what about your horses?"

"I promised the girls a stay in London, and I have a lot of damage to smooth over now, courtesy of my brother. Besides, I do not think I could spend eight weeks apart from you. Somehow you have worked your way into my very blood, and I would no sooner separate myself from my own heart than I would the woman I love."

"How much do you love me?" she asked, sliding over to his side of the carriage. He was large and took up most of the cushion, but he shifted so that she would have room. She leaned inward and kissed his chin. "Do you love me this much?" She kissed his cheek next. "Or this much?" Her soft lips planted on his while her hand drifted to the front of his trousers and closed over his hardness. "Or this much?"

He grasped her wrist and spun lithely off the cushion so that he was kneeling before her on the carriage floor. "I will show you how much I love you. Happily. Every day, for the rest of our lives," he promised as he inched the hem of her dress upward.

And he did.

Epilogue

Ivy and Owen's wedding was simple but beautiful. It took place in a field while red, orange, and russet leaves drifted over them. The girls carried baskets of flowers, and they dashed around in little white dresses, leaving trails of mum petals wherever they went.

Barnes attended, along with Diane, and rather than their usual fighting, there was an awkward air between them. Ivy wondered what had happened, but before she could ask, the dowager swept into the banquet room and stiffly congratulated them. She had decided to move to the dowager house tucked farther back on the property, and had readily agreed that the girls would remain in the main house. Everyone was delighted with the arrangement.

Hours of feasting followed the ceremony. By the end of the afternoon, Ivy's cheeks felt like they were going to crack from smiling, and she wanted nothing more than to go upstairs with her new husband, but he was nowhere to be found.

A short walk later, she discovered him behind the stables with his eight sisters.

"No, no, Ollie," he said. He strode toward his sister, his cravat loose around his neck and his hair tousled. "You must embrace impact. I know it is frightening to be hit, but once you are struck a few times with the foil, you will realize it is not so painful, and it will allow you the freedom to practice braver attacks. Here, let me show you." He opened his body to her, and Ollie gripped the fencing foil with a giggle, her ribbons trailing from her hair and her dress askew. "Go ahead, strike me."

Ollie exchanged an unsure look with Ophelia, who nodded her approval.

"Do not worry, Ollie. It will not hurt me. You will see. Go ahead."

Ollie leaped forward and thwacked her brother solidly across the chest. He staggered backward, theatrically clutching his coat. "My God," he gasped, "I have been proven wrong. I think... I have been killed."

The girls squealed and raced toward him, piling on top of him until he fell over. They pretended to nurse him to health, while Ophelia came to stand at Ivy's side.

"You do not want to join in?" Ivy asked the eldest girl. She wrapped her arm around her shoulders and gave her a squeeze.

"No, I am too old now."

"One is never too old for fun."

Ophelia bit her lip and turned her face to Ivy. "I think we will be happy now, Miss Bennett. I *feel* happy. And hopeful. I have not always."

"You must call me Ivy," she said. She brushed aside one of Ophelia's curls. "And, yes, Ophelia. As long as we all have one another, we will be very happy indeed."

By the time the nursemaid came to collect the girls, the foil was in Owen's hand and no one was the wiser. They raced into the house after kissing both Owen and Ivy good night, exhausted but smiling.

Ivy walked toward Owen, and he tossed the foil aside. It was dusk, but she could still hear music and laughter in the direction of the feast.

His green eyes shone in the light of the glowing lamps set around the barn as he wrapped his strong arm around her waist and pulled her close, as naturally as if he had done it a thousand times before. She felt as if she belonged here, wrapped in his embrace, breathing in his scent, and soaking in his love. Because Owen Brackley, as grouchy as he was, had a lot of love to give.

"I must soon share the good news of our wedding with Saxony," he murmured in her hair, nodding toward the barn behind them. "If he is lucky, he might one day find a mare as clever and spirited as my wife. Perhaps Olivia Peppersnort the Third."

Ivy laughed and lifted her face to press her lips to his jaw. "I love you, Lord Owen Brackley the Scowly."

He bent his head and ran his nose down her neck. "And I love you, Lady Ivy Brackley, the Lantern of My Life. You have lifted the darkness for all of us, and I..." He paused, his throat working. "I cannot believe I have the honor of basking in your sunshine and being your storm cloud when you need one."

She met his mouth in a soft, lingering kiss. Then he swept her into her arms and carried her to Brackley Manor, which they planned to crowd with many, many happy memories.

Acknowledgments

I want to thank my agent, Emily Sylvan Kim. We started this journey together with Emily (Leverton, that is), and I'm so proud of how far we've come. Thank you for your unending support.

Thank you to my editor, Junessa. You took a chance on this series and I'll forever be grateful that you did. Our historical romance journey ends here, but I've enjoyed working with you to put the love stories of these intrepid governesses into the world.

I also want to thank the following people:

The wonderful team at Forever: Jordyn Penner for your insightful edits; Dana Cuadrado for publicity and marketing, Becky Maines, copy editor; Daniela Medina, cover designer (thanks for giving me three beautiful covers!); Jeff Stiefel, interior designer; Rebecca Holland, managing editor; Samantha Segreto, production editor; SongMi Lee, manufacturing coordinator; and Erin Cain, production coordinator.

The historical romance community for loving and continuing to read historical romance. Everyone who has read one of my books and recommended them to others—you are the best! Thank you so much for your support. I write these books for you!

All of my writing friends and online communities, reviewers and ARC readers, conference organizers and librarians and indie booksellers—you're all so incredible and I've cherished getting to interact with you.

My family and friends: Each of you has shown up and supported me in so many different ways, and I am so, so grateful to have you in my life.

My husband and children, who never doubt me and always cheer me on.

Lastly, all the historical romance authors who've inspired me, entertained me, and brought me joy—thank you for your words and stories. It's been an honor joining the historical romance shelf with this series.

About the Author

Lindsay Lovise writes historical and contemporary romances with brave heroines, along with creepy young adult books. Although she earned degrees in English and teaching, she always knew she wanted to write stories about love. When she's not writing, Lindsay is reading (probably romance), drinking coffee, and avoiding laundry. She currently lives in New York, but she was born and raised in Maine, where the winters make for perfect reading weather.

You can learn more at:
LindsayLovise.com
Instagram @LindsayLovise
Facebook.com/LindsayLoviseAuthor

RAISING READERS
Books Build Bright Futures

Thank you for reading this book and for being a reader of books in general. We are so grateful to share being part of a community of readers with you, and we hope you will join us in passing our love of books on to the next generation of readers.

Did you know that reading for enjoyment is the single biggest predictor of a child's future happiness and success?

More than family circumstances, parents' educational background, or income, reading impacts a child's future academic performance, emotional well-being, communication skills, economic security, ambition, and happiness.

Studies show that kids reading for enjoyment in the US is in rapid decline:

- In 2012, 53% of 9-year-olds read almost every day. Just 10 years later, in 2022, the number had fallen to 39%.
- In 2012, 27% of 13-year-olds read for fun daily. By 2023, that number was just 14%.

Together, we can commit to **Raising Readers** and change this trend. How?

- Read to children in your life daily.
- Model reading as a fun activity.
- Reduce screen time.
- Start a family, school, or community book club.
- Visit bookstores and libraries regularly.
- Listen to audiobooks.
- Read the book before you see the movie.
- Encourage your child to read aloud to a pet or stuffed animal.
- Give books as gifts.
- Donate books to families and communities in need.

Books build bright futures, and **Raising Readers** is our shared responsibility.

For more information, visit **JoinRaisingReaders.com**

Sources: National Endowment for the Arts, National Assessment of Educational Progress, WorldBookDay.com, Nielsen BookData's 2023 "Understanding the Children's Book Consumer"